Praise for

Into the Deep

"Just when I think Colleen Coble can't possibly outdo her last novel, she does it again! *Into the Deep* has everything: suspense, romance, danger, and a spiritual thread that's delicately woven into the story's fabric. Readers won't be disappointed with the fabulously satisfying end. If you haven't tried the Rock Harbor Series yet, you're missing a treat!"

DENISE HUNTER,
author of *Mending Places*

"Colleen Coble keeps the action tight throughout *Into the Deep,* with surprising twists to delight the most avid of suspense readers. I want to revisit these characters often!"

HANNAH ALEXANDER,
author of *Hideaway* and *Safe Haven*

"*Into the Deep* has it all, from murder mystery to a corporate intrigue to the many challenges of the blended family. Colleen Coble has a talent for creating believable characters who live in and deal with our complicated real world."

DEANNA JULIE DODSON,
author of *In Honor Bound, By Love Redeemed,* and
To Grace Surrendered

"Colleen Coble has done it again! A tightly drawn storyline, set within the endless complexities of a small town in Michigan's Upper Peninsula."

RANDALL INGERMANSON,
author of *Oxygen* and *Premonition*

"Colleen Coble knows how to keep the pages turning with characters I grew to love and amazing plot twists and turns that kept me guessing till the end. As satisfied as I was at the perfect conclusion to this series, I was sad to see it end."

DEBORAH RANEY,
author of *A Nest of Sparrows* and *Playing by Heart*

"A gripping and emotional ride. I loved *Into the Deep*! Colleen Coble is a master at characterization and setting. I feel I took a trip to Michican's Upper Peninsula, and I can only hope Bree and the gang will be back!"

KRISTIN BILLERBECK,
author of *What a Girl Wants* and *She's Out of Control*

"Once again, Colleen Coble creates a pressure-cooker environment for her characters, then proceeds to turn up the heat. In *Into the Deep,* situations and relationships seem hopelessly snarled, but Coble manages to unravel the tangle and weave all the threads into a thoroughly satisfying ending."

CAROL COX,
author of *Sagebrush Brides*

Into the Deep

Other Books by Colleen Coble

Without a Trace
Beyond a Doubt

Into the Deep

COLLEEN COBLE

WESTBOW
PRESS

A Division of Thomas Nelson Publishers
Since 1798

visit us at www.westbowpress.com

Published in Nashville, Tennessee, by WestBow Press, a division of Thomas Nelson, Inc.

Publisher Note: This novel is a work of fiction. Names, characters, places, and inci-dents are either products of the author's imagination or used fictitiously. All charac-ters are fictional, and any similarity to people living or dead is purely coincidental.

Library of Congress Cataloging-in-Publication Data

Coble, Colleen.
   Into the deep / Colleen Coble.
     p. cm.— (The Rock Harbor series ; 3)
   ISBN 0-8499-4431-7 (trade paper)
   1. Upper Peninsula (Mich.)—Fiction. I. Title.
   PS3553.O2285158 2004
   813'.54—dc22

2004006639

Printed in the United States of America

04 05 06 07 08 — 6 5 4 3 2

For my brothers and sister-in-law,
who believe I can do anything:

Rick and Mary Rhoads
David Rhoads

1

Swarms of black flies tried to find a way past the netting around Bree Nicholls's head. Every inch of her body was swathed in some kind of covering in an effort to foil the insects, but from the stinging at her ankle, she knew some had breached her defenses. She paused and swatted at the biting pain. Michigan's Upper Peninsula might be the best place to live at other times, but June was pure misery in the deep woods.

Her German shepherd–chow search dog, Samson, wagged his curly tail in an effort to dispel the clouds of black flies buzzing around his head. He raced ahead of her, pausing occasionally to look behind as if to say, "Are you coming?"

Naomi O'Reilly, Bree's best friend and search-and-rescue partner, panted to keep up. "You think he's dead?" she asked.

Bree didn't pause to answer. It was a useless question anyway. The only way to answer that would be to find the body. She thrashed her way through the clinging blackberry bushes onto a small beach fronting Lake Michigan. The beach had managed to hold back the encroaching North Woods and seemed almost hidden by the sunlight-choking tall trees surrounding it. The sandy area was already full of deputies and searchers. She scanned the shore for her brother-in-law, Sheriff Mason Kaleva, and saw his bulky form directing the searchers about to begin dragging the lake.

She almost groaned when she saw who was standing beside him. Ranger Kade Matthews's gaze met hers, and she wished she could leave. But this was a small community, and people already talked enough about their breakup. She tried to smile but feared it was more of a grimace when Kade's own expression darkened.

Samson bounded across the damp sand to greet him. Kade scratched the dog's ears, then walked away to join other rangers and Mason's deputies at the water's edge. As head of security on the Kitchigami Wildlife Preserve, he had every right to be here, Bree told herself, hurrying to join Mason and Samson. At least she wouldn't have to pretend nothing was wrong. But if this breakup had been the right thing, why did it hurt so much?

"Anything?" she asked Mason.

Mason shook his head. "This is a heck of a way to introduce the new residents to Rock Harbor. The chamber of commerce coaxed the lab to open here by painting a pretty picture of all the recreation in the Keweenaw. Now it will look like the area is unsafe."

"He might just be lost," Bree reminded him. "Maybe he never went out on the lake."

"He was due home four hours ago," Mason said. "His fishing gear is still by the water. Besides, he's a no-show at his son's fifth birthday party. Not like him at all, according to his wife."

She couldn't argue with that, and it didn't bode well. She glanced at her watch. Two o'clock. Her son, Davy, was at the party with his friend Timmy, Naomi's stepson. The sound of the waves seemed louder, and a few raindrops hit her arm. "Storm's coming. We'd better get out there."

Naomi and her dog, Charley, hurried toward her. None of the other Kitchigami K9 Search and Rescue members had arrived yet. Bree turned back to Mason. "You have a boat for us?"

Mason nodded his head toward a dinghy. "I thought you'd like something low to the water. It's got an engine as well as oars."

"Perfect. You have the scent article?" Mason handed her a paper bag. She unrolled it and then another paper bag inside the first one. "Come, Samson."

The dog eagerly sniffed the sock inside the bags then woofed softly. Bree handed the bag to Naomi, and Charley sniffed it as well. Both dogs turned and looked out toward the lake. Not a good sign. Bree had hoped the man had put in to shore somewhere. He was a scientist, not a sailor. Only people experienced with Lake Superior had any business out on its capricious waves.

Once they were in the boat, Mason shoved them off. Samson immediately went to the bow. The wind blew his thick, curly fur back from his head. "Find him, Samson," Bree urged. The dog whined, and his tail dropped between his legs. The hope of finding new resident Phil Taylor alive began to wane.

Naomi had the motor barely putt-putting along. She steered it slowly back and forth across the inlet near the beach. The clouds were already turning darker, and a drop or two of rain plopped into the water. Charley and Samson had their noses in the air. Samson gave a howl, then strained toward shore near an outcropping of rock called Three Indians.

"Over there!" Bree pointed and Naomi turned the boat.

Charley whined and turned his head back to look at Naomi. Samson howled again then launched himself into the four-foot swells. Biting at the water, he paddled toward the rocks.

"Samson, no!" The way the waves were pounding the rocks, Bree was afraid her dog would be tossed against the granite and killed. The dog hesitated then turned and paddled back to the boat.

"Over here," Bree shouted to Mason. "Bring the nets here." She tossed the anchor overboard and hauled Samson back into the boat. The average water temperature in Lake Superior was only forty degrees, and she shivered when seventy pounds of cold, wet dog landed next to her. She pulled a towel out of her ready-pack and began to dry him off.

Anything was better than facing what her dog's reaction might mean. Though she'd had her share of searches ending badly, she was never prepared when it happened. Rubbing the towel rhythmically over her dog's wet fur, she prayed for Phil Taylor's family.

"He's got a wife and three kids," Naomi said, her gaze on the boats beginning to drag the lake.

Bree nodded. "I met her at the Suomi last week when she invited the kids over for the birthday party. She seemed so sweet. Poor woman."

"You don't suppose he went swimming here, do you? It's too early in the season to even think of getting in that water. I wouldn't get in it until July."

"I don't know. Some people new to the area just don't know any better." Bree watched until one of the searchers shouted, then she turned her face away as the nets found what they were looking for.

Mason pulled his boat alongside Bree a few minutes later. "It's Phil. Your boys are at their house, right? You might as well come with me to tell his wife. I think she'll need a familiar face. She's so far from her family."

Bree wanted to refuse, but she hunched her shoulders and nodded.

The Taylors lived in a small cottage at the edge of Rock Harbor. A rental, the cottage seemed to cling for dear life to the thick woods behind it as it looked over a small cliff at Lake Superior's seasonal fury. The storm had passed by but the effects still lingered; monster waves crashed against the rocks below.

Children squealed in the yard, and Bree could see Davy stomping in a mud puddle. No matter how often she looked at her son, she marveled at the perfection of his compact body, a miniature version of his dead father. Her vision blurred as her gaze wandered to Adrian. He was fatherless now, too, but just didn't know it. Life seemed so unfair at times.

"Those boys are covered in mud." Naomi's voice was resigned.

Adults mingled with the children, and Bree glanced at her watch. "It's pickup time. Maybe we should wait until most of the people are gone to break the news to Denise."

Mason hesitated, then nodded. "I hope the storm didn't flood the mine where the new lab is set up. It's the craziest thing I've ever heard. Who in their right mind would try to grow plants inside a mine?

And for what purpose when there are perfectly good places to grow it outside?"

"They're sure tight-lipped about it," Naomi agreed. "But MJ Pharmaceuticals must know what they're doing."

"You'd think so. Hilary was ecstatic when she heard they'd be employing nearly fifty people. Especially with her reelection coming up in a few months."

Naomi nodded. "She's always on top of everything. I wish she'd slow down."

Bree knew her sister-in-law would never do that. She and Rob, Bree's deceased husband, were as alike in temperament as they were in looks, both focused and driven when they attacked a project. "How is Hilary feeling? I haven't seen her since last week."

"Sick of taking it easy, but feeling pretty good. You should see the bedroom. She's transformed it into an office complete with fax machine. Her secretary comes there every morning. She's nearly four months along now. Just another two months, and we'll all breathe easier."

Denise was giving prizes out for the last game. She turned, and her expression changed when she saw Bree's Jeep. The one-year-old twins clutched her legs, one on each side. Kneeling, she scooped them up and came toward the car. Bree and Mason got out and waited for her.

"Did you find him?" Her lips trembled, and she pressed them together.

"Maybe we should go inside." Mason said.

She didn't seem to hear him. "Phil isn't usually so irresponsible. Did he say why he didn't let me know he would be home so late?"

Little Abby had her thumb in her mouth and smiled winningly at Bree. Alex began wailing, his fists rubbing his eyes.

"May I?" Bree held out her hands for the crying child. To her amazement, Alex came right to her and cuddled against her shoulder. With Davy now nearly five, it was hard to remember when he'd been this small.

"He's not usually so outgoing with strangers," Denise said. She shuffled Abby to the other hip. "Did Phil say what time he'd be home?" Her voice was high and jerky, and she didn't look at either Bree or Mason.

"Mrs. Taylor, I'm afraid I have some bad news," Mason began.

"Oh, don't tell me he wrecked the car." Denise gave a nervous laugh. "I told him he needed to get new tires before we moved up here."

"No, the car is fine. But I'm afraid Phil isn't. We found his body in Lake Superior, ma'am, just off Three Indians beach area."

Denise stared at them, her mouth slack. She blinked through glazed eyes. "Wha . . . what are you saying? Wait, I don't understand."

"I'm sorry, Mrs. Taylor. I'm going to have to ask you to come down to the morgue and identify your husband's body."

Abby nearly slipped from Denise's grasp, and Naomi grabbed her.

Alex began to cry as his mother shrieked. "Shh, it's all right, little one," Bree whispered. But it wasn't. Nothing would be all right for this little family for a long time.

The adults and children turned at the sound of Denise's desperate cries. Mason took the widow's arm and helped her into the car.

"I'll take care of the children," Bree promised. "Just let the dogs out of the Jeep. I'll need Samson here."

Mason nodded and opened the back door for the dogs. Charley went to nose the ground at Naomi's feet while Samson jumped out and raced to join Davy. The little boy turned and caught sight of his mother. Worry rippled across his face, and he looked down at his wet, muddy clothes. Bree smiled at him, and his face cleared. He threw his arms around the dog and turned back to his friends.

"We should feed the babies and put them down for a nap," Naomi whispered.

Bree nodded. "Let's tell the others what is going on first. They have to be wondering."

Yancy Coppler lumbered toward her like a genial bear. Bree had liked the researcher the minute she'd met him. He reminded her of Santa Claus with his head of white hair and neatly trimmed beard. She'd heard he was still recovering from a nasty divorce, and she couldn't imagine a woman ditching him.

"Trouble?" he asked when he reached her.

She nodded. "Phil drowned in the lake."

He winced, and his pale blue eyes watered. "Ah, poor Denise." He glanced at the twins. "Is there anything I can do? The rest of Phil's team is here too." He blinked and rubbed his forehead.

"Just tend the kids until their parents pick them up," Naomi said.

"I can help with that," he promised. He hesitated. "Do we know what happened?"

Bree patted a wailing Alex on the back. "Looks like he drowned while fishing. Samson found him just off Three Indians rock."

A muscle worked in his jaw. "Phil was a great guy. We're going to miss him at the lab. He did all my computer work. I'm hopeless at it. I guess I'll have to break down and hire an assistant. But that's minor compared to what Denise and the kids will be going through."

Bree watched him walk slowly back to the adults huddled by the sidewalk. She recognized the other scientists on the team. Chito Yamamoto, the youngest of the researchers, took a step back when Yancy began to speak. A Japanese-American, Chito had a three-year-old daughter here at the party. Ian Baird, who had thinning blond hair and clothes that rarely matched, was distant and single, though from the glances he was sending Nora's way, he seemed eager to change that. Nora Corbit and Lola Marcos were also single, both in their fifties. Denise had told Bree they considered themselves grandmothers to the Taylor children. Bree hoped they'd be of special help to Denise now.

The head of the lab, Cassie Hecko, stood with her assistant, Salome Levy. They both stopped talking when Bree approached. The two older women glanced toward Bree and nodded, then turned to take charge of Adrian and his friends.

Bree and Naomi carried the squalling toddlers into the house. The kitchen's aromas of fresh-baked cake and hamburgers made Bree's stomach growl. She hadn't eaten today. After several minutes of rummaging through the cabinets for a cookie or something to distract them, she found saltine crackers. They both accepted one and began to quiet.

"Mum-mum-mum," Abby said.

"We'll go see Mommy in a minute," Bree assured her. It was nearly suppertime, so maybe they were hungry. Naomi found some jars of baby food in the cupboard and heated them in the microwave.

By the time they'd fed the children and settled them down with toys, the childish squeals and shouts from the front yard had abated. Bree and Naomi stepped onto the back porch. Davy, Timmy, and Adrian, the Taylor's five-year-old, played quietly with boats in a nearby mud puddle. The adults stood huddled together, talking softly.

Lola Marcos squeezed Bree's hand when she and Naomi joined the group. "Bless your heart, *chiquita*. Those poor children." Her gray hair, straight as seaweed, swung against her shoulders.

Nora Corbit was the opposite of Lola. Where Lola was round and soft, Nora was thin and sinewy. But her stern face wore the same expression of compassion. "I still can't believe it," she said.

Bree nodded. "Thanks for staying to help out." She heard Samson growl, a hostile sound she rarely heard from her good-natured dog. She whirled to see what was wrong. He approached the woods and stopped in a stiff-legged stance. His ears laid back, snarls like she'd never heard issued from his throat. Her gaze went past him to Davy, and she gulped.

A gray wolf was five feet from her son. Its teeth bared, it crouched as if to jump on the unsuspecting boy. A crushing weight on her chest smothered her warning, and only a strangled cry emerged. Time seemed to stop as she saw every detail of the wolf's menacing approach. A patch of hair was missing from its back right leg, and the pointed teeth it bared at her son seemed to grow.

She felt as though she moved against the power of Superior's waves as she sprang to grab Davy, but with an easy bound, Samson put himself between the wolf and her boy. He planted his body as a guard.

His feet sank in the mud, and the growl he uttered was unlike any Bree had heard from her placid dog. He lunged at the wolf, and the wild animal drew back just before Samson's teeth would have sunk into its throat.

Bree's feet finally carried her to her son. She snatched Davy to her chest and ran to the cottage. Naomi was on her heels with Timmy in her arms. Lola had Adrian. With the children safe, Bree turned to watch. The wolf fell back then circled the dog. Samson seemed no match for the heavier, more muscular wolf, but stood firm. Its teeth snapping, the wolf leaped on Samson. The two animals melded into a snarling ball of fur with occasional flashes of bared fangs. The sound of snapping teeth nearly froze the blood in Bree's veins.

"Stay here!" Bree told everyone. She thrust Davy into Yancy's arms. She needed a weapon. Frantic now, she charged around the house to the Jeep. Her bear spray was in her ready-pack. She flung open the door and dragged the sack toward her. The battle behind her reached a frenzy. She upended the backpack and dumped the contents on the wet grass. Her hand finally closed around the bear spray. She popped the top off then rushed back to her dog.

But Samson needed no help. With a last growling lunge, his teeth clamped down on the wolf's leg. The wolf yelped and managed to struggle away, then crashed headlong to the woods. Samson started to go after him.

"Samson, no!" Bree shouted.

Her dog shook himself, then turned toward her and whined. He looked toward the woods and gave a final growl, then trotted to Bree, satisfaction and triumph in every line of his body.

Bree fell to her knees and embraced him. "Good boy," she cooed, running her hands over him. He had some bites that would need treatment, but he was too proud of himself to flinch when her hands touched the injuries.

"Man, that was really something!" Ian Baird rushed to where she knelt with the dog. "I've never seen a dogfight like that."

"What an incredible animal," Nora said. "He saved your little boy. That wolf would have had him in another second."

"I've never seen the like," Yancy panted, rushing to join them.

Bree buried her face in Samson's fur. He smelled of wet dog and blood. She felt disjointed, like she would fall apart if someone said another word. "I love you, Samson." He licked her face, and she began to cry. It was either let the tears fall or faint, and tears seemed the stronger of the two reactions.

"He's going to need tending," Naomi said. Her face was the color of the white beach below them. "You take him to the vet, and I'll stay here with the kids."

"Thanks." Bree managed to get to her feet. "Let me check on Davy first." She wanted to run her hands over him the same way she'd just done with Samson, to make sure he was all right. She hurried to the back door where the boys stood peering out. They were more excited than frightened.

Samson followed her into the kitchen. She wanted to pick him up, but knew she couldn't transfer her own fear to her son. Samson nudged her hand then stopped, his ruff raised. He whined and went to the back door. Sniffing the floor, he whined again then lifted his muzzle and howled. He tucked his tail between his legs and hunched down.

He was signaling a death scent.

2

The streets of Rock Harbor were choked with cars, a sure sign summer had come to the U.P. Ignoring the posted no-parking zones, motor homes had been left in haphazard abandon while their occupants loitered along the outdoor displays of thimbleberry jam and local honey.

Kade Matthews grimaced when he couldn't find a spot to leave his pickup. There was no use in getting ticked off though. This was how it was every summer. And the money the tourists spent kept the town going the rest of the year. He finally found a space he could squeeze into across from the Suomi Cafe. He got out of his truck, then dodged a family in the middle of the street, gawking over the architecture of the town clock.

The cafe was doing a brisk dinner business. Molly, her hair scraped back from her skinny face, brought him a cup of coffee as soon as he slid into a booth. "What happened at the lake today, eh? I heard a body was found." Her Yooper accent was always more pronounced when she was excited, and today it was thick enough to butter the *nisu* in the display case.

"Then you know more than I do. I left when the sheriff took over." He studied the menu though he knew it as well as the contents of his own cupboards.

"Hey, you heard the latest Yooper joke?" Molly didn't wait for Kade to answer. "You know you're a Yooper if your mosquito repellent doubles as your aftershave."

Kade grinned. "I heard you're a Yooper if you think the sign saying 'Fine for Parking' means this is a really good spot."

She laughed and nodded toward the street thronged with cars. "Looks like all da trolls are the real Yoopers."

Anyone living below the Mackinac Bridge, otherwise known as Troll Turnpike, was called a troll. The ongoing joke in the U.P. was that trolls were easy to spot because they locked their houses when they left and locked their car doors even in Escanaba. No real resident bothered with locking anything. Kade wasn't even sure where his house key was hiding.

He grinned at Molly and ordered a pumpernickel and rye sandwich with chips, then turned to stare out the window. Seeing Bree today had shaken him.

"I thought I'd find you here."

His sister's voice interrupted his thoughts, a circumstance he welcomed since his thoughts persistently drifted to Bree. He glanced at his watch. Six o'clock. "You're off work early." The Coffee Place didn't close until eleven, and he'd thought Lauri had to work until then.

Lauri slung her tall, slim form onto the seat across from him. "The smell of the espresso was making me sick, so Cutler let me go a little early."

She did look a little green. Kade pushed his glass of water toward her. "Need something to drink?"

She shook her head. "Food is what I need. The morning sickness doesn't usually bother me if I eat breakfast, but I was running late this morning so I didn't eat anything. All I've had today is a bagel." She told Molly to bring her a chicken-salad sandwich and a Dr Pepper then turned to Kade. "Okay, give. What's going on out at the lake? Bree called for me to come help search, but I had to work."

"Phil Taylor was reported missing. I found his fishing rod and gear out by Three Indians. When I left, Bree and Naomi were trying to find him. Molly said she heard they found a body, but don't quote me."

"Who's Phil Taylor?"

"One of the new scientists in charge of things out at Rock Hound Mine."

Lauri shook her head. "Seems crazy to put a lab in a mine. And they're growing stuff in there, I hear. One of my customers this afternoon told me he saw them hauling in what looked like plants."

Kade grunted. "Sounds crazy, but with lights I suppose you can grow plants anywhere. And there would be plenty of humidity in there."

Lauri didn't answer but stared at him, a thoughtful expression on her face.

"What? Do I have dirt on my face?"

She scowled. "I suppose you didn't even speak to Bree, did you? You are as stubborn as the summer mold. It's been two months and you haven't even tried to hear her side of things."

"What is there to talk about? She prefers her fireman Nick. She can have him."

"You make me so mad! Bree too. She's just as stubborn as you. If one of you would just apologize, everything would be fine."

"I have nothing to apologize for." Kade crossed his arms over his chest.

Lauri narrowed her eyes. "Men never apologize," she said.

She seemed about to launch into another tirade, but Kade shook his head. "Did you go for your doctor's appointment this morning before work?"

"Yep, everything is fine. The doctor says the baby is healthy." She accepted the Dr Pepper Molly brought her and swished her straw through the dark liquid absently.

Kade frowned as he watched her. The past two months had brought a definite softening of her attitude toward him, but the cost had been high. With his sister now four months pregnant and only seventeen herself, the future terrified him. Lauri was his responsibility, and the thought often made him break out in a cold sweat in the early hours before dawn.

So far he'd failed miserably. With Bree as well as his sister.

⸙

Superior Forensics was in charge of the kitchen now that it looked as though Phil had been murdered. Bree wished she could fix Denise a cup of tea, but they'd been banished to the living room. Naomi had taken the boys to Anu's.

The bereaved wife rocked back and forth in the armchair by the window. "He can't be dead," she murmured.

The living room was pleasant and homey with lots of family pictures scattered on the various end tables and walls. The blue and yellow color scheme would be cheerful in other circumstances. Toys lay scattered on the carpet, and the room looked every inch a happy home. Bree knew it would be a long time before much laugher echoed here again.

"I'm so sorry, Denise," Bree said, kneeling in front of the woman. "I know what you're feeling. My husband died nearly two years ago in a plane crash." Her eyes burned. She remembered every minute detail of how she heard the news about Rob. They were etched into her memory forever. She held Denise's cold and shaking hands tightly.

Samson pressed his nose against Denise's leg and gave it a comforting lick. His wounds, mostly around his head, had been bandaged, giving him a wounded-hero appearance.

"I need to do something," Denise said. "Call our family, I suppose." Fresh tears erupted. "I don't know how I can tell his mother. He's her only child."

Bree winced. "I could call for you."

"No, no, I should do it. It would be worse to hear it from a stranger." She rubbed her eyes, then looked at Bree. "No offense."

"None taken. I think I have some Pepsi in the Jeep. Can I get you one? I have some pistachios as well."

"No thanks. I couldn't eat anything. I suppose you think I had something to do with Phil's death." Denise wiped her red nose as fresh tears welled. "There has to be some mistake. When I left to go shopping, Phil was getting his things together to go fishing. He promised he'd be back by ten to help me with Adrian's party."

"No one is accusing you of anything."

"You didn't see the way the sheriff looked at me. He thinks I killed him." Denise buried her face in her hands.

Bree touched her shoulder. "Mason will figure it out. Tell me about your morning."

Denise gulped. "I went out to the lab to pick up some papers for Phil, then went to get groceries."

"What papers did you pick up?"

Denise hunched her shoulders. "He said it was just some notes on the project. It was just a bunch of squiggles—made no sense to me. He had an idea and wanted to work on it over the weekend."

"Did you talk to anyone at the lab?"

"No. No one was around, so I just used his key for the office, grabbed the papers, and left."

Bree knew she had no business getting involved in this murder. Mason hadn't asked for her help, and Denise wasn't a personal friend, but something about the woman tugged at her heart. Maybe it was the death of her husband. Bree told herself to keep her nose out of it, but somehow she knew that wasn't going to happen. Denise deserved answers, and so did those children.

"Where are those papers now?"

Denise pointed to the sofa table. "I laid them there."

Bree stood and went to the table. "These?" She glanced at the notes. They were filled with formulas that would likely make no sense to anyone but him.

Denise nodded and burst into tears again. "What am I going to do without Phil?"

Bree went to her and embraced her. Phil and Denise had brought the kids to church since they'd moved to town. "Just hang on to God," she whispered.

"I am," Denise said in a choked voice. She shuddered and made an obvious attempt to regain her composure.

Once Denise was calm again, Bree probed with a gentle voice. "Was Phil happy here in Rock Harbor? Did he mention any conflicts at work?"

Denise grabbed a tissue from the box on the table. "No. He was thrilled to get to move up here. He and his dad used to come up every autumn for a fishing trip. He went on and on about how much I'd love it here, how great it would be for the kids. And this project at the lab was something he was really excited about."

"What was he working on?"

"I don't know. He wasn't allowed to talk about it, not even with me."

"Did he know all the other scientists who transferred here?"

Denise nodded. "They'd already started putting the project together in Dayton." She stopped and stared into space. "He and Yancy were especially close. They headed up the project."

No wonder Yancy had been upset. Bree hated to be questioning Denise. "No clue about the project?"

Denise seemed to gather her thoughts. She wiped at her eyes. "I know it's something really important to the company. The last patent they had was challenged in the courts and they lost. The company really needs this new project to be done right. And they're on a tight deadline—two months. Phil was determined to be their golden boy."

Now he would never spin another centrifuge or write another formula. And, more important, he'd never see his children grow up.

"Bree, we're ready for you and Samson now." Mason stood in the doorway, a worried frown on his face.

She leaned over and squeezed Denise's hand. "Is there anyone I can call for you?"

Denise shook her head. "I'll call my mom, and she'll come right away. It will take her ten hours or so to get here from Indiana because she won't fly." She buried her face in her hands. "I just can't believe this," she whispered.

"I can stay tonight," Bree offered.

"I'll be all right. The pastor is on his way over. When he gets here, I'll call Phil's mother too." Her voice trembled.

Bree nodded then snapped her fingers at Samson, who got to his feet and followed her.

Mason led the way to the kitchen. "Forensics is done. I want Samson to see if he can follow the scent from the kitchen to any other places where the body might have been laid."

Bree still had the scent article they'd used at the lake. She pulled it out of her backpack and gave Samson a fresh sniff. His tail swished eagerly as she rubbed his ears. "Search!" she told him.

He whined then went to work. His customary death-scent responses—drooped tail, howling, whining—manifested immediately as he nosed the spot he'd indicated earlier.

"Not there, Samson. We already know about that." Bree pulled him away from the site. He went to the kitchen door and scratched at it. Bree let him out, and he bounded through the darkness of the backyard to the driveway. He sniffed the ground beside the driveway and began to howl again.

Mason directed the two forensic technicians to see if they could gather any more clues, and they rigged bright lights around the area. Bree called Samson and told him to continue to search. He raced back and forth across the yard. Samson worked in a Z-pattern, his nose in the air as he tried to pick up another scent. At one point he seemed to sense something near the end of the driveway, but in the end, he wandered back to Bree with his tail drooping.

"The body must have been put in a car. Samson's not getting a scent beyond here."

The forensic team was busy picking up hair and other debris in the driveway. "See if there are any tire marks we can use," Mason told the men.

Samson stood with his ears sagging, and Bree knelt beside him. "You did good, boy." She glanced at Mason. "Would you hide? He's had a rough day."

"Sure." Mason handed her his hat. "You can use this." He jogged to the back of the garage.

Bree waited a few minutes then thrust the hat under Samson's nose. "Go find him, Samson. Find Mason."

The dog's tail began to swish, then he bounded away with his nose in the air. He crisscrossed the backyard until he found Mason's scent, then raced in the direction Mason had gone. Moments later Samson came back to Bree with his tail held high and a stick in his mouth to show he'd found his quarry. Bree allowed him to lead her back to Mason.

"Good boy!" Mason rubbed the dog's ears. "He's a real treasure, Bree. I hear he drove off a wolf this afternoon."

"He's our protector." Bree knelt and buried her face in his fur. "Good dog, Samson."

Her dog whined and licked her face. He pulled away and went to her Jeep. "I guess he's ready to go," Bree said. "He probably misses Davy. He'll be disappointed to get home and not have him there. I should probably go by Anu's and let him see that Davy is okay."

"And make sure yourself," Mason said with a teasing grin.

"That too," she agreed.

"I'll let you know what we find out. This is sure a stumper. The Taylors have only been in town two weeks. Who would want to kill him that quick? From what I've seen of the man, he seemed amiable."

"I wonder if it had anything to do with the lab. He had Denise pick up some papers for him, but they just look like formulas he was working on. Did you find anything in his car?"

Mason rubbed his chin. "Nope. Just fishing stuff. But his car looked like it had just been vacuumed. Could we take Samson out to check it?"

"Sure. You want me to call Naomi and Charley too?"

"Samson should be enough. If you get a questionable response from him, we can call in some other dogs then."

Mason's phone rang, and he answered it. He listened a few moments, then he closed his eyes and pressed his lips together. "It was the coroner. Phil's death was from a gunshot wound."

3

Cassie Hecko stretched the kinks out of her back and surveyed her domain. The lab equipment gleamed atop the stainless-steel cabinets and counters. Her supplies had been safely stowed out of view. She had a big job ahead of her, made even bigger by Phil's death. Her smile dimmed with regret. She would miss Phil's humor.

Salome Levy poked her head in the door. In her early thirties, she was unmarried, a commonality that made the two more like best friends than boss and assistant. Cassie always felt a twinge of envy when she looked at Salome. She was gorgeous with black hair that shimmered in the sunlight. Today she wore her curly hair loose, and it reached nearly to her waist.

"Ready to check out the growing chamber?" Salome asked. "I want to stop at the supermarket on the way home. I thought I'd make fettuccine tonight for dinner if that sounds good to you. I can't let you show me up. The lasagna you fixed last night was fabulous. I thought your dad was going to lick his plate!"

"I'll just like it because I'm not cooking." Cassie grinned and snagged a green army jacket from the hook on the back of the door and slung it over her fatigues and T-shirt.

"That's the only reason you were willing to rent me a room," Salome said with a grin.

Though it was nearly eighty today, the mine's hallways would be closer to fifty until they got to the growing chamber. "Everything set up?" Cassie asked.

Salome nodded. "The lighting was installed Monday, and all the seeds were set out yesterday and today. They seem to be happy in their new home."

"Let's take a look. I want everything in order by the time Marc comes to check us out."

Before they could leave the room, the phone rang. Cassie raised her eyebrows. "I didn't think anyone had the number yet. It has to be Marc. He's like a terrier on a scent. I thought maybe when he married Yancy's ex-wife he'd lighten up." She walked toward the desk.

Salome grimaced. "I don't know how you put up working for him. I would have quit the first week."

"You just have to know how to handle him. I grew up with a mother like him, so I know all about walking on eggshells. You tread lightly and get ready to run at the first sign of a frown." Cassie grinned to show that her past didn't bother her any longer. People never looked deeper than a smile.

She reached the phone and answered it. "Cassie Hecko."

The strange voice on the other end made her blink. "You must shut down your godless operation or face the consequences."

"What?" Cassie pulled the phone away from her ear. Was this some kind of joke? The voice sounded as if it had been masked by some digital device. "Who is this?"

"You've been warned. Do what I say or face the consequences." The caller clicked off.

Cassie slammed down the phone. "Great. The kooks have found us already."

"Don't let it bug you. They're everywhere." Salome held the door open for her, then they went down the hall and through the security gates into the copper mine. The smell of water-borne minerals and the sound of dripping made Cassie feel a bit claustrophobic, as though the rocks would crush her. The loony-tunes call didn't help her mood.

The passageway emptied into a cavernous room over a hundred feet in diameter and nearly as tall overhead. Tables arranged in rows on the concrete floor were laden with plants. The jagged rock walls were painted white, and lights glowed so brightly overhead that Cassie reached for her sunglasses and put them on.

"Whoever came up with this idea was brilliant," she said. "No insects or diseases to worry about down here, and we can control all the growing parameters. These plants should shoot up fast."

"And we're self-contained. There's no danger of the plants propagating in the environment. We just need to keep this under wraps. If the media finds out, we'll have environmental nuts crawling over us like ants at a picnic. I guess they think these plants are going to sprout feet and walk out of here."

Cassie nodded. "The team knows to keep quiet. And it shouldn't take long. Not with the scientists we have."

"And you're the smartest of the bunch," Salome said. "We'd be years behind the competition if it wasn't for you and your dad."

Cassie shifted, uncomfortable with the praise. "I just like the excitement of discovery. Dad did most of it." She looked away. "I just hope we can make our deadline."

"It's too bad he won't be in on the final wrap-up, huh?" Salome squeezed her shoulder. "He's proud of you though."

"Too proud sometimes."

"Is that what drives you? I've often wondered if you were trying to prove yourself to your dad."

Salome was closer to the truth than Cassie liked. As roommates, they usually just skimmed over the top of deep issues, and she was surprised Salome had picked up on that. "I've never felt I needed to prove anything to Dad," she said firmly. The truth was much more complex, but Cassie had hopes that the next few months would prove her statement true.

"Well, if we don't make our deadline, none of this will matter. The company will go under, and our competitors will win," Salome pointed out. "I just wish your dad could help us. Locked inside that mind of his is stuff no one else knows, not even Yancy or Phil."

"Speaking of my dad, I should check on him. He's been a little disoriented since the move." She pulled out her cell phone and punched in the number.

"Hi, Dad, how's everything?" She tried to keep her voice cheerful as she waited to see what his condition was today.

"I can't find my microscope," Bernard Hecko answered in a querulous voice. "Did you move it, Cassie?"

"It's in the garage. I haven't had a chance to unpack it yet. Stay in the house, though, Dad, and I'll get it out tonight."

"My work won't wait. I'll get it out myself." He put down the phone without turning it off.

Cassie could hear him mumbling. Then a door opened, and she knew he had gone to the garage. "I need to run home," she told Salome. "Dad's not having a good day."

"Oh dear. I'll hold down the fort here." Salome bit her lip. "Um, Cassie, how much longer do you expect to keep him at home? Don't you worry he'll wander off?"

Cassie felt the old, familiar sense of failure. "I can't stand the thought of a nursing home."

"At least he'd be safe. I think you're making a mistake to trust him alone. You never know when an Alzheimer's patient will take a turn for the worse."

"Tell me about it." Cassie grabbed her backpack and swung it to her shoulder. "I'll be back as quick as I can."

"Stop by Phil's and ask Denise if she's seen his notes," Salome called after her. "I've turned his office upside down looking for them."

Surrounded by thick forest about fifteen miles from Rock Harbor, the Ketola cabin sat in a tiny clearing barely big enough for the house. The nearest neighbor was five miles away and never visited, a state of affairs Jonelle Ketola knew her husband, Zane, intended to maintain. The crows cawed from the trees as Jonelle followed him to the dog pens. His two pit bulls, Bruck and Trickster, lunged to the wire fence to greet him.

He tossed their meat to the ground in each of their pens. He and Jonelle both knew better than to hand-feed the dogs. They were liable to make a meal of any slow fingers.

Bruck, the bigger and meaner of the dogs, growled at Trickster to stay away until he was done, but the younger dog had speed and agility on his side, and he lunged forward for his share. Bruck turned to snap at him, but his teeth closed on empty air. He turned back to his meal.

Jonelle shuddered, but Zane smiled. "He's in good form for the fight."

"He scares me," Jonelle said. She wished he'd get rid of these dogs. When the baby came, she wouldn't be able to sleep a wink for fear they'd get out and attack her child. Her hand strayed to her stomach.

Zane saw the movement and put his arm around her. "I'm just doing this for you and the baby, you know that. No kid of mine is going to go without like I did." He narrowed his eyes, and his mouth grew pinched. "He's going to go to college and have some status in the world."

Jonelle had to wonder if it was status for their child that Zane really wanted, or a proxy status for himself through their child's accomplishments. She returned her husband's hug. He just wanted what was best for them. She had to remember that.

A sleek gray Acura drove along the gravel lane toward them. Zane released her. "What's he want now?" He grabbed a beer from Jonelle's hand and went to wait by the porch. The car stopped in front of Zane, but for several long moments, no one got out. The windows were tinted so darkly, Jonelle couldn't see what he was doing. An uneasy stirring in her stomach made her half sick.

The driver's door finally swung open, and Simik got out. In his forties with gray touching his black hair at the temples, he was dressed in a spotless blue pinstripe suit. "Zane," he said. "Ma'am."

Zane's partner always gave Jonelle the willies. The schemes he'd gotten Zane mixed up in sometimes kept her awake at night. She could tell by the look on Simik's face he had another moneymaking scheme up his sleek suit sleeve. She'd never heard his first name, but his last name was enough to strike fear in her heart.

Simik's eyes gleamed as he looked around the yard. "Our troll in town has a proposition for us."

"Oh?" Zane asked.

Jonelle suppressed a sigh. The man's connections to bigger dog gambling rings had reaped huge financial benefits for Zane, and her husband wasn't about to walk away from him, even though dogfights were illegal in all fifty states and danger lurked in Simik's muddy eyes.

"When's the next fight?"

Zane shrugged. "Next month."

"You have a worthy opponent for Bruck?"

"No one stands a chance against Bruck, and you know it."

"Our troll is willing to pay thirty thousand dollars for a dog he's found who can take him on. And he'll bet heavily in the actual fight."

Zane gave a bark of laughter. "It's too easy taking money from our little patsy. He's soft and weak. He always thinks he can recoup his losses on the next fight. You'd think by now he would have learned not to bet against Bruck. There's not a dog alive who can take on my lean, mean killing machine."

"Seriously," Simik said. He took a step closer. "He says he saw this dog drive off a wolf a couple of days ago."

Zane frowned. "So what? Bruck has killed plenty of wolves in his career. I trained him against wolves."

Jonelle knew it was a lie, but Zane liked to maintain some mystique concerning his dogs. Still, Bruck was a fearsome dog. He had been bloodied but never beaten in the three years he'd been in the ring. The muscular dog was at the height of his strength and ferocity. He was unbeatable. The graveyard behind the cabin held more dog carcasses than Jonelle could count—all casualties of Bruck's mean streak. And Zane made sure he stayed mean. He fed the dogs only as much as they needed to maintain their strength, and they were always hungry for more. That gave them an edge over their softer opponents. And the steroids Zane fed them only added to their ferocity.

Jonelle had tried to sneak them food, but she was always punished for it.

Simik leaned forward. "Our troll says this dog has to be seen to be believed. And I'd like to see him lose his money on it."

Jonelle wondered what Simik had against this "troll." She'd seen the way Simik had sucked the man deeper and deeper into the gambling ring, almost as though it was a personal vendetta to bankrupt him.

"What ring did he see him in?"

"Not a ring. In town." The other man pulled a handkerchief from his pocket and wiped his face. "This heat could break any day. I thought the U.P. was supposed to be cool."

"We get our hot spells just like anywhere else."

"You ever heard of Samson? He's the search dog Bree Nicholls works."

Zane squinted his eyes. "Yeah, I seen him around. Big mutt, looks mostly German shepherd. That him?"

"Yes," Simik said eagerly.

"He's soft. I wouldn't waste Bruck's time on such an untrained animal."

"The troll says he'll go so far as to make it double or nothing in the ring," Simik said with a contemptuous curl of his lip. "You just have to get the dog into good enough shape that we can convince the troll and the rest of the betters he has a chance against Bruck."

Jonelle's eyes widened. Zane wouldn't refuse such a plush deal.

"I thought he was already into you for twenty thousand."

"He is. I want everything he's got."

"How's he going to talk the little gal into letting us kill her dog?"

"That's where you come in. You're going to need to snatch him."

"That's your job."

"You've done it before and have the equipment and know-how to deal with a dog Samson's size. I'll pay you five thousand just for the snatch." Simik took out his wallet.

He held out a roll of hard cash. Jonelle saw the greedy look on her husband's face, and her heart sank.

"Make it ten," Zane said. "I'm the one taking the chances."

"Ten thousand dollars for something that will take you all of an hour including driving time? Are you nuts? You stand to make half of the thirty the troll is willing to pay to get him trained." Simik pocketed his money and turned to go.

"Okay, six then."

The other man paused and drew the money out slowly. "Okay. But you've got to do it soon. I want to have time for you to starve him a bit and make him meaner. We have to make this believable."

Jonelle finally got up the nerve to speak. "I've seen that dog around town. You realize he's famous? They won't take his disappearance lightly. There will be a massive search."

Simik shrugged. "Yeah, but they won't find him. You'd better see to that."

"But—"

"Shut up, Jonelle," Zane barked.

Jonelle gulped. She'd heard about the little boy, just like everyone in the area. Lost in the woods with a hermit for nearly a year, he'd only been reunited with his mom for about seven months. It seemed hardly fair to snatch his pet. And without a doubt the boy's mother would search the forest until she found the dog. Zane wasn't thinking.

Zane turned back to Simik. "I'll do it," he said finally. "When you want me to get him?"

"The sooner the better. Once you beat a little meanness into him, we'll have an unprecedented attendance at the next fight. You have the knock-out drug?"

"Yeah, I got it. That dog is as good as dead."

⊗⊰⊱⊗

Cassie kicked off her shoes at the door and padded across the thick carpeting. The last few days at the lab had been grueling, but she relished the challenge. An enticing aroma of vegetable soup drew her toward the kitchen. Her stomach rumbled. She'd thought it was her turn to cook, but she wasn't complaining.

"I heard that," Salome called from the kitchen.

"I thought I'd beat you home. When you said you were going shopping, I was envisioning your usual all-day marathon." Cassie dropped onto a bar stool and propped her elbows on the granite counter. "Where's Dad?" Bubbles, Cassie's sheltie, lay on the floor by the stove. She got up and came to greet Cassie. Rubbing her dog's ears, Cassie watched Salome stir the pot.

"Asleep on his bed. I found this in the microwave." Salome shoved a file folder across the counter to Cassie.

Marked "Top Secret," Cassie had seen it before. "Dad can't let go of his research. It just breaks my heart." She flipped through pages of outdated research, skimming in vain for details from the project her dad had been working on with them. She tossed it onto the counter.

"You can't blame him for clinging to it," Salome said. "It's a hard fall from top of the research field to puttering around an empty house all day. And he was close to solving our problems before his memory failed."

"He could still do it if he had a couple of really clear weeks."

"I don't think that's going to happen."

The gentleness in Salome's voice was nearly Cassie's undoing. She dealt with it better when she didn't have to face sympathy. "He'll be fine," she said emphatically. "I'm going to find a cure."

Salome didn't say anything, she just kept stirring the soup. "We should be ready to eat in just a minute. You can start on your salad if you're starving."

"I can wait. How about if we eat out on the deck?"

"Sounds good." Salome pulled hot bread from the oven and put it in a basket. "What took you so long? You said you were just popping in on the lab for a minute. You never rest, not even on the weekend."

Cassie snagged a hunk of French bread, burning her fingers in the process. "Things are a nightmare at the office. Phil's death has left every-thing in turmoil. I really need his notes."

"Didn't you swing by to ask Denise?"

"I hate to disturb her now. Maybe in a few days, if they don't turn up on their own. Hey, I hopped on the pharmacy's Web site and put in a request to refill my asthma prescription. You're coming in late tomor-row; can you pick it up for me?"

"No problem." She looked up at Cassie. "Did you see the news-paper?"

"No, what is it?"

"A fringe environmentalist group has found out we're altering tobacco plants. They're predicting dire consequences." Salome tossed the paper at her.

"The media will be all over us. And more environmental groups will be coming out of the woodwork." She groaned. "I wonder if the nut who called the lab the other day was with this group."

"Could be," Salome said.

"Let's not worry about it now. I'm starved. I'll get Dad."

"He already ate. I think he's asleep."

"Okay, you grab the bread and I'll carry the bowls."

The women got the food to the patio table. The soft light of the fading day cast long shadows over the backyard before deepening to near black at the edge of the forest. One of the shadows moved, and Cassie squinted toward the neighbor's yard.

A woman dressed in crisp black slacks and a double-breasted red jacket waved to them. "Hi, neighbors. I just moved in." She stepped into their yard and came toward them.

Her black hair hung in a glossy curtain on her shoulders, making Cassie feel dowdy and plain. She stood to greet the woman. "We're fairly new ourselves." She put out her hand. "Cassie Hecko and my associate, Salome Levy. My father lives here as well, but he's asleep."

"He must be the scholarly gentleman I found in my kitchen this afternoon." The woman laughed.

"Oh no! I'm so sorry." Cassie wanted to hide under the table. "He was in your kitchen?"

The woman nodded. "I'm Marika Fleming. I've been wanting to meet you. May I?" She pointed to the chair.

Cassie nodded. "I'm so sorry about Dad. He has Alzheimer's."

"Not a problem. I'm a sucker for old folks." Marika sat in the chair, her smile still intact.

"You want some soup?" Cassie sat in the chair beside her. Marika waved off the offer with a smile.

"I'll get the salad," Salome murmured, slipping away through the sliding door.

"I represent NAWG," Marika began.

"The environmental group?" Cassie's warm feelings toward the woman began to evaporate. The North American Wilderness Group, better known as NAWG, was notorious for their underhanded actions.

Marika held up her hand. "Yes, but don't judge me on that. I want to help. I'd like to be your point person to help make sure things don't get out of hand at the lab."

"In spite of what the newspaper might report, I have everything under control," Cassie said.

Marika's smile faltered, then came back full wattage. "That's wonderful, but support from an objective third party couldn't possibly hurt anything. Could I see for myself?"

"I'm sorry, we don't allow anyone inside. It's part of our safety rules to make sure no seeds or plants escape from our contained area. The more visitors we have traipsing around, the more likely it is for a seed to be carried out on shoes."

"So you *are* growing new plants."

Too late Cassie realized she'd given away too much. She stood. "I really need to go check on my father. I'll try to keep a better eye on him."

"Don't let me run you off. I can take a hint." Marika stood too, her smile still friendly. "Just remember, I'm here to help if you need me." She gave a little wave and went back to her own yard.

"What was that all about?" Salome asked, carrying two bowls of salad through the door.

"I'm not quite sure," Cassie said with her gaze on the woman's back.

4

$\mathcal{C}$assie and Salome ate their dinner, then carried everything back inside. As they loaded the dishwasher, the doorbell rang.

"Another interruption," Cassie said. "You keep working and I'll get rid of them." With Bubbles on her heels, she hurried to the door.

She flung the door open and blinked in surprise. Bree Nicholls and Sheriff Mason Kaleva stood on the doorstep. Samson stepped forward, and he and Bubbles sniffed one another. Bubbles barked excitedly and raced off with Samson right behind her.

"Er, come in," Cassie said. She had a feeling she knew what was coming, but the questions were getting tiresome.

Bree looked around. "You've made this place your own pretty quickly. When Steve and Fay Asters lived here, it was much more sterile. I like it."

Cassie smiled. "It's still a work in progress." She pointed to the chairs and sofa. "Have a seat. I'm sure you didn't come out here to see what changes I've made in the house. Sorry I've been missing the training sessions, Bree. I've been really busy."

Bree looked at Mason, and he cleared his throat. "I need to ask you some questions about Philip Taylor. Your assistant lives here as well, I've heard. Could she join us?"

"I'll get her," Cassie said. She had Salome join them in the living room.

"So what do you need to know?" Cassie asked once they were all seated.

Mason uncapped his pen and fumbled in his pocket for his

notepad. "How well did you know Philip? Had he worked for you long?"

"About three years. He and the rest of the team worked with my father, when he was still a researcher. You knew Phil longer, didn't you, Salome?"

Her assistant nodded. "I worked with him on a project in Arizona for two years before we both came on board here. He was very conscientious and knowledgeable. More so than any other member of our team."

"Why all these questions? I thought he drowned," Cassie put in. The tension in the room seemed almost unbearable to her. She didn't look at Bree.

"That doesn't now appear to be the case. What was Phil working on?" Mason asked.

Cassie and Salome looked at each other. How much should she reveal? She chose her words carefully. "We're working on proteins that might aid in the treatment of diabetes." He didn't need to know their work went deeper than that.

"How many scientists are working on your project? And where did Phil fit into the mix?"

"Eight," Cassie said without hesitation. "Me, Yancy Coppler, Chito Yamamoto, Ian Baird, Nora Corbit, Lola Marcos, Salome, and Phil. I'm looking for someone to replace Phil, but that may take a while. He was brilliant."

"And you have how many employees?"

Cassie looked to Salome for the answer. Her assistant didn't let her down. "Fifteen right now," Salome said promptly. "But we have plans to expand the workforce to nearly fifty."

Mason continued writing in his small pad. "Anyone have a grudge against Phil? Did he ever seem agitated or afraid?"

"Good grief, no. Phil was the most likable guy on our team, next to Yancy, maybe. Of course, that might not be saying much. We can be a bit opinionated and set in our ways, but he was very genial."

Salome nodded. "If someone was going to get killed because they were obnoxious, it should have been Chito Yamamoto. He's the one always picking a fight. He wants to make everyone do things his way."

"Did this Chito and Phil ever argue?"

"They had their professional differences. But Phil was usually the peacemaker in the bunch. Are you thinking he was murdered?"

"He was shot," Mason said. "That means murder, or at the very least, manslaughter."

Murder. Cassie bit her lip. "I had a threatening phone call," she said slowly.

Mason looked up sharply. "I don't have a record of that."

"I didn't call. It's not an unusual occurrence."

"Male or female?"

She shrugged. "I couldn't tell. They were using one of those machines that mask your voice."

"You think the call might be related to Phil's death?"

"I don't see how. The person didn't mention Phil. I was just told to shut down the lab or face the consequences."

"When was this?" Mason wanted to know.

Cassie thought back. "Two days ago. The day after Phil died."

Bree needed some downtime after the past few frenzied days of the murder investigation. She'd promised Davy a picnic today, and since Phil's funeral wasn't until the afternoon, she packed a basket and drove out to the dock where her small dinghy stayed. The water on Lake Superior rolled in a seemingly endless realm of brilliant blue that matched the sky overhead.

Davy, his life preserver cinched snugly around him, sat at the bow with his arm around Samson, who wore a doggy smile as the wind blew in his face. Bree guided the dinghy into the inlet. The breeze kept the black flies off them and relieved the heat of the day. Near the end of the inlet, Bree killed the engine. The water and sky were placid here, with the exception of gulls dipping and veering overhead, their caws hoarse and loud.

She waved at the scuba club members on the shore. Several of the lab employees had joined the local club, and she counted ten divers out today. She recognized Ted Kemppa, the Larson men, and Carson Meeks, Samson's vet. Yancy Coppler popped his head up from the water and waved as well.

Bree smiled and closed her eyes for a moment, turning her face to the sun to soak up its warmth. Their picnic basket contained all the refreshment they'd need for the day, and a Styrofoam cooler held bait for the cane poles that lay on the floor of the boat. Davy had been begging to go fishing for days, and she couldn't have ordered up a better day for it. He'd asked if Nick could go along, but Bree hadn't extended the invitation. Davy was way too attached to the handsome fireman, especially when Bree wasn't sure the friendship he offered them could—or should—ever lead to anything more.

A sound caught her attention, and she squinted through the bright sunlight toward a figure on the shore.

"Help!" The woman on the bank waved to her frantically.

Bree could see no cause for alarm, but she guided the boat to shore. "I'm so glad you're here," the woman said breathlessly. About fifty, she wore jeans and a short-sleeved shirt. Red welts from bug bites peppered her arms in spite of the pungent odor of Deet, which the breeze brought to Bree's nose.

"Is something wrong?" Bree asked, rolling the netting back down over Davy's face as the black flies swarmed them. She tied her own netting as well and pulled on gloves before she and Davy got out of the boat.

"My Lacy is missing." The woman wrung her hands and looked back toward the woods. "We've been camped at Kitchigami Campground for two days. I let her out to relieve herself this morning, and she hasn't come back. I've called and called for her. One of the other campers told me about you and your dog and pointed you out to me."

"Lacy is your dog?"

The woman nodded. "She's a Chihuahua. Can you help me look for her?"

Bree nodded, though she had a feeling it would be useless. Likely a wolf or coyote had taken one look at little Lacy and decided she would make a tasty breakfast. "What's your name?"

"Oh, I'm sorry." The woman held out her hand. "It's Carol Matchett. I'm from Detroit."

"Are you here alone?"

Carol shook her head. "My best friend, Alice, is with me. She's a writer and is doing research up here, so I came along to keep her company. We're supposed to leave tomorrow. I've got to find Lacy!"

"We'll do what we can." Bree squeezed the woman's hand. "I'd like to let my dog sniff Lacy's bed or food dish or anything else you have that belongs to her."

Carol's face brightened, and she took off down the trail to the west. Bree held Davy's hand and followed with Samson. Campers, motor homes, and tents packed the campgrounds like mushrooms popped up in a moist meadow. Carol led them inside a fifteen-foot camper and showed them her dog's things. Samson sniffed around Lacy's bed and wagged his tail. He whined and went to the door. Bree told him to find Lacy, and he ran toward the road. Bree followed with Davy. Samson's headlong rush along the gravel road ended at the parking lot. He stopped and sniffed around the area then turned toward Bree, his tail drooping.

Bree frowned when her dog was unable to find the trail. She'd have bet money an animal had taken the little dog. One had, but it was apparently of the two-legged variety.

"Why is he stopping?" Carol demanded.

"Someone seems to have taken Lacy away in a car," Bree said. "Samson can't track a car unless the window is down, and this one evidently wasn't. I'm sorry. Likely some other family met up with Lacy and fell in love with her too."

Carol wrung her hands. "You have to find her," she wailed.

"I'll call the sheriff and ask him to be on the lookout for her. That's all I can do." Bree dug out her cell phone and punched in the number. The dispatcher promised to pass the word along, and Bree clicked off her phone. She squeezed Carol's hands. "I'm so sorry," she said. "I'll be praying for Lacy's safe return. I can only imagine how you feel. Samson is part of our family, and we would be devastated for something like this to happen to him."

"Thank you." Carol wiped at her eyes.

"Call me if you find Lacy." Bree gave her a business card.

The woman's sorrow over losing her dog put a pall on the bright day. Bree unpacked lunch and sent Davy and Samson to gather sticks for a fire to roast their hot dogs. She spread the blanket on the sand and began to pull out the contents of the picnic basket.

"Need some help getting the fire started?"

Bree turned toward the familiar voice and stared up into Kade's face. He wore a look of trepidation, as though he wasn't sure of his welcome. His windblown hair made him seem boyish, but the breadth and height of him was all man. Bree stood slowly. She felt breathless, and then felt stupid for it. This was the man she'd once thought she might spend the rest of her life with. Gazing into his eyes, she told herself her physical reaction to his presence was just because he'd frightened her.

"Kade, you startled me." Her cheeks felt hot, and she turned her back to finish preparing the lunch. She felt rather than heard his cautious approach. "What are you doing here?"

"I've missed you. Lauri mentioned you were going to be out here."

His low voice was nearly in her ear. All she'd have to do was turn and put her cheek against his chest. That simple gesture might be enough to mend the tension between them, but Bree felt paralyzed, unsure of how he really felt. How she felt. His steady strength and integrity drew her as always, but the memory of the way Davy's face lit up in Nick's presence was enough to reinforce her reticence.

Kade cleared his throat and stepped back when she didn't answer. Bree whirled, afraid he'd left. "I . . . I've missed you too." His gaze probed her face, and she felt vulnerable and exposed. Since the night Anu's husband had returned to town, they'd barely spoken.

He smiled and started to step closer, but Samson came leaping from the forest with Davy on his heels. The dog carried a stick in his mouth, and Davy had an armload of twigs. The boy skidded to a halt when he saw Kade. A scowl darkened his heart-shaped face, so like Bree's own.

"What's he doing here? I don't want him here."

"Davy, that's enough," Bree said sternly. "Apologize at once."

Davy thrust out his lip. "Sorry," he muttered. He refused to look at Kade but walked stiffly toward his mother and dropped the wood at her feet. "I wanted Nick to come."

Kade knelt with one knee on the sand. "You can have more than one friend, Davy. I thought we were getting to be friends."

Davy glanced at him quickly then looked away. "I want Mommy to be friends with Nick."

Bree winced, but Kade didn't even blink. "Mommy can be friends with me and with Nick. She doesn't have to pick just one friend either."

Bree stared at him. This was new. Kade's jealousy of Nick was what had brought about this impasse between the two of them. Before Davy could answer, the brush rustled, and they turned to look.

Nick came striding through the trees. His smile faded when he saw Kade standing beside Bree. He recovered his smile. "Am I too late for lunch?"

"Nick, you came!" Davy scrambled toward the fireman and flung himself against his legs.

Nick hoisted the boy into his arms. "I thought you wanted me to come. You sound surprised. I told you I'd try to make it."

Bree's jaw tightened. "Davy invited you?" She could sense Kade's withdrawal, and she felt suddenly angry with both Nick and Kade. The hostility emanating from both of them made her want to walk away from the whole situation. Maybe she should quit seeing Nick as well. Just focus on her son. Davy might like the fireman, but he'd soon get over it.

But looking at the boy's rapt face as he gazed up at Nick made her resolve fade as quickly as the morning mist over Lake Superior. Davy had come so far in the past seven months. She couldn't do anything to jeopardize his adjustment after all he'd been through.

"Davy, would you see if you can find a few more sticks?" If things got tense, she didn't want him to overhear. But neither Davy nor Nick seemed to hear her.

Kade slowly took his hand from his pocket then held it out to Nick. "Fletcher, I think it's time we called a truce. Bree and Davy aren't bones to be fought over. They can be friends with both of us. Let's start there."

Nick's eyebrows went up almost to his hairline. With obvious hesitation, he reached out and grasped Kade's hand. "We can give it a shot. Just so you know I don't like to lose."

"Neither do I," Kade said quietly.

Bree was tempted to grab Davy and get back in the boat. She wasn't sure either of them really wanted her for herself. They were like two dogs marking their territory. "Hey, you two, don't talk about me like I'm invisible. You're not even asking me what I want!"

Kade nodded. "You're right. What do you want?"

"I . . . I . . ." Bree's voice trailed off. "I don't know what I want, but I don't want either of you using . . . others . . . to get to me." She glanced at Davy.

"You know me better than that." Kade scowled.

"I'd never do that either," Nick said. He ruffled Davy's hair with a gloved hand. "Me and Davy are buds just because we want to be, right?"

"Right!" Davy squirmed to get down. "Come see the fish I caught, Nick."

Nick set him down, then followed the boy to the lake's edge. Left alone with Kade, Bree felt tongue-tied all over again. She knelt and put an arm around Samson, rubbing his ears. She didn't want to meet Kade's eyes. "Want some lunch? I have plenty." She continued to babble under Kade's steady gaze. "Lauri hasn't been to practice in a couple of weeks. What's she been up to?"

"I didn't come here to talk about Lauri," he said. "She's been telling me I'm an idiot for letting you go, and I finally came to my senses. I'm not going to make this easy for you, Bree. I'm not going to let Fletcher win by default. So I want us to start over. Are you willing?"

Starting over sounded good. Bree looked away. "I don't know, Kade. I've got too much going on for serious thought right now."

Kade seemed to accept her ambivalence. "How's the rest of the family? Hilary doing okay?"

"She seems almost overly happy, as though if she just ignores the problem with the pregnancy, it will pass. I'm so afraid of what she'll go through if she loses the baby." It felt good to talk to Kade again, to share her worries with him. His level head and calm manner always lightened her cares.

"Lauri is doing the same thing. She's determined that Naomi will be the one to adopt her baby, but Naomi and Donovan still haven't decided what is best for them. They're praying about it."

"I think Naomi's leaning that way though."

"I'd like to talk to her about it, but Lauri wants to handle everything herself." He picked up a stick and poked at the fire. "It's hard to let her handle this on her own."

Bree nodded. "How is the baby wildlife center doing? Landorf laying off your case?"

"Pretty much. He's basking in the media attention. The center is packed to near capacity right now. Someone brought in two eaglets yesterday. You should bring Davy by to see them."

"He'd love that. Maybe on Friday? I could bring him out after story hour at the library."

Kade nodded. "I'll be back to the center by around three. Come over then so I can show you around." He bit into a pretzel. "Anything new on the investigation?"

"Mason said Phil didn't drown. He was shot with a .44 magnum. We visited Cassie yesterday, and she seemed reluctant to say too much. I'm not sure how long Phil worked for her, so maybe it's just that she doesn't know much. And she's protective of her facility."

Talking to Kade, Bree felt as though the sun shone brighter and the trees turned greener. She hadn't been aware of just how much her estrangement from him had affected her until now. Samson bumped his head against Kade's hand. Kade laughed and then scratched the dog's ears. Bree's throat tightened at how much even her dog wanted to be around the big ranger. She just had to be sure what was right for Davy.

5

*R*ock Harbor Mortuary was packed by the time Bree made it to the parking lot. She left the windows down for Samson and went inside with Davy. She glanced around. Rock Harbor residents were out in force to support Denise, even though Phil was a newcomer. Bree took Davy's hand and walked into the crowd.

"There's Adrian, Mommy," Davy said. He pulled his hand from hers and ran forward to see his friend.

Denise stood by the casket with Adrian by her side. Bree pressed her arm. "How're you doing?"

"Okay," Denise said. Her eyes were red and puffy, and she avoided looking Bree in the eye. "Thanks for bringing Davy. He'll help Adrian stay occupied. Where's Samson?"

"In the Jeep." Bree watched Adrian show Davy a toy fire truck. They walked off to a secluded corner and squatted on the floor to play. Bree turned back to Denise. "Can I help with the twins today?"

"They're taken care of." Denise nodded to a corner. Bree spied the twins being carted around by Lola Marcos and Nora Corbit. Ian Baird stood stiffly beside Lola. He looked uncomfortable in his gray pinstripe suit, which had been unfortunately paired with a plaid shirt. As always, Yancy hadn't bothered to dress up. He wore a red-denim shirt over blue jeans and boots. He was coaxing a smile out of the babies.

Bree touched Denise's hand. "I have some food in the Jeep I thought I'd drop by."

"Fine," Denise said vaguely, reaching out to take the hand of the man in line behind Bree.

Feeling dismissed, Bree moved through the crowd to join Phil's colleagues. "You're a natural with children, Yancy," she told the researcher.

"I love kids. I wish I got to see my daughter more." He broke off and looked toward the door. Bree turned to look and saw an older man.

"That's Bernard Hecko," Lola said.

"Cassie's dad?" Bree asked. She glanced around for Cassie but didn't see her.

Nora nodded. "Poor man has Alzheimer's. He was a brilliant researcher until just a few months ago. It hit him fast."

Bernard ambled toward the group. "There you are," he said, beaming. "I've found it, Yancy! The missing piece of the puzzle. But I can't find my notes. Someone has moved them."

Chito squared his shoulders, and his jaw flexed. "You're causing a scene, Bernard. Go home. You don't need to be here."

Bernard pulled away. "You just want my notes," he shouted. "Everyone wants my notes."

Nora and Ian exchanged glances. Bree could see everyone turning to stare. Denise would be devastated if the funeral turned into a circus.

"I'll take care of him; he likes me," Yancy whispered as Bree started to move forward. He took Bernard's hand. "I've got something I've been meaning to ask you," he said. "Let's go to your house and talk about it." He led Bernard toward the door. "And I'll help you look for your notes, okay?"

Bree's own relief was reflected on the faces of the rest of the research team. "It's so sad," Lola said. "We'd have this project finished if Bernard hadn't gotten sick."

Abby reached for Bree. She scooped up the toddler and found joy in the soft little body. She nodded toward the baby's mother, who was sitting in a chair staring off into space. "She doesn't seem to be doing very well."

Chito shrugged. "About like you'd expect. She's always been a bit weak."

Nora scowled at him. "She's in shock, you moron! She hasn't slept since Friday. Poor kid."

Chito frowned back at her. "You're such a bleeding heart." He stalked off.

"Is that her mother?" Bree nodded toward a woman walking with determination toward Denise. She had the same nose and chin as Denise.

Nora nodded. "She's been hovering pretty closely. We told her we'd watch the twins today so she could tend to her daughter."

"What's up with Chito?" Bree asked.

Ian grimaced. "He's in one of his moods. Let him go. He'll talk archeology with anyone who'll listen and then he'll be fine."

Lola wrinkled her nose. "I'm glad he's not zeroing in on me. I'm sick of hearing about it."

"I take it he's an amateur archeologist?" Bree asked.

"Haven't you heard him droning on and on about it?" Nora yawned. "Snoresville. He's interested in the Ojibwa tribe now. Wants to get an amateur dig going at the burial site on Eagle Island. He's been exploring some underwater ruins."

"How fascinating," Bree said.

"Chito's all right," Ian said. "Nora just doesn't like him because he doesn't listen to her golden nuggets of wisdom." His voice held an edge.

"Drop it, Ian," Lola said sharply. "No one wants to hear your views anyway."

Bree could sense the hostility between the two researchers. "Do you all dive? I saw Yancy in the water earlier today."

Lola nodded. "It started with Yancy. He got hooked on scuba, then talked us into taking lessons. His new formula depends . . ." she broke off. "Sorry, I shouldn't be talking about it."

Ian shrugged. "Women can't keep their mouths shut," he snapped. "But I doubt Bree would understand it anyway."

"Probably not," Bree agreed. "I've gone down a time or two, but it always scares me. I like my feet firmly planted on terra firma."

Ian gave a curt nod and walked away.

Bree raised her eyebrows and looked at Lola. She frowned and shrugged before turning in the opposite direction.

"They were dating," Nora said as soon as Lola was out of earshot. "It never pays to date a coworker. I tried to tell them. Now we all have to deal with the fallout until they get over it."

Bree spotted Nick coming in the door. She waved at him, and he joined her and Nora. She introduced them, but Nick barely acknowledged her presence.

"I was wondering if you were here," Nick said.

Bree noticed how he ignored the baby in her arms. He'd always spent a lot of time with Davy, and she'd often wondered if he really liked all children or was using Davy to get to her.

"How long are you off-duty?" she asked.

"Three days. I thought we might take Davy out fishing one day."

"I'll have to see. I need to do what I can to help Mason find the murderer."

"Yeah," he looked around and lowered his voice. "Surely you'll need a break sometime."

"You could take Davy and go one afternoon," she offered.

He frowned. "It's not nearly as much fun without you."

He sounded like Davy when he didn't get his way. The pouting was even less attractive in a grown man. Bree forced a smile. "I'll see if I can get away a few hours."

His face cleared, and he smiled. "How about I take you to dinner when this is over?"

"I'm exhausted. I just want to stay home and veg out." Just thinking of smiling and keeping up with Nick's energy made her tired. What did that say about how she really felt about him?

"Tomorrow?"

"Okay. Why don't you come to the house, and I'll fix us dinner."

"Is it safe?" He grinned. "I'd rather take you both out."

Bree couldn't help but compare him to Kade. The big ranger never made her feel her cooking was sub par even though she knew it was. But Nick was a gourmet cook in his own right. No wonder he found her offerings to be less than adequate.

She decided not to make an issue out of it. Why should she complain about not having to cook? "As long as I get to pick."

He groaned. "You'll just pick the Suomi. I want a good steak. Let's go into Houghton."

"Davy hates steak."

"Steak joints have hamburger."

She didn't know why she was being difficult, but she was tired of accommodating everyone else. "Let's go for pizza."

"Fine. I can endure pizza for one night." He gave her a quick kiss then went toward the receiving line.

"Handsome man," Nora said. "His whole attention was on you."

"He's a fireman," Bree said.

"I thought I heard you were seeing that *bonito* ranger," Lola said.

"I was." Bree changed the subject. Her love life confused her, so she could only imagine how it looked to others.

The next day a storm front had pushed out the bright summer weather and replaced it with a cold drizzle more characteristic of autumn than late June. Weather in the U.P. was always unpredictable, and June could be capricious. Bree had learned to always carry jackets as well as yellow slickers for her and Davy in the Jeep.

"I hate rain," Naomi grumbled beside her in the Jeep.

Bree's cell phone rang. "Grab that, will you?" She tossed her cell phone to Naomi.

Naomi answered it. "Kitchigami Search and Rescue. Naomi speaking." She listened a moment. "Just a minute, you'd better talk to Bree." She covered the mouthpiece. "It's Cassie. Her father is missing."

Bree pulled off the edge of the road. This lane was too narrow to try to negotiate while on the phone. "Cassie? What's wrong?"

Cassie's voice was barely recognizable. "I came home for lunch to check on Dad. He's nowhere to be found. Bubbles and I have been looking, but . . . Can you bring Samson and see if you can find him?"

"I'll call in the team." She looked out at the drizzle. "I don't suppose he has a jacket on?"

Cassie's sigh was loud in the receiver. "I have no idea. The last I saw him this morning, he was in pajamas." She gave a hiccup. "This is my fault. I should have put him in the nursing home. I knew it wasn't safe to leave him."

"We'll be right there. The dogs will find him. The moisture in the air actually helps them." She clicked off the phone and dropped the gearshift into drive, then turned the Jeep around and headed toward town. Naomi made the necessary calls to the team. They dropped Davy off with Anu at Nicholls' Finnish Imports, then drove out to Cassie's house.

Cassie and Bubbles were waiting curbside when they got out of the Jeep. Bree let the dogs out and went to join them.

"You've got to find him, Bree." Cassie's face contorted. Samson whined and pressed against her leg as if to offer comfort. She dropped to her knees and buried her face in his fur.

Bree put her hand on Cassie's head, but she knew the best comfort would be to find her dad. "Do you have a scent article?"

Cassie raised her head and nodded. "I'll get it." She seemed to collect herself, then went to the door. The rest of the team began to arrive while Bree waited for Cassie to return. Once she had the search article, Bree sent her team out. She took Samson into the open field next to the house and let him sniff the socks Cassie had brought out in paper sacks. Samson sniffed the bag and began to wag his tail. He crisscrossed the field with his nose in the air then headed toward the woods across the road.

Bree glanced at the darkening sky and winced. The storm clouds obscured the sun and made the interior of the forest even darker. Hypothermia set in quickly in these conditions, especially with the elderly. An added problem was the density of the forest. The trees were so close together they were hard to walk through.

Cassie loped along beside her as she ran after her dog. Charley shot past them and raced after Samson. Naomi jogged behind them. They entered the woods, and their progress slowed. Brambles tore at Bree's jeans, and she had to force her way through the thick tangle of vegetation. Crushed evergreen needles stirred the air with pine scent.

"How old is your father?" Bree asked, pushing a tangle of vines out of her way.

"Sixty-five."

"Young for Alzheimer's."

"He's got the early-onset kind," Cassie said, panting as she tried to keep up with Bree. "Some of the time he's pretty good. It's just that you never know when he'll get one of his fuzzy days and go wandering."

"I didn't see him when I was at your house last week. He's done this before?"

"Never. I hoped this day wouldn't come, though Salome tried to warn me." Her voice sounded thick. "He sleeps a lot—he was napping when you were there—and he's not any trouble. I'd hoped to keep him home until . . ." Cassie looked away.

The dogs began to bark, then Samson came running back to Bree with a stick in his mouth. Charley was right behind with a small branch as well. "They've found him!" Bree petted her dog. "Show me, Samson."

Samson, his tail waving proudly, led her toward a stand of white pine. The tree limbs drooped close to the ground. She couldn't see into the thick branches, but the dog stopped in front of it and barked. "Shh. Quiet, boy." He whined and pressed into the branches.

Bree stooped and peered under the trees. A heavy scent of pine wafted up her nose. "Mr. Hecko, are you in there?"

"Doggone dogs. Won't give a body peace at all." The grumble from under the pine boughs sounded strong, and Bree looked over her shoulder at Cassie and smiled. "Sounds healthy enough," she said.

"Daddy, come out from under there," Cassie said. Her voice sounded strained.

Bree parted the boughs and shined her flashlight into the shadows under them. The man sat on a bed of pine needles. His hair stuck up on end, and he had five pens clipped to his pajama top. A fancy calculator was in his pocket, and he clutched a small microscope. "You ready to go home, Mr. Hecko? It's almost time for supper."

He shrugged then crawled on his hands and knees out from under the trees. Once in the open, he brushed the debris from his pajamas. He looked pale, and he was shivering. Bree whisked a solar blanket from her ready-pack and wrapped him in it. He clutched it around his chest, and she noticed his hands. Long, slender fingers like those of a pianist. They looked firm and supple and younger than his age.

"I've got work to do. The lab is expecting me," he muttered.

"Let's get you inside." Bree took his left arm, and Cassie took the other. They walked him out of the woods and across the road to the house. Naomi called in the rest of the team and dismissed them, then called the ambulance.

Bernard was shivering so hard by the time they got to the house, Bree was beginning to worry. They got him inside, and Cassie wrapped an electric blanket around him while they waited on the ambulance.

"My discovery will benefit the world," he muttered. "You have to finish it, Cassie."

"I will, Daddy." Cassie thrust a cup of hot tea in his hands. "Drink this. It will help warm you."

"I can't find my notes. Did you take them?"

"No, you filed them away, remember?"

He nodded. "I must find them. The research is so important." He touched Cassie's face. "You're a good girl, Cassie. I never told you how glad I am you're continuing my research."

"You told me, Daddy." Tears spilled over Cassie's lashes, and she stood and stepped away. "What am I going to do, Bree?"

"I think you'll have to hire full-time help for him. Either that, or—" Bree looked away.

"Or a nursing home," Cassie concluded. She rubbed the tears from her face with the back of her hand.

Bree wished she could help. Mr. Hecko seemed a fine man, and she could tell he and his daughter were close.

Bernard scratched his chin and looked up at Bree. "You look just like your mother when I first met her," he said.

Bree smiled. The poor guy must be mistaking her for Cassie, though they didn't look alike as far as she could tell. "Are you getting warm now?"

Mr. Hecko continued to stare at her. "I never thought I'd see you again, Bree."

How did he know her name? She'd never met him. Her attention caught on the gold ring on his pinky finger. A black slit ran through the center of the yellow stone and resembled the eye of a tiger. She stared at it, wondering where she'd seen it before. A sick feeling made her gulp.

She stared into his face then glanced at Cassie. The younger woman wore a strange expression—maybe resignation? Bree looked back at Bernard Hecko's ring. A familiarity settled over her. Her pulse thumped against the skin in her neck, and she felt almost faint as she remembered where she'd seen the ring—and Bernard.

She remembered a man her mother called Uncle Bernard. Bree used to twist a ring just like that around on his finger. He said it belonged to a tiger named Meow. She still remembered the stories he told her about the big cat.

Her gaze traveled back to his face. He was smiling at her. Her throat constricted. "You're not . . . Uncle Bernard?"

He smiled, and his eyes cleared even more. "I see you looking at Meow. You remember, don't you? Even though it's been so long, you still remember." His voice quavered, and his eyes reddened.

Bree gripped his hand. "Uncle Bernard, it *is* you."

He patted her hand. "It's me, my girl. You haven't forgotten your old man."

Her old man. What did he mean? Bree tried to pull her hand away. "I never figured out how you were related. Are you my father's brother or my mother's?"

His smile faltered, but he tightened his grip on her hand. "Neither, Bree." He swallowed, and his Adam's apple bobbed in his wrinkled neck. He looked at Cassie. "I can't tell her, Cassie. You'll have to do it."

Cassie stepped forward. Her voice was resigned. "He's your father, Bree. Our father."

Her father? Bree shook her head. "No. You're wrong."

The last trace of fogginess in Bernard's watery green eyes disappeared, leaving his gaze lucid and clear. He gripped her hand so tightly she winced. "Your mother never wanted you to know who I really was. She thought people would talk." He shook his head. "Like they weren't already."

With every passing moment, he seemed to become a different man, focused and alert. He raised a hand that steadied the closer it got to Bree's cheek. "So pretty," he crooned. "You were always so pretty. Your hair is a little darker now than it was when you were a little girl."

Bree felt frozen in place. She glanced around for Naomi. The sympathy in her friend's eyes steadied her.

"You had a little girl," she muttered. Bree remembered a small, solemn child who followed her around. She tore her gaze from Naomi's and studied Cassie. "Cassandra? You were Cassandra?"

Cassie's face was full of emotion: hope, fear, trepidation. She went to the coffee table and grabbed her purse. She pulled out a faded picture and handed it to Bree. "See if you recognize the children," she said simply.

Bree stared at the photo. She recognized her smiling mother and Uncle Bernard. Her own five-year-old self sat on the floor in front of them with her arm around a little girl with dark curls. The resemblance between the two children was remarkable, only Bree had red hair and

Cassie had brown. Bree glanced back to Cassie. Cassie's green eyes swam with tears, and Bree knew where she'd seen those eyes before. Looking back at her from the mirror.

"Breathe," Naomi whispered in her ear. She put a steadying hand on Bree's arm.

6

$\mathcal{B}$ree wanted to bolt from the house. She stared into Cassie's face. "You're my sister?" she croaked past a throat that felt wrapped in Spandex.

"Yes." Cassie thrust out her chin as if daring her to deny it.

Bree forced herself to ask questions she wasn't sure she wanted to know the answers to. "He moved away when I was six. How did you know where to find me?"

"Your mother sent him pictures and updates."

The very idea of her mother doing something so mundane and normal seemed unreal. She'd never even known her mother to take any pictures. There were her school pictures, but half the time her mom didn't buy but one sheet. "And your mother?"

"She died when I was ten."

"Did she know about me and my mother?"

"I doubt it. She didn't notice much of anything."

Cassie must have sensed Bree's panic, for she put her hand on Bree's arm and stopped her flight. "He loved you and your mother very much, you know."

Bree shook her head. "That doesn't make any sense. A father who loved me wouldn't have left me to deal with an alcoholic mother. He never so much as sent me a birthday card."

Cassie blinked and frowned. "I don't remember her drinking. She always smelled of lilacs, and her skin was so soft."

Bree looked away. Sometimes she remembered a laughing, smiling mother who baked cookies and read to her, but the memories were so buried by scenes of broken dishes, cursing, and slaps that she'd thought the others were merely fantasies. Could her father's leaving be what changed her mother? Her memories were so jumbled. Maybe her mother had been different before Bernard left. She didn't want to think about that. This raking up of memories was like pulling the scab off a wound.

She turned away from Cassie and yanked her fingers through her hair. All she wanted now was to get away and think about this. Her insides felt cold, like frosted glass. One more revelation and she would shatter into shards, each one cutting until she bled from a thousand wounds.

When she had herself under control again, she looked up to meet Cassie's anxious gaze. Bernard regarded her with a smile that seemed to say he knew she would welcome him with open arms. Her stomach churned with acid. "I'm sorry, you've caught me off guard. I hardly know what to think or feel." She wanted to scream, to ask how their dad could abandon her to slaps and screams instead of hugs and kisses. This man didn't even know her.

"I have the letters and photos if you'd like to see them," Cassie offered.

Bree shook her head. "No. Not now." The wail of the ambulance rattled the windows. Her work here was done. She took a deep breath and focused on Naomi's face. "Let's go, Naomi." She didn't dare look at Cassie or Bernard. Only those close to her would see her cry.

Saddle leather creaked as Kade rode Moses along Ribbon Trail. Glimpses of blue juxtaposed themselves against the thick green foliage, but he didn't have time today to slow his horse and enjoy the lake panoramas. It would take him at least an hour to ride out to Ribbon River, where a hunter had reported dozens of fish floating dead in the water.

He crested the hill and looked down into a meadow. Banks of wild-flowers made the thought of possible contamination that much more disquieting. He urged his horse, Moses, down the final leg of the trail to the creek. The black flies swarmed, but luckily his insect repellant was still potent. The nuisance of the bugs should ease in a few days.

As he reached the meadow and dismounted, he heard rustling in the brush. Probably fishermen. He tied Moses to a tree and swatted a black fly on his arm, then trod through the underbrush in the direction of the sound. Stepping from the shadows of a stand of white birch, he found a woman kneeling beside the river. She wore a pantsuit and what Kade assumed were once fashionable shoes.

She definitely wasn't a fisherman.

As he approached the river, he could see dozens of dead fish floating among the lily pads. In the open water, dozens more rode the current, their white bellies turned up to the black flies that feasted on them. Bile rose in Kade's throat at the odor. What could have caused this? There was nothing upriver that could have wreaked this devastation. The only operating lumbermill was downstream.

The woman saw him coming and stood. She wiped her hands on her slacks and left smears of moisture. Her smile seemed genuine.

Kade nodded. "Ranger Kade Matthews. What's going on here?"

The woman cleared her throat then spoke in a husky voice. "That's what I'd like to know. I'm with NAWG."

North America Wilderness Group. Kade had heard of them. They had their fingers in nearly every radical environmentalist activity that went on in the northern states. The group had been linked to everything from factory bombings to the destruction of bioengineered crops.

"Someone call you?"

The woman's smile widened. "You and I are on the same side, Ranger. We're both wearing white hats. There are creek chubsuckers dead here, and they are on the endangered species list. This can't be allowed to continue."

"I agree. That's my job," he said. He knelt and looked through the dead fish. The woman was right. He saw at least two of the endangered fish floating in the carnage. "This is bad," he muttered.

The woman nodded. "Would you be willing to talk to the media about this? I plan to call the networks as soon as we get back to town. We need all the attention we can get to find out what happened and stop it."

Kade stood and wiped his hands on his pants. "I don't think so. I'd rather face a charging bear than a camera any day." Her lips twitched, and he saw the amusement in her eyes.

"I can handle the media," she said.

She reminded him of someone, but Kade couldn't place the woman's face. Her dark hair was coiled atop her head, and her chiseled features added to the regal look. Someone else Kade knew carried herself like a princess, but the memory just wouldn't surface.

"You handle the media then, and I'll track down what's causing this," he said.

"Only if you can do a better job than your predecessors. They let the Michigan grayling go extinct." She smiled. "But you look quite competent."

"The department did what it could to conserve the fish," he said. "Sometimes nothing we do helps."

She nodded. "I didn't mean to cast blame. I've heard about you and your conservation efforts, Mr. Matthews." She stepped away from the river. "I'll be in touch."

"You look familiar. What's your name?"

She blinked and looked away. "Marika Fleming. But we've never met. I'd remember someone like you."

Fleming. The name didn't ring a bell. He tipped his hat and watched her walk out of the meadow and up the slope covered with wildflowers.

He turned again to look at the fish. He had to figure this out and prevent it from happening again. He didn't want any fish to go extinct on his watch either.

He swung into the saddle and proceeded down the path along the river. Several times he saw what appeared to be dumping spots. Empty five-gallon buckets and trash littered the sites. But what could have been dumped with such catastrophic effect? He took water samples from each spot, labeled the bottles, then grabbed the buckets and lashed them to the saddle. He'd have them tested to see if they were tainted.

Ribbon Trail petered out at an outcropping that rose thirty feet to a high, rocky shelf overlooking the river. Kade dismounted and looped Moses's reins around a shrub. He climbed to the top of the cliff. From the view here, he could see nearly the whole watershed basin. The wilderness looked pristine. If he hadn't seen the fish with his own eyes, he would have thought the water running through here was as pure as it looked.

The old copper mine that MJ Pharmaceuticals had converted to a lab lay upstream, just beyond a stand of aspen. He dragged his binoculars out of the pouch at his waist for a better look. He brought the lenses to his eyes, and the figures jumped into focus. Two people in white lab coats were entering the mine. Yancy Coppler and Nora Corbit. He put his binoculars away and climbed down to his horse. He'd need to head over to the mine and take a good look at their waste disposal systems. But that would have to wait. First he'd have the buckets tested. Then he'd have a better idea of what to look for.

"What's the matter, boy?" Jonelle Ketola crouched at the fence and peered in at Zane's prize pit bull. Bruck was pacing the containment area on stiff legs. Jonelle didn't dare put her hand in the pen when the dog was in this state. She hoped he would calm down soon.

Zane yanked her back from the fence. "Careful. He's pretty agitated. Maybe the dose of steroids and cocaine needs to be adjusted. He ain't focusing like he should. I'll cut tomorrow's dose in half." Zane stood, watching the dog prance around his pen. "He's a fine specimen, the best dog I've ever had. Look at those muscles."

Jonelle nodded. Thick muscles rippled under the sleek, black coat. The dog would rather die than lose a fight. His reputation had spread far through the country's underground dogfighting networks.

It was getting hard to find someone willing to pit his dog against Bruck, but she knew what her husband planned. If he could get his hands on Samson, the event would attract hundreds of spectators. Everyone wanted to see Bruck lose. The dog's defeat would satisfy the personal vendetta of some owners who had lost their dogs to Bruck's drug-induced bloodlust. Their desire for Bruck's defeat would blind them to Zane's schemes.

Jonelle held up the bowl. "I've got their food."

"You're all dressed up. You heading to Houghton?"

"Yeah, I want to start getting some baby stuff." She tried to hand him the food, but he pushed it away.

"Take it back. I'm not feeding them today. They have a practice match tonight. Simik brought me some bait dogs."

Jonelle grimaced. "I hate it when you use those dogs. They don't hardly know what's going on. Can't you use rabbits or something?"

"It's not the same. Just remember, this is all for the baby. If we didn't have the dogs, you wouldn't be going shopping. You're too soft-hearted."

She slipped her arms around his waist. He embraced her with one arm, but his attention was on the dogs. "I need your help today, so don't go gallivanting off to town just yet."

She sighed, and her smile faded. She let go of Zane and started to lean over the fence to throw a treat to Bruck. The dog growled low in his chest then lunged at her. She snatched her hand back just in time. She had better keep her mind on her surroundings instead of day-dreaming about the baby.

"I just told you not to feed him. He's liable to leave you with a stump. Besides, I don't want you making him soft."

The dog growled again and leapt up on the fence. He could smell the food and wanted it ferociously, which Jonelle knew was just the state Zane liked to keep him in. He grabbed up the cattle prod and zapped the dog with it. Bruck yelped and snarled, but slunk away. Jonelle flinched.

"He needs to spend some time on the treadmill," Zane muttered. "Burn off some of that energy."

"What are you wanting help with?" Jonelle linked her hand through Zane's elbow.

"A dognapping."

She groaned. "Zane, you already got some dogs. Let it be." Her heart sank. She didn't want him to take that Samson. He was a pet.

"This dog's going to bring in some good money. Don't feel too sorry for him. He'll give Bruck a good fight."

"I don't think Bruck can be beaten. Isn't that good enough for you? Do you want him to fight until he is finally bested, or do you want him to go down in history as the greatest fighting dog ever?"

"He's not ready to retire. Look at him; he's still in his prime. I'll know when the time comes."

She sighed. "What do I have to do?"

"Just drive the truck."

She sighed but followed him to the truck. They drove to town in silence. She knew he could sense her disapproval by the way he turned his head and stared out the window at the passing scenery.

"We could do a lot with the money," he said abruptly. "Put up another barn and maybe start to breed Bruck. With the prices I could get for tough pups, we could put that new room on the back of the house you been wanting."

Jonelle had been bugging him about that new room for two years. But she wasn't sure the price tag was worth it.

They reached the edge of town. "How do you know where to find this dog?"

"We'll drive past where he lives. Go that way."

Jonelle drove out Negaunee toward the lighthouse. The thick leaves hid the structure until they passed the Blue Bonnet. "There it is," he told her.

Jonelle sighed but drove on.

"Let's see if he's in the yard."

Jonelle nodded and slowed the truck. They crept past the lighthouse, but the yard was deserted and no Jeep was parked in front. "They must be gone," he muttered. He drummed his fingers on his leg. "Head to town," he ordered. "There are two other places to check."

"We can't snatch a dog in the middle of downtown," she protested.

"We won't. But maybe the kid and the dog are with the aunt or the grandmother. I got both their addresses."

He had her cruise by Anu Nicholls's neat cottage, but nothing stirred there. Then he directed her to the edge of town. "There he is!" He pointed to the handsome dog lying under an oak tree in front of a large home on the hill. "What a beauty! Look at the muscles on him."

Jonelle looked at the dog. And she watched the avarice on Zane's face as he drank in the sight of the big dog.

"Looks to be part shepherd," he muttered. "And he's been trained for endurance. He won't die quick."

"Are you nuts? That's the sheriff's house!"

He blinked, then his smile spread. "It just makes it a challenge, darlin'. Park here." He put on a heavy coat and gloves.

The dog lifted his head when Zane approached. Jonelle shook her head. Funny how most dogs could sense danger.

"Hey, Samson," Zane said softly. From his pocket he pulled a steak in a plastic bag. "Look what I have for you." He opened the bag and held out the meat.

Jonelle grinned when the dog sniffed it then took it delicately in his mouth but didn't eat it. Zane may have been outsmarted. Samson continued to eye Zane warily.

"Eat it, pooch."

Jonelle knew the meat was laced with a sedative. Samson laid it on the porch and gave it a lick.

Zane pulled a choker leash from his pocket. She wasn't sure he could get it around Samson's neck. The dog seemed pretty wily. Jonelle glanced at the curtained windows. Someone could come any minute. They needed to get the dog and get out of here.

He held out his gloved hand. "Take a whiff, Samson. I'm okay."

The dog showed his teeth but took a delicate sniff of Zane's proffered hand. Samson's hackles didn't go down though. Jonelle felt her admiration for the dog rising. This was one smart animal. He knew when to be wary.

Zane harrumphed and stood. "I'll have to use the stun gun. You can't blame anyone but yourself, pooch."

He jogged back to the truck and got it out of the back. "He's not taking the bait."

"So I see," Jonelle said through the open window. "Just leave him be, Zane. He seems a really nice dog. I saw his picture in the paper, and he saves lost people. Besides, he's that little boy's pet."

"Shut up!" He strode back to the dog.

Jonelle held her breath. Samson lay with his nose to the untouched steak. Zane didn't waste any more time trying to coax the dog. He loaded the dart in the gun and aimed it at the dog. "Sweet dreams."

The dog flinched and yelped when the dart struck his flank. He turned to bite at the dart, then got to his feet and started toward Zane. Samson staggered as he neared, then crumpled into a heap.

Jonelle shuddered at the smile of satisfaction on her husband's face. Zane slipped his hands under the dog and started to lift him. He grunted with exertion. "I might need your help, Jonelle. This is one heavy dog."

She started to get out of the car, but he managed to heft the dog to his chest and stagger toward the truck.

"Hey, you there! What are you doing with that dog?" A pregnant woman stood on the porch. A little boy ran past her down the steps.

"Let go of my dog!" The child reached Zane before the woman and pummeled his legs. "Give me back my dog!"

Zane shook the boy off. "Get away from me, kid."

The boy clung to his leg like a limpet, and the dog started to slide from his arms. Holding her stomach, the woman came running across the yard. Dropping the dog, Zane shoved the kid away and ran for the safety of the truck.

He waved the gun. "Stay back or I'll shoot!"

"Samson!" The kid wailed and flung himself onto the prone body of the dog.

The woman stopped suddenly and bent over double. "Davy, go get the phone," she said, clutching her stomach.

"Samson's dead!" The kid was crying in earnest now.

"No, he's not, but I have to get help." The woman groaned.

Jonelle spared one last look as Zane flung himself into the truck. Even from here, she could see how pale the woman in the yard was.

"Get us out of here!" he shouted.

As the truck roared away, she had one last glimpse of the woman in agony.

7

The bubble light on top of the sheriff's car in front of Hilary's house was rotating, but the deputy had turned off the siren. Bree jammed her foot on the brake and threw the Jeep into park. She was out the door practically before the vehicle stopped moving.

Davy was crouching over Samson. Wailing, he kept trying to rouse the inert dog. When he saw Bree, his face screwed up even more, and he broke into noisy sobs. "Make him wake up, Mommy."

Bree knelt by her son and pulled him onto her lap. She was almost afraid to touch Samson. Her heart was beating loudly in her ears, and she felt faint. She reached out and touched the dog. Warm. And his chest was still moving up and down. Relief came in a sweet flood. "He'll be okay, sweetheart. He's just sleeping." She saw the dart on the dog's flank and pulled it out. She started to toss it away with an angry gesture, but instead laid it on the ground. Mason might need it for evidence.

"Where's Aunt Hilary?"

"In the house with Uncle Mason." Davy rubbed at his eyes. "I want to play ball with Sam."

"Dr. Meeks is on his way here. He'll take care of Sam." She needed to check on Hilary but couldn't tear herself away from Davy and Samson until more help arrived.

Why Samson? Did someone need to use him to locate something or someone? His tracking ability was the only thing that set Samson apart from other dogs. But if that's what it was, all they had to do was ask for her help, and she'd gladly give it. And Davy could have been hurt as well.

"Make him wake up, Mommy," Davy sobbed again. He buried his face against her shirt.

"The vet will be here any minute," she said, hugging him.

The ambulance screamed down the street and stopped in front of the house. Bree looked up from her intent concentration on her dog. "Was Aunt Hilary hurt?"

Davy nodded. "She was holding her tummy and crying."

Bree winced and closed her eyes. *Please God, let Hilary and the baby be all right.* She stood with Davy in her arms as another car pulled in behind the ambulance. She recognized the vet's car. The paramedics raced past her, and she waited until Dr. Meeks knelt by Samson.

"I'll take care of him," the vet promised, opening his bag.

She put Davy down. "You stay here in case Samson wakes up and needs you," she told him. She dreaded to see what was happening inside the house.

Hilary's sobs, mingled with Mason's deep, soothing voice, came through the bedroom door. A hopeless quality about her sister-in-law's cries broke Bree's heart. She walked slowly toward the bedroom. Reaching the doorway, she paused and peeked inside. Papers were strewn on the floor, probably from the book Hilary had been working on. The paramedics were taking Hilary's vitals. Mason held her hand. Her mascara had run in rivulets down her face.

"Hil?" Bree said softly.

Hilary's face crumpled still further. "I lost the baby, Bree."

"Oh no." Bree closed her eyes, but the tears leaked out anyway. She went to the bed and sank to her knees. "I'm so sorry, Hil. Has anyone called your mom?"

Mason nodded. "I did. She's on her way."

Bree didn't know what to say. She reached out and squeezed Hilary's hand. The comforting words she wanted to say felt trite. Only God knew if Hilary could get pregnant again. It had been a miracle the first time, and Bree wasn't sure if God would grant more than one of this type.

"Di . . . did the man hit you, Hil?"

Hilary just shook her head without answering. Mason slid a side-long glance at Bree. "She ran outside when the guy tried to take Samson. The pregnancy was already pretty shaky." His voice trembled.

Guilt swept over Bree. If Davy and Samson had been with her, maybe this wouldn't have happened. "I'm so sorry," she whispered.

"Not your fault," Mason said.

Hilary turned her head away, and Bree wondered if it was because she couldn't bear to look at her. Maybe she was being too sensitive, but she could almost feel the accusation radiating from Hilary.

"Kulta," Anu whispered from the doorway.

She went to her daughter's side, and Bree tiptoed out of the room. She felt aimless and wished Kade were here to hold her. Wrapping her arms around herself, she went outside.

"How's Samson?" she asked the vet.

"Drugged. He's going to be okay, maybe tired and achy for a few hours. But he's strong. I gave him something to counteract the sedative, and he should be rousing soon. See he gets plenty of water." The vet snapped his bag shut and stood. "You have any idea what this was all about?"

"I wish I knew. Another dog, a small one, was taken a few days ago. But it's probably just coincidental."

Dr. Meeks rubbed his chin. "Maybe not. I've heard that a couple other small dogs have come up missing lately."

Samson began to stir. Bree sank to her knees and ran her hands over his curly coat. He raised his head and licked her hand. She gave a shaky laugh and buried her face in his neck, breathing in his familiar doggy scent.

"Thanks, Dr. Meeks," she murmured. At least Samson would accept her comfort, even if Hilary wouldn't.

"You're quite welcome. I don't often make house calls, but Samson is someone special." He nodded to Bree and Davy and went toward his car. "Call me with any questions," he called over his shoulder.

By now, Samson was struggling to get up. He licked Davy's hand, then stood on wobbly legs. Davy threw his arms around the dog's neck.

Bree resolved to keep a closer watch on both Samson and Davy. "Come to the house," she told Davy. He led the dog toward the front door, passing the paramedics on their way out.

Inside the house, Bree gave her son some crayons and a coloring book Hilary kept for him and went back to the bedroom. Standing outside the door, she heard Hilary's heartbroken voice.

"It's all the dog's fault. If I hadn't been running to save him . . ."

Rubbing the tears from her face, Bree stepped into the room. "Is there anything I can do for you, Hilary?"

"No." The answer was muffled. "Just go home and get that dog out of here."

Anu sent Bree a pleading glance, and Bree tried not to be hurt. Hilary was just reacting out of pain and desperation.

"It's not Samson's fault, Hil," Mason said, taking his wife's hand.

Hilary closed her eyes, and her face contorted. She swallowed, and her chest heaved. She opened her eyes and held out a hand to Bree. "I'm sorry, Bree. It's not your fault or Samson's. It was an accident. I just want to blame something, someone." Her chin wobbled. "Forgive me."

Bree squeezed Hilary's cold fingers. "It's okay, Hil," she said. "I understand. Call me if you need anything."

Mason pressed his lips to Hilary's hand, then laid it down and followed Bree down the hall. He caught her at the door to the living room.

"Sorry, Bree. She and Samson have never been the best of friends. You know how she is about dogs. She'll be up and down like this for days."

"I know." Bree looked away. She couldn't bear to see the pain in Mason's eyes. This was as hard on him as it was on Hilary. "I'm so sorry about the baby."

"Thanks. Thanks for understanding."

"No problem. I love Hilary. I wish I knew what's happening."

"I heard Bertie Smith's two poodles are missing."

"Dr. Meeks mentioned other missing dogs, but they're all small ones. You think they're all connected?"

"Yesterday Doug Montgomery wondered if a dogfighting ring has cropped up somewhere nearby," Mason said. "They typically use small dogs for training, bigger dogs like Samson for the real deal. It might be a hunch worth looking into."

She frowned. "I'm going to have to watch over Samson like a hawk. I can't let anything happen to him. It would crush Davy. Me too." Bree glanced into the living room where Samson lay with his head on Davy's lap while her son colored. Her two boys. To get to either of them, they'd have to go through her.

Naomi stirred the whipped cream into her mocha and took a sip. Timmy sat beside her, his thin legs swinging happily as he licked his sugar-free chocolate cone. "Want to go to the park when we're done?" she asked him. Emily was at her best friend's house for a sleepover, and Naomi was enjoying this one-on-one time with Timmy.

"Can we go to the park?"

"Sure."

A woman stepped through the door to The Coffee Place. The pharmacist, Terry Alexander, waved to her from his table in the corner. She waved back, then walked to the counter and ordered black coffee and bought twenty dollars in Lotto cards. Her dark hair gleamed above a red sweater that showed way too much cleavage, and her black jeans were tight enough to show her liver working, as Naomi's grandmother used to say. Naomi stared, trying to place the woman.

Steve Asters came in. His eyes widened when he saw the black-haired beauty, and his gaze cut to Naomi. He raised his voice a bit. "Marika O'Reilly, I didn't know you were back in town."

"It's Marika Fleming now. I've been married and divorced again since I was here last." She smiled up at Steve in a way that suggested she wouldn't mind considering him for the role of husband number three.

Marika? Naomi stared. She had seen her picture in Emily's room. Naomi nodded her thanks to Steve for warning her, then took Timmy's hand. "Let's go," she whispered.

They'd almost reached the door when Marika turned and saw them. Her eyes zeroed in on Timmy's face, and recognition spread across her face. She took a step toward them. "Timmy," she said softly.

Timmy stopped and pulled his hand from Naomi's grasp. "Hello," he said, licking his cone. "Are you here to buy some berry stuff?"

"Don't you know me, Timmy?" Marika approached and knelt before the boy. A myriad of emotions rippled across her face as though she were an actress not sure what part she was supposed to play. Longing, consternation, love, all mingled into a visual kaleidoscope that left her mouth sagging.

Timmy looked at her curiously. "Hello." Something in Marika's face must have alarmed him, and he took a backward step.

Naomi wanted to snatch him into her arms and dash out the door, but she stood rooted to the floor. She felt horrified yet not surprised. With all the calls Marika had made lately to Donovan, she'd been half expecting something worse than phone calls. Here it was.

How long had Marika been in town? Had Donovan seen her and not mentioned it? Naomi tried not to think her husband would keep something like this from her, but next to Marika, Naomi felt plain and dowdy. She wished she'd taken the time to curl her hair this morning instead of pulling it back into a French braid. And she'd just grabbed faded jeans and a T-shirt when she got out of the shower this morning. There wasn't a stitch of makeup on her face.

"I've missed you, Timmy." Marika drew closer.

Timmy regarded her. "Are you my mom's friend?"

The children had begun to call her Mom, and at first Naomi had been taken aback, but Donovan thought they needed the stability of a mother and had encouraged it.

Marika's eyes narrowed, and her upturned lips went straight and white. Spots of red darkened her cheeks. Her eyes filled with tears. "I'm your mom, Timmy. Don't you know me?"

Timmy's eyes grew large. He backed away from Marika, clutching at Naomi's jean-clad leg. "I want to go home, Mom."

Marika swayed and grasped Steve's arm to steady herself. "I'm your mom, Timmy. Me. You've seen my picture, haven't you?"

"I want my mommy," he sobbed, reaching for Naomi.

His tears broke the paralysis that had held Naomi in place. She lifted Timmy into her arms. He wrapped his legs around her waist and buried his wet face in her neck, jamming his dripping cone into Naomi's braid. The warm, moist feel of his breath strengthened her.

"Please. Give me my son," Marika said, holding out her arms.

"I think you need to take this up with Donovan," Naomi said, starting for the door. "Timmy doesn't remember you, and I'm sure you don't want to scare him."

Crying now, Marika came after her. "Just let me hold him a minute."

The other woman's pitiful plea did not match her stance—shoulders jutting slightly forward and fists clenched—and Naomi shook her head. "I'm sure Donovan will allow reasonable visitation." She reached the door and pushed it open.

Marika followed her outside. "I want more than visitation." Her attempt at a smile was more of a grimace. "You're Naomi, right? I'd like us to be friends, please. For the sake of the children."

Naomi would rather open her arms to a barracuda. She wanted to ask why Marika had abandoned her children, but Timmy didn't need to hear them squabbling. His small chest was heaving. He needed to be out of this situation. She'd get Davy and head to the library, do whatever was needed to distract her son.

Marika made no more move to stop them, and Naomi gained the safety of her car. She buckled Timmy into his car seat then sped away. She found it impossible to keep from looking in the rearview mirror. Marika hadn't moved from her spot on the sidewalk and still stared after Naomi's car.

Naomi didn't want to feel sorry for her, but she couldn't help it. If Timmy had been her own child and he'd run from her into the arms of another woman, she would have been hurt too. Bree would have been crushed if Davy hadn't recognized her when he was found in the woods after missing a year. But unlike Bree, Marika had brought this all on herself. Naomi didn't want to think about what had coaxed the woman back into town. Whatever it was, it surely spelled trouble.

The stereo was pounding out the "William Tell Overture." The music was so loud, Cassie could feel it in her bones when she entered the house. Bubbles was cowering in the corner, her paws over her ears. Cassie stepped to the stereo and flipped it off.

"Dad?" she called. Bubbles followed her to the living room, but no one was there in her dad's chair. "Maybe he's napping, though how anyone could sleep through that noise is beyond me," she told Bubbles. The dog followed her down the hall to her father's room. His bed was empty.

So was his closet.

Cassie stared into the room. Dresser drawers hung open, their contents missing except for a lone sock that lay draped over one drawer. Not again. Panic clawed at her chest. She ran down the hall to the family room. The sliding glass door stood open.

She stepped onto the back deck. "Dad!" Only a crow answered from atop the phone line. Where could he have gone? She raced back inside, rushing to the refrigerator to see if he'd left a note. The smooth, stainless surface held no hint to her father's whereabouts. She glanced in her office and found things out of order there with some of her files lying on the floor.

Her hands shaking, she dialed Bree's number. She should have called the nursing home after the last time, but he'd seemed so much better. She was dumped into voice mail. Her voice trembled as she left a message. Then she turned to her dog. "Come on, Bubbles, maybe you can remember enough to help this time." She ran to her dad's room. His hamper still held dirty clothes. She lifted Bubbles to the opening. "Sniff, girl."

The dog whined and wiggled to be let down, but Cassie pressed her head into the pile of dirty laundry. When she was sure Bubbles had gotten a good whiff, she put the dog down. "Find Dad, Bubbles. Find him!"

The dog cowered on the carpet and whined again. Cassie felt like picking her up and shaking her, but it wasn't the dog's fault they hadn't been to training in months. She ran her hand through her hair and went to call the sheriff's office.

While she was looking up the number, the phone rang and Cassie grabbed for it. "Bree?" she said breathlessly.

The phone was silent, though she thought she could hear someone breathing. "Who's there?" she demanded.

"Cassie?"

She closed her eyes, relief coursing through her. "Dad? Where are you? I'll come get you."

"I need you to bring me my notes," he said, his voice shaky.

"We'll worry about your notes later. Tell me where you are."

"They're in an orange folder. Or was it blue?" her father continued, his tone worried.

"Dad, where are you?" She heard a clatter; then the phone clicked. "Dad, Dad?" The phone was dead. Cassie threw it across the floor where it spun to a stop under the coffee table. Her blood was pumping along like a river to the falls. Wait, she had caller ID. She fell to her knees and scrabbled for the phone.

Out of network. Where had he called from? She wanted to cry but knew she didn't dare give in to the luxury of tears. She grabbed the phone book again to call the sheriff. The phone rang again, and her pulse raced.

"Dad?"

"Come get me, Cassie. Come get me now."

Bree felt afraid to leave Samson and had the dog shadowing her every minute, which meant Davy stayed close by her side too. Her appetite was gone, both from worry about her dog and the situation she faced with her newfound father and half-sister. She talked it over with Anu on the phone, though she'd known what her mother-in-law would say.

"You must forgive him, *kulta*," Anu had told her. "As a Christian, you are commanded to harbor no bitterness."

Bree wished she had Anu's strength of faith. Bleary-eyed from lack of sleep, she drove to town. She pulled into a spot in front of Nicholls's, then took Davy's hand and skirted a motor home parked too far from the curb. She opened the door to the store and held it for Samson and Davy to enter. Her mother-in-law was on her knees arranging a display in the front window.

"Grammy, we're here," Davy said.

"So I see. Come give your grammy a hug." Anu settled back into a seated position on the floor and held out her arms.

Davy rushed to throw his arms around her, then smacked his lips against her cheek. "Me and Mommy are going to go see my new aunt and my grandpa. I didn't know I had another aunt besides Aunt Hilary. And this isn't Grandpa Abe."

Anu's gaze skittered quickly to Bree's face in a probing look. Bree smiled to hide the trepidation she felt, but Anu stood and dusted off her hands.

"I have fresh *pulla* in the display case, my *lapsi*. Eino will give you some milk to drink with it if you ask."

"Yay!" Davy tugged on Samson's collar. "Come on, Sam. You can have a bite too." The dog looked as eager as Davy. The two moved quickly through the store to the back where Anu's bakery case was filled with Finnish treats.

Anu took Bree's arm and guided her to a secluded corner away from the ears of the tourists who thronged the store. "You do not seem too sure of this sister, *kulta*. I see unease in those green eyes of yours."

Bree looked away. Anu sometimes saw too much. "I don't think I could have faced seeing him until I talked to you and you helped me get some perspective."

"It will get easier as you get to know them both."

"I don't know how to get to know them," Bree said. "I only have vague memories of Cassie and m—her father." She couldn't say the words "my father." She'd lived so long with believing there was no father in her life that it was hard to even admit she might have one who had loved her.

"Give them a chance, my Bree," Anu urged. "They've come a long way seeking you. It took much courage for them to come here and tell you who you really are."

"I know, but what's their goal? It's impossible to recapture those lost years."

"You all carry much baggage. Perhaps together you can find healing."

"I don't want them to hurt Davy."

"Such a loss not to know our boy." Anu glanced toward Davy with a fond look. He was tossing bits of *pulla* to Samson and eating some himself. He wore a milk mustache. "I think they only want to be part of your lives."

Bree thrust out her chin. Maybe she was being overprotective, but Davy had gone through enough, and she didn't want him to face more trials. A stupid wish, when she stopped to think about it. Life was full of battles and challenges. She couldn't keep everything from him, no matter how hard she tried. The realization frightened her. "I don't want him scarred."

"Nor do I," Anu said quietly. "But there is never so much love in our lives that we can afford to reject it when it is offered."

"I don't know for sure the Heckos are offering love."

"Try to hold your misgivings for now. Wait and see. I feel sorry for them both."

"You feel sorry for everyone," Bree pointed out. She managed a smile. "I should be more like you. It's hard to trust after being hurt."

"I am protective of you and Davy," Anu said. "If I thought Cassie and her father intended hurt, I would tell you to stay far away." Anu caressed Bree's hair, and Bree leaned into the touch. "*Kulta,* it is time you let go of that bitterness. We have talked of this before, and I have backed down when I saw your pain, but no more. You must ask God to release it. He is with you, even in the deep places of hurt."

Bree pulled away and jumped up. "I'm going to be late to Cassie's. I have to go."

"You can't run when God is telling you to do something, my Bree. He will make you miserable until you give in. Your childhood is in the past. Let it go."

Bree didn't answer. "Davy, it's time to go meet your Aunt Cassie and your Grandpa Bernard."

Her son swiped the back of his hand across his mouth and stood. "Come on, Sam." He and the dog scampered across the floor to where she stood. "See you later, Grammy."

"I will be praying for you, *kulta,*" Anu said quietly. "You know what you must do. I will pray God will give you the strength."

Bree kissed Anu on the cheek. It wasn't her mother-in-law's fault Bree's childhood had been so miserable. "Love you," she whispered before taking Davy's hand and hurrying to the door.

8

*M*otor homes and trucks pulling campers plied the road in both directions as Bree drove her old Jeep out to Cassie's house. It was hard to think of it as Cassie's house when Steve and Faye Asters had built it and lived in it all the years Bree had lived in Rock Harbor. Standing on the front porch with Davy's hand in hers, she told herself the only reason she'd accepted Cassie's invitation was because she wanted to help protect the younger woman.

Cassie answered the door only moments after Bree pressed the bell. Her expectant smile did much to lighten Bree's anxiety. "I've had an awful week, but knowing you were coming helped. Dad wandered off yesterday again. He even took his clothes." Her eyes watered. "I don't want to do what's necessary, but I have an appointment with the nursing home." Her gaze dropped to Davy's face, and she stooped. "Hi, Davy. Remember me?"

Davy's grip on Bree's hand tightened. "Sam remembers you," he said, running his other hand over the dog's head. Samson's ears perked, and he barked.

Cassie laughed. "Samson and I are old friends. Come in," she said, stepping aside. "I'll tell Dad you're here." Bubbles scrambled to touch noses with Samson.

"I almost didn't come," Bree said, following Cassie to the living room. "Anu convinced me it was what God would want, so here I am."

Cassie made a face, and Bree felt an inner urging to share her faith with this newfound sister. She tried to resist it, then thought that giving in might help justify her decision to come. "Davy and I would love for you and Salome to come to church with us on Sunday."

Cassie shrugged. "Thanks, but I'm pretty busy at work. I've been working seven days a week right now." She told Bree and Davy to have a seat, then left to get her father.

It was going to take more than a casual invitation to get through to Cassie. Bree smiled at Salome sitting in an overstuffed chair by the picture window that looked out on Lake Superior. "Looks like you're in another world," she said.

Salome put down the book she'd been reading. Bree strained to see the title. *What a Girl Wants* by Kristin Billerbeck. "I loved that book too," she said.

Salome grinned. "A little chick lit angst makes my own woes seem small." She stretched.

"Any more threatening calls from wackos? I'm not sure Cassie is keeping me informed."

Salome shook her head. "Just the one. I told Cassie it was a prank call."

"I hope this isn't just the lull before the storm," Bree said.

"Terry said . . ." Salome began then stopped.

"Terry Alexander?"

Salome flushed and nodded. "I was talking to him at the Suomi. He said he got a prank call like that the other night too. Just kids."

Her manner seemed too diffident to Bree. Was she hiding something? Surely a young woman as beautiful as Salome wouldn't have a romantic interest in Terry. He was older and starting to lose his hair. And he was also married.

Salome stood. "I think I'll send my brother an e-mail before lunch." She smiled at Davy. "I have a collection of Star Wars figurines you might want to play with," she told him. "They're in the chest over there." She pointed to an intricately carved Chinese chest in the corner. Davy's face brightened.

"What do you say?" Bree prompted.

"Thanks, ma'am."

Salome laughed. "I think I feel insulted. It's the first time I've ever been called ma'am." She went toward the door while Davy opened the chest and began to pull out Star Wars toys.

Cassie came back in the room. "Have a seat. Dad will be out in a few minutes. He's just finishing his bath." Cassie sank into the chair Salome had vacated and pointed to the love seat across from it.

Bree perched on the edge of the seat. "Is your dad okay?" She still couldn't say "my dad."

"He seems fine. But I'm going to have to make a decision. I've been afraid to even leave the house; he's been wandering lately. I can't put it off much longer."

"I'm sorry." Bree wanted to feel some connection to Cassie and Bernard, but the old resentment kept rearing its head. "Um, how's progress on your project?"

"Phil's death set us back a bit." Cassie shrugged. "But there have been no more calls at least."

"Do you think the calls might be related to Phil's murder?"

Cassie looked away and played with a strand of her hair. "No . . . yes . . . I don't know. Some strange things have been happening at the lab."

"Like what?" Bree leaned forward. This was more up her alley than facing the relational issues between them.

"Some environmentalists have been hanging around for one thing. Asking questions, poking around the perimeter, that kind of thing."

"Have they threatened you?"

Cassie shook her head. "The media has been crawling all over the place. My neighbor, Marika Fleming—she's with NAWG—has offered to help. I'm thinking of letting her. She doesn't seem to be like the rest in her group."

"Marika is your neighbor?"

Cassie nodded. "You know her?"

"I've heard the name." Was it coincidence that Marika had moved in next door?

"Maybe she could funnel some of the media attention away from us. There is one other thing," Cassie said. "When I was looking for Dad yesterday, I noticed my office had been searched. But it was probably just Dad." She looked uncomfortable. "I shouldn't have said anything. I'm sure it's nothing."

"What could anyone want from you?"

"I have no idea. I asked Dad about what he was looking for, and he said they were looking for his notes, that he hadn't been in my office."

"Who are 'they'?"

"I have no idea. I never know what Dad's thinking anymore." Cassie smiled through a pained look. "He's good, but he hasn't worked on the project in three months, and the work he did six months before that was pretty jumbled."

"Could someone really want his notes?"

Cassie hesitated. "I think he's just rambling. He claims he's come up with something special, but when I question him about it, he forgets. I'm sure it's nothing. I think both he and I are imagining things."

"I could have Mason run a fingerprint check."

Cassie shook her head. "I'm being silly. I didn't ask you here to talk about that anyway. I want to talk to you about us. And Dad."

Every muscle in Bree's body tensed. She had been hoping to avoid this conversation.

Kade rode Moses toward the Ten Mile Peak campground. There had been reports of a marauding black bear rummaging in the trash, and he had just enough time to check it out. He carried a tranquilizer gun with him. If the reports were true, he might have to move the bear to another area of the park. Most bears would take whatever food was easy to get, and the park had installed bear-proof dumpsters a couple of years ago to discourage the animals from coming into camping areas. It had been working so far.

He paused near the stream and let the horse catch a drink. He stretched his legs in the stirrups and listened to the water gurgle through the rocks. He sighed, thinking of his sister. If Naomi and Donovan didn't take the baby, he didn't know what they'd do. Whenever he tried to talk about a contingency plan with Lauri, she blew up.

Pulling Moses's head up, he continued on toward the campground. Voices carried to his ears from just around a bend in the river. Angry voices. He tensed and rounded the bend. Two figures stood in the meadow.

Kade had seen the man talking to Marika around town, and Molly at the Suomi had introduced them earlier in the summer. Yancy Coppler's hands were clenched at his side, and he was in Marika's personal space. She had her arms crossed over her chest and didn't seem inclined to back away. Kade couldn't blame him for being mad. NAWG had caused the lab nothing but grief.

"Anything I can do to help you?" Kade asked, reining in Moses.

Yancy's head jerked up. He shook his head as though to clear it and gave a weak imitation of a welcoming smile. "Ranger Matthews."

Kade leaned back in the saddle. "Everything okay out here?"

"He was just ordering me off the property once again," Marika said, smoothing her slacks. "I have a perfect right to be on park property, isn't that right, Ranger?"

"As long as you aren't breaking any laws."

"I never break laws," she said, smiling.

He smiled back at her. There was something very engaging about her. "You got a minute?" He didn't wait for her answer but dismounted and walked toward them after tying Moses to a tree.

She glanced at her watch. "I need to get back to town by two, but I have time." she said.

"I wondered what your group hopes to accomplish here. I tested some five-gallon buckets that had been left by the river, and they contained traces of lawn chemicals. Your group wouldn't have something to do with that, would they?"

She raised her delicately shaped eyebrows. "I want to save the fish, not kill them, Ranger Matthews. Have you been inside the lab yet? I still think it's coming from there."

"Not yet, but I will. You were near where I found the buckets." He'd done some research on her organization, and the rumors of arson and violence had alarmed him.

"But I had nothing to do with it."

She regarded him steadily, and he was inclined to believe her. He softened his tone. "What about your cohorts?"

"You seem determined to pin this on NAWG. The lab director is your girlfriend's sister, you know. I can see why you'd want to believe the lab has nothing to do with it."

Yancy scowled. "You're way out of line, lady."

Kade shrugged. "And she's your neighbor."

"True. I'd like to help them, but she won't let me."

Her warm smile disarmed him. "You know, the NAWG doesn't exactly have a stellar reputation, Marika. Everywhere they've gone, there have been bombings or vandalism."

She grimaced. "I've been trying to change that. Don't color me with the same brush."

If she wasn't telling the truth, she was sure a smooth operator. "I'll take your word for it," he said, smiling in spite of himself.

Her smile deepened, and dimples flashed in her cheek. "Even if the lab isn't killing the fish, it's wrong to genetically alter things in our world. If those plants escape into the wild, it could devastate the ecology."

Yancy shook his head. "Come on, Marika, this is the U.P. Do you honestly think tobacco can grow here? Our growing season is too short. The plants would die before they ever propagated themselves. You're not making sense."

That seemed to get to her, because she colored. "I have to go. I can see you're not at all concerned about the truth." She walked down the path toward the parking lot.

Yancy swatted at a cloud of gnats. "You think her organization is behind the dead fish?"

"I don't know. She seemed sincere," Kade said.

"Our research is at a crucial point right now. Phil's death was a devastating blow. He knew things about the process no one else knew. We can't have any more disruptions."

"Sounds like you need to make sure Cassie's completely filled in, or get it down on paper just in case."

"Oh no, no, I wouldn't trust it to paper, not with everything that's been happening." He swiped at the gnats again. "Dratted bugs. Kill one and a hundred more swoop in to take its place."

"Our father wants to see you and Davy as much as he can while he's lucid, Bree. Sunday dinner every week, just like a real family." Cassie meant to make her half-sister agree, no matter how many objections Bree might raise. "He wants to be part of your life."

Bree glanced at her son playing with the figurines. "Davy, why don't you take Samson out to potty." Once the boy obeyed, she turned back to Cassie. "I don't think so, Cassie. We're not ready yet. We're here today because you insisted, but I'm not sure I'm ready for a real relationship with expectations on his part. I can stop in occasionally, but not all the time."

"You're not ready, or Davy isn't ready? Don't you think he'll like getting close to a new grandpa before it's too late?"

"I think Bernard gave up any rights he had to me and my son long ago." Bree thrust out her chin. Her lips thinned to a straight line. "You can't expect to waltz into our lives and have us be one big happy family overnight. I don't buy this loving-me-from-a-distance stuff."

Cassie bristled. "Why don't you ask him about it yourself? You're judging and condemning him without a hearing."

"Maybe I am. But he condemned me to a rotten childhood. I couldn't choose then, but I can choose now. And right now I choose not to put myself or Davy in a potentially painful situation. We can get together at holidays, maybe."

Cassie curled her fingers into her palms. "I've noticed you have no family of your own around, Bree. Your family is your dead husband's family, no one of your own flesh and blood. Aren't you the least bit curious to know your own family?"

That seemed to reach Bree, because she inhaled harshly and looked away. "I always wanted a sister," she admitted. "But I'm not sure I can trust you. You knew who I was when you first came, didn't you? And all this time you've been sitting back, coming to my training sessions, watching me. Everyone in town accepted you at face value. You were just scoping me out, weren't you?"

Heat moved up Cassie's face. "It sounds awful when you put it like that."

"You could have told me who you were when you first came. If your father hadn't wandered off, would I know who you were even now?"

"Maybe. I was waiting for the right time to tell you."

"When? Christmas? You've been here over two months." Bree's voice rose, and she looked away. "Where's your rest room?"

Cassie told her, and Bree went down the hall. That hadn't gone well. Bree seemed adamant about keeping them at arm's length. Davy came back inside with Samson. The little boy sat beside her on the sofa, and she put her arm around him. The warmth of his small body seeped into her. Her nephew. It seemed surreal. All these years with no family except for her dad, and now she had a nephew. And a sister. At least Davy had no trouble accepting her affection.

She'd find a way to break through Bree's reserve. Davy began to fidget. "Where's Mommy?"

Bree came back into the room, and Davy ran to her. "Mommy, I want to see my new grandpa! When's he coming?"

"Soon, sweetie." Her gaze questioned Cassie.

"I'll go check on him in a few minutes," Cassie said.

"Why don't you take Samson out in the backyard and play Frisbee?" Bree told Davy.

Her tactic to distract him worked. He called to the dog, and they both scrambled for the sliding glass door to the back.

Bree sat on the sofa and rubbed her hand through her hair. "When did you learn about us?"

"Last summer. I found the pictures and letters from your mother when I was looking for some research notes Dad had squirreled away."

"Research notes. I've gathered he's a scientist. What did he do . . . before . . . ?"

Cassie nodded. "Our present formula was his brainchild, though Phil and Yancy have refined it." She smiled. "Poor Dad can't let go of it. He insists he found something even more wonderful. That's the worst thing about his disease—he can't quite figure out what has really happened and what hasn't."

"Did you confront him about the pictures as soon as you found them?"

"Yes." Cassie couldn't help the scowl that tightened her mouth.

"I can see by your face it wasn't a welcome revelation."

"I couldn't believe he would keep something like that from me." She finally met Bree's gaze. "I remembered you so well. I idolized you and cried for you for months after we moved away. I was angry with him when I found out you were my sister all these years and I never even knew it."

Bree's stony expression softened. "I remember you too. I used to pretend you were my little sister."

Cassie couldn't bear to look at Bree, so she picked up a picture she'd laid out and handed it to her sister. "Remember this? We were at the park by the river."

Bree took the picture and stared at it. "I remember. You spilled Kool-Aid on your new dress."

"You gave me one of your T-shirts to wear. I still have it."

Bree's head jerked up, and her eyes went wide. She swallowed. "This is hard, Cassie," she whispered in a husky voice. "Can I see the rest of the pictures?"

The request caught her off guard. "Sure." Cassie got the box from the closet shelf and opened it. She pulled out a packet of letters held together with a wide rubber band. "Here are the letters." Bree needed to read the letters first. They would explain everything.

Bree just looked at them for a moment. She finally reached out to take them. Barely glancing at the top envelope, she laid them beside her.

"Don't you want to read them?"

"I can't just yet."

"You won't understand if you don't read them."

"I doubt I'll understand anyway." Bree glanced in the box. "These the pictures?"

Cassie pulled a small photo album from the shoe box. "You can tell he looked at it a lot. See how tattered the plastic is?"

Bree looked down at the album in Cassie's hands. "Cold and neglect can do that to plastic too."

Cassie gritted her teeth, the warmth of the moment broken. "You're determined not to understand, aren't you? He loves you!"

"You'll have to forgive me if I don't believe that," Bree said. "I wouldn't treat Samson the way he left me to be treated."

"He had no choice."

"We always have a choice. I don't believe in the victim mentality."

"You're acting like a victim right now! You have the choice to give him a chance to explain himself, and you've already made up your mind."

Bree withdrew, and Cassie knew she'd scored a point. Spots of color stained Bree's cheeks. "I can't stand any more hurt in my life," she mumbled. "And neither can Davy."

"Would you just look at the pictures?"

Bree looked away.

"Take them! I was so wrong about you," Cassie burst out. "The first time I met you, I thought you were the most extraordinarily brave woman I'd ever seen. But you're nothing but a coward."

Bree jerked her head around. "I'm not afraid."

"Aren't you? Why else would you refuse to look at pictures that can't hurt you? Why else would you deny your own father his dying request?"

"Dying?"

"Yes, dying. Alzheimer's is a killer. But even more, he has cancer." Cassie wished she could snatch the words back. Her father had asked her not to tell Bree. He didn't want her to know until they had a chance to get to know one another.

Bree blanched. "How bad?"

"Inoperable brain cancer," Cassie snapped. She rubbed her eyes. "I'm taking him to the nursing home tomorrow. We both know it's time. He's been wandering more. I have no choice. Satisfied at his punishment? The man who abandoned you will get his just desserts. All we want is a normal family dinner here once a week."

"I never said I wanted him to be punished." Bree rubbed her forehead. "This isn't easy, Cassie."

"I never said it would be. But you can make his final days happy. Is it too much to ask to visit him once a week?" Cassie was prepared to beg if she had to.

Bree sighed and bit her lip. She flipped open the photo album. "I never knew my mother took these." She studied the photos of herself as a small child, maybe seven or eight. "All my school pictures are here too."

"I told you—he kept tabs on you." Cassie wanted to force her to see the truth. "You're a mother. Have you never made a mistake with your son? All parents do things they wish they could go back and change."

Bree didn't meet her gaze. "I'd never abandon Davy."

"Dad had a lot going on in his life right then. He loved you though."

"Then why didn't he ever contact me?"

Cassie nodded toward the door. "Here he comes. Let's ask him."

9

Naomi felt glum as she sat on the park swing. Watching Timmy laughing on the teetertotter outside the library, she wondered how she could protect the children from the coming upheaval. Donovan had been shaken at the news of Marika's return, and the last few days they'd both held their breath. Emily had been the worst, screaming she wanted to see her mother.

It had to be hard to be an abandoned kid.

The black flies had fled into the warm, dry air, and Naomi lifted her face to the sun. The swing swayed beneath her, and she felt the tension ease from her shoulders. She would spend this time praying like she should have done right from the first. God would see them through this trial.

Charley barked and ran back and forth between her and Timmy. Strange the park was so deserted today. It was an ideal day for being outside. A glint caught her attention, and she turned to look. Lauri's old Plymouth was pulling in beside her car.

"How'd you know where to find me?" Naomi called, watching Lauri walk toward her with her characteristic long, swinging strides. The girl got prettier every day. Pregnancy had brought that characteristic bloom to her complexion, and Naomi was surprised at the intensity of the envy that stabbed her. She would never be more than just passably pretty, though Donovan swore she was beautiful.

"I didn't. I was driving by on my way to work. I was early so I thought I'd stop for a minute." Lauri sat in the swing beside Naomi.

"You look marvelous." Naomi knew what Lauri wanted.

"I feel pretty good." Lauri made a face. "I'm just glad the morning sickness is over." She kicked the toe of her sneaker into the dirt and pushed the swing into movement. "I wondered if you and Donovan had made a decision yet on the baby?"

"I wish I could give you an answer," she said. "For lots of reasons, I'd like to do it, Lauri. But we're still adjusting to married life, and I'm not sure bringing another child into the mix with Timmy and Emily is the right thing to do. We're still praying about it."

Lauri's smile faded. "When do you think you'll know? The uncertainty is really bugging me."

"Sorry." Naomi smiled at her and put all the plea she could into her gaze. "Just give us a little more time, okay? Have you thought about what you'll do if the Lord tells us no?"

Lauri frowned. "Not really. I don't think he'll say no."

"Um, just because we want something badly doesn't mean God is going to do it."

"The Bible says he will give us the desires of our heart."

Naomi shook her head. "It says, 'Delight yourself in the Lord, and he will give you the desires of your heart.' When we're delighting in him, our desires come in line with his, not his with what we want."

"Then what good does it do to pray?" Lauri's lower lip trembled like a child's.

"What do you think prayer is supposed to accomplish? God isn't like a genie in a bottle who will do whatever we ask. Prayer is about talking with God, getting to know him, learning to love the things he loves. He's preparing us to be fit citizens for the kingdom to come, and his goal isn't to give us everything we want in this world. Don't you want whatever God knows is best?"

"Well, yeah, I guess. But it seems so obvious."

"But we can't see the end result. You just have to trust God to see the beginning from the end."

"Trust is hard for me," Lauri admitted. "I keep thinking about how much I prayed when Mom got sick. The preacher had been talking about trust, and I told God I'd trust whatever he knew was best. Then Mom died, and I felt like it was all my fault."

"Oh, sweetie, I'm so sorry. I know it's hard to lose your mom, but God had a purpose in it. We likely won't see it this side of heaven though." Naomi wondered what God's purpose was in letting Marika back in their lives. Telling Lauri to trust him was one thing, but it was harder to do when it was her own happiness at risk. What if Donovan took one look at Marika and discovered he still loved her? She gulped and pushed her swing. Better not to even think about it.

"You have to adopt my baby, Naomi," Lauri burst out. "If I give it to an adoption agency, I'll never see it again. At least I'd be able to watch him or her grow up."

So that's what this was all about. "I thought you didn't want to stay in Rock Harbor, that you wanted to spread your wings and fly away."

"I did. I mean, I do! But I'd know right where you were and that the baby was all right."

"I'll talk to Donovan," was all Naomi could say. It wasn't fair to Lauri to keep her in limbo.

Bree didn't know what she was doing here. She'd determined not to let herself be coerced into sitting and talking over old times. But Cassie had somehow managed it. Bree couldn't deny the emotional tug she felt toward her sister. She remembered a lot more than she'd told Cassie she did. The times when "Uncle Bernard" and his daughter were around had been the best days of her life.

Davy sat between her and her dad while Cassie watched from the armchair. Bernard Hecko was fully dressed today. He wore twill trousers and an oxford shirt. The five pens he'd had on his pajama pocket were now lined up in his shirt pocket. His red hair was neatly combed instead of sticking up.

With gentle hands he caressed Davy's head. "I've got a piece of candy for my favorite grandson." He pulled a piece of caramel from his pocket. "Here you go."

"Thanks." Davy took the candy and began to unwrap it. "I didn't know I had another grandpa."

Bernard smiled. "I didn't know I had a grandson for a while either."

The camaraderie between the two amazed Bree. How could they pick up as if they had always been secure in their relationship, when she felt tongue-tied and inadequate? Cassie was smiling too, but all Bree wanted to do was bolt for the door and not look back.

Bernard—it was still hard to think of him as her father—looked up at her. "We could go outside. I had a slide and swing set put in yesterday."

"Yay!" Davy raced for the door. He turned. "Hurry up, Grandpa!"

"I'm coming, I'm coming." Bernard got up and shuffled to the door.

Bree followed, her steps lagging. She knew he wanted to talk to her without Davy overhearing. She should not have brought Davy on her first visit.

Davy ran toward the swing. "Watch me, Mommy!" He turned to make sure he had all their attention, then clambered to the top of the slide and slid down. Samson barked and raced around him.

Bernard made his way to a yard chair and sank down. He patted the chair beside him. "Sit down, Bree. We can talk."

Just what she didn't want to do. She glanced at Cassie and saw her intent stare. *Coward,* her eyes seemed to say. Stiffening, Bree sat beside Bernard and folded her arms across her chest.

"Finally I get to see how you've done all these years," Bernard said. He stretched out his legs in front of him and searched his pocket for a piece of hard candy.

"You could have found out at any time by picking up the phone and calling me."

He glanced at her from under his heavy brows. "I thought it best not to confuse you."

"You thought wrong. It might have given me some stability."

"You had your mother."

"Oh? You think a drunk could give me a stable life? It might not have been so bad if she'd been a sloppy drunk. But she was a mean one." Bree rolled up her sleeve and showed the scar she usually kept hidden. "See this? She jabbed me with the fireplace poker for snagging her hose when I washed them for her. I'd show you more but they hardly matter. The scars on my heart will never heal."

Bernard stared at the scar. Furrows creased his brow, then he closed his eyes and shook his head. "I didn't know," he said. His eyes reddened, but he didn't look away.

"How could you? You never called." She'd said more than she intended. But he needn't expect to be greeted with open arms for his sacrifice in staying out of her life.

"I'm sorry," he said. "I was transferred to Florida. Things were pretty much over between your mom and me, and I thought I'd be too far away to be much of a dad anyway. I knew she drank a little, but I never realized it was to that extent."

"You just had your fun and took off, right?" Bree didn't try to keep the contempt from her voice. Maybe her mother's drinking had gotten worse when Bernard left. She was too young to remember how it had all started.

"I know it looks that way." His voice sounded weary, and he rubbed his head.

"Is your headache bad today, Daddy?" Cassie asked, her voice low and anxious.

"Not too bad, Cassie. Not too bad." He rubbed at his head again. "I wanted to marry your mother, you know," he said. "She said she didn't want to break up my marriage."

"Hadn't she already?"

"Will you just shut up and let him explain?" Cassie burst out. "You're so stinking rude."

"Rude?" Bree stood and clenched her fists. "You're the one who insisted I come. This isn't easy for me." All the years of heartache washed over her in a wave of painful memories. This man could have made her childhood so much different, but he hadn't cared enough.

"Sit down."

Bernard's commanding voice stilled her restless movements. She turned and stared at him. The firmness in his voice was at odds with the plea in his eyes. Though every part of her being wanted to get out of here and forget this entire conversation, she slowly sank back in the chair. "Ten minutes, no more," she said. "I have things to do today."

"My wife was ill, a mental illness that made her shriek and cower every time I came near her. I had to put her in a facility and find someone to care for Cassie. I thought you were in the good care of your mother." He sighed and dropped his head. "Maybe I wanted to believe it—I don't know. Worrying about Cassie and my wife was more than I could handle. I had no idea things had been bad though. I'm sorry, Bree. Will you forgive me?" He reached over and grabbed her hand.

Forgive him? She tried to say "of course," but the words stuck in her throat.

She pulled her hand away and stood. "I'd better get Davy. My students are waiting."

This was going to be the hardest day of her life. Cassie tried to keep the tears from spilling over as she drove her dad to Rock Harbor Nursing Home the next morning. She still didn't know if Bree would agree to her request for a regular family meal, and that made the day seem even bleaker.

Her dad reached over and patted her knee. "Don't cry, Cassie. It's best this way."

His sweet words only added to her guilt. He was lucid again today, and she wanted to pretend to herself he'd stay this way forever, that he'd never have another blank day in which he wandered off. She knew better.

"This is a really nice place, Dad, and it's only two miles from the house," she said with false enthusiasm. "I'll stop in and see you every day, and you can come home every Sunday."

He didn't answer, and she glanced at him. Her heart sank at the dullness gathering in his eyes.

"Did you bring my files?" he asked.

So quickly he was gone. Cassie blinked hard. "I've got them," she promised.

"I can't let them fall into the wrong hands." His sly look faded to confusion again. "My research is too important."

Naomi dried her hands on the dishtowel and hung it up to dry. Donovan had been uncharacteristically quiet ever since he got home, and her stomach clenched with the waiting to see what was wrong. She had a feeling it had something to do with Marika. The two weeks since she'd run into her husband's ex-wife had trudged by with a sense of waiting for the other shoe to fall.

She was ready to get it over with.

"You having trouble with that, sweetie?" Naomi noticed the frown on Emily's face as she worked on her homework.

"No," Emily said, her gaze on the paper and a stubborn line to her lips. "I don't need *your* help anyway." She stood.

Naomi sighed. She thought Emily hated her now that Marika was back in town. "You need to wash your hair tonight when you take a shower."

Emily picked up a glass of water on the table and dumped it on her head. "There. It's washed. Now leave me alone!"

She rushed from the room, and Naomi followed. "I will not have you talk to me like that, young lady!" she called. Emily didn't answer but rushed into the bathroom and slammed the door. Just as Naomi reached the door, she heard the lock click. She rattled the doorknob. "I want to talk to you, Emily."

"Go away!" Emily shrieked the words. "I hate you."

Naomi's hand fell from the knob, and tears burned the back of her throat. She swallowed hard. Donovan was going to have to talk to Emily. She went down the hall in search of him.

Donovan was in his recliner with the news blaring and the paper in his lap. He dropped the paper to the floor and patted his leg. She collapsed onto his lap, and he nuzzled her neck.

"Um, you smell good. My favorite scent of baby shampoo and cooked cabbage." There was laughter in his voice.

Naomi chuckled. "Your son still insists any other shampoo will burn his eyes, and you're the one who wanted the fried cabbage. The rest of us won't touch the stuff." She settled against his chest. She would talk to him about Emily later. Right now, she needed this comfort.

Donovan played with her hair. She could sense a stillness in him, as if he was biding his time to tell her something. "How was your day?" she asked tentatively.

His hand stopped caressing her hair. "Um, not so good," he said.

Naomi sat up and looked into his face. His blue eyes had an anxious squint. "What happened? Did Marika come by?"

He nodded. "Worse, she brought her lawyer with her. She wants to have the kids this weekend."

Naomi felt like a fist had landed in her solar plexus. "What did you tell her? We can't let her take them. What if she runs off with them? She can't be trusted, Donovan."

"You and I both know that, but I'm not sure we can convince a judge of that fact. She has parental rights. Her lawyer was quick to point that out." He wrapped a strand of her hair around a finger. "I think she's changed. She's making a conscious effort to control her temper, and she seems to genuinely care about the kids."

Naomi tensed. "Her track record tells a different story."

"She says she was emotionally unbalanced during that time because I mistreated her."

"What?" Naomi curled her hands into fists. "You don't even kill spiders, but carry them outside! Is she nuts?"

Donovan gave a faint smile and kissed her nose. "It's good I have you for a defender." He sighed and ran his hand through his hair, leaving the black strands standing at attention. "I'm not sure we have a choice, sweetheart. It's Emily's birthday, and Marika says she's missed three birthdays already and doesn't want to miss another."

"And whose fault is that? Not yours!" Naomi wanted to break something, preferably Marika's head. "Now she's back here as some kind of environmental crusader! Every time I turn around someone is gushing about how wonderful she is to care so much about her hometown."

"She was always one to get involved in a cause. I'm surprised she's stuck with this one as long as she has. She said she's been working for this organization since she left here."

"Well, I don't want her taking Emily on her birthday. I have a party planned for her with all her friends."

Donovan's arms tightened around her. "You know as well as I do that Emily would love to spend her birthday with her mother."

"She hates me," Naomi murmured. "I wish you'd talk to her."

"I'll try."

"So what did you tell the lawyer?" She was afraid to hear the answer. Donovan's tight jaw said it all.

"I told her she could have the kids for the day but not overnight."

"Why did she have to come back? We were so happy." Since Marika's return, the progress Naomi had made with Emily had eroded. The little girl had withdrawn and begun to call Marika on the phone the minute she got home from school. From the hopelessness in her husband's voice, she knew he felt he didn't have a choice. A part of her wondered if he had even fought to avoid this or if one look at Marika's beauty had made him cave.

"I'm still happy; aren't you?"

"Yes, but she's messing everything up." Naomi scowled.

"What's that face mean?" Donovan ran his fingers along her jaw.

Naomi had to know. She knew the question would upset him, but she couldn't live with this uncertainty gnawing at her like Charley with his favorite chew toy. "Do you still have feelings for her?" she asked in a small voice.

"For who? Marika?" Donovan gave a bark of laughter. "Oh yeah, I have feelings for her. Dislike and distrust. But that's all." He cupped Naomi's face in his hands. "You're my wife, and I love you. Don't ever doubt that. My years with Marika weren't happy, not one of them. The honeymoon wore off in a month, and I wondered how I could have been so stupid. I thought the children would make things better, but nothing helped. She was still just as wild and volatile. I've never said this, but the only thing I really felt when she left was relief. I didn't believe in divorce, but she gave me the easy out." He kissed her. "Can you still love a coward?"

The relief she felt nearly made her cry. "With all my heart," she whispered. She snuggled against his chest again. "We need to decide about Lauri's baby too. Have you given it any more thought and prayer? She needs to know so she can make plans. I'm leaving it up to you."

Donovan nodded against the top of her head. "Yeah, I've thought about it. And prayed about it." He cleared his throat. "I don't think we should do it, Naomi. We've got so much on our plate right now with Marika. More turmoil wouldn't be good for the kids or for our marriage. And I'd like to have a baby of our own sometime."

Naomi closed her eyes, unable to stop the prick of tears. That was her heart's desire too. She thought about carrying a baby in her own body, the child of their love for one another, and the vision filled her heart with a joy she'd never thought she'd feel. "When?" she asked.

"Soon. Let's wait until this thing with Marika settles down and then start trying. I'm already thirty-six. I want us to have time to ourselves when we retire. I'm going to talk to a lawyer myself tomorrow and see what our choices are about Marika. We need to get it resolved, even if we don't like what we have to do. There has to be some way to protect the children."

Naomi didn't know when she'd been happier. She thanked God Donovan felt the same way she did about having a child. But how could she tell Lauri no?

10

Her students clustered around the yard with their dogs. Bree found it hard to keep her mind on the training. Her father's pleas coupled with the pictures of her as a child had rattled Bree more than she wanted to admit. She didn't know what she would have done if she hadn't had an excuse to leave. The past few days, her mind had been filled with turmoil and confusion.

"You're all doing terrific," Bree said. "I want you to be working toward FEMA certification now. The Federal Emergency Management Agency certification isn't easy, but you're all committed and your dogs are up to the challenge. There's a training session in Milwaukee in three weeks. I'd like all of us who can to go to that. Are you game?"

"Even Zorro?" Lauri put in eagerly.

"Especially Zorro. He's come a long way this year. You should be proud." Bree studied the faces clustered around her. They were more than students; they'd become close friends and part of her life. "You've studied water searches, man-trailing, death response, and now it's time to learn disaster preparedness. It's a tough job though. You have to be physically conditioned for climbing over rubble, but even more important, the job takes mental conditioning to face the lack of hope when only bodies and not living victims are pulled from collapsed buildings. But I think you're ready for it."

"I'm in," Eva Nardi said. Lauri called her a Nordic goddess, and the description fit her six-foot statuesque frame.

"I'll need to see if someone can watch Gretchen," Karen Siller said. "But she can probably stay with my mom. How long would we be gone?"

"Over a three-day weekend. But it will be worth the trip," Bree promised.

"I'll have to ask Kade," Lauri said. "Or you could ask him. He'd say yes if you asked."

Bree's cheeks heated at Lauri's pointed look. "I think I'll let you handle that."

Lauri knelt and scratched Zorro's ears. "He'll do anything for you."

"From the mouth of a child," Naomi muttered under her breath.

Bree shot her a quelling look. "I'll see about making motel arrangements. Are you all okay with sharing a room? Other than you, Ryan. I'm afraid you'll have to pay for it yourself."

"No problem. I'll find something to do," the quiet paramedic answered with a sly look at Eva. She smiled back at him.

"We had a call this morning about looking for a runaway who's been missing for two months," Bree told them. "I'd like as many of you as possible to go with me. This will be something new for you as we go through the boy's room and let the dogs look for distress smells. It's doubtful we'll find the boy, but we might be able to tell a little about his state of mind. I told the parents we'd come over late tomorrow afternoon."

The group began to disperse. "Can we talk?" Lauri asked Naomi.

"I was planning on it," Naomi said. "We have any Pepsi left, Bree?"

"In the refrigerator."

"Come with us," Naomi mouthed over her shoulder as she and Lauri went toward the Kitchigami Search and Rescue building.

What was up? Bree hurried after them. She and Naomi hadn't had much time to talk the last few days.

Inside the building, Naomi handed out soda. She pulled her long, single braid over her shoulder and twisted it in her hands, a sure sign she was nervous.

"Pistachio?" Bree asked, splitting a nut with her thumb.

"Thanks." Lauri took a handful, but Naomi refused, though she didn't make her usual comment of dislike but instead chattered away about last night's reality TV show.

"You're going to say no, aren't you?" Lauri said, sounding near tears.

Suddenly understanding her friend's anxious manner, Bree took Lauri's arm. "Let's all sit down," she suggested.

Lauri made no move to resist as Bree tugged a folded chair into the office. Tears sparkled on her lashes.

Naomi shut the door behind them. "I'm sorry, Lauri," she said. "Donovan and I talked it over, and we both feel this wouldn't be the right thing for our family. The kids are in so much turmoil already with their mother back in town, and we don't think we can disrupt them even more."

"But what am I going to do?" Lauri's voice was plaintive.

"There are so many couples who really want a child," Bree said. "You won't have any trouble finding someone to take the baby."

"But I want it to be someone I know and trust." Lauri turned to Bree. "What about you, Bree? Davy needs a brother or sister."

Bree gaped. The thought had never crossed her mind. She turned the idea over in her mind slowly then shook her head. "He needs the stability of knowing he has my undivided attention right now," she said. "I'm sure he'd adjust to a brother or sister if he had to, but I don't think now is the time. And your baby needs a loving father as well as a mother."

"Maybe I should just abort it!" Lauri crossed her arms over her chest and glared at them.

"You know you don't mean that," Bree said, careful to keep her voice gentle. "You still have plenty of time to find an adoptive family. I'll help you look. There are probably several in town who would love a baby."

"My life is a mess," Lauri wailed. "I thought it was all settled, and now you've spoiled everything!" She jumped up and rushed out the door, slamming it behind her so hard papers flew from Bree's desk.

Naomi's hand shook as she passed her palm over her forehead. "I hated to do that. I know she was counting on me taking the baby."

"I understand though," Bree said. "It's a lot of responsibility. "What's happening with Marika?"

"Donovan is checking with our lawyer. But we think we have a good case since she abandoned them. For one thing, we can insist on supervised visitation, which will go a long way toward easing our fears about her running off with the kids. He's going to write her a letter detailing what we expect. We'll probably have to go to court." She sighed heavily. "Emily has been throwing tantrums that have to be seen to be believed. I don't know what we're going to do."

"Let's pray together right now," Bree suggested. She chuckled at the surprise in Naomi's face. "I know I'm a baby Christian, but I've learned that much."

"You're a good friend," Naomi said, taking her hand. They bowed their heads and prayed for God to guide Naomi's situation and to keep the children safe.

Jonelle leaned on the fence and watched Zane work Bruck. The dog's powerful muscles moved as he loped along on the treadmill.

Zane glanced up and saw her. "I have to get that dog today. The big match is in just over three weeks. We need him to put on a good show by then."

"Why should you care? You don't want Bruck to lose," Jonelle said.

"I don't want the fight to be one-sided either. The spectators might feel they aren't getting their money's worth. I want the betting to go high for this one—really high. Then me and Simik will rake in the dough."

Jonelle tossed corn to the chickens scratching in the yard and didn't answer. He wouldn't listen anyway. A big car came up the driveway. She rolled her eyes. Simik again.

He got out of his car and walked toward Zane. "Zane." His voice was tight. "We got a problem."

"Yeah?"

"The troll is getting antsy. He's offering more money to snatch the dog, but it has to be today or he's going to get someone else."

"What a patsy! He's paying us to snatch the dog, and then he thinks that mutt will really beat Bruck." Zane rubbed his hands together. "We're making money off him in a double whammy."

Simik leaned against the fence and watched Bruck. "The troll is itching for that dog to fight. If we won't get the dog, he'll go elsewhere. We can't let that happen. I want to control the game and bankrupt the jerk. You get that dog and make him mean enough, the troll is sure he can beat Bruck."

It was a complex game the men were playing, Jonelle thought. Make the troll think Samson has a shot at Bruck, then get him to bet everything he has on the fight.

Zane snorted. "It's easier said than done. People are watching now."

"Don't whine to me about it. You've already screwed it up once."

"You didn't offer to help!"

"You said you could handle it. You've never had a problem before."

"Yeah, we'll get the stupid dog today. You tell the troll it's a go."

"All right, but don't disappoint us again." Simik nodded to Jonelle, then got in his car and drove away.

Zane stared after him with his fists clenched. "Sometimes Simik drives me crazy."

"You really going to get that dog today?" she asked, bending over her strawberry patch to pull weeds.

"I have no choice. You need to come with me to drive the truck."

"I'm not going." Jonelle stood with her hand in the small of her back. "I want no part of taking that dog from the boy. Give it up, please, Zane." She put a heartfelt plea in her voice.

"Why can't you ever be on my side? This is for you, for us. It's just a dog, for Pete's sake!"

She sighed. "I am on your side. But I don't like this business, Zane. You're smart. You could do something else."

He gave a bark of harsh laughter. "Like what? Cleaning toilets?"

"There's nothing wrong with cleaning toilets," she said. "I do it."

"Not for long. With this money, we could afford a maid." He glanced at his watch. "Let's go."

"Let me wash my hands." She dusted the garden dirt from her fingers.

"There's no time. You're fine." He grabbed her arm and hustled her to the truck.

"I want no part of this," she protested as he pushed her into the seat.

"When will you learn these dogs are not your pets? You're too soft on them. They're here to make money."

She crossed her arms over her chest and frowned. There was no getting through to him.

They pulled into Rock Harbor. Late afternoon sun cast long shadows in the passing yards.

"Perfect timing," Zane said, with a smile. "Folks will be fixing supper. The woman will probably let him out to pee." He glanced at her. "You still sulking?"

"No. Let's just get this over with. I don't want to end up in jail."

Driving down Negaunee Road, he kept glancing in the rearview mirror. "No one's following us."

The road was clear as far as she could see. Even the Blue Bonnet looked deserted.

First he drove by the lighthouse. Smoke billowed from the backyard, and the aroma of grilled meat wafted through the open window of the truck.

He grimaced. "I hope they're not all outside."

He turned the corner and Jonelle caught a glimpse of people in the back. The kid tossed a Frisbee to the dog. Samson was a magnificent animal. Even though she didn't want to see him hurt, she could understand why Zane yearned to see the dog in action. Heavy muscles moved under his thick fur. He'd give any dog a run for its money, though Zane would deny any chance he might beat Bruck.

The little boy threw his arms around the dog, and Jonelle had to look away. "Look at how much that little boy loves his dog, Zane. You can't do this."

"Just shut up, okay?" He drove into a pull-off in the woods and killed the engine. "We'll wait."

She inhaled the aroma of grilled meat. "If I'd known we were going to be all night, I would have brought something to eat. The smell of that food is driving me crazy."

"I got some apples in the back."

"Apples aren't steak. We could go get some dinner and come back."

"I'm not going anywhere."

"How about if I run after some pasties? It would only take a few minutes. You can stay here and watch."

"And what if I find the perfect time to snatch the dog and you're not here? I'd be screwed."

She wanted out of here. Watching the perfect family was driving her crazy. "They're still grilling. They'll be out there for a while yet."

Zane peered through the shadows. "Drop it. You're not going anywhere."

Jonelle opened the door and got out. "I'm not a child, Zane."

"Sometimes you act like it," he got out and slammed the door. Reaching into the back of the truck, he pulled out his tranquilizer gun.

Jonelle followed him. They crept along the edge of the woods to get a closer look at the dog. The woods crowded close to the yard on the east side and hid him from view to within ten feet of the fence.

Jonelle knelt in a carpet of wildflowers. The voices carried to her on the wind.

The ranger flipped the rib-eye steaks over. The woman sniffed the sizzling aroma and groaned. "Aren't those done yet? I'm famished."

"Almost. If you didn't ruin a steak by wanting all trace of pink gone, they'd be finished. You need to discover what steak is all about. I don't know how you eat that shoe leather."

Jonelle sighed at the good-natured love in the man's voice. She didn't think Zane had ever talked to her in such a gentle, teasing way.

"A good chef can cook it tender even if it's well done."

"Yeah, well, you're free to try it."

The woman's tinkling laugh came. "I didn't mean me and you know it. I'm just learning to boil water."

"I wasn't going to mention that."

"You know when to shut up," she told him. She turned to her son. "Davy, come wash up for dinner."

Jonelle pressed her fingers against a headache just starting to throb. They were going in. There was no stopping Zane now. She sighed.

She watched the little boy scuff his toe in the dirt. "Aw, Mommy, me and Sam was having fun."

How would he react when his dog was missing? Jonelle was thankful she wouldn't be around to see the trauma to the kid.

"You can come back out after dinner," the woman said. Samson raced after the Frisbee again. He caught it and carried it with him as he settled into a patch of rhubarb. "Come on, Samson, let's go in."

The dog laid down.

"You don't want to stay out here," the woman said.

He whined.

Take him with you, Jonelle thought. Her gaze went to her husband. She could see the intent in his shoulders as he crouched with the tranquilizer gun.

Jonelle froze when the dog lifted his head and growled softly in Zane's direction. The woman didn't seem to hear him, for she turned toward the door.

"Okay, but just until dark. The gate's locked, and the only way in or out is through the house."

"Steaks are done." The ranger carried the platter of steaks toward the back door.

Their voices faded as they vanished inside the house. Zane shifted, and Jonelle heard the rustle of vegetation. The dog growled again, his eyes seeming to pierce the shadows that concealed them. Zane brought the gun up and sighted it. The dog's growl intensified, and he got up and walked toward where they crouched.

"Perfect," Zane whispered. His finger tightened on the trigger. "Just a little closer." He pressed the trigger, and the dart zinged through the air and buried itself in the dog's left flank.

He yelped and Jonelle tensed, then relaxed as a burst of laughter from the house covered the dog's noise.

Samson staggered a few more feet then collapsed. Zane nodded with satisfaction. "Hand me the cutters."

Jonelle pulled some fence cutters from her pocket and handed them to him. He cut the fence and bent it back enough to crawl through to reach the inert dog lying four feet from the fence. Grasping the dog's leg, he dragged him through the fence.

Jonelle didn't like the rough way he handled the dog. "Give him to me," she said.

"He's too heavy." Panting, Zane hefted him into his arms and carried him toward the truck. He dumped him in the area behind the seat. "Run the windows up. We don't want the search dogs to be able to track him."

11

"Hey, this is really good," Kade brought another forkful of potato casserole to his mouth. "I should drop off a note from Lauri more often. Maybe I'd get invited to stay again. What's in here?"

"You sound surprised." She didn't want to tell him what was in it because he claimed not to like sour cream.

He grinned. "Sorry. I know how hard you've been working on learning to cook. I wanted to praise your efforts."

"So this is just sucking up and it isn't all that great?" She tasted the casserole herself. It wasn't even burned.

"That's not what I meant at all. It's delicious. Isn't that right, Davy?"

"I like Grammy's cooking," the little boy said. "But Mommy makes the best peanut butter and jelly."

Bree grinned. "He hasn't learned diplomacy yet."

"That's no way to make a woman happy," Kade told Davy. "Your mommy needs to know she's the best at everything."

Davy took a bite of his hamburger. "Mommy's the best mommy, but Grammy is the best cook."

Kade and Bree laughed, and the sound of their mingled amusement gave Bree a funny feeling in her chest. It was almost painful. She'd missed times like this with Kade so much.

They ate dinner, then Kade helped her carry the dishes to the kitchen while Davy got a book out to read.

He appeared a few minutes later. "I can't read without Sam."

"Go call him. He's probably ready to come in now. I'm surprised he hasn't been whining at the door for the scraps of meat."

"Okay." Davy went to the back door and yelled out the screen. "Come here, Sam!"

Kade scraped scraps onto a plate. "He'll be one happy dog with this stuff. Zorro loves it when we grill."

"Samson does too." Bree began to load the dishwasher.

"He's not coming, Mommy," Davy complained.

"What's with him? I hope he's not getting sick." Bree wiped her hands on her apron. "I'll get him. You go read your book and I'll bring him to you." She stepped onto the back stoop. "Samson! Come here, boy!"

There was no answering bark. Frowning, she stepped into the yard. It was starting to get dark, so she had trouble seeing the spot where her dog had been lying. She approached the area but didn't see Samson. "Samson, where are you?" Her gaze roamed the yard and focused on a bumpy shape out by the fence, but in the dark, it was hard to make out what it was. She jogged to it. As she got nearer, it came into focus.

It wasn't something by the fence; it *was* the fence. Bent and pushed out to make a hole. The breath left her body. "Samson," she wheezed. But the yard felt empty. Her hands went to her face as the truth began to sink in. "No, no," she whispered. Her cries grew louder. "Oh, dear God, not Samson!"

She turned to run to the house but felt she was moving in slow motion. She had to get the other dogs. They had to find him before it was too late.

Anu arrived within minutes to whisk Davy away. Bree was still shaking by the time the dog teams arrived. Naomi had even called Cassie but couldn't reach her. Mason arrived before the dogs and found only tire marks in the pull-off near the fence. There was no telling if the marks were old or fresh.

Bree watched the dogs roaming the yard and tried to pray, but she couldn't settle her thoughts enough to do more than just whisper,

"Please God, please God," over and over in a mantra of desperation. She couldn't bear to think of what her dog was going through. He'd known a life of love and comfort. Would the people beat him? Starve him? Did they take him for a fight? Samson could fight, but it wasn't his nature.

Soon it looked as though the entire town had rallied for her dog. Molly from the Suomi came along with several of the teenagers who worked at The Coffee Place.

Mason waved them all over to him. "We're going to have to have some organization. I'm going to divide you all into teams and assign grids for you to search. We've got a vast amount of area to cover. They're surely long gone from these woods."

"They can't be far," Bree objected. "They've been stalking Samson. They have to live in the area somewhere."

"But we know how vast the North Woods is," Mason pointed out. "They could be only twenty miles from town but down some cow path. Did anyone see any strangers around today?"

Molly snorted, her Yooper twang heightened by her agitation. "And who would notice, eh? We've had tourists crawling all over town for a month."

The others agreed. Steve Asters nodded. "I bet we had thirty people from out of town use the ATM today."

"What about people you've seen around but don't know much about?" Kade put in. He had been organizing his ranger buddies who had shown up to help. He stepped closer to Bree and put his arm around her.

His presence made her feel as if she'd been given a spot aboard one of the *Titanic*'s lifeboats. She turned and buried her face in his chest. Nick hadn't shown up, though he'd been called. He was never one to be in a hurry though.

The townspeople looked at one another, but no one offered up a name. The insular quality of the community ran deep. They wouldn't tattle on a neighbor without good reason. Despair ran through Bree in a cold stream. She had to find Samson. She couldn't imagine her life without her dog.

"We'll find him," Kade whispered.

She clung to him, sensing his resolve in his taut muscles. "We have to," she said. "We have to find him, Kade. Tonight."

He didn't answer. "Tonight," she said again insistently.

"It's dark, Bree," he said. "We'll do the best we can, but if the dogs don't pick up a scent, we'll have to hit it again tomorrow. It may take a lot of tedious work just going down every lane and every trail."

She pushed him away. "I'm not stopping until I find him." Stalking away, she went to join the dog teams. Naomi had brought out Samson's bed and was letting the dogs sniff. They seemed to sense the sobriety of the night. Charley stood with his tail down, almost as if in mourning. Zorro and Bubbles huddled together in a frightened pose. Eva's and Ryan's dogs nosed the bed, their tails wagging as they smelled the scent of their friend.

The other dogs followed Samson's lead. How would they work without him? She'd never thought of this problem. She should have trained them without Samson on occasion to prepare them to work without his lead. Rubbing her fists against her burning eyes, she swallowed the lump growing in her throat.

The teams released the dogs to search, and Charley took off toward the cut fence. He dashed through it, and Naomi scrambled after him. Bree ran after them both. She knew her dog wouldn't still be in the woods here, but she couldn't deny the leap of hope the dog's eager response gave her.

The dogs followed the trail to where Mason had found tire tracks. Charley ran down the road a few yards then stopped and began to wander aimlessly. Bree's eyes began to burn as she struggled to hold back the tears. There was no clear trail.

Kade rubbed his scratchy eyes. The other searchers had gone home around one this morning for some rest, but he and Bree had taken Charley and Zorro and continued to look. Dawn gradually cast a pink glow over the leaves and vegetation, but the full brilliance of the morning sun made his exhaustion seem heavier. He glanced at Bree. The dark circles under her eyes made her look even paler. There was almost no color in her face or lips, only the bright crown of red hair.

He read weariness in the droop of her eyelids and the dogged way she put one foot in front of the other. If he tried to make her stop, she'd just snap at him, but he had to make the attempt. She wouldn't help Samson by killing herself.

"Hold on a minute." He paused and pulled out his canteen. "We both need to rest."

She glanced at her watch. "I should call Anu and check on Davy."

"Good idea." Any idea was good if it made her stand in one place. "Have a seat." He pointed to a moss-covered log.

She settled onto it and pulled out her cell phone. "I don't know if I can get a signal back here."

"We're on a small rise. You might get one."

She punched the button then closed the phone. "No signal."

"I'm sure Davy is fine. Anu will keep him distracted." If Kade could only distract Bree. He wanted to free her from this burden, but this was something he couldn't fix. He didn't want to tell her that most dogs taken this way were never seen or heard from again. His own heart could hardly bear the thought of magnificent Samson suffering at the hands of the kind of men who would do this. He clenched and unclenched his hands.

"Are we going to find him, Kade?"

Bree's green eyes looked too bright, probably with tears. Kade looked away from the pain etched in her face. Love could be more painful than he realized. "We'll find him." He tried to put power and conviction in his voice but feared he was failing when he saw her face crumple even more.

She buried her face in her hands. "I want Samson. I want to put my face in his fur, to feel him lick my face. I can't stand it, Kade. I just can't. Why would someone do this? It's inhuman! Maybe he was taken for a dogfighting ring, but what if it's for medical tests or something? He could be tortured or cut up!"

He knelt and took her in his arms. Her whole body heaved with the force of her grief. She buried her face in his chest. She was depending on him, and he couldn't let her down. He had to find Samson. "I'll find him," he whispered. "No one will quit until we find him. The dognapper wanted Samson so persistently, I can't believe it was for medical research."

She pulled away and ran her hand over her face, leaving dirty tracks on her cheeks. "How could God let this happen? This is pure evil, Kade."

"I know," he soothed. "But God never promised we wouldn't have trials; he just promised to go into the deep waters with us. He'll bring Samson out the other side." His own faith wavered. Sometimes God didn't intervene and evil had its way. He could only pray this wasn't one of those times.

"I shouldn't be surprised," she said, after a long pause. "God let Rob die, and Anu experienced the heartache of losing both her husband and her only son. Steve's wife was murdered. Peter Thorrington is dead. Evil won those rounds."

"Only in this life," he reminded her. "Evil never really wins. Palmer and Max are paying for what they did. They'll have more consequences when they face God."

She was shaking her head. "I just don't know how I'll even explain this to Davy. I was hoping we'd find Samson right away, and I wouldn't have to go home and answer his questions. He and Samson are like blood brothers."

"Why don't you go check on him and I'll keep looking?"

Her gaze searched his face. "You're exhausted too."

"I'm tough." He grinned to lighten the moment.

"I know you are," she said softly. "I don't know what I'd do without you, Kade. You've been my rock."

He kissed her cheek and turned her toward his parked truck. "I'll run you home and feed Charley and Zorro. Then I'll start in the quadrant near Black River."

She nodded and they drove to town. He stopped in front of Anu's house.

"Why don't you try to sleep a few hours? We'll be no good without some rest." She glanced at her watch. "It's nearly seven. Let's meet at eleven and go back out."

"Okay. I ought to let Lauri know how things are going anyway. She'll be worried." He kissed her goodbye, and she got out. As she walked toward the house, he could see the dread that dragged her steps. Davy would be crying for his dog. He didn't envy her that encounter.

Bree let herself into the house with her key. Maybe they were both still asleep and she could just close her eyes for fifteen minutes. Fifteen minutes and she'd be fine. Tiptoeing, she moved down the hall toward the living room. The sounds of movement and voices in the kitchen brought her up short.

Anu was talking to Davy. Her heart lurched. There would be no avoiding his insistence. Last night when he'd realized Samson was gone, he'd gone around the yard shouting for him until Anu forcibly carried him off.

Bree sighed and squared her shoulders. She stepped into the kitchen. Davy saw her and jumped off the bar stool.

"Where's Sam, Mommy? I want him now." His lower lip stuck out, and he stared at her with accusing eyes.

Bree knelt and pulled him closer. "We didn't find him yet, sweetheart."

His lips quivered, and his eyes filled with tears. "You promised you'd find him!"

"I know, and I'm trying. So are Charley and Zorro and the other dogs, but so far they aren't picking up his scent."

His eyes grew huge. "Maybe *she* found him. We have to go to the cabin!" He tugged on her hand.

"Sweetheart, Rachel isn't there anymore. She went to Chicago, remember?"

He hesitated then nodded. "But she might have come back and taken him."

"Why would she do that? You don't have to worry. She's not coming back."

"She might take Sam since she can't have me," he said.

"Oh no, she wouldn't do that. She knows you love him. She loves you and wouldn't want to hurt you." If there was one thing Bree knew about Rachel Marks, the woman who had found Davy after the plane crash, it was that she loved the boy. She'd loved him enough she intended to keep him as her own son.

But the woman was unstable. She'd proven it by ignoring the reality that Davy's own family would be searching for him. Could she have taken Samson? Bree glanced at Anu and saw the same question on her face.

"I'll just give Mason a call," Anu said, going to the phone.

While Anu spoke in low tones, Bree lifted Davy to his bar stool again. "What do we have for breakfast?"

"Grammy made *panukakkua*. But I don't want any. I want Sam." He began to cry in earnest, sobbing so hard Bree wanted to cry with him.

She lifted him from the stool and cradled him in her arms. "It's okay, sweetheart. Kade and I are going back out to look for him in just a little while."

Davy refused to be comforted and finally cried himself to sleep in her arms. Weary beyond belief, Bree glanced up at Anu. "What did Mason say?"

"He called while he had me hold. Rachel answered the phone. She's been nowhere near Rock Harbor since she left last November."

Bree's shoulders sagged. "It almost would have been better if she had him. At least she wouldn't mistreat him."

"Let me take the boy. You are done in. Go lie on the couch for a while." Anu took Davy from Bree's unresisting arms.

"Call me if Mason phones," Bree said, trailing after her down the hall. Anu turned right toward the bedrooms, and Bree went to the living room and collapsed on the sofa. She was sound asleep almost before her head hit the cushion.

She awoke with her heart trying to climb out of her chest. She sat up, breathing hard and trying to make her heart stop racing.

"You were having a nightmare," Anu said, standing in the doorway. "I was about to wake you. You kept crying out."

"I think it was about Samson, but I can't really remember," Bree said, rubbing her palms over her face. "What time is it?"

"Ten thirty."

"I've got to move. Kade is picking me up in half an hour. Is Davy okay?"

Anu nodded. "He slept about half an hour then awoke. Naomi came to take him to play with Timmy. She said to tell you Donovan is staying home with the children today and she'd be back here to hook up with you and Kade."

Bree absorbed the information for a moment. She was too tired to think.

"I have some eggs and bacon ready for you. You must eat."

Bree knew her mother-in-law was right, but her stomach rebelled at the thought of food. She stood and followed Anu to the kitchen. The aroma of toasted *nisu* began to clear away the cobwebs in her brain. "Smells good," she said with more gusto than she felt.

"Mason called."

Bree's head jerked up. Why hadn't Anu told her right away? "And?"

"No sign of Samson. He's running a match on the tire track he found by your house."

"That won't do much good if it's an old one."

"Yes, but we know the dognapper has tried to get Samson at least once before. There is a chance this tire track is his. Mason got a description of the truck Hilary saw to see if it might be the same type as the tire track. Negaunee is not a well-traveled road, and this is an obscure pull-off."

"Good point. How long before he'll know something?"

"A couple of days."

"That's too long!" Her dog had been gone for over twelve hours now. Twelve hours! That was a lifetime in dog years. She felt trapped in quicksand, powerless and frantic to escape.

12

Cassie moved her fins in unison with Salome as they swam side by side through the clear water. Underwater all her cares seemed to be as distant as Mars. Two days ago, rain had rendered visibility at only twenty feet or so, but today the murkiness was gone, and the clear water of Lake Superior allowed her to see nearly a hundred feet.

The hiss of her regulator didn't distract from her enjoyment of the underwater world. She wore enough weights to allow her to walk along the bottom. They'd found the special algae she sought somewhere along this cliff, but Cassie couldn't remember exactly where it was located. Maybe fifty feet from Three Indians rock. Then Salome pointed, and Cassie nodded when she saw what she'd come here for. She swam to the rock, and she and Salome began to scrape the algae off the rock.

They worked with the unison of friends used to each other's movements. Cassie wished she could work down here all the time. The lab wasn't nearly as inspiring as this ethereal world below.

In fifteen minutes Cassie had all she needed for now. And just in time. She was pulling hard at her air, feeling light-headed. She pointed toward the surface, and Salome nodded, then followed her up to the light. She surfaced and climbed into the boat anchored off Three Indians rock.

Gasping, Cassie clambered up the ladder behind her. "My air was running out," she said. "I must not have gotten it fully recharged."

"You okay?"

"I'm fine. I just feel a little nauseated. I'll be okay by the time we get to the lab." Cassie fingered the algae. "I'm eager to see how this does with the plants. Let's get back to the lab."

They were back within fifteen minutes. Cassie hung up her wet suit to dry in the restroom, put a white lab coat over fatigues, and hurried to her office. The bright lights kept the lab from feeling like it was underground. The equipment around her hummed as Cassie peered at the algae with a microscope. She hoped this would be the breakthrough for the plants. She worked quietly, trying to ignore her growing discomfort. Beads of sweat broke out on her forehead, and her vision blurred. She felt sick and weak.

The phone rang, and she answered it. From the hum, she instantly knew it was the voice synthesizer.

"I warned you. Now you have to pay."

The phone went dead in her hand, and she put it back in its cradle. "Stupid nut," she muttered. He was going to make her life miserable. She dabbed at her forehead.

Salome pecked on the door. "There's someone here to see you, Cassie. A park ranger."

Cassie took a swig from her bottle of water, and her vision cleared. "Be right there." An interruption was the last thing she needed. Besides, the corporation's policy was to have no outsiders in the lab. "I'll see him in the reception room." She followed Salome down the hall to the reception area. A man in a brown park service uniform stood by the bulletin board perusing the articles Cassie had instructed Salome to put up— articles about other labs working on various projects with proteins that might cure anything from cancer to diabetes.

The man turned at the squeak of Cassie's rubber-soled shoes on the tile floor. She recognized him immediately as Kade Matthews, Bree's friend. She'd seen him when she stopped to see if Bree had found Samson. He looked tired.

"Ranger Matthews. Did you find Samson?" The room felt hot and close. Cassie picked up a magazine and began to fan herself with it.

The ranger shook his head. "No sign yet, but we haven't given up hope. I'm here on another matter. I found some dead fish downstream from the mine. So far we've been unable to determine the cause, and I need to take some samples of what you're dumping." Kade looked around the room.

The hint of accusation put her on the defensive. "Our business is curing, not killing. We're not dumping anything. If you have dead fish, it's not our problem."

"You're not dumping anything? What about your septic?"

"Totally self-contained. We have an aeration system that purifies the water even better than your city sewage system. So I suggest you look somewhere else for your fish killer." She had to get him out of here so she could lie down a little while. Could running low on air have caused this reaction? She blinked rapidly to clear her vision.

Kade smiled in a placating way. "I hate to disrupt you, but I really need to take a tour of your facility, see for myself."

"I'm afraid that won't be possible. This facility isn't open for public inspection."

"I'm hardly the public. Surely you can understand I need to make certain the lab isn't the cause of the environmental problems. If we can't handle this now, I'll have to come back with the sheriff. I don't want to do that. And I'm a trustworthy sort of guy. Really."

Cassie bit her lip. The last thing she needed was a major investigation. Her boss would think her incompetent and might replace her. She couldn't risk her father's lifetime of work over a policy that probably didn't apply to this situation anyway. "Very well. But I must ask you not to share anything you see here. Competing pharmaceutical companies would love to get their hands on what we're doing."

"I'm not in the habit of shooting off my mouth," Kade said. "If you're clean, I'll be the first to leave your work alone. And Bree is special to me. I wouldn't do anything to hurt your sister."

Her sister. Finally someone was being nice about the connection between her and Bree. Cassie's vision cleared even more. She could get through this. "Follow me. You'll need a lab coat. We can't have any contamination in the growing area." She took him to a room and had him change, then led the way down the brightly lit hallway. "This is the growing chamber."

Kade peered at the lush plants. "What are these? They seem to be growing well here."

"A genetically altered tobacco plant. Tobacco is one of the easiest of all plants to grow. We're harvesting a special protein for our research."

"What will it do?"

"I'm afraid I can't tell you that. It's enough that you can see what we're growing and that we're no threat to your environment."

"What if this genetically altered plant escapes to the outside world? Could it grow and harm native plants?"

"In the first place, it couldn't escape. A mine is a perfect place to maintain security and total self-containment. And in the second place, it couldn't grow in this climate. So the ecology is safe."

"A mine seems an odd place to grow plants."

Cassie nodded. "The high levels of carbon dioxide make the plants thrive. They should flower in five weeks instead of ten. The yield is much higher than we could get outside as well."

Kade didn't answer as he followed her through the rest of the tour and examined the lab's septic system. A few minutes later she deposited him at the door to the mine. "I hope I was able to set your mind at ease about our work here," she told him.

"Very impressive. But I think I'll snoop around the grounds a bit and see if I can find anything seeping from the mine."

"You won't find anything. We're clean as new snow." Suddenly dizzy, she swayed and put her hand on the back of a nearby chair.

"I think I'll look just the same."

Salome appeared in the doorway. "I could use your help, Cassie."

Cassie wanted to tell Salome she'd be right there, but her lips refused to form any words. Lights danced in a gathering darkness that clouded her eyes. "I don't feel too well," she muttered. The strength ran out of her legs, and she tried to prop herself up with the chair.

"Catch her!" Salome shouted.

Bree parked in front of the Suomi Café. She'd avoided coming here since Samson had gone missing. Molly's sad face would threaten her composure, but she decided to chance it this morning. Mason came out of the bank and waved at her. She waited for him to join her by the door to the Suomi.

"You find something?" she asked eagerly.

Her hope dimmed as he shook his head. "Sorry." he asked.

"How about Phil's murder?"

"The researchers are squeaky clean, except for one count of breaking a restraining order during a divorce proceeding—Yancy threatened his ex and her boyfriend with a gun—and another one for reckless driving. That would be Chito. No help there."

Before Bree could answer, the ambulance screamed by, followed by Cassie's car. Bree caught a glimpse of Kade's face, white and strained, as he crouched over the steering wheel. The car barreled down the street, then turned onto Rock River Road toward the hospital.

"I suppose I'd better go see what all that's about," Mason said. "You want to come along?"

"Yeah, that's Cassie's car." Bree maintained an appearance of calm she didn't feel. She hoped Cassie was all right.

Bree hopped into the passenger seat. Mason drove to the hospital and turned his car into the parking lot. Cassie's car sat crossways at the emergency-room entrance. Bree jogged up the sidewalk toward the doors.

Bree paused inside while Mason went to the reception desk. Two nurses were running down the hall, the rubber soles of their shoes squeaking on the tile floor. They disappeared into the examining room. Kade came out moments later. His gaze lingered on Bree's face, and the slow smile that lifted his lips made her feel she was riding the Magnum roller coaster at Cedar Point, but the smile did nothing to brighten the shadow in his eyes. Whatever was wrong was very serious.

He reached her side and took her arm, steering her toward the waiting room. "How did you happen to get here?"

Mason answered for her. "We saw you speed by the Suomi. What's going on?"

"Cassie got sick while I was at the lab. The way the doctors are acting, it looks serious." Kade released Bree's arm and sat in a chair. The lines around his eyes were etched and strained.

Bree had been so cold to Cassie the last time they'd been together. What if she died before they got to be real sisters? "Is she going to be all right?"

Kade hugged her. "She collapsed pretty suddenly. I've been praying for her."

"Could someone have tried to harm her?" Bree wanted to know.

Kade shook his head. "I don't see how. Cassie took me on a tour before she got sick. There doesn't seem to be anything dangerous on site."

"What are they doing out there?" Bree had been wanting to know that for weeks. She knew they were working on finding a new drug, but that was all.

"She didn't say exactly, but they're growing plants."

"We already knew that much."

"You know how pharmaceutical companies are. They're paranoid about someone else getting a drug out first." Mason stood and stretched. "We'll find out all about it sooner or later."

"What if it's something dangerous? We know nothing about the process or any side effects to the community. Maybe what she was working on caused her to collapse. Did you see the lab itself?" Bree asked.

"No, just the growing area. She let me inspect the wastewater system too. It's not causing any problems with the fish."

Salome came down the hall. Her long dark hair was in disarray, and worry shadowed her eyes.

Bree stepped to meet her. "How is she? Can I see her?"

Salome bit her trembling lips. "The doctor thinks she'll be all right, though he asked me for her next of kin . . ." She stopped as her voice broke.

That would be Bree and their dad. The thought was like a blow to her gut.

"Any idea what's wrong with her?" Mason asked.

"The doctor says it looks like an overdose of something and asked what medicines she's taking. She takes a beta blocker for her migraines and a pill for her asthma. The beta blocker she buys through a mail-order pharmacy. I picked up her asthma refill a couple days ago. They're running tests on her now."

"What kinds of tests?" Mason wanted to know.

"Toxicology, I think. Though I can't imagine Cassie taking more than she should. She is very level-headed and careful to take her medicines exactly as prescribed."

First Phil Taylor was shot, and now Cassie lay dangerously ill. Bree told herself it was likely a coincidence, but unease mixed with her worry.

They sat silently in the waiting room for nearly an hour before Dr. Richmond came out. He'd only been in town a month, having taken Dr. Max Parker's place. The bags around the doctor's eyes made him look older than his forty years. Bree wondered if he'd slept last night.

"Looks like there was a mix-up at the pharmacy," he said. "She was supposed to be taking theophylline for asthma, but somehow the pharmacy filled propranolol, which she was already taking. When she doubled it up, it slowed her heart."

"How could a mix-up like that happen?" Mason asked. He uncapped his pen and dug out his notepad.

Dr. Richmond gave a weary sigh and sat in the chair beside Bree. "I have no idea. There are fail-safes to keep this from happening, but some studies say that medical error is the cause of death in a full third of cases."

"She's not going to die!" Bree held out her hand to the doctor.

"She's holding her own, but the asthma has complicated things," Dr. Richmond said.

Salome put her hands to her face. "This is crazy," she whispered. "I picked up part of that refill a few weeks ago, but the pharmacy was short on pills, and I just picked up the rest a few days ago. She can't die."

Bree went to her and put her arm around her. Salome's shoulders stiffened, then she turned and buried her face in Bree's shoulder.

Bree held her tight and looked at the doctor. "Explain to me what happens at the pharmacy."

Dr. Richmond shrugged. "I called Terry to see what could have happened. He's as puzzled as we are. According to the computer, the refill was right, but the written prescription is for theophylline. This was the second time it had been refilled, and the last one under that number was for theophylline. Somehow between the first refill and the second, the drug listed in the computer changed. Even that partial refill Salome mentioned was for the right drug."

"How could that happen?" Mason wanted to know.

"Beats me. Terry is checking his paper copies to see if he can get to the bottom of it."

"I think I'll stop at the pharmacy and see what he's found out," Mason said.

"You think the mix-up could be related to Phil Taylor's murder?" Bree asked.

Everyone turned to look at Bree, and she saw dawning horror on Salome's face. "The phone threat," Salome whispered.

Bree looked at her. "You picked up the prescription. Did you notice anything strange at the pharmacy?"

Salome chewed on her lip. "Not really strange. I browsed through the aisles for some Tylenol and shampoo, then picked up the prescription."

"Was Terry behind the counter?"

Salome shook her head. "He got called to the front of the store, and the technician gave me the prescription."

"Who was it?"

"I don't know. She was blond, midtwenties."

"Deanna Chester. She's good. Nothing else out of the ordinary?"

"There was a big argument right in front of the pharmacy. Deanna had to ask them to leave."

"A fight? What kind of fight?"

"Lola and Ian. It embarrassed me to see them argue like that in public, but I'm not their mother. I could have crawled under the counter when Deanna asked them to leave."

"Lola's got to be ten years older than him," Bree observed.

Salome shrugged. "Live and let live."

Bree made a mental note to ask Deanna about the incident. "Deanna gave you the prescription and didn't ask any questions?"

"She started to ask me something, then Ian and Lola started going at it, and she just handed it over and took my money."

"I wonder if she noticed the discrepancy then got sidetracked. We'll have to check that out."

"Enough talk," said Dr. Richmond, rising. "I need to get back to my patient." The doctor glanced at Bree. "She wants to talk to Bree, so come along."

Bree and Kade exchanged a look. The connection that seemed almost spiritual at times between her and Kade had not gone away. She smiled at him, and he winked. For some stupid reason, she felt like crying.

She dragged her gaze from his face and hurried after the doctor. "She wants to see me?"

"So she says." He stopped at the door to her room. "But keep it short, and don't upset her."

Cassie lay on the white sheets with her eyes closed. Her complexion was pasty, but she seemed to be breathing easily. Skirting the tubes attached to the young woman, Bree went to her bedside. Before she could say anything, Cassie opened her eyes.

"You came," she whispered. "You've got to help me, Bree."

"What can I do for you? You need something from home?"

"I'm scared. The person called again and said I'd have to pay the consequences."

Bree tensed. "You think the caller had something to do with your getting sick? The doctor said it was a pharmacy error."

"I don't know." Cassie struggled to sit up. "He called again just before I got sick. What if he switched my medicine?"

"Do you have any idea who the caller could be?"

"Jackson Pharmaceutical wants our formula."

Bree felt in over her head. "Jackson Pharmaceutical?"

Cassie gestured toward the table. "Could I have some water?"

Bree held the cup and straw to her lips, and Cassie took a sip. "Thanks. Jackson is our biggest rival. They're trying to bring our drug out first, and they want to slow us down."

"Tell me about Jackson Pharmaceutical and this formula."

"They are working with the same protein we are, but we're further ahead. At least we were before Phil died." She sighed.

"How do you know this?"

Cassie coughed. "We have someone on our payroll inside Jackson. They are just beginning the process. We'll have ours patented in a few more months if we can move forward. Theirs is years away."

"You've worked hard," Bree observed. "Are you sure it's going be effective?"

Cassie nodded. "It has to be."

"Who else is working on the project?"

"Why don't you go out to the lab tomorrow and talk to all of the employees? Begin to dig into what's going on."

This was her sister. She had to help her. What if someone was really trying to hurt her? Samson was depending on her too. She had to try to help them both.

"I wish we had Samson. He might be able to scent whether there have been any intruders. We need to keep the lab as secure as possible," Cassie said.

Bree rubbed her forehead. "Mason has resources I don't have. We'll have to let him help us."

"I don't want him there."

"Then I'm not coming out either." Bree crossed her arms over her chest. "I have a child to raise and a dog to find. Mason is better equipped to deal with this kind of thing than I am. I don't want anything to happen to you, but I can't do it alone."

"Okay."

"One other question now, about Salome. You said she picked up your prescription. Did you happen to look at the name of the drug?"

Cassie shook her head. "Didn't even occur to me. It was a refill—I've been taking this drug for ages. No big deal."

Except it had turned into a huge deal.

An older building on the corner had been razed to make way for the new drugstore, and its squat facade looked out of place amid the Victorian buildings that lined the downtown. Tourists crowded the store, buying bug spray and other camping essentials. Bree pushed her way through the aisle. She spied Mason's bulky form.

"You talk to Terry yet?" she asked when she reached him.

"He's not back from lunch. Deanna said he was due any time."

"I want to talk to her anyway. Salome mentioned that fight, and I want to know more." Bree motioned to Deanna, who waved, then spoke to a coworker before exiting the pharmacy booth to join them.

"I'm so sorry about what happened to Cassie," Deanna said. She glanced from Bree to Mason as if wondering which one would accuse her first.

"Salome said there was an altercation in front of the pharmacy counter yesterday just as you were about to ask her something. Do you remember what you were going to ask her?"

"Just the standard line about whether she had any questions about the medication," Deanna said. She bit her lip. "I wish I'd caught this."

"You had no way of knowing," Mason said.

She sagged at the sheriff's words. Relief lit her blue eyes. "I . . . I wondered if I was going to be charged," she admitted.

"Could we see the written script?"

"I have it right here." Terry Alexander came up behind them.

He'd been the pharmacist for as long as Bree had lived in Rock Harbor. A genial man in his thirties, he parted his hair just above his ear and swept the wispy strands over the center bald spot. He held out a paper.

Mason scanned it, then handed it back to Terry. "Can you decipher it? It looks like it says theophylline."

"It does," Terry said grimly. "But that's not what the computer says. I don't understand how this could happen. We carefully check every prescription when it's loaded into the computer."

"Tell us how it works," Bree suggested. "If I dropped a prescription off and said I'd pick it up later, how would it be processed?"

"Either Deanna or I would input it into the computer along with the other prescriptions. We'd double-check to make sure it was put in properly. Then the computer would spit out the prescription and one of us would fill it. We check it against the paper script the first time to make sure it's right." Terry held out a computer printout. "This says we put it in right, and it was refilled once as theophylline. But that's not what the computer says now, and that's not what was refilled this time."

"So it's just checked against the written script the first time it's filled? If I get a refill, you don't recheck?"

"That's right."

Mason frowned as he read the printout. "So what you're suggesting is that somehow between when you put this prescription in the computer and filled it once and when it was filled the second time, it somehow changed to another medicine? That makes no sense. A computer glitch of some kind?"

"I've never heard of a computer glitch like that," Terry said. "I know it sounds crazy, but I don't know how it happened. What's even crazier is that the first part of the second refill was right—the partial Salome picked up a couple of weeks ago. It's just this remainder that was wrong."

"What about cybercrime?" Mason asked. "Could someone have gotten into the computer and altered the prescription?"

Bree wanted to shake her head. It sounded like something out of a novel or a movie. How would a tiny burg like Rock Harbor attract someone with that kind of computer savvy? This wasn't New York. "There has to be another explanation," she said.

Terry shook his head. "I'm telling you, there's no other way this could have happened. I think Mason is on to something." He waved the paper at Mason as if to emphasize the point.

"Is there any way we can find out for sure if someone cracked into the computer? And don't you have some kind of—what's it called—firewall?"

"Sure, we have a firewall, but a determined cracker can get past most anything."

"I read about some cybercrime detection company in Detroit," Mason said. "I think I have their information back at the office. I'll contact them. In the meantime, can you print out any logs you might have, Terry?"

"Sure, but I'm no computer expert. I probably won't know where to look to find the ones that might help us."

The import of what was happening began to sink into Bree's consciousness. If someone deliberately altered Cassie's prescription, then it had been a murder attempt.

13

The man and woman moved through the dark house. Their flashlights pushed back the inky blackness only a few feet. Carpet muffled the sound of their footsteps, though there was no one in the house to hear. The dog lay snoring in the front room after being fed drug-laced hamburger.

She knelt by the desk and began to riffle through it while her partner searched the filing cabinet. They had to find it. They worked quietly; only occasional grunts from the man by the filing cabinet and the sound of metal drawers sliding disturbed the almost eerie silence.

She slammed the final drawer shut, frustration making her careless. "It's not here. We're going to have to search the whole house."

"What if the other woman comes in?" he asked.

"She's been conveniently delayed by our friend."

They started in Cassie's bedroom.

The aroma of the tea mingled with the scent from the potted roses lining the patio. It was good to be home, though she'd only made it as far as the living room sofa before deciding to sit outside. Bree had brought her home, then gone out to search for Samson.

Two days in the hospital had seemed like an eternity. Cassie settled onto the chair and propped her feet on the deck railing. She'd just relax awhile and watch the sunset. Salome wouldn't be home for another hour—she'd gone to her Pilates class—and the silence spoke to Cassie's heart.

The phone rang, and she grabbed the portable. "Hello."

"Cassie, I've been trying to reach you for days." Her boss's voice was impatient.

"Sorry, Marc, I was in the hospital."

"Whatever for?"

Like her boss really cared. "Just a drug mix-up at the pharmacy. I'm fine."

"No wonder, since you're in the boonies. The pharmacy probably still uses things like eye of newt. I tried to tell you to find a more up-to-date location, but you were insistent."

It was a familiar complaint. Cassie tried not to grit her teeth.

Marc barreled ahead. "Why didn't you call me the minute Phil died? Is the project in jeopardy?"

"I'm on top of things," Cassie said evenly. She didn't need her hand held, but she doubted Marc would ever realize that.

"How on top of things? Is his death causing a delay?"

"Nothing I can't handle."

Marc huffed on the other end of the line. "You're skirting the issue, Cassie. Tell me in one-syllable words. Are we going to make the deadline?"

Cassie bit her lip. "I don't know yet," she enunciated.

There was silence on the other end of the line for several seconds, then Marc sighed. "How much of a delay?"

"I'm hoping not more than six months."

"Six months!"

Cassie held the phone away from her ear. "Yancy is trying to fill in the holes as best he can."

"What about your father?"

"He's in a home now. I don't think he'll be any help."

"Is there anything you can give him to temporarily stimulate his memory?" Her boss's voice was calculating.

If there was, she would have done it long ago, but Cassie was too disgusted to say anything.

"Cassie, are you there?"

"There's nothing we can do to help Dad. I've got the best minds working on it. It will be okay."

"If it's not, we're all in trouble. The company will go down the tubes, and you'll all be out of a job. Tell your researchers to get off their duffs and *get me that drug!*"

The phone crashed in Cassie's ear, and she winced. She punched the off button and laid the phone on the table. She'd hoped to avoid this conversation until she had things more in order at the lab. Sighing, she got up to get her phone book in the office. She'd call Yancy at home and see how things had gone the past two days.

She went down the hall to her office and pushed open the door. Blinking in dismay, she glanced at the papers strewn on the floor. Someone had ransacked her office. She grabbed the phone to call Mason. He promised to come right over.

Her nerves were a jangled mess. She kept looking out the window into the now-dark backyard. What if the intruder was still out there? She couldn't understand what anyone would want here. All her records were at the lab. But what else could they want?

Bree paused and wiped the perspiration from her forehead. This fruitless search had brought back too many memories of what it had been like to look for Davy all those months. She wouldn't be discouraged if she knew the outcome would be the same, but she had a sinking feeling two miracles were unlikely.

Zorro scampered through the grass with Charley, both dogs not as focused as usual without Samson to follow. She didn't know how she could keep going back to Anu's to face Davy's hopeful face that crumpled into tears when she arrived without his dog. She felt like she'd knocked on every door in a twenty-mile radius, but no one had offered a shred of evidence. And no one seemed to know about a dogfighting ring.

If that's even who had taken Samson. She couldn't bear to think of him being mistreated. Setting her jaw, she whistled for the dogs and got back to the search.

"I thought that sounded like your whistle." Kade pushed through some brush into the clearing where she stood. "You look beat."

"I am. What are you doing out here?"

"Just patrolling and watching for signs of Samson while I do it."

Her eyes filled with tears. "I'm beginning to think we're not going to find him, Kade. What will I do if he's gone forever?"

He stepped close, and she threw herself in his arms. She'd tried to be strong for Davy, but she was tired, so tired. He smoothed her hair and held her while she sobbed out her fear and frustration. Finally spent, she pressed her cheek against his damp shirt and breathed in his familiar scent.

"Don't give up hope yet."

"I'm trying not to." She sniffed and pulled away to scrub at her cheeks.

"You're strong, Bree. You can get through this."

She knew her anger was out of proportion, even as the bitter words burst from her lips. "I'm tired of being strong. I want to let someone else carry the burden for a while." She pulled away and turned and ran after the dogs.

He called after her, but she didn't pause. Only God could carry this burden, and she knew just where to find him.

Kade started after Bree, then an inner sense told him to leave her alone. He turned and went back to Moses. There was nothing he could do for her except to find her dog, and though he didn't want to admit it to Bree, he was beginning to think she was right about Samson never being found.

His cell phone rang, and Lauri told him her car was dead. Glancing at his watch, he told her he'd take care of it while she went on to work. He dropped his horse at the ranger station stable and drove his truck to town. Ranger Matthews to the rescue. Some days he felt like that's all he did.

He parked his truck outside the Ace Hardware Store. Lauri's battered red Plymouth sat across the street. He popped the hood and jiggled the spark plug wires. He got out his key and tried to start it. Nothing. When Lauri said it was dead, she wasn't exaggerating. Not a sound came from the engine.

He went back to peer under the hood, but he'd probably have to call a mechanic. Minor problems he could fix, but this seemed major. He pulled out a few spark plugs and wiped them off, then reseated them. The engine still wouldn't fire. Sighing, he went to Nicholls's to wash his hands and call a tow truck.

Donovan looked up when the bell on her door jingled. "Hey, guy. I assume you're looking for your sister? She went to work."

"I know. She called from there and said her car was dead. It is. I just need to wash up and borrow your phone book."

"Sure. The rest room is through here." Donovan led him through a break room and flipped on the light. "I'll get the phone book."

Kade washed his hands. Donovan tossed him the phone book when Kade joined him at the counter. He thanked him and called to have the car towed to the mechanic.

"Coffee?" Donovan asked when he hung up the phone.

"Sure." He followed him to the back room past the display of plumbing supplies.

"You take it black, don't you?"

"Yep." Kade accepted a Little Mermaid mug. "Nice," he said, holding up the cup.

Donovan grinned. "Emily's castoffs. Hey, at least it holds coffee." Donovan studied his face. "You look as low as Naomi when she burned last night's cake."

Kade tried to smile, then gave up the struggle. "It's Bree. She's driving me crazy. One minute she's hanging on to my shirt crying her eyes out and the next she's pushing me away."

Donovan took a swig of coffee. "Time to be a man, my friend. Take a stand and tell her how you feel."

"She knows how I feel." He hunched his shoulders and sipped his coffee.

"You're sure? Have you ever told her what you want and that you love her?"

"Not in so many words. I wanted to give her space to grieve for Rob and for Davy to adjust."

"Rob has been gone nearly two years. You want her to grieve her life away with a misplaced sense of guilt?" Donovan pulled a chair out with his booted foot and sat down. "Have a seat. This may take a while."

Kade grinned. "You have some advice from the heights of your married wisdom?"

"Naomi has taught me a lot. Sometimes a woman needs a man who takes a strong stand, someone who looks her in the eye and helps her make difficult decisions. A woman wants a leader."

"I've always thought of myself as a leader. It's been hard to stand back and do nothing. I've had to pray for strength every day."

He leaned back. "I think you're praying for the wrong thing. Be yourself, Kade. Bree needs your strength and leadership even if she hasn't admitted it to herself. Fight for her."

"How? With Fletcher in the picture, Davy won't give me the time of day. Bree notices that."

"Davy needs leadership and guidance too. Show him the father he wants in his life is you. Win him the same way you'll win Bree. Not with flowers or candy, but with a strong sense of purpose and a firm hand for the future. And don't leave God out. I couldn't function as a dad without God giving me some help."

"You make it sound easy. Have you seen how he hardly looks at me?"

Donovan nodded and shrugged. "And I've seen the way you cater to him—Bree too. Almost as if he is in charge. *You* be in charge, Kade. In a loving but firm way."

Kade leaned back in his chair and let the front legs come off the ground. "You've given me a lot to think about," he said.

"Don't just think about it. *Do* it. Now. Today. Naomi and the rest of the team are meeting Bree at the training center about now to help with the search." He gave Kade's chair a good-natured kick, forcing Kade upright again. "So quit sitting around and get out there."

Donovan's intense blue eyes boring into him made him feel he could do anything. What did he have to lose, really? He was getting nowhere by doing what he thought Bree wanted.

"Okay," he said finally. "I'll give it a shot."

Every muscle in Bree's body ached from her earnest trek through the woods today. Fruitless, just as every search had been so far. She'd stopped to pick up Davy from Anu's and had distracted him by having him help her clean the yard in front of the SAR building. Davy scooped the debris into a small wheelbarrow and carted it to the ditch along the back of the property, where it could safely decompose. The physical work helped in another way as well—it helped keep her thoughts about Samson at bay.

"How about something to drink?" she asked Davy.

"Juice?"

"I've got some in the fridge. You want to run get it?"

"Okay. Come on, Charley. You can help."

Bree watched Davy link his fingers under Charley's collar and stroll toward the building. Bless Naomi for letting Davy spend so much time with her dog. She didn't know how he would have gotten through the trauma of losing Samson without Charley's slobbery comfort. Her son had come so far, and she feared this setback. He'd started to make occasional midnight forays into her bed again.

As she put the rake away, Bree heard a vehicle's tires crunching along the macadam road that led back to the training center. It was a bit early for the rest of the team. She shielded her eyes from the warm July sunshine as she waited to see who was paying her a visit. A surge of adrenaline quickened her pulse when she recognized Kade's truck. He must have gotten off work a little early.

She mentally shook her head at the way she still tracked his movements. It was time she got over that. Thrusting her hands in her pockets, she waited for him by the bench near the parking lot.

Bree's gaze lingered on his broad shoulders and the way his muscles flexed against his shirt when he slammed the truck door and came toward her. "Hi!"

"Hi yourself." He walked straight to her and embraced her.

Her arms went around him, and she laid her head on his chest. He smoothed her hair, then tipped her chin up and kissed her. Breathing in the scent of his skin, a warm masculine aroma, she felt a tingle that started in her toes and moved up to her chest in a wave of heat.

"I've missed you," he whispered.

She managed to regain her composure and pull away enough to catch her breath. "You just saw me." She laughed and wondered if he heard the shakiness in her voice.

"I mean I've missed being with you like this. I want to talk to you," he said. He grabbed her hand and pulled her down beside him on the bench.

"You seem very, uh, eager," she said. "Is something wrong?"

"No. Everything is right." He splayed her hand out and ran his fingers across her palm.

Every nerve in her hand seemed to spring to life at his touch. She pulled her hand away and tucked it into her lap. "What's going on?" She eyed him.

His smile was wide and confident. "I figured out what I want, and I'm going to work to get it."

Her heart sank. He was moving to California, taking that promotion he'd been offered once before. She swallowed and tried to think of something positive to say when all she wanted to do was burst into tears.

"Aren't you going to ask what it is?" He reached over and took her hand again.

"Sure. What's up?" she managed to say.

"You and Davy. You're what I want. So I'm giving you fair notice right now. I'm going to woo you. Fletcher isn't going to win you by default. I've been stupid, but I'm finally waking up. I thought you needed space, so I was trying to give it to you. But it's separated us for long enough. It's time for us to make plans for the future. Plans together. Losing Samson and watching you hurt makes me want to take care of you, to share your burdens."

She stood, needing to pace to relieve some of the tension building in her chest. He kissed her hand and pulled her down onto his lap. She hesitated, then went willingly.

"I know we have some problems to work out, but I know we can do it, Bree. I love you. I've loved you for months."

The *love* word, what she'd been longing to hear. "So why are you just now saying it?"

"You've tried to hold me at arm's length because you weren't sure you were ready to hear it. I won't be put off any longer. I know you love me, even if you're afraid to admit it to yourself. I'm going to show you your trust isn't misplaced. I'm not like your father, Bree. I won't leave you."

Bree felt overwhelmed, but a part of her was powerfully drawn to this new Kade, this man with fire in his gaze and determination in his voice.

He held her gently. "Don't run from this, Bree. That's what you usually do. You run off and hide somewhere so you don't have to admit your feelings. You're afraid, and it's okay to be afraid. I'm scared too. But I'm not letting that stop me anymore."

Panic flared in her chest and she felt almost desperate to get away. She wriggled away. "Let go, Kade. I can't think about this now. Davy needs me." She knew she was being irrational, but she seemed helpless to stop herself.

The light in his eyes faded, and he let her go. She sprang to her feet and took a step backward.

"Look at me, Bree."

Her heart seemed about to pound out of her chest, and she raised her gaze to meet his. She swallowed.

"Look in my eyes. I won't leave you. Tell me you don't love me and I'll go."

The love in his eyes brought stinging moisture to her eyes. "I . . . I can't."

"Then tell me you love me."

"I'm not ready yet, Kade."

He stood. "Then I'm going to be here when you are. But I'm not going to make it easy for you to keep putting me off. You need some-one who will love you forever, who will be there when Davy wakes with a bad dream, when you're sick or scared. Davy needs a little brother or sister. We belong together. I think you know that."

The funny thing was, she *did* know that. She'd always known it. So why did she run from him? Was it something in her genes—some fault she'd inherited from her mother? She didn't want Davy to have to carry her baggage. But she didn't know how to let go and trust Kade.

"Mommy, here's your juice." Carrying two glasses, Davy came across the yard.

"Hey, buddy." Kade squatted to eye level with Davy and held out his hand for a shake.

He was smiling with a confidence Bree had never seen before. This new Kade was thrilling but disconcerting.

"Hi, Kade." Davy looked at Bree, then cautiously took the hand Kade was holding out.

"Hey, you're breaking my fingers! When did you get so strong?" Kade winced and shook his fingers as if they hurt.

Davy's half-frown turned to a genuine grin. "Look at my muscles." He pushed up the sleeve of his T-shirt and flexed his arm.

Kade felt it and raised his eyebrows. "That's a bicep. And it's a beauty." He pressed again. "Rock hard. I can't even push it in. Want to see how to make it even bigger?"

"Yeah!" Davy's eyes went wide.

"Let's see how many pull-ups you can do." Without waiting for Davy's answer, Kade hoisted him to a tree branch. "Grab hold there, big guy."

Davy grabbed the tree branch, and Kade explained what to do. Bree watched, almost not believing her eyes. She didn't know what had brought about the change, but it stirred her heart in a way she'd never felt.

14

Jonelle hated to do errands like this. The envelope with the money inside almost seemed to radiate heat from the passenger seat. What if she got stopped? How would she explain all that money? Zane never should have put her in this position. She should have refused to go, but she wanted to get to a phone and call her mother.

She'd managed a quick pat on Samson's head before she left, and the mournful look in his eyes broke her heart. Sometimes she was tempted to call his owner and tell her to come get him. But she couldn't do that. Zane would end up in jail, and where would that leave her and the baby?

Her nerves felt stretched as tight as the skins drying in the racks on her back porch. She saw Simik's car parked by the Tastee Freeze at the edge of town and pulled the truck in beside him. Simik made her nervous even when Zane was around. He was married, but the look in his eyes when he saw her didn't seem as though he was remembering the ring on his finger.

His gaze flickered over her when she walked toward his car, and his oily smile made her want to run.

He ran his window down. "Get in the car, and we'll talk."

"Zane sent you this." She thrust the bulging envelope in his hand. "I don't need to get in."

"I need to count it. Get in." His voice brooked no argument.

Sighing, Jonelle went around the car and got in on the passenger side. The rich leather upholstery welcomed her like an old friend. When she was growing up, her dad had always had fancy cars like this one. She rubbed her hand over the downy soft seat.

Simik's pudgy fingers rippled through the bills in the envelope. "All here," he said. He stuffed the envelope into the dash pocket. A paper fell onto the floor, but he was smiling at Jonelle and didn't notice. "I've been watching you, Jonelle. You're too good to be stuck in that hole."

"Zane's good to me," she said, her fingers creeping to the door handle. If he made a move, she'd bolt.

"Want some ice cream?"

Her stomach rumbled, and she realized she hadn't eaten all morning. It was nearly eleven now. "Okay," she said. "Superman."

He laughed. "Just like a kid. I'll be right back." He got out of the car and went to the counter.

Jonelle looked around the car curiously. Simik was an enigma to her. Smooth and suave but with rough edges. She saw the paper that had fallen onto the floor. Glancing to make sure he was still occupied, she picked it up and unfolded it.

Scanning it quickly, it seemed to describe a job offering a great deal of money to a Philip Taylor. She'd heard that name before, but where? Chewing on her lip, she glanced out the window and saw Simik coming toward the car. She stuffed the paper into her jacket pocket.

"Here you go." Simik handed her a triple-size cone.

"I can't eat all that," she protested. She took the cone and hoped he didn't notice her hands shaking.

"You could use a little fattening up." He got in beside her and began to eat his cone.

The flavor proved how boring he was. Vanilla. Who ate vanilla these days when there were so many flavors to choose from? Jonelle took a lick of her cone. How quickly could she get out of here?

"How did someone like you get hooked up with Zane? He's just a good ol' boy, and you're too good for him."

Sometimes Jonelle wondered the same thing. She shrugged. "The usual story. He was the high school jock, and I was the head cheerleader. We thought he'd go on to pro football, but he blew out his knee. My parents tried to stop me from marrying him, but I loved him. I still do, of course," she added hastily. She wiped her sticky fingers on her jeans. "I've got to go. Thanks for the ice cream." She slipped out of the car before he could stop her.

Only when she was back in her truck did she realize she still had the letter.

❧

Naomi felt at the end of her rope. She'd searched with Bree yesterday afternoon, and she was still too tired today to deal with this. Timmy had been impossible all morning. One minute he was lethargic and tearful and the next he was running around the house in circles. She was ready to toss him in the backyard. If Charley had been home to play with, she might have done it too. Timmy seemed to get mad about nothing today, and she wondered if Marika's appearance had affected him as much as it had Emily.

"That's it—no more," she told him when he suddenly shrieked at the top of his lungs and lunged at Emily for getting a cookie without getting him one. Naomi picked him up by the waist. Kicking and screaming, he fought her.

She carried him to the living room. "You sit here until you calm down."

He looked at her piteously. "I don't feel good, Mom. My stomach hurts."

Naomi felt Timmy's head. His skin felt cold and clammy under her fingers. "Are you getting sick on me?" she asked.

He nodded listlessly. "Maybe."

"We'd better check your blood sugar." She went to the kitchen and got the supplies down off the high shelf. He'd had his shot this morning, but his agitation and quarrelsome nature clicked in anyway. It looked, smelled, and acted like a sugar reaction. She told herself it might be a cold or the flu, but his sudden lethargy was beginning to scare her.

Timmy began to cry when he saw the tester.

"This is the new one, remember? It doesn't really hurt," she soothed. "Just don't look and you won't even feel it."

He continued to sniffle. Naomi evaluated his color and didn't like what she saw. He looked pasty. Was he trembling? She couldn't tell if it was from fear or because he was sick. The test over, she glanced at the results and nearly gasped. His sugar was dangerously low, lower than she'd ever seen it. She wasn't sure what to do.

She grabbed orange juice from the refrigerator. "Here, sweetie, see if this makes you feel better. We'd better take you to see the doctor." The juice might help, but with his symptoms and his blood sugar this low, she wasn't about to take any chances.

Timmy drank the juice. After about fifteen minutes, a bit of color began to come back to his face. Naomi dialed the phone and explained to the nurse what had happened.

"Take his count again in fifteen minutes," the nurse told her. "If it's not normal by then, bring him in."

Naomi anxiously watched the clock. Timmy began to fidget and cry when she got the tester again. She soothed him as best she could and checked his blood sugar. Better, but still too low.

"We've got to go see the doctor," she told him. She called Donovan and told him what was happening. He promised to meet her at the office.

Emily seemed surly as they rode to the doctor's office. "You okay?" Naomi asked her, keeping a worried eye on Timmy.

"I'm okay," the eight-year-old girl said. "My mom is supposed to call today. If she calls while we're gone, I'm going to be mad at you."

Marika again. Naomi wished she could turn the clock back to the days when they were a new family, happy and learning to love one another. Emily had been a different child then. "She'll call back."

Emily glowered at her. "Why did you have to marry my dad? My mom says she could have come home with us if it weren't for you. You've spoiled everything."

Naomi swallowed. She didn't want to hurt Emily by pointing out her mother was the one who left them. "I'm sorry you feel that way," she said, her voice low. "But I don't think your dad would have let your mom come home even if I wasn't here."

Emily pressed her lips together and turned to stare out the window. She muttered something.

"What, sweetie? I didn't hear you."

Emily turned to glare at her. "I said I hate you! I wish you'd go away."

"Stop it, Emily!" Timmy shouted. He leaned over and punched her on the arm. "You're being mean to Mommy."

"She's not our mommy!" Emily shrieked so loudly the veins stood out in her neck.

"She is so. I don't like the other mommy." Timmy rubbed his eyes and began to cry.

Naomi's eyes stung, and she blinked rapidly. She had to find a way to get through to Emily.

⁂

Donovan met Naomi in the hospital emergency-room entrance. He took his son from her arms. "How bad is he?"

"I don't know, but I didn't want to take any chances." Naomi grabbed Emily's hand as they went inside. The little girl tried to pull away, but Naomi held tight. Emily needed her support, whether the child realized it or not.

They reached the emergency room, and a figure rose from a chair in the waiting room.

"Mommy!" Emily jerked her hand from Naomi's and raced to throw herself against Marika, who gripped her hand and hurried to meet Donovan.

"Who called *her*?" Naomi whispered.

"I did," Donovan said.

Naomi nearly stopped in the hall, then had to run to catch up with her husband's long strides. "Why?" she panted.

"She's his mother. It was the right thing to do."

Naomi felt a stinging in her face as though she'd been slapped. Marika had been gone for two years, letting other people care for her children, then all she had to do was waltz back into town and pick up where she left off. "I see," she said carefully.

Further conversation was impossible as the nurse took Timmy back. "Just his mother and father can come now," she said.

Donovan stopped and looked back at Naomi. "I want my wife with me."

The nurse started shaking her head, but Donovan grabbed Naomi's arm. "She's coming with me."

Warmth spread through her at his insistence. "It's okay," she whispered. "Emily needs someone with her. I'll stay."

Marika pushed Emily at Naomi then sauntered off with Donovan like a queen with her escort.

Naomi stirred the scrambled eggs without much energy. The TV in the living room was blaring out the *Sesame Street* theme music, so the kids would be occupied for a while. She'd brooded for two days about Donovan calling Marika. She knew she should talk to him about it, but the hurt was still too fresh.

"Breakfast almost ready? I'm late." Donovan dropped a kiss on the top of her head and went to the hall without waiting for an answer.

Donovan was a man of habit and ritual. Every morning he showered, dressed, kissed her, got the newspaper, and read it while he ate his breakfast. Sometimes Naomi wanted to grab him by the shoulders when he came down and tell him he couldn't read the paper this morning. She could just imagine the look on his face.

Things were busy at the store, Naomi knew that. He was still just as tender and sweet when he came home at night, but his distraction rattled her. She'd known marrying a man with a family would be different than being a newlywed with no other people in the house, but she hadn't realized how little time there would be for just the two of them. Their time alone was practically nonexistent.

Donovan came back in the kitchen with the paper in his hand. "Gosh, I'm late." He opened the paper, grabbed his coffee, and took a sip.

Naomi pulled out a chair and sat at the table with him. "I need to talk to you."

He lowered his paper. "Something wrong?"

He still wasn't really listening. She could tell it by his tone and the way his eyes kept straying back to the headlines.

"Yes. Very wrong. Please put the paper down and look at me."

His eyebrows rose, but he did as she asked, folding the paper and setting it off to the side of his plate. "You sound mad. Did I do something?"

She almost relented at the tone of panic in his voice, but steeling her resolve, she folded her hands in front of her and stared at him hard. "You shouldn't have called Marika."

"I'm sorry. I thought it best." He put his hand out, palm up, the way he did when he wanted to hold her hand. She ignored it.

"What would you have done if she wasn't in town?"

"You're not making any sense. I couldn't have called her if I didn't know where she was, now could I? But since I had her number, I thought she should know." He smiled and put an arm around her. "I never meant to hurt you, princess."

At his pet nickname, she almost wilted. But this battle needed to be fought now. She slid out from under his embrace. "I realize that, but she abdicated her rights when she deserted you and the children." She saw him wince but rushed on anyway. "I just think her presence was upsetting to the children. They still are trying to find their way in this whole mess. It's not like Timmy's life was in danger. I had it under control."

He was silent.

"What—you don't think I'm handling it?" she demanded.

"Don't get mad at me. I know you're trying your best," he said. "But Timmy never used to have these sugar swings. He's had two in a week now. We need to figure out what he's eating."

"You think I'm feeding him stuff he shouldn't eat? I follow his diet to the letter! And I set the timer for his shot. It's not my fault, Donovan. Does Marika say it is?"

He shrugged. "I haven't talked to her about it."

"But you've been thinking it." She sat back, deflated and near tears.

"I didn't say it's your fault. You're putting words in my mouth." He grabbed her hand and didn't let go when she tried to pull it away. "Look at me. I know you would never hurt Timmy. But we all need to work together to figure this out. That includes Marika."

Jealousy boiled in the pit of her stomach. She'd never felt it before and didn't like the way it made her breath come in short gasps.

She swallowed the rage. "Why don't you start giving him his shot? Then you'll know it's done right." She stood and went back to the stove. She turned the heat on under the skillet and poured the egg mixture into it.

His chair scraped against the floor, but she didn't turn to look.

"I can almost see the steam coming out of your ears," he whispered in her ear. He slipped his arms around her waist from behind and pulled her against his chest.

Naomi stiffened. He shouldn't think a few sweet words would mellow her out. Her eyes burned, and she blinked rapidly.

"I'm sorry, Naomi. You're doing a phenomenal job with the kids, the house. My life was a mess before you came. But even more, you've filled up all the lonely places." His lips roamed to the side of her face and down to her neck.

Determined not to cry, she sagged against him. "I'm afraid of Marika," she said in a small voice.

Donovan laughed. "She's more pitiful than scary."

"You're not a woman. I've heard for years how beautiful she was and how much you loved her."

"*Loved* is the operative word there. That was over long before she left. You're more than just beautiful—you're good. Your beauty is inside and outside both. Marika's was merely external. You have nothing to fear from her."

His breath whispered across her neck and she shivered.

Nothing to fear. She prayed that was true. Then why did she feel that her happy home teetered on the brink of disaster?

The doorbell rang, and she turned in his arms. Kissing him quickly, she pulled his hands from her waist. "You want to get that? I'll finish these eggs and you can eat."

He turned with obvious reluctance and went down the hall. The front door opened, and she heard the murmur of voices. It almost sounded like Mason, so she wondered if she was needed for a new search. She slid the skillet off the heat and followed Donovan to the door.

Mason stood with his hands in his pocket and an apologetic expression on his face. He nodded to Naomi. "Morning, Naomi."

Donovan was staring at a paper. "Marika is suing for custody of the kids," he whispered.

Naomi gasped and brought her hand to her mouth. "Oh, Donovan."

"Sorry, Donovan," Mason said. "I know this comes as a shock. For what it's worth, I doubt she has a snowball's chance."

Donovan's big hand crushed the paper, and he tossed it into a corner. "She's not getting my kids."

Mason's eyes were kind, and he nodded toward the wadded up paper. "That won't solve anything. You'll be getting another one in the mail you'll have to fill out."

"We have to call a lawyer," Naomi said shakily. "Will we have to go to court?"

Mason nodded. "Try to keep the kids from having to testify though."

"They're not stepping foot inside a courtroom." Donovan slipped his arm around Naomi's waist and drew her to his side. "How's she getting the money to do this? She doesn't have anything."

Mason shrugged. "All I know is she's doing it. So you'd better get prepared."

15

*B*ree trudged into Nicholls's Finnish Imports. Anu stood folding T-shirts at a display table. Her bright smile dimmed when she saw Bree's face.

"Ah, *kulta,* I see your day on your face. You need a hug. Come here." She held out her arms, and Bree allowed herself to be wrapped in them.

"He's gone, Anu. I think he's gone for good."

"It's only been a week, Bree. Do not give up yet. I've been praying, and I believe we will find our Samson."

Bree pulled back and looked into her mother-in-law's face. "Really, Anu? You really believe that?"

"I know it in my heart. You must believe too."

"I wish I could." Bree stepped away and fished in her pocket for a tissue. "Where's Davy?"

"He is fine, *kulta.* Naomi has him."

"How's Hilary doing? I haven't talked to her since Samson was taken. She called and left a message on my machine. She said she was so sorry about Samson."

"In spite of her dislike of dogs, she likes Samson more than she admits."

"I'll take your word for it." She poured a cup of coffee from the pot on the counter. "What did you and Davy do today?"

"I took Davy to visit his grandfather." Anu said.

"When does Abraham expect to be moved to the state prison?"

"Soon, perhaps as early as next week. I wanted to see him before he went. The pastor has been to see him every few days, and I have hopes that he will accept Christ soon."

Anu's face was glowing, and Bree gave a slight smile. "It amazes me that you can still show concern and love for him after he deserted you for thirty years. You know all he did, but you can still forgive him."

"To harbor bitterness would accomplish nothing," Anu said. "It would hurt me more than it would harm him. God loves him just as much as he loves me. All people are able to be redeemed."

"I don't know about that," Bree said.

"Ah, I see by your face, you are thinking of your parents. You must let go of that bitterness, *kulta*. If you do not root it out, it will send its tentacles into every area of your life. It was your mother's birthday recently, no?"

Bree shook her head. "I sent a card and got the usual response: nothing. I didn't expect anything other than maybe a request for money. I guess I'm surprised even that hasn't come through. She hasn't called in over a year."

"Maybe she is sober now."

Bree gave a short laugh. "I've been accused of being a Pollyanna, but even I know better than to hope for something like that."

"God can transform even a life like your mother's."

Bree knew Anu meant well, but she'd never met the drunk who raised Bree. Bree usually thought of her mother as Dolores instead of Mom. Such a warm, fuzzy endearment like "Mom" or "Mother" didn't apply to a hot-tempered woman who spent nearly every evening passed out on the sofa.

"What of your father? Have you been to see him?"

Bree shook her head. "I've been too busy looking for Samson."

"You cannot search every minute, *kulta*. Take time for your father. You don't know how long you have with him. There is much time to make up."

"I don't really know him. I'm not even sure I want to."

"Did your mother ever talk about him?" Anu rubbed her thumb over Bree's hand in a soothing motion.

Bree shook her head. "She flew into a rage whenever I mentioned him. I learned not to ask. What I hate him for is that he left me at her mercy. He couldn't have loved me or he wouldn't have done that."

"I'm sorry, *kulta*. It is obvious the scars are still very painful."

At the softness in Anu's voice, a lump lodged in Bree's throat and refused to be swallowed. She was turning into a regular fountain. This pain wasn't something new to deal with—she'd lived with it for years. So why was it all of a sudden resurrecting itself like this?

Bree's cell phone rang, and she answered it with a sense of relief.

Mason's voice came over the line. "Denise just called. Philip's papers are missing."

⁂

Denise met Bree and Mason at the front door. Her hair looked like it hadn't been combed all day, and the children were still in their pajamas. Bree scooped up Abby and followed Mason's broad back into the living room.

It looked like an Ojibwa windstorm had blown through.

"Sorry about the mess," Denise said. "I haven't felt like cleaning."

Bree looked around carefully and realized the disarray was simply from living with three children. "How do you know someone was here?"

"Because the file is gone." Denise pointed to the table where Bree had seen it last.

"Maybe one of the kids moved it," Mason said.

Denise shook her head. "It was there last night when I went to bed. And the back door was ajar when I got up this morning. Someone was here." She clasped her arms around herself.

Mason glanced around. "I could dust for fingerprints, but there were so many people here the day Phil died, I'm not sure it would do much good."

Denise pushed her tangled hair out of her eyes. "Are we in danger—me and the kids?"

"I doubt it. But I'll have a deputy watch the house. Though it looks like the thief got what he came for. What was this file?"

"Just some formula notations Phil was working on."

Mason frowned. "Why didn't you give them to Cassie?"

"I'd been meaning to, but I never got around to telling her I had them."

She hadn't gotten around to a lot of things, Bree thought, looking around the dirty house.

Zane took a coiled whip down from the nail on the porch wall.

"What are you doing with that?" Jonelle asked, her voice rising.

"I'm going to teach that dog to fear me. He actually tried to lick my hand this morning. I don't have much time to make him mean."

Jonelle caught at his hand. "Please don't, Zane. It's my fault. I've been petting him." She couldn't let him hurt the dog.

Zane's face flushed, and he clenched his fists. "You know better than that, Jonelle! I've told you to leave my dogs alone."

"I know, and I will. Give him another chance, please. Don't hurt him for something that's my fault!" She grabbed the whip out of his hand and ran down the porch steps.

"Come back here with that!" Zane roared. His heavy boots thumped down the steps after her.

Jonelle put on another spurt of speed and reached the river behind the house. She hurled the whip into the fast-flowing river with all her might. Zane grabbed her and spun her around. She held up her hands in front of her face, certain he would actually hit her this time. Though he'd never raised his hand to her, she knew she'd pushed him past all reason this time.

"Don't look at me like that," he said, dropping his hand from her arm. "I wouldn't hurt you, Jonelle, don't you know that?"

Tears spurted from her eyes at his suddenly gentle tone. "I know, Zane. I was just scared for a minute. I know I shouldn't have bucked you like that. But I like Samson."

He shook his head ruefully. "You'll be the death of me. I'll try cocaine and steroids instead. He won't feel a thing."

"Oh, Zane, give him back." She caught at his arm. "Please, just let him go. He'll be able to find his way home."

He shook his head. "Sorry, Jonelle. He's my ticket to a lot of money."

A political dinner was the last place Bree wanted to be. She knew it was important, but she was emotionally and physically exhausted. She entered the community center and glanced around as she listened to the excited buzz of conversation. The Rock Harbor Community Center had been built by early residents during the heyday of the Copper Queen mining era. Mine money showed in the elegance of the oak paneling and the coffered ceiling overhead. Crystal chandeliers shimmered above Bree's head, and her shoes echoed on the marble floors.

She spied Anu at the punch table and made a beeline for her. Her mother-in-law looked slim and lovely draped in a blue silk dress that caught the light from the chandeliers.

"Ah, *kulta*, I was wondering where you were."

"Lauri was a little late from picking up a pizza for supper for her and Davy."

"I was almost late myself. Abraham called."

"How's he doing?"

"Very well, I think. I worried when he was transferred to Detroit, but it seems to be the best place for him. He has begun to attend a Prison Fellowship service and is asking even more questions."

Bree tried to hide her surprise. She'd thought Abe Nicholls was too hard-hearted to ever admit he needed the Lord in spite of Anu's assertions that he was listening to her witness about Christ. But she knew nothing was impossible for Jesus. "Has Hilary agreed to see him yet?"

Anu shook her head. "Abraham writes her every week, but I believe she has thrown away all the letters."

Bree understood how her sister-in-law felt. The man who'd deserted Hilary as a small child had returned only to try to take possession of a fabulous green diamond, not to see his daughter or wife. It was hard not to be bitter. Her gaze wandered to Hilary, in a dress the same color as the infamous diamond. She had a hard edge about her tonight, just like the stone too. The mayoral reelection would be here in a few more months, and Hilary was determined to win her third term. Sometimes Bree wondered if it would be the best thing for Hilary to lose the election. She depended too much on it for her sense of who she was.

"I'm surprised the doctor let her attend this little shindig," Bree said. "She's still not herself since the miscarriage."

"You know my daughter. She promised to sit and rest, but look at her." Anu made a sweeping motion with her hand. "She hasn't sat down yet."

"We'll have to take care of her."

"I see she has managed to bring most of the new residents into her camp," Anu said, nodding toward the group of researchers from Cassie's lab. "Steve Asters seems quite smitten with Cassie Hecko. She looks lovely tonight."

"At least she's not in her fatigues and army boots," Bree agreed, watching Cassie smile up at Steve. "Steve could use some female companionship. He's been alone too much since Fay's death. I wouldn't mind having Steve as part of the family."

"It's nice to hear you admit you have a family now," Anu said.

"I'm going to follow your advice and take time to get closer to them. I told her I'd come to Sunday dinner this weekend."

Anu smiled her approval, then she nodded to the left. "I see you have had much male companionship," Anu said. "The young fireman seems to be following you everywhere. I see him now looking for you."

Bree saw Nick scanning the room and stepped behind a pillar. Anu raised her eyebrows. "You are avoiding Nick?"

"Just for a while," Bree said. "I wanted to mingle, and Nick demands too much of my attention."

Anu was silent a moment. "So you aren't in love with him?"

"I don't know. He hasn't been around much since Samson disappeared. And Kade . . ."

"You know with your heart." Anu's voice held a touch a humor.

"Maybe." Bree brushed a curl out of her eyes. "But Nick's good husband material."

"Why do you think so?"

Bree shrugged. "Don't you think so too? He loves kids, he's got a stable job, he is very attentive. When we're together, I mean."

"I thought you said he was too attentive."

"That too." Bree laughed, but Anu didn't smile.

"What about Kade?"

"What about him?" Bree looked away.

"Don't try to hide your eyes from me. Have you considered the real reason you want to avoid Nick?"

"And what's that?"

"Because you're in love with Kade."

Bree finally met Anu's gaze. "Maybe. I'm feeling I might be ready to face the future now. And I always thought Kade would be a part of that. I just don't want to make a mistake. Davy and I are getting along fine, but I know he needs a father."

"And you need a husband."

"I don't *want* to need a man though. I think that's what I'm struggling with the most. Am I ready to go into a life where I have to answer to someone else?"

"You answer to God now," Anu pointed out.

"And I still struggle with that. It's a trust issue. I always knew I couldn't trust my mother. My father wasn't around, so he was obviously untrustworthy too. It's hard to believe even God won't fail me someday." Bree could hardly believe the things she'd been thinking about had really come out of her mouth. She bit her lip and wished she could take them back.

But Anu just smiled and squeezed Bree's arm. "We all struggle with that. How can we trust someone we can't see or touch?"

"Exactly! My parents in this life have failed me. It makes it hard to think of God as a father."

"That's what faith is all about. And our struggles with that issue can make us stronger for the battle. As long as you keep asking questions and looking to God for the answers, your faith will grow. Never be ashamed to admit you have questions. God is big enough to handle them."

Bree hugged her mother-in-law. "You always make me feel better," Bree said.

"Now about Kade," Anu began.

Bree released her and stepped back. "I still need to do some thinking about that issue. And praying."

Anu looked like she had more to say, but Hilary joined them. "What are you two doing hiding over here?"

"Just gabbing. You look great." Bree kissed her sister-in-law.

"Thanks. I'm tired though."

Now that she was closer, Bree could see Hilary's pallor under her makeup. "You need to sit down. Now."

"I know. I probably shouldn't have come, but I don't want to lose the election."

"How about some punch? You could sit over on the couch and I'll bring people to you." She cringed inside at what she'd have to do, but Hilary needed to rest. Her eyes looked droopy and almost feverish.

"You hate to mingle," Hilary said.

"I can do it when I need to."

"I might take you up on that," Hilary said. "I didn't get rest today with getting ready for tonight."

"You *will* take her up on it." Anu took Hilary's arm and steered her toward the sofa.

Bree smiled and began to move around the room. She saw Chito in the corner looking lost. "Seems like I've been seeing a lot of you scientist types lately," she said, joining him.

He didn't look at her and shoved a piece of cheese in his mouth. "Yeah, I guess."

"I've been wanting to talk to you, and this seems as good a time as any." Bree leaned against the marble post. "I heard you often argued with Phil. What were your disagreements about?"

Chito scowled. "I don't know who told you that, but it's wrong. Phil could be opinionated and didn't like it when anyone disagreed with him."

"Funny, I heard he was very congenial."

He stuffed another piece of cheese in his mouth. "It was a facade. He thought he was another Einstein."

"And you didn't think so?"

"I may be young, but I have a good mind," Chito snapped. He put his empty plate on a table. "You'll have to excuse me. I need to talk to someone."

Bree watched him hurry away. She could see he might be difficult to work with. And he had a temper. Could Phil have pushed him too far? Though it was hard to imagine any of Phil's friends could have killed him, most murders were committed by someone known to the victim.

She shook her head and started toward the punch table. Nick fell into step with her.

"There you are," he said. "I've been looking for you."

"I was talking to Anu. I need to mingle and direct people over to Hilary. She's resting."

"I'll help you."

"Thanks. You know how I hate crowds." He was a good man. She just wished she could feel about him the way he seemed to feel about her.

They moved through the crowd, talking with bankers, lawyers, and just good, middle-class people, urging them to stop by and chat with

Hilary. Nick's lighthearted banter flowed like Rock River in the spring rains. He made it look so easy. Bree watched him as he talked. He moved his hands, touching people on the shoulder and looking them in the eye. He gave every person he talked to his undivided attention.

Then Bree caught sight of Kade's dark head at the door. She hadn't thought he was coming. Her heart seemed to shift into slow motion, pumping first ice then heat through her veins. Didn't her reaction to him tell her something? Nick, sweet as he was, had never affected her the way Kade did. The way Kade had declared his love for her had kept her awake at night.

Kade saw her, and the way his lips turned up in a slow smile was for her alone. She'd never seen him smile like that at anyone else. While Nick made her feel special, he could do the same with anyone in the room. Kade kept his special glances and smiles just for her. She knew she shouldn't blame Nick for being charismatic, but she couldn't force her heart to stop responding to Kade.

She left Nick chatting with Barbara McGovern, the bank owner's wife, and moved to meet Kade. She caught the scent of his spicy cologne. Though he was dressed in a dark blue suit, he had his hands shoved in his pockets, and the familiar stance heightened the sense that he would never change. He was like Three Indians Rock, solid and standing firm against the winds and waves that battered his life.

"Hi." Kade's smile reached his eyes.

"Hi yourself. I thought maybe you'd be the only resident to miss this bash."

"Landorf wanted to chew me out. He must have been hungry."

"Want me to yell at him?"

"Nah, I can handle him. We're getting along okay for the most part. He's mellowed. Maybe I have too."

If he continued to look at her like that, she was going to melt into a puddle on the floor. She couldn't look away from his gaze.

He tucked her hand into the crook of his elbow. "Where's Hilary? I should say hello."

"On the sofa. She's feeling tired." They started across the room. "Anything new going on out at the forest?"

He frowned. "Still no sign of who dumped the chemicals that killed the fish. My money is still on the environmental group. Maybe not Marika herself, but her group."

"She's too pretty to be guilty, is that it?" Bree laughed.

He grinned. "I didn't say that, but she's quite a looker."

Was the sick feeling in the pit of her stomach jealousy? Bree curled her fingers into her palms. "She's suing Naomi and Donovan for the kids."

"She's never far from trouble, is she?" Kade said, shaking his head.

"And we've been having plenty of it. Speaking of which, I've started wondering if someone is intentionally targeting the lab."

"What do you mean?"

"Well, Phil's dead, and someone has broken into both Cassie's home and Denise's home, looking for something. Whoever it was stole some of Phil's notes. And what about Cassie's medicine? It would take a person with a special knowledge of computers to change that prescription, especially from the outside."

"Who would have that kind of knowledge about computers? It almost sounds like it could be a prank, and Cassie was just unlucky."

"I'm more inclined to think it might be another brainy scientist."

They started toward Hilary again. The mayor smiled warmly when she saw Kade with Bree. "I wondered if you were coming, Kade," she said. She patted the seat beside her. "Sit down and talk to me for a while."

Kade settled on the sofa beside Hilary. Bree marveled at how far the two had come in the past nine months. Hilary had been violently opposed to Bree dating Kade. Now she'd accepted him fully and disliked Nick. If only she could get all members of her family to agree, maybe her life would be easier.

16

Kade rode his horse along the trail to Big Frog Falls. He lifted his face to the patch of sunlight streaming through the trees. Those who lived in the U.P. relished the summers with the long days of sunshine. There was a special quality of light to the North Woods, a golden glow that lifted his spirits. The late afternoon rays of sun threw long shadows in the woods.

Moses snorted and tossed his head, chewing at the bit occasionally as he ambled among the wildflowers, the blooms nearly to his belly in some places. Kade kept a sharp eye out for wolves. The report of the wolf that had tried to attack Davy was troubling. Wolves usually avoided contact with humans, and luckily there had been no more reports in recent weeks.

He passed a campsite, dismounted, and checked the ashes. Cold. Satisfied, he started to get back on his horse when he heard voices in the ravine farther to his left. He tied Moses to a tree and trod through the thick forest in the direction of the sounds. He heard something whimper. Not human, maybe a pup. Kade couldn't tell. But the distress in the animal's voice quickened Kade's steps.

He broke through the tree line and looked down into a clearing in the ravine. Three young men crouched around a white Chihuahua in a pen. They poked it with sticks and laughed when it whimpered again. Kade started to shout at them then decided to first get a better look at what they were doing. He burned to charge them with something. If there was one thing he hated, it was to see an animal mistreated.

He didn't recognize any of the men. They were all in their twenties, as near as he could tell. One was Hispanic, the other two Caucasian. The two light-skinned men looked like brothers, both with thin noses and scraggly beards. They were so bony, they looked unhealthy. The Hispanic looked younger than the other two, and he seemed uneasy with the poking and laughter of the other men. He saw two more dogs in cages facing a pit made out of plywood. The dogs—both pit bulls and nasty looking—snarled and paced in their cages, obviously eager to get at the little white dog.

"Let's get this over with," the Hispanic man said.

"You're too soft, Manuel," one of the other men said. "We need to savage this guy up a little if he stands a chance against the dogs. We want them to be ready to fight when they meet up with Bruck."

"They don't stand no chance against Bruck anyway, and you know it." The one they called Manuel shuffled his feet and looked around.

"We get their bloodlust up with a fresh kill, and they might," the other man said. He jabbed at the white dog. It cowered with a yelp.

Dogfights. Kade would like to throw these three in with this "Bruck" they were talking about and see how they liked his teeth. Even though it was a felony in most states, dogfights had been on the upswing all over the country in recent months. He thought of Samson, and the reality facing Kade now made him feel sick.

He would need to call for backup. He couldn't handle three men by himself. But if he waited, the little dog would be dead in a few minutes, for both of the Caucasian men started toward the cages to release the pit bulls. Kade grabbed his cell phone and keyed it on quickly.

"Send backup," he whispered, giving his coordinates. "And call Mason." He clipped his phone back in place and checked to make sure he could pull his gun easily. The men had reached the cages and had their hands on the cage doors. "Park Security. Stop right where you are," he ordered.

The men froze. One uttered a string of obscenities and pawed for his gun. Manuel took off running for the pickup parked at the top of the ravine. "Hold it!" Kade barked. As the other man's gun swung up,

Kade pulled his own gun. He fired a shot over the fleeing man's head for good measure. "Hands in the air!"

All three turned slowly to face him as they raised their hands over their heads. Kade had only two sets of handcuffs with him, but they were in his saddlebag. "Over here, now!" The men shuffled through the brush toward him.

"Hey, man, we wasn't doing anything," one man whined.

"What's your name?" Kade asked.

"Bart Sommerville. This here's my brother Brandon."

"Shut up," Brandon hissed. He glared at Kade. "You got no call to hold us. These is our dogs."

"Looks to me like you were about to have a dogfight. That's a felony in Michigan."

"Hey, come on, Ranger, you can look the other way. No one cares about a little friendly dogfight." Brandon's eyes gleamed. "I got money in my pocket. I'll give you a thousand bucks to let us go."

"Dogfighting and bribery; you're working yourself in deeper and deeper," Kade said through gritted teeth. It was all he could do not to bury his fist in the man's mouth. He glanced toward the dogs, hoping they weren't so far gone they were unable to be rehabilitated. As long as they weren't aggressive to humans, they could often be saved. He would check with Bree. She would know what to do.

Kade held the white Chihuahua—Lacy, the tag said—in one arm while he drove along the road toward the SAR center with the other. Mason had taken the men into custody and transported them to town. He passed Lauri going the opposite direction and waved, but she didn't see him. Her face seemed set and strained.

He told himself he wasn't taking the dog to Bree just to score some points with her. It made sense she'd know if a dog was missing. Her team found more than people; they found pets and possessions as well. Bree had her fingers on the pulse of most everything that went on in the county. It was nearly time for the team to meet her for the daily search for Samson. He pulled in behind Bree's Jeep and got out.

Charley bounded to meet him, and he knelt and petted the dog for a minute. Lacy touched noses with Charley and whimpered, reminding Kade of his mission. Charley followed him to the building.

The building seemed deserted when he stepped inside. The lights were off in the big training room, and his boots echoed on the painted concrete floor. Charley padded with him through the dim room, illuminated only by late afternoon sun sifting through the building's two small windows.

The door to Bree's office was closed, and he tapped on it lightly. Lacy whimpered again. Her experience with the pit bulls had obviously unnerved her. Of course, the Chihuahua breed wasn't known for its bravery, he thought with a grin. He patted the small dog on the head. "It's okay, girl."

"I'm in here," Bree called.

He pushed open the door and found her filing papers in a cabinet. The way her face lit up when she saw him warmed his insides.

"What do you have there?" Her gaze settled on the white dog.

"I found this little girl about to be fed to some pit bulls." He described the scene and how he'd rescued her, then turned the men over to Mason. He loved watching the expressions change on her face, from curiosity to horror to admiration. If he had a hundred years to sit and watch her face, it wouldn't be enough time. Like most redheads, she burned instead of tanned, and her nose was peeling. Her green eyes watched him with an intensity he'd always found invigorating. Bree never did anything halfway. When she finally committed herself, it would be with her whole heart. He found he was willing to wait and to work for that day, if she would only look at him like this all the rest of their lives.

Bree got up and came toward him. She put her palms on the sides of his face and kissed him. "Thank you," she said, her eyes grave. "You have a heart like Samson's."

Kade's own ears grew warm. "High praise I'm not sure I deserve," he said, depositing Lacy in her arms. "I was just doing my job."

"We both know that's not true," she said. She ran her hands over Lacy's body. "She seems okay."

"The dogs hadn't gotten to her yet. But she would have been toast in about thirty seconds, if she lasted that long. The pit bulls were vicious."

"Where are they now? Maybe they know something about Samson!" Hope lit her eyes.

"In custody. Mason said he was taking the dogs to the animal shelter, but he was talking about having them put down."

"No! Is he sure that's necessary?" She grabbed the phone and dialed.

Kade listened to her tell Mason not to do anything until she evaluated the dogs. All the time she talked, her long fingers rubbed Lacy's ears, and the little dog relaxed under her ministrations. "What about Lacy?" he asked when she hung up.

"I think I know who she belongs to." She reminded him about the woman she and Davy had met out at the lakeside campground several weeks ago. "That has to be the owner." She flipped Lacy's tag over and found a number on the back. "I'll call and tell her you've found her dog. She'll be thrilled. Lacy seemed very important to her."

He waited while Bree notified Lacy's owner, and then followed her outside. "How about dinner tonight after the search?"

She hesitated, then shook her head. "I think you'd better get home to Lauri. She's pretty upset. Besides, I want to talk to those men."

"I saw her tearing out of here. I figured Zorro hadn't done well."

"No, it's not that. She asked me again about taking her baby. I had to tell her there was no way I could do that. A baby needs a mother and a father both."

Kade's high spirits deflated immediately. Did that mean she wanted nothing to do with Lauri's baby? "Naomi's decision really rattled her." He sighed and leaned against the doorjamb.

"I know. I felt bad for her. But Naomi's life is in total turmoil right now."

"I'm not blaming her, but I know how much it meant to Lauri. I'll have to see what our options are. I wouldn't mind keeping the baby. Actually, it's hard to think about giving away part of our family to strangers. It wasn't so bad when I thought Naomi would raise it."

"I have an idea, but I can't talk about it yet," Bree said.

Kade raised an eyebrow. He was curious but knew better than to try to press her. "We'd better get to town and talk to Mason."

"I'll call the team and tell them to get started looking for Samson without me." Her smile faltered at the mention of her dog.

Mason's cruiser was parked in front of the Suomi Café, and Bree pulled her Jeep in beside it. Kade jumped out of his truck with Lacy and followed Bree inside. Mason had a cup of black coffee in his hand. His eyebrows winged up at the expression on her face.

"Have you interrogated those men yet?" Bree asked.

"I did. They confessed to fighting dogs." Mason set his coffee on the table and invited Bree to sit. He glanced up at Kade. "You find that dog's owner?"

"Yeah, Bree called her. She's coming to get Lacy and should be here soon. We told her to come to your office, so I'd better get over there."

Mason nodded. "I'll be along in a few minutes. Let me talk to Bree first and I'll join you. Don't let the owner leave if she shows up before I get there. I want to ask her some questions."

Kade nodded and turned to Bree. "Call me later, okay?" he said softly. "I'll be praying for you. Want to meet me for breakfast in the morning?"

She nodded, and he pressed his lips against her forehead. She clung to him for a minute, feeling a bit like a swimmer clinging to a rock amid deep waves. Kade always made her feel so safe. When he and Lacy were gone, she asked Molly for a cup of coffee.

"Did they mention Samson?" she asked.

Mason shook his head. "They're not talking about the bigger fish out there. I offered them a deal, but they just clammed up."

"Could I talk to them?"

"Sure. But I don't think you'll get anywhere."

Bree exhaled, then nodded. "It's worth a try. How's the investigation going on Phil's death and Cassie's change in prescription?"

"Slow, though I did hear from the computer expert about Cassie's drug scare. Seems the pharmacy computer was definitely broken into. The scrip was changed."

"That sounds really scary, Mason. How can any of us know we're getting what we should be taking?"

"I'm having the paper run a warning tonight. Everyone needs to examine their prescriptions carefully, know what they're prescribed, and make sure what they get is what they've been taking. And for the near future at least, Terry will be comparing all the refills to the original written orders."

Bree shivered. "Scary stuff."

Mason nodded. "It's going to be hard figuring out who changed that scrip. About as hard as figuring out who killed Phil Taylor."

"No clues yet?"

He shook his head. "Nothing really. Forensics went over the kitchen again, but they still haven't found anything unusual. They dusted the living room to see if there were any prints left there when the perp took the file, but it had been wiped clean except for Denise's prints and the kids'."

"You don't suspect Denise, do you?"

Mason shrugged. "I'm not ruling her out."

"I can't imagine her being capable of hurting anyone."

Molly put Bree's coffee on the table. "I couldn't help overhearing," she said. "I'm thinking you would want to know what happened here a couple of days before Phil died, eh?"

"What did you see?" Mason asked.

"I try to stay out of our customers' business, but sometimes you just can't, eh? Phil and Denise have been coming in several times a week ever since they moved to Rock Harbor. They didn't get along real well, but they had a lot of pressures with the babies and all. But a couple of days before he died, they really got into it here." Molly shuffled, distress on her face.

Mason took out his notepad and pen. "Can you remember exactly what was said?"

"She told him she wished she'd never married him, that he was a weasel and not a man."

"Could you tell what the fight was about?" Bree asked.

"It sounded like she wanted him to loan her brother some money. He called her brother 'shiftless and no good,' which really got her going. He finally slammed out of the café and left her here with the kids."

"Did she say anything to you?" Mason was busy jotting down everything Molly said.

"She just cried awhile, then when she got ready to leave, Phil came back in and apologized. They acted like nothing was wrong as they left, but it bothered me to see the kids crying and upset."

"Everyone fights sometimes," Mason said. "But I'll check it out. You want to come talk to the men now?" he asked Bree.

She nodded and got up.

But no matter how much she begged, the men turned stony faces to the wall and refused to answer any of her questions about Samson.

17

Cassie rubbed her burning eyes and pushed away from her microscope. The nursing home had called when Dad got fractious, and she'd arrived late last night to find him in quite a state. He'd been pitiful, dressed in three layers of clothes and carrying a packed suitcase. He hadn't known where he was going. He was getting worse.

She squeezed her eyes shut. Her sister had been no help. Bree didn't seem eager to welcome her new sister with open arms, and Cassie reminded herself how much of a shock it must have been to hear the truth. At least she and Davy were coming to dinner tomorrow. Hopefully Dad would be having a good day. And if Bree never warmed up, well, Cassie had dealt with being unwanted before. It wouldn't be anything new. Her mother hadn't talked to her from the time Cassie was five until she'd died when Cassie was ten.

She was just turning back to her microscope when a rumble started under her feet. It built until the beakers on the counter rattled, and one fell to the floor, shattering into sharp pieces. An earthquake? Cassie jumped up, crunching through the glass to the door. In the hall, workers were running toward the entrance. Her mouth dry, she fell into line with the rest. Maybe the mine had caved in somewhere, and they were all trapped here. She tried not to think like that as she exited into the reception area.

"What happened?" Yancy asked. No one seemed to know.

Yancy Coppler's forehead glistened with perspiration as he went to the door. "Maybe it was just an earth tremor," Cassie said. "We need to get out of here just in case."

Nora Corbit clapped her hand over her mouth and moaned. "We're all going to die."

"Don't be silly, *chiquita*," Lola Marcos said. She went to the door and yanked on it. It opened easily, and she went through the air lock to the other door. It opened also, and a collective sigh of relief echoed through the reception area.

The relief turned to consternation, however, at the sight outside the mine. Hundreds of people marched in front of the mine, most carrying signs like "No Genetically Altered Plants" and "Keep the Environment Safe."

The crowd saw them and charged toward the door. Cassie yanked a stunned Nora out of the way and slammed the security doors into place seconds before people began pounding the metal door with their fists. "Back inside!" she shouted, ushering the rest of the employees back into the reception area. She shut and locked the second door. "Chito, call town for help before these nuts get in here."

The slight-built man nodded and went to the phone. "The line's not working," he reported moments later.

"Cut?"

He shrugged. "Maybe."

"Anyone have a cell phone that works here?" Cassie looked from face to face, but everyone shook their heads. She'd forgotten to recharge her own cell phone. She fought a rising sense of panic then took a few deep breaths. "They can't get in here, and they can't stay out there all night. The mosquitoes will run them off."

"What if we tried talking to them—explaining what we're trying to accomplish here?" Lola suggested.

Cassie grimaced. "You ever heard of reasoning with an angry mob?"

"It's worth a try. We don't have anything to lose. But be careful," Yancy warned.

"Go out the hidden side door," Chito said.

Cassie nodded and went down the hall to a small hallway that led to the left. The others followed her. When she reached the door, she held up her hand. "Listen." From the other side of the metal door she could hear fists pounding. "They've found this exit too."

"They seem to be getting madder," Nora said fearfully.

With no way to communicate with the outside world, Cassie felt like she was trapped under water without her air tank. "There's no reason to panic," she said, as much for her benefit as anyone else's. "We have food and drink in the vending machines. We're not going to starve. We'll just wait it out."

"I have to get home to my family," Chito said. "My wife and I are invited to a dinner party in our honor tonight. I have to be home by five."

Cassie glanced at her watch. "It's almost that now. When you don't show up, will your wife come looking for you?"

Chito looked away. "Probably not. She'll just think I got involved in work and forgot. She will try to call, but the phone is out."

"What if they're out there all night? There's nowhere to sleep in here." Nora paced nervously.

Cassie didn't relish the idea of sleeping in the straight chairs or on the floor herself. What did the protesters think they'd accomplish by this? The lab wasn't going to close up shop and go away.

The rumble came again. It seemed to emanate from the direction of the growing chamber. Dread froze Cassie's limbs. "The growing chamber!" She turned and ran down the hall to the door at the end.

"Wait, Cassie, don't go in there!" Yancy shouted. He grabbed her as she wrenched at the door. A puff of dust flew from under the door as the rumble continued. Cassie stood on tiptoe and looked through the window into the chamber. Smoke and dust billowed in clouds and she couldn't see the plants at all.

"My plants," she whispered.

Yancy pulled her away from the door. "I think a bomb has gone off in there," he said. "It's not safe."

Cassie's eyes burned, but not from the dust leaching into the hall from the growing chamber. She wouldn't cry, not in front of her colleagues. They were looking to her for leadership and strength. But right now, the last thing she felt was strong. Their work of months had just been destroyed.

Samson snarled and saliva dripped from his muzzle. Jonelle watched sadly as the big dog staggered around the pen, lunging at the stick Zane prodded him with. The drugs seemed to have done their work all too well.

Zane laughed and poked the dog again. Samson grabbed the stick in his mouth ferociously.

"Bring me the video camera," Zane called. "I want some film of him like this to circulate. Those bets will come pouring in."

Jonelle brought the camera to him. "Aren't you afraid he'll kill Bruck?"

"Nah, it's all show. Bruck'll make mincemeat out of old Samson here. This dog has been a pet too long."

Jonelle longed to do something to save the dog. But it was probably too late.

"Look, Mommy!" Davy pointed out a small deer crossing the road in front of them.

She slowed the Jeep and allowed the animal to meander to the other side. "Are you excited?"

Davy nodded. "Can I hold the baby eagle?"

"I don't imagine that would be good, but we'll ask Kade how much they can be handled. I've never seen an eaglet myself."

Bree tapped her fingers against the steering wheel. Her breakfast with Kade this morning had been canceled, and the amount of disappointment she'd felt had surprised her. She wanted to speed to the wilderness center but forced herself to do a sedate forty-five.

"Timmy wanted to come too. He cried when Aunt Naomi said no."

"We could have brought him. I should have told Naomi it was okay." Bree pulled into the Kitchigami Wilderness Preserve parking lot. The lot was nearly full with campers, motor homes, and SUVs. She heard the sound of children from the lot behind the baby-wildlife building. She let Davy and Charley out of the Jeep, and they followed the noise.

Kade was demonstrating how to feed baby raccoons. The partially grown coon was perched on his shoulder with its tail curled around the ranger's neck. When he finished, the children moved to the next display.

Kade turned, and his face lit up. "Hey, I was beginning to wonder if you were coming."

"Can I pet the baby eagle?" Davy pulled his hand from Bree's and ran forward.

"Sorry, buddy. He doesn't like being handled. He might peck you." Kade ruffled Davy's hair.

The little boy stuck out his lower lip and pulled away. "You're mean! I want to pet him."

"Davy, mind your manners," Bree said.

"Sorry, chief. You can pet the deer though. I'll even give you some food for him."

Davy ignored the offer. He ran down the bark pathway to the aviary. "Can I pet these birds?"

"I know one who likes to be handled." Kade turned and whistled. "Mazzy," he called.

A squawk came from the birch tree behind him. A flutter of black feathers swooped from among the leaves and settled on Kade's shoulder.

"She's still hanging around? I thought she had forgotten you." Bree picked up a piece of corn and held it out to the starling.

"She probably would if I'd quit calling her and feeding her. I should have let her go fully wild, but she's like my kid." Kade put his finger under the bird's feet, and Mazzy stepped onto it. He held the bird out to Davy. "Put your finger out, and she'll come to you."

Davy giggled and held out his finger. The starling hopped onto it and perched. "Her feet feel funny. What did she eat when she was a baby?"

Charley barked at the bird, and Kade laughed. "I found her on the ground before she even had feathers," he said. "I fed her watered-down cat food for weeks until she could eat on her own."

"Can I keep her?" Davy asked.

"She doesn't like to be in a cage. She gets to town quite a bit. Next time you're going into the Suomi with your mom, call her name and see if she's around."

Charley barked again, then Mazzy squawked. She lifted from Davy's hand and disappeared into the tree again.

"Mazzy!" Davy called.

The bird squawked but refused to come back. "Sorry, big guy," Kade said. "She'll come back when she's hungry again."

"What else do you have here right now?" Bree asked, starting down the path toward the other pens.

"Some deer, a badger, and an owl." He lifted Davy over the fence and handed the little boy a bucket of corn. "Whitey likes corn," he told him. Davy ran to feed the little deer. Charley whined and put his paws up on the fence. Kade petted him. "He'll be back in a minute."

"You're doing a good job here," Bree said.

Kade flushed. "Thanks."

Bree couldn't keep her gaze from lingering on his face. "How's Lauri?"

"Okay. She's talking about keeping it."

"And you don't want that?"

"I keep trying not to think about what I want. She'll lose the rest of her childhood if she does. And I'm not sure she's ready to be a mother." He glanced at her. "I have to be honest and say I'm not sure I want the responsibility I know will fall on me. She's almost grown, and I could begin to think about my own life, my own future. My own family."

The plea in his blue eyes made it difficult for Bree to breathe. She knew he wanted a future with her. "The right woman wouldn't mind helping to raise her baby," she said.

"How would you feel about it?"

The intense blue of his eyes darkened, and she knew the question was more than rhetorical. "I'd be okay with it," she whispered. She'd be more than okay with it. She loved babies, but she wasn't about to bare her heart that way. She'd told Lauri she couldn't adopt her baby on her own, but perhaps that responsibility would be different if it were shared with Kade.

The expression on his face was a heart-stopping mixture of yearning and tenderness. He took off his hat then took a step toward her. Her chest tightened. Before he reached her, Davy called to him.

"Hey, Kade, I want out. I have to go to the bathroom." Davy danced around the pen, then tried to climb the fence by himself.

Kade's face darkened with disappointment, but he turned with a good-natured shrug. "I need to get out on rounds in the forest anyway."

Bree didn't know if she was relieved or disappointed when he went to grab Davy from the pen.

"I love this color!" Naomi laid a garnet-red shirt over herself and pirouetted. She wanted to forget her troubles and just enjoy the day.

"It brings out your hair and eyes," Bree agreed. "I'd look hideous in it." She glanced out the window. "Wonder what all that's about?"

Naomi joined her at the window. The pharmacist Terry stood talking with Marika. He had his hand on her arm and was gazing down at her with a yearning expression on his face.

Anu came up behind them. "It's probably nothing. I believe they dated in high school."

"It looks like something," Naomi said.

"How far do you think Terry would go for Marika? Far enough to change a prescription?" Bree asked.

"I can't believe that of Terry," Naomi said. But there certainly seemed to be something to the couple. Marika gave the pharmacist another pretty smile, then got in her car and drove away. "Forget it," she said, turning to Bree. "We're shopping. What do you like here?"

"How's this?" Bree held out an army-green denim shirt.

"Eew! You always go for such drab colors. But they look good on you. Bet Kade would like you in it."

Bree blushed. "I saw him this morning. I took Davy out to see a baby eagle."

"How did that go?" Naomi kept the sweater and continued to look around Nicholls's Finnish Imports. Anu had told the girls they could have first pick of the new shipment from Finland.

"Kind of awkward."

"It will get better." Naomi's smile felt king-sized today. Donovan had taken the children to the store with him this afternoon to give her a little break, and she intended to milk every minute of enjoyment from it. After the stress of the past weeks with Marika popping up everywhere she turned, she wanted to laugh and giggle with Bree like the old days. Davy was with his Aunt Hilary, and it was like old times.

"Let's go for lunch. I'm starved," Bree said. "I want to start the search in quadrant three this afternoon."

"Lunch is my treat," Anu announced.

The women paid for their deeply discounted purchases, then went down the street to the Suomi Café. After Molly seated them at their booth and took their order for beef pasties, Anu leaned forward and squeezed the hands of both younger women. "I thank the two of you for allowing me to join your fun day. Not many women your age would welcome an old woman."

"Hey, where'd that come from?" Bree's smile faded. "We always like being with you. And you're not old! You're barely in your fifties."

Anu smiled. "I know sometimes you young ones must talk about private matters."

"We don't keep anything from you," Naomi said. "Besides, I need your help today to get through Bree's thick head."

Bree's eyebrows arched. "Why do I have the feeling I'm not going to like this? You'd make a great Dread Pirate Roberts. I didn't even see this ambush coming. Save me, Anu!"

Anu's gentle smile widened. "As you wish," she said, chuckling.

"Inconceivable!" Naomi retorted.

The three women laughed. It felt good to giggle like schoolgirls. When was the last time she'd laughed this way? Naomi stretched and felt the last of her gloom drift away. "I bet Anu knows what we're going to discuss," she said smugly.

Anu shook her head. "Do not pull me into this too soon. You are doing just fine on your own, Naomi." She tipped her chin into her palm and smiled.

"Sure, throw me to the wolves," Naomi muttered. She pulled her long braid over one shoulder and twisted the thick rope of hair around her fingers. "You ready to get back with Kade?"

Bree went still. She took a sip of coffee. "Do we have to talk about this?"

"Don't blow it this time! I'd hoped one of you would get off your high horse long enough to break the ice forming between you. I bet it was Kade, wasn't it?"

Bree looked down and played with her napkin. "Maybe," she said. "But I have to think of Davy. I'm not sure he's ever going to like Kade."

"Does that mean you're going to give Kade the cold shoulder again—all because Davy prefers Nick?" Naomi wanted to shake some sense into her friend. Couldn't she see Kade was the right man for her?

"No," Bree muttered. "He's—different now somehow. Truthfully, I'm finding it hard to resist him."

"Well, maybe you're learning some sense then. Kade is worth a dozen Nicks."

"Did someone mention my name? Nick Fletcher stood at their table, his handsome face in his customary smile that said all was right with his world, and if it wasn't, then he'd make it that way with sheer determination.

"Nick, hello," Bree stammered. "We were just having lunch."

"So I see. I stopped by to grab sandwiches for the guys at the station."

Nick's muscles filled out the fire department's light blue shirt to perfection. It was no wonder he had turned Bree's head. But he was flashy, where Kade was quiet and steady. The fireman wasn't a bad man—he was just the wrong man for Bree.

"I thought I might bring a pizza over Monday if you're free, Bree," Nick said, taking the bag Molly brought him.

"That would be great," Bree said. "Davy will be glad to see you."

"Only Davy?"

"Me too, of course," Bree's smile was distracted.

"Good then. I'll see you around six."

As he walked away, Naomi leaned forward. "See what I mean? It's all about Davy. That's no way to build a relationship. Someday he'll be grown and gone. Then what?"

"I like Nick," Bree protested.

"Yes, but you love Kade. You're just too bull-headed to admit it."

"Naomi is right, *kulta*," Anu said. "Though you must always be conscious of your son's happiness, a strong marriage is not built on what a child wants. If his mother is happy, Davy will be happy. He will take his cue from you."

"What if I don't know what I want? I don't want to hurt either one of them."

"What is it you want? Who makes you feel alive and happy? Safe and secure? Whose name does God seem to be whispering in your ear?" Naomi sat back, certain her words had struck pay dirt.

"How can I tell who is God's will? Maybe neither one of them is right. What if God doesn't want me to remarry at all until Davy is raised? Anu, you stayed single." Bree turned to her mother-in-law.

"Do you feel God is asking you to remain single?" Anu asked, a frown knitting her brow.

Bree thought a moment. "No, not really. I didn't mean that. But just because you've got honeymoon stars in your eyes doesn't mean everyone else needs to rush out and get married, Naomi. I don't want to make a mistake. I've seen too many men come and go in my mother's life. She only ever loved my father, but she made do with other men. And a bottle."

"This isn't about your mother."

"In some ways it is. I carry her genes. What if I'm looking for the same things she was—excitement, romance. I've been thinking about things since Bernard and Cassie came into my life. I don't want to repeat her mistakes."

"If you can so clearly see what drove her to make poor choices, why do you have so little sympathy for her?" Anu tempered her hard question with a soft smile.

Bree hunched her shoulders. "Enough about my mother. It's been hard enough facing my past with Cassie and Bernard here."

"Have you seen them lately?" Anu asked.

"My father called yesterday to talk to Davy. I'm going over for dinner tomorrow."

"You might not have much time." Naomi knew how hard this had to be for her friend. "I think it's great he's come looking for you. It's time to let go of your childhood."

"I'm afraid to trust either of them."

"You haven't given either of them a chance," Naomi pointed out.

"My life is going in a different direction. I'm happy with the way it is. But I admit—" she broke off.

"Yes?" Naomi wanted to know.

"It's painful to see how my life could have been different if it weren't for my parents' selfishness. They both made mistakes, and Cassie and I have paid the price."

"Your mother has suffered too," Anu said gently.

"She didn't suffer. She drowned everything with alcohol." Bree moved restlessly. "Look, let's talk about something else."

"You're going to have to face it someday." Naomi said. "We all make mistakes as parents. God is the only perfect parent."

"This one is going to take a little while to gear up to." Bree's smile was strained. "Take off your Dread Pirate Roberts persona, and let's talk about something else."

18

Kade heard the ruckus before he saw it. Shouts, cries, and the sounds of a crowd of people stomping through the vegetation carried on the wind. He urged Moses into a gallop. He blinked as the scene at the mine came into view.

An angry mob stormed the entry to the lab. Men pounded on the door with their fists, and women waved placards and signs. The news media was here as well.

Telling them the water samples he'd taken had come back clean would fail to sway a mob like this. He needed help. Wheeling Moses around, he climbed to the top of a hill and managed to get a signal on his cell phone. The ranger station promised to send help and to notify the sheriff for more assistance. Waiting would be a good idea, but it went against his instinct. Was everyone inside all right? He knew Bree would be worried about Cassie.

Deciding he couldn't just wait here, Kade rode along the side of the mine. There was a side entrance back here somewhere. With luck, the mob wouldn't know about it either. One side entrance was thronged by more people, but Kade knew of another, more hidden one that only life-long residents of Rock Harbor knew about. Vegetation crowded in on both sides of the trail, raspberry bushes reaching out prickly fingers for him as he passed. He left Moses tied to a tree at the trail and forced his way through the thorny bushes. A dead oak tree, split by lightning several years ago, marked the overgrown entrance if he could just find it.

Ah, there it was. He pulled the vines off the door and revealed the small entrance. It might not even be usable anymore. Sometimes these old mines caved in along some of the veins, though he'd always heard this one was in good shape.

The door didn't budge when he yanked on it. Probably locked from the inside. "Cassie!" he pounded on the door. Maybe she would hear him. "It's Ranger Matthews." He continued to jiggle the knob.

Nothing. He pressed his ear against the door but could hear no sound on the other side. He kicked it a few times, then turned to go. But a slight scraping sound stopped him. He paused and put his hand on the door handle. "Hello? Anyone in there? It's Ranger Matthews. I'm here to help."

He winced at the screeching sound. Then the door creaked open a few inches. He saw Yancy Coppler's round face peering out at him. "It's me, Yancy. Let me in."

The door swung fully open. The rest of the crew crowded behind Yancy. Kade caught a whiff of smoke and gun powder. "Are you all right?"

Cassie stepped out from behind Yancy. "Yeah, but my plants aren't." Her red eyes and quivering lips told their own tale of the day's trauma.

"What happened?"

"Someone set off a bomb in the plant room. All the tobacco plants are destroyed. I'll have to start all over again." Her eyes brimmed with tears, and she ran her hand over her eyes. "You'd better get in here before they see you. They're a bunch of kooks."

He slipped inside and shut the door behind him. Yancy threw the bolt into place. The acrid odor of smoke burned Kade's throat and he coughed. "Help is on the way. Show me what happened."

Cassie led him to the door of the plant room. Piles of rock and rubble barred his entrance into the room.

"It's not safe," he told her when she started to step over the rocks. He peered into the room but couldn't see much for the haze of smoke and ash. "How did they get in?"

"I have no idea. We thought our security was airtight." She gave a bitter laugh. "They claimed no security was safe enough to keep these plants from escaping. I guess this proves their point about the danger. If they can get in, someone could transport the plants out. I'm going to have to see what I can do to make sure this doesn't happen again."

"You're continuing?"

Her face was grim. "Of course."

Nodding, he took her elbow and led them all back to the reception area. "Have a seat." He sat on the edge of the receptionist's desk while the lab personnel gathered around.

"Someone tell me exactly what happened today."

Cassie sighed and told him.

"So no one was inside as far as you know?"

"We didn't see anyone."

"Could they have gotten in and planted the bomb last night?"

"I would imagine that's what happened."

The older guard shook his mane of white hair. "We was here all night, missy. It was real quiet. I don't see how anyone could have got in without us knowing about it."

"Has everyone been through a security check?"

Cassie nodded. "Extensive security check. And we all get one yearly."

"When was the last?"

"About ten months ago."

Someone here could have developed connections with the organization outside since then, but to what purpose? Kade stared at the faces turned up to his. He didn't really know any of them well. "Any of you know Marika Fleming?"

The blank faces didn't change at first, then Salome nodded. "She's our neighbor."

Would Salome blow up the lab? Kade didn't think so. He frowned, and his gaze lingered on Salome's face. It was pale and set, and he wanted to dismiss his suspicions. She was Cassie's friend; she couldn't be guilty. But the suspicion wouldn't die.

"Who does your computer work?" he asked abruptly.

"Phil used to do most of it. Now I do," Salome said. "Why?"

"Just thinking." Maybe he was barking up the wrong tree, but something didn't feel right about it. How could anyone get into the mine without help? But why would Salome or any of them want to destroy their own work?

The security measures here rivaled Fort Knox. His gaze met Cassie's, and he saw the same confusion in her eyes. If there was an internal problem, it was her worry.

And he had a feeling Bree would be right in the middle of it as well.

The crowd's roar seemed to soften, and Kade looked toward the door. "I'm going to see what's going on out there," he said.

"I'll back you up," Chito said.

From his tone, Kade knew Chito was hoping for the opportunity to fight. Clenching his teeth, Kade went to the door and peered out. He almost didn't believe what he was seeing.

Marika Fleming stood at the head of the crowd. "You're not helping matters," she shouted. "This is wrong! All of you go home. I'll handle things. I'm with NAWG, and I can tell you this lab is harmless. I've called the sheriff, and he'll be here any minute. If you don't want to go to jail, get out of here."

The crowd muttered and complained, but it was slowly beginning to disperse. Kade heard the distant sound of sirens, and the mob began to move faster.

Bree rubbed her throbbing head. Two weeks without her dog. She didn't think she could stand another minute of it. Sitting in the Suomi, she saw the sympathetic glances diners threw her way. It was all she could do to stay seated with Naomi and Anu gone. Glancing at her watch, she saw it was almost time to meet the team. Naomi had run home to change clothes.

Molly brought her another cup of coffee. She wiped her streaming eyes. "I about can't work for worrying about Samson. I've been saving him a soup bone. You bring him in as soon as you find him, eh?"

"I will," Bree choked out. *When* she found him. Not *if.*

Mason came through the door and saw her. His face grim, he joined her. "Those men still aren't talking," he said.

"What can we do?" she whispered.

"We're doing all we can." He ordered coffee and breakfast. "Even Hilary went out to look with me last night. How's Davy?"

"Too quiet. Anu has been keeping him busy." She desperately wanted to hear good news of some kind. "Hilary must be doing better."

His gaze flickered to her, then away. "She still cries most every night." He ran his hand through his hair. "She tries to cry softly, but I still hear her. I don't know what to do. I feel so guilty. If she had another husband, she could probably get pregnant again. As it is, the doctor says it's doubtful."

"What about adoption? I mentioned it to Hilary a little while ago, but she got mad."

"Don't take it personal. She gets mad at most everything these days."

The weariness in Mason's voice tugged at Bree's heart. "Did you know Lauri needs to find adoptive parents?"

His eyes widened and his mouth went slack. "Lauri's baby," he said as if he'd never heard the words. "Naomi's not taking it?"

"Nope. She and Donovan have enough on their plates right now. Do you think Hilary would consider it?"

A dawning hope transformed Mason's face with color. "That's a great idea, Bree! When is the baby due?"

"Around Thanksgiving, I think. Let me call Kade and ask." Any excuse to hear his voice. His calm manner helped still her terror of what could be happening to Samson. She punched his number on her cell phone.

"Ranger Matthews."

Her heart went into overdrive at the sound of his deep voice. "Hi, it's me."

"Bree?" The surge in his voice told her he was glad she'd called. "Out on your afternoon search yet?"

She gulped. "No. I'm meeting the group in an hour to search some more. Listen, I'm talking to Mason. When is Lauri due?"

"November fifteenth. You need to get out here to the lab. Mason too. There's been an explosion. Can you get him?"

"He's right here. I'll tell him. Is Cassie all right?" Bree asked, urgency raising her voice.

"Everyone is fine. But we need to figure out who did this." He paused. "Why are you asking about the baby?"

"Mason wants to talk to Hilary about it."

"That would be great!"

"Don't get your hopes up," she warned. "Hilary may shoot them down."

"Lauri has been depressed ever since she found out Naomi and Donovan wouldn't take the baby. She'd be thrilled."

"Don't say anything to her yet. I wouldn't want her disappointed if Mason can't talk Hilary into it."

"I won't. Hey, I want to take Davy to ride go-carts, get his mind off Samson. How about it?"

"I'll be out searching."

"We'll go after dark."

She wanted to be looking for her dog every minute, but Davy needed her too. "Okay," she said finally.

"We can visit the bookstore in Houghton and go for pizza afterwards. How does that sound?"

"I'll tell Davy."

"How about I bring Lauri too? If she'll come."

"She'll come if you ask her nice."

"I can be nice."

"So I'm finding out." She loved this teasing banter between them. She'd forgotten what it was like. A tingle started at her toes and finally settled in her stomach, warming the ice she'd been encased in ever since Samson was taken.

"I'll see you then. I love you."

He hung up before she could answer, but she sat there with her mouth open. So much for the words being hard for him to say. He'd sounded almost poetic.

"There's been an explosion at the lab. Kade needs us out there. He said they're all okay though."

Mason sighed. "I'd like just one calm weekend." He checked his cell phone. "Looks like I missed a call. Probably the lab."

"I haven't been on a go-cart since I was twelve," Lauri said. "You quit taking me."

Kade grinned at the sulk in her voice. "I can always let you out at the movies." He knew she wouldn't miss this outing. She'd been talking about it ever since he got home.

"You can ride with me if you forgot how," Davy offered.

In the backseat of Bree's Jeep, Lauri leaned over and ruffled his hair. "I think I can remember."

Kade reached across the seat and linked his fingers with Bree's. "Just one big, happy family," he whispered.

"Except for Samson," Davy said sadly.

Kade felt Bree's fingers tighten, and he squeezed them reassuringly. "We'll find him," he whispered.

She squeezed his hand in return.

"Cassie seemed glad you came to help. Are you sure you're up to this tonight? I'm sure you're tired."

"I'm fine," she told him. "I'm worried about her though. The level of violence keeps escalating. I'm not sure where it will stop."

"Mason is on it. Let's not worry about anything tonight."

Bree nodded her agreement.

"Hey, Davy," Kade said, "I had to move a bear the other day."

In the rearview mirror, he saw Davy's eyes go wide. "A bear?" the little boy squeaked.

"Yep. A big black bear. I got to the campsite and he was just sitting there like he owned the place. He'd filched a sack of food from one of the cabins and was just munching away."

"Like Yogi," Davy quipped.

"Just like Yogi. Only we can't let the bears do that. When they get used to taking food from people, they can get dangerous. So I called for help, got him tranquilized, and we had him taken to a remote part of Ottawa."

"Did he scratch you?" Davy swiped his hand like a bear paw and growled.

"No, I was careful. But he was a big one."

"Samson can beat anything," Davy declared. "We should find him so he can protect you from the bears."

"Samson doesn't like to fight," Bree said. "He's a good dog."

Kade caught Lauri's eye in the rearview mirror. She nodded when she understood his facial expression and turned to distract Davy.

Bree turned the radio noise to the back and lowered her voice. "Have you seen any more sign of the dogfighting going on? I heard in town yesterday that another small dog came up missing. If we could maybe watch other dogs in town, they might lead us to Samson."

"I hadn't heard that." He shook his head. "I haven't seen anything, but I've been watching. There's no guarantee it's a dog ring, Bree. You know that."

She moved restlessly. "I don't know who else would have taken him."

"I've been driving around the woods, stopping at a few cabins and looking for dogs. If I find any other pit bulls, it would bear more investigation."

"Only pit bulls?"

"They're the most common dog used in these rings. They've been bred to fight to the death."

Bree shuddered. "We have to find Samson."

19

"We clean up the debris, and we'll be back in business in no time." Cassie knelt and tossed a handful of rubble into the Dumpster they'd hauled in this morning. She was unutterably weary. After yesterday's violence, she'd lain awake in her bed watching the clock tick through every hour.

"I don't know, Cass, it looks pretty bad. Makes you wonder if we're not supposed to be here. Maybe the environmentalists are right, and this is the wrong thing to do." Salome knelt to help her.

Yancy laughed. "You sure you didn't help them, Salome?"

Salome shot him a poisonous glare. "Don't even joke about it, Yance. I'd like to kill whoever did this."

"Quit teasing her, Yancy," Cassie said.

Salome lowered her voice so Yancy wouldn't overhear. "I'm scared, Cassie," she said. "I've been thinking about looking for another job. This is just getting too dangerous."

Cassie blinked. "You can't leave now, Salome. Our success here means more money than we can imagine! You'd lose your bonus. Besides, when this drug hits the market, you'll be able to name your own price at any other pharmaceutical company."

"That won't do me a bit of good if I'm dead," her friend said. "We all survived it this time. But what about the next time? If I leave, I'll be safe."

"Has someone been threatening you? I've never known you to quit anything."

Salome looked away. "Nora is scared too. We all are."

"So you're all about to jump ship and leave me with no one?" Cassie grabbed a whisk broom and dustpan and brushed aimlessly at a clean spot on the floor. She didn't trust herself to speak.

"I'm sorry, Cassie." Salome touched Cassie's arm. "You should go too."

"I'm not leaving my job! This is my baby—our baby, Salome. You've been with me from the beginning. Please, we can't let them win. This is our big chance to prove we're somebody. If we quit now . . ." Her voice broke.

"You care too much about what other people think," Salome said softly. "Your life is more important than a new drug."

"It's for my dad," Cassie said. "It's not just for the glory."

"That's what you say. But I don't think it's true. For you, it's always been about proving yourself. Grow up, Cassie. The world doesn't revolve around you. I have plans for my life, plans that don't include getting killed before I have a chance to marry and have a baby."

"I have this under control," Cassie said through gritted teeth.

"Do you? Or does it have you?" Salome flipped her hair out of her eyes and stooped to pick up debris.

Cassie put her hands on her hips and sighed. Yancy was watching her. She cleared her throat. "I'll get out my backup cuttings and we'll get them transplanted once this mess is cleaned up."

"You have backups? When did you decide to do that?" Yancy leaned over his round belly and picked up a large piece of debris. Huffing, he carried it to the Dumpster and heaved it in.

"With the hoopla from the environmental group, I thought it might be a good idea."

"Where are they stored?" he asked. "You're lucky they weren't in here."

"No kidding! I have them in the refrigerator in my office."

"Hiding with the shriveled apples and the green cottage cheese," Nora quipped.

"Very funny. Get to work, you." Cassie pushed her.

Nora chuckled and joined the other workers cleaning the room. "Did anyone call Ian?"

"I tried," Lola said. "There was no answer. But I think he said something about going fishing on his day off. Maybe he went out for dinner after. I left a message on his machine."

"He might have gone out of town. He'll be back tomorrow, but I'll try to get hold of him again later today," Cassie said.

By noon most of the debris had been cleared away, leaving only one corner to be finished. All the lights had been destroyed, but they could continue to use the temporary ones for now. A local carpenter had promised to come today to build more plant tables, and Cassie was expecting a shipment of potting soil and containers tomorrow.

The fanatics may have slowed them down, but they couldn't stop their research. She would find a cure for Alzheimer's if it killed her.

She heard a sharp intake of breath from Chito Yamamoto. He backed away from the final corner where he'd been working. "Call the sheriff." His voice was high and strained.

"What is it?"

"There's a body. I think it's Ian."

Rain dripped from the thick canopy of leaves above Bree's head. The moisture created almost a halo of mist in the clearing. All of her search team had assembled in spite of the weather. Sporting yellow slickers, they slogged through the mud to join her.

"I appreciate you coming," Bree said when rumbles of their grumbling reached her ears. "I know it's lousy weather, but consider it good training. Sometimes people get lost in this kind of weather. Knowing how to search now could be the difference between life and death. And Samson is out there somewhere, waiting for us to find him."

The group's grumbling petered out. Bree saw Lauri and Eva exchange glances. "What?"

Eva dropped her gaze to the ground. "I wonder if it's time to give up, Bree. He's probably been taken out of the area. I don't know how we could ever find him."

"Ooh, did we crawl out of the wrong side of the bed this morning?" Ryan Erickson asked. The paramedic looked fresh and alert. "We aren't giving up until Bree says it's time to give up."

Eva glared at him but didn't answer. They'd had a "thing" for about two weeks, but now that it was over, they were at loggerheads again. Bree grimaced. The day was shaping up to be lousy.

"I'm not ready to give up yet," she said quietly. "I still feel Samson is around here somewhere."

"Feelings don't tell us where to search," Eva pointed out.

Bree ignored her comment. "We'll do some training, then go out and search for Samson. We're going to work on cadaver scent today," she said.

"I hate this kind of work," Eva grumbled.

Naomi shot her a quelling look. "All of us would rather find living people, especially the dogs, but we're going to be faced with this sooner or later."

Bree nodded. "I'm going to sprinkle some cadaver scent on gauze and let your dogs smell it." She prepared the pad and dropped it into a paper bag. "Whichever dog finds it first, I'm giving away a twenty-dollar certificate to the Suomi Café."

The grumbles changed to smiles.

"Let's get on with it," Lauri said.

Bree held up her hand. "I've already hidden the scent tube. It's not going to be as easy as you think. I buried it six feet underground."

"Hey, that will take all day for them to find it," Eva said, frowning.

"Charley is exempt from the contest," Naomi put in.

"Wait here. I'll call you when it's ready. I want to watch the dogs work."

"I'm going to look over the grid map and figure out where we want to search for Samson today," Naomi said.

Bree shot her a grateful look. Her best friend knew how worried she was. "Be right back," she said.

Jogging through the scent of pine and mud, Bree felt her tension slip away like the ebbing of Superior's tide. The wilderness sustained her, like an infusion of lifeblood into her soul. God felt just a whisper away out here, and she knew he was in control of everything, even the trauma Hilary and Mason were going through and the trial she was facing with losing Samson. She whispered a prayer for them all and lifted her face to the stinging rain.

She found the fake burial site, then stationed herself in a tree stand to watch the dogs work. She spoke into her walkie-talkie to Naomi. "Okay, we're all set. Send them out." She settled her back against the bark and watched as the dogs zigzagged through the woods. Charley found it first of course, but he didn't count. Then Zorro nosed the spot and began to bark. Bree grinned. He was turning into a fine search dog.

Once all the dogs had found the site, she dropped from the tree and congratulated the workers. Lauri was awarded the gift certificate, and she carried it like a badge of honor. Together they all started back to headquarters to meet Naomi.

Walking through the thick vegetation, Bree stumbled over something lying on the ground in a bed of wildflowers. It moved yet didn't feel like a stick. She stooped and peered under the vegetation. A gun lay hidden under a patch of jack-in-the-pulpit. Bree started to pick it up, then drew back her hand. Phil had been shot with a .44 magnum. She was no expert on guns, but Rob had one made by Smith and Wesson, and this looked just like his. She'd better call Mason in on this. It just might be the murder weapon.

She pulled a flag from her ready-pack and stuck it in the ground by the gun so she could lead Mason here. She took out her GPS system and marked down the coordinates. It wouldn't do to lose the gun now. Hesitating, she decided she'd better take it with her. If it was gone by the time she got Mason back here, he would have her hide. She took out a plastic bag and pencil, then lifted the gun with the pencil and dropped it into the bag. Maybe forensics could get some prints off it.

She grimaced. There was no telling if it was even the murder weapon. More likely someone had just lost it. Her cell phone rang, and she grabbed it. "Bree Nicholls."

"Bree, it's Cassie."

Her sister's voice sounded strained. "Could you come to the lab? Ian's dead. Whoever it is seems to be planning on killing us all, one by one."

Jonelle breathed a sigh of relief when Zane's pickup disappeared around the bend and was swallowed by the trees. Grabbing some salve, she shot out the back door to the dog pen. Samson lay in the corner, his head on his paws. He growled when she approached.

"It's okay, boy," she said softly. She opened the gate and approached him cautiously. She didn't think he'd hurt her, but after the way Zane had treated him, there was no telling. The dog growled again when she touched his flank, but he didn't snap at her.

The stick Zane had used on the dog had left cuts, and she cleaned the wounds with peroxide. Samson whimpered but seemed to know she was trying to help him. She smoothed salve on raw skin and patted his head. He licked her hand, and it was all she could do not to cry. She wished she had the courage to save him.

Superior Forensics personnel were still combing the room, but it was likely the blast had destroyed any evidence. Cassie sat with the rest of the crew in the reception area. Clasping her icy hands together in her lap, she tried to make sense of the way her life had come crashing down around her.

She couldn't close out the image in her mind of Ian's still body crumpled like a broken doll under the debris.

Mason handed her a cup of coffee, and she wrapped her fingers around it, letting the warmth seep into her cold hands. Salome sat on one side and Nora on the other.

Mason pulled up a chair in front of the group. "So no one thought to make sure where everyone was?"

"I took a head count," Cassie said. "But Ian was off that day. I thought it odd he didn't show up today to help get things back in order, but I just assumed he'd gone out of town." Guilt gnawed at her stomach. Could he have been saved if he'd been found?

"Was he acting funny this past week?"

"Ian always acted funny," Yancy muttered.

"What's that?"

"He was a strange bird." Yancy leaned back in his chair.

"Explain, please."

Nora cleared her throat and glanced around before offering her opinion. "No one ever got close to him. He never talked about his life outside the lab, he was picky about anyone looking at what he was working on, he dressed in clothes that didn't match. He was odd in a lot of ways."

"You dated him for a while. Were you angry with him for breaking up with you?"

She flushed. "I did the breaking up. I couldn't abide a man who never shared what he was thinking."

"Why are you asking these questions?" Cassie demanded. "Surely you don't think he had something to do with the explosion?"

"Could be," Mason said. "I want to look at all the possibilities."

Cassie noticed he looked pale and a little haunted, like he hadn't gotten much sleep. He rubbed his forehead, and she looked back into her coffee cup. His life wasn't any of her business.

Mason glanced at the security guards. "Did Ian come in the night before the explosion?"

Both guards nodded. "He said he had some stuff to work on. That wasn't unusual for him though," the older guard said. "He came in most every night."

"Anyone else here that night?"

The guard nodded. "Pretty busy night, actually. Yancy, Chito, and Lola came by. Even you," he nodded to Cassie.

"Me too," Salome said. "I wanted to check on those cultures."

Mason sighed. "Maybe Superior Forensics can tell us more."

"You think he might have been killed setting the bomb?" Yancy wanted to know.

"Either that or he was just in the wrong place at the wrong time. The autopsy should tell us the cause of death."

Cassie set her coffee down on the table beside her. "What if someone is targeting us? All of us? I wish Bree would get here."

The media was already at the scene when Bree arrived. Naomi had taken Davy home to play with Timmy. She pushed through the crowd and found Mason. Dark circles ringed his eyes, and she wondered if he'd gotten any rest this past weekend.

He saw her and lifted his hand. "Got another body," he said.

"Cassie called it murder."

"I'm not saying that yet. Could be an accident. He might have been in the wrong place at the wrong time, or he might have been planting the bomb and it went off too soon."

"Why would he bomb his own work?"

Mason shrugged. "Maybe he has links to an environmental group."

"What about a rival pharmaceutical group? Cassie has talked about Jackson Pharmaceuticals. Could they have bombed the facility?"

"Maybe. But my instincts say there was someone helping on the inside. You ever try to get in this place?" He shook his head. "It's like trying to break into the national vault."

Cassie interrupted Mason. "Thanks for coming so quickly." Her hair stood out from her head like she'd just run her fingers through it.

Bree hesitated, then reached out and put her arms around her sister. "You've had a rough week."

Cassie's eyes filled with tears, and she leaned her head against Bree's shoulder. The gratitude in her eyes made Bree feel ashamed. She was just going through the motions. They both had the same blood running through their veins. She wanted to open her heart to Cassie but didn't know how.

Mason took out his notepad. "Are you sure you have all the entrances and exits closed up except for this one and the ones along the west side?"

Cassie shrugged and dropped Bree's hand. "We got a map of the mine from Steve. Want me to get it?"

"That might be helpful. I have a hunch we have another way in here you know nothing about."

When Cassie left to find the map, Bree pulled Mason aside and showed him the gun she'd stumbled over.

"Where'd you find it?" He took the plastic bag and peered in at the gun.

"Out near the training center. I marked the spot. You think it could be the murder weapon?"

"We should only be so lucky." He pocketed it. "I'll have ballistics test it."

Cassie came back with the map in her hand. "Here it is." She unrolled it on a nearby desk.

Bree and Mason peered over her shoulder as she traced her finger along the passageways they had open.

"The only way to know is to follow every passageway to the end and see what we've got," Mason said. "Can I take this?"

"Let me make you a copy. I'd better keep the original." She flagged down the receptionist and told her to make a copy for Mason.

"I'll get some men on it." He nodded to Cassie and Bree then strode off to talk to Deputy Montgomery.

Cassie gripped her hands together. "I'm scared, Bree. Every time I turn around, something else bad happens."

Bree nodded. "Do you have any enemies?"

"Personal ones?" She shook her head. "Not that I know of. But the company is another story." She took a deep breath. "Come to my office where we can talk in private. There are some things you should know."

The desperation in her voice puzzled Bree. "If it pertains to the deaths, we'd better have Mason join us."

"Let me tell you first. I need to talk now and he's busy." Cassie led the way to her office and shut the door behind them.

Bree looked around curiously. The office was devoid of most personal effects save for one small photo on the desk. She picked it up and recognized the man holding a girl. Uncle Bernard, her father.

Cassie's gaze lingered on her face. "That's me when I was ten. I'd just won the science fair. Daddy was so proud."

Their father was smiling at Cassie. There was love and pride in his face.

Cassie lost no opportunity to show how lucky she'd been growing up with a father. Bree put the frame back on the desk. "At least you had him around. I had a succession of fathers, each one more indifferent than the one before."

Cassie bit her lip but said nothing. She sat in her chair and put her elbows on the desk. "I haven't been completely honest with you," she said. "Our research here is a little more critical than I've indicated. It may provide a cure for Alzheimer's, not just diabetes. I'm afraid Jackson knows what we're really researching."

"You think they might be behind what's been happening?"

"I know they are. We've been paying an informant, Leif Lindell, at Jackson. He says they're in a frenzy over it."

"The sabotage I can understand. But why murder?"

"If they can knock out our scientists, who would be left to finish the testing? They'd have clear sailing ahead and be able to rush the drug to market."

"Couldn't they still bring their drug out? Just with a slightly different formulation? Other drugs are like that."

"Yes, but the first one always makes the most money. We intend to be first." Cassie leaned forward. "I *will* be first."

Bree understood Cassie's hope, but surely any drug she found now would come too late to benefit their father. "I'll tell Mason about it and we'll see what we can find out."

People thronged the sidewalk outside the pharmacy as Bree pulled into town. Terry was running a special on a shipment of troll dolls, and it seemed as though all the tourists wanted one. She walked through the store to the back, where she found Terry with his wife, Regina.

Regina faced him with her fists clenched. She leaned forward slightly from the waist with her face in Terry's. "I've had it," she hissed. "It was nearly midnight when you came in last night. I know you're seeing someone. I can smell the reek of her perfume all over you. Don't bother coming home tonight. I'm sure she'll be glad to put you up." She whirled and barreled down the aisle, nearly knocking Bree over.

"Sorry," she muttered, brushing past Bree.

Terry's eyes were rimmed in red. "Sorry about that. We've been having a few problems."

Bree's mind sped through the possibilities. Could Terry be connected to Cassie's troubles somehow? She remembered the way he looked at Marika. And even Salome seemed taken with him. "I wanted to ask you a couple more questions about procedures here."

"Come to my office where we can talk in private." He led the way to his office.

Bree stared at the bald spot on the back of his head. She'd always liked Terry. Could Marika be the woman he was seeing? And if she was, did it even matter? She couldn't imagine how infidelity could be tied in with the attempt on Cassie's life.

"Have a seat." Terry adjusted the blinds and let the sunshine into the office.

The decor was early seventies garage sale. Bree sat on a green chair with a torn vinyl seat. "I wanted to ask you about Deanna."

He flushed. "Don't believe everything my wife says."

"Excuse me?" Bree shook her head. "I haven't talked to your wife about this."

His cheeks grew a dull red. "I thought maybe you overheard us as you came up." He shook his head. "Never mind. What about Deanna?"

Deanna must be the other woman. At least this wasn't something she needed to poke into further. Relief made her smile more warmly than she intended. "Is there any chance she—or you for that matter—could have been filling another prescription and accidentally changed Cassie's?"

He shook his head. "No. Like I told you before, we run reports to check everything we do. Besides, I thought Mason's expert found evidence of the hacking."

"Yes, he did. But I'm trying not to overlook anything." Bree watched him fidget and not look her in the eye. Maybe there was a connection she was missing.

20

*T*here was nowhere to park outside the Suomi Café, so Bree pulled into a spot across the street and down a block. It would be like this for another month—at least until the end of August. Then the tourists would depart and leave the townspeople to enjoy their town themselves.

Taking Davy's hand, they crossed the street with Charley following them. "Want some chocolate milk and a bagel for your afternoon snack?" she asked.

"With cream cheese," Davy proclaimed.

"And some thimbleberry jam, maybe?"

He nodded. "I'm hungry."

"Me too." She opened the door for him, and they stepped inside.

Molly's expectant gaze glanced behind Bree as though looking for Samson, and her eager look dulled as she saw Charley instead. Molly took the pencil from behind her ear. "What can I get for you two?" She didn't ask about Samson, and Bree was grateful.

Bree gave her their order, then she and Davy began to do the games on the back of the paper place mats. The bell at the front door jingled, and she looked up. Hilary stepped inside the café. Charley stood to greet her and pressed his nose against her leg.

She flinched away. "Beat it, you mangy hound."

"Why don't you like dogs, Aunt Hilary? Charley likes you. Samson does too."

Hilary's chin quivered, and she looked away. "I'll buy you a stick of peppermint candy." She dug in her purse and handed him some money.

His question forgotten, he scampered to the candy counter at the front of the store.

"Sit down. I'll get you coffee." Bree waved to Molly.

Hilary slid into the booth opposite Bree. Except for the lost look in her eyes, she seemed her normal self, every blond hair in place and her clothes perfectly accessorized.

Hilary tilted her chin up. "Don't look at me like that. I don't want pity."

"I'm sorry, Hil. I know you're hurting. We were all looking forward to the baby."

Hilary stirred cream into her coffee. "I'm going to repaint the nursery and turn it into a guest room."

"Don't do it yet. Talk to the doctor again."

Hilary shook her head. "I already did. Mason had another sperm test. It was even worse. We'll never have another baby." Her eyes looked almost feverish.

Bree's eyes burned, but she didn't dare cry, not here. It would upset Hilary even more. "Have you thought about adoption?"

"I don't want to raise someone else's baby."

"Look at how you love Davy. He's not your own, but you love him as if he were. I think you have enough love in your heart to share."

"I don't want to go there," Hilary burst out. "I can't stand another disappointment. The mother sometimes changes her mind."

"What about Lauri's baby?"

Hilary was shaking her head even as Bree spoke. "Mason mentioned it, but I don't want to run the risk. Can't you understand that? You have no idea how devastating this loss was to me and Mason. We wanted our baby, and now we'll never have him. It was a boy, you know."

"I hadn't heard." Bree's voice broke, and she cleared her throat. "I know about loss, Hilary."

"But God pulled a miracle out of his hat for you, didn't he? You still have Davy."

"But I lost Rob."

Hilary dropped her head. "I know. I'm sorry. But it seems so unfair. This is an ocean of pain I'm swimming in. I'm barely treading water." Tears pooled in her eyes.

"But God is there with you," Bree said. "He goes even into the deep places of pain with us."

"I know that, but I don't *feel* it."

Bree fell silent. She knew about the darkness in the night when her prayers didn't seem to go higher than the border on the wallpaper. "Your mom always says feelings are fleeting. It's hard, I know. I'm not as wise as Anu, so I can't advise you much. When I have dark times like that, I try to remember Romans 8:28, where it says all things work together for our good."

Hilary gave her a withering glance. "This can't possibly be for my good."

"I know it doesn't seem that way." Bree realized she'd probably said the wrong thing. "I'm sorry. But just think about Lauri's baby."

"I told you. It's a closed subject." She folded her arms across her chest.

Bree tried one more time. "Don't bottle all that love up inside. It will grow bitter."

"Too late. I'm not risking my heart again."

Denise's house looked silent and empty, but Bree knew she had to be home. Her van was parked in the driveway. Bree pressed the doorbell and heard it echo from inside. The sound of a baby crying rose above the bell.

When Denise opened the door, Bree's heart lurched. The woman looked like she hadn't combed or washed her hair in days. It hung in oily strands around her face. Denise's eyes were dull and apathetic. She blinked when she saw Bree and tried to muster a smile but only managed a twitch of her lips.

"Hi, Denise." Bree smiled and hoped it was a better attempt than the one Denise had made.

"Oh, um, Bree." Denise shifted Abby to her other hip. "Come in."
She backed away from the door and pushed her hair out of her eyes.
"I'm a mess. Sorry the house is in such a state. I can't seem to get the
energy to do much to it."

"It's fine," Bree assured her. She stepped over the newspapers piled
by the door and tried not to look at the dirty dishes on the hall table.
Davy found Adrian right away, and the two friends dashed off to play.
Toys as well as dirty diapers and empty containers of baby food littered
nearly every inch of floor. She should have come sooner. Poor Denise
knew hardly anyone in town.

"Would you like some tea?" Denise looked vaguely out the window
as though she couldn't stand to look Bree in the eye.

"No thanks, I just had some coffee." Bree reached over to tickle
Abby's tummy. "Where's Alex?"

Her eyes went wide. "Oh my gosh, I left him in the tub!"

Bree froze. "Alone?"

Denise didn't answer but sprinted toward the hall, and Bree raced
after her. It felt like she was moving through molasses. She strained her
ears to hear some sound from down the hall.

Denise hurtled through the doorway into the bathroom with Bree
on her heels. Alex was lying facedown in the tub.

"Oh, dear God, help us," Bree said. She pushed past Denise and
scooped up the baby. He wasn't breathing. "Call 911," she ordered, laying him across her legs on his stomach. She pressed on his tummy and
water trickled from his mouth. She glanced up to see Denise still standing there with her hand over her mouth. "Do it. Now!" She practically
screamed the words and Denise finally began to move.

Sobbing, Denise turned and Bree heard her steps fade. She turned
her attention back to the baby. "Come on, Alex, stay with me," she
whispered. "Please, God, we need some help here." She laid him on the
floor and began to administer mouth-to-mouth. She stopped and put
her head to his chest. There was still a heartbeat.

She bent over him again, covering his mouth and nose with her own and breathing in small puffs of air. His small chest rose and fell with her breaths.

"The ambulance is on the way," Denise said, standing in the doorway.

Bree didn't stop to look at her. "Pray, Denise. He's still not breathing."

Her total focus on the baby, she ignored Denise's intake of breath and soft sobs. "Come on, Alex," Bree muttered. "Breathe, baby."

In and out, in and out. Her arms ached with tension, and she could feel every pore in her face as she put her whole heart into saving the baby. Finally Alex coughed. Coughed and took a breath of his own. He sputtered and water flew into Bree's face. She rolled him on his tummy, and he vomited, then began to cry weakly.

The distant *wah-wah* of the ambulance grew closer, and Bree breathed a sigh of relief that help was almost here. "Thank you, God," she whispered.

Denise fell to her knees and kissed her son's forehead.

"Ma-ma-ma," he cried.

"Mommy's right here, sweet boy," Denise said, pressing her cheek against his.

The ambulance sounded right outside the door. Bree raced down the hall to throw open the door. "This way." She directed the paramedics to the bathroom. Denise had to step out of the room too as the men checked out the baby.

"He looks like he's going to be fine, but we'd better take him to the hospital for observation," one of the men said. "His mother had better come as well."

"Let me get Abby," Denise said.

"I'll keep her," Bree said. "You can ride in the ambulance with Alex."

Denise was crying hard by now, and she nodded gratefully. "Take my van if you come to the hospital. The car seats are already in there."

The paramedics carried the wailing child toward the ambulance.

Denise scurried after them. "The keys are on the kitchen counter," she called over her shoulder.

"I'll stay here unless you need me to come," Bree said. "I can bathe Abby and get her down for a nap."

Denise stopped and turned. "I don't know what I would have done if you hadn't been here, Bree. Thanks."

Bree saw the gratitude in the young mother's face and felt a glow of thankfulness. "I'm just glad I was here too. You'd better hurry. They'll leave you behind."

Denise nodded and left, slamming the door behind her. The quiet descended, and Bree felt the tension ease out of her shoulders. That had been close. Another few seconds and she doubted she could have saved Alex. God had been good to them all today. But he was good every day. Just sometimes she noticed.

She checked on the children. Adrian and Davy were playing with trucks. Bree smiled when she saw Abby asleep on the carpet. Perfect. She could tackle this house while the baby slept. She decided to start with the kitchen. It looked like every dish in the house was dirty. The sink overflowed with pots and pans while plates and cups mounded the counter and table. When had Denise last cleaned? Before Philip died? That was more than a month ago—eons when you had children.

The dishwasher was empty, so she loaded it first then washed what wouldn't fit by hand. It took her an hour to get the kitchen in order. Then she changed the sheets on the beds and found a basket in the laundry room she used to begin to pick up the toys while a load of laundry was spinning.

Abby awoke, and Bree had Davy and Adrian help her pick up the living room toys. By the time she'd bathed Abby, she felt like she'd worked on an assembly line all day, and it had only been a few hours. But the house looked great, vacuumed, neat, and orderly. She called her search-and-rescue team and told them she'd be delayed. Karen promised to take charge of the search for Samson and call if they found anything.

It was after eleven when she heard a car stop outside. Relief loosened her chest. She peered out the window and saw Mason's car. Denise got out with Alex in her arms. Bree opened the door and stepped to the front stoop.

"You should have called me. I would have come to get you."

"I didn't want you to have to bring the kids out." Denise looked dreadful. The skin around her eyes was so dark she looked like she had been in a fight. Her lips were colorless, and her complexion seemed yellow and frail.

"I fixed some vegetable soup. It's still hot," Bree told her. "If you want to trust my cooking, I'll fix you a bowl."

"I don't think I could eat anything."

Alex was sleeping in Denise's arms. "I'll put him to bed for you. Abby just finished her lunch, and she's playing in the living room with the boys." She took Alex, though Denise didn't seem to want to let him go. And who could blame her? She'd almost lost him. Carrying him through the house, she gently laid him in his crib.

When she'd cleaned the room earlier, she thought about how Phil had probably helped pick out the furnishings here, the train wallpaper border, and the teddy bears that lined the shelf around the room's perimeter. There were several framed pictures of Phil with the twins, and Bree felt a real bond with Denise and her children.

Bree needed to be a friend to them.

"You cleaned the house," Denise said when Bree went back into the living room. "You didn't have to do that. I just can't seem to focus on anything. Mom came for the funeral, then had to go home. She wanted me to go with her, but I can't leave until I know who did this to Phil."

"That's one reason I came by earlier," Bree admitted. "I want to find out who killed him too."

Hope brightened Denise's eyes. "How can I help?"

Bree glanced at her watch. Karen and the rest of Bree's team were probably breaking for lunch. "Let's go back over the days leading up to the murder. Did Phil receive any strange phone calls or letters? Did he act oddly?"

Denise shook her head, her eyes dulling again. "I've racked my brain trying to think of something, but there was nothing, only . . ."

"Only what?"

"Just his job offer. That wasn't out of the ordinary though. He was always getting calls from headhunters wanting him to apply for some research job. His expertise was well-known."

"What company was this?"

"Jackson Pharmaceutical. They offered him a half-million-dollar bonus if he'd bring the formula for what he'd been working on with him and move to their company. He told them no. He was happy where he was, happy in Rock Harbor. He loved it here. Besides, he didn't own the formula." Her eyes filled with tears. "I'd never seen Phil so happy. He talked about building a big house overlooking Lake Superior and living here forever." She swiped the back of her hand over her eyes.

"Where is Jackson based?"

"Milwaukee. Phil hated Milwaukee, which was another strike against them."

"What was he working on—do you know? Was it that wonderful? Cassie said it was an Alzheimer's drug."

"That's all I know."

Bree sighed. Nothing added up to a reason for murder.

Kade smiled when he heard the giggling voices from inside the cabin. Sounded like Lauri had her friends over for the night. After last year's brooding silence, when Lauri withdrew from her normal friends, the sound gladdened his heart.

Lauri sat on the floor with her friends Dinah and Ruthie. They were playing Yahtzee. The cabin was filled with the aroma of cookies and popcorn.

"Smells good. Any cookies left for me?"

"On the counter," Lauri said.

He went to the kitchen, open to the living room, while the girls finished their game. He poured a glass of milk and grabbed a handful of cookies before sitting at the table. Zorro nosed his leg, and Kade broke off a small piece of cookie and tossed it to the dog, making sure it contained no chocolate.

The girls' game ended, and Lauri's two friends got up to leave. "I have to pick up some milk and bread at the store on my way home," Ruthie said.

"Want to come spend the night tonight?" Dinah asked Lauri.

Lauri hesitated, then shook her head. "I have to work early in the morning, and I'm tired. I'm always tired. I'll be glad when this baby is born."

She looked down at her belly, round but still small, and Kade saw the flash of disappointment that crossed her face. It had to be hard to be seventeen and pregnant when all her friends were still carefree. He polished off the last of the cookies and gulped down his milk, then put the glass in the dishwasher.

Lauri said goodbye to her friends, then dropped disconsolately onto the couch. "I'm so sick of being pregnant," she announced.

"I know. I could tell." He walked to the couch and sat beside her. "It will be over before you know it. I found a place today I wanted to talk to you about." He pulled a brochure out of his pocket. "This organization helps place babies for adoption into good Christian homes. I made an appointment for us for Tuesday. I took a day of vacation."

Lauri gave it only a cursory glance before tossing it to the coffee table in front of her. "You know I don't want to give my baby to just anyone, Kade! I want it to be someone local."

"That's nuts though, Lauri! Do you think the adoptive parents are going to be okay with you just dropping in to check on how they're raising your baby? Once you sign those papers, you have no rights."

"I wasn't going to just drop in," she said, plucking at her hair in a sulky manner. "But I'd see the kid around town. I'd know if it was okay."

"You've got to trust God in this, kiddo. These would be good Christian folks, people who are desperately longing for a baby. You could be an answer to their prayers."

"No!" She stood and went to stare out the window.

Her arms crossed over her chest, the rigidity in her stance told Kade not to push too hard. What could he do? She wouldn't let him help her make the decision. "You have to decide something, Lauri. The baby will be here in four months. That's not a lot of time to find someone."

"If I don't find someone, I'll just keep it." She turned then, tears shimmering in her blue eyes.

A wave of love swept over Kade. She was his baby sister, the one he'd always protected. Yet now he couldn't save her from the consequences of poor choices she'd made. But if she kept the baby, he would be paying the price right along with her. He'd do it willingly, but he was sure she'd never calculated the cost to him.

"I see," he said. "You haven't even discussed this with me, Lauri. This is something we should decide together, since I'd be the one supporting you both."

"Oh, it's all about money now, is it?" She flung her blond hair away from her face.

"No, it's not about money," he snapped. "It's about responsibility and maturity. You're seventeen. Who do you think is going to watch the baby while you go back to school? Who is going to buy it clothes and diapers and formula? Not you. It would be me. And I'm not saying I would be unwilling to do it. But don't you think you should be discussing this with me and not assuming good old Kade will just step and do what you want?"

Anger flared in her eyes. "I can do it myself," she shouted. "I don't have to go back to school. I'll keep my job at The Coffee Place and take care of the baby myself."

"With what?" Kade wanted to throttle her. She had no idea of the work or cost of maintaining a household or raising a child. She was scarcely more than a child herself. "You couldn't afford rent on your wages, let alone diapers and formula. And child care. It's expensive. I suppose you could just go on welfare and let the state support you while you have baby after baby."

Too late he realized he'd gone too far. Her face blanched, and tears pooled in her eyes and ran down her cheeks.

"Is that what you think of me?" she whispered.

He wanted to apologize, but the words lodged in his throat like a fishhook.

"You think I'm so stupid I'd do this again? I'll never get in this kind of trouble again! If there's one thing I've learned, it's boys aren't to be trusted. They want only one thing, and once you give it to them, they disappear."

Kade winced at the bitterness in her words. He wanted the best for her—college, a husband and family someday. But her cynicism would have to go. "I'm sorry," he finally managed. "I didn't mean that. I know you better than that. But you're not making sense, Lauri. A baby isn't some doll you can just pick up and put down when you please. Children are a lot of work. I heard you laughing and giggling with your friends. That would be gone if you had a baby to care for. You'd be talking about the best baby food and the new tooth the baby just grew, and they'd still be laughing about the prom and the hottest boy in school. You would soon find you had nothing in common."

"Well, stab me in the heart," Lauri said, with a dramatic wave of her hand. "But I don't have much choice, now do I?"

"I brought you a choice," he said pointing to the brochure.

"That's no choice at all. I have to find someone local."

Seeing the obstinate expression on her face, Kade knew it was her way or not at all. He was just going to have to find an adoptive family here in Rock Harbor.

21

Cassie put her book down and glanced at the alarm clock. It was only ten, but she was too tired to read any longer. A lake shower had blown in early, and she'd thought to sleep well tonight. It was over now, and the fresh scent of wet pine wafted in her open window. It should have made her sleepy, but it didn't. She was too keyed up about the family dinner today.

She turned out the light, then rolled over and punched her pillow. The moonlight on the trees outside cast moving shadows on her wall, and she wished she'd opted for blinds. Out here in the boonies, she hadn't thought she would need to totally shutter the windows, but since the explosion at the lab, she felt open and vulnerable.

She was exhausted but her mind raced. She tossed and turned for what seemed like forever, but another glance at the clock told her it was only ten thirty. Maybe a cup of herbal tea would help her sleep. The thought of getting out of bed wasn't appealing though.

A shadow flitted across her wall and vanished. She raised her head and stared. What was that? She listened. The wind had picked up and now whistled through the eaves and moaned through the pines in the backyard. The shadow moved again, and she saw the clear outline of a figure. It looked like he was carrying a gun. Bubbles lifted her head and growled.

She tried to call out to Salome but no words came, just a strangled sound. Rolling off her bed, Cassie crept to the window and peeked out. There he was, outlined against the shed, a hat pulled low over his head and a rifle under his arm. He was staring at the house, but thankfully not at her window. His attention seemed to be on the back door.

Cassie sank back to the floor, pressing her face against the cool wood. Her heart thudded against the floor and she could feel the reverberations against her cheek. She crawled to the phone and dialed 911. The line was busy. Bree. She'd come. Just as she dialed the number, she heard the glass in the patio door shatter, and Bubbles began to bark.

Bree answered, and Cassie whispered into the phone. "Come quick; someone's in the house." She slammed down the phone and turned off her light. Racing down the hall, she saw Salome in the kitchen putting a tea bag into a cup of hot water.

"Hide!" she screamed. A boot kicked out the rest of the glass, and the man started to move through the shattered door. She caught a glimpse of Salome's terrified face as Cassie dove for the light switch and flipped it off. They both slipped into the pantry.

The scent of flour and packaged goods mingled with the sharp tang of fear. Salome's breath came in gasps. He had to hear them. Cassie slipped her hand along the wall, and her fingers closed around the broom.

"Stand back," she whispered to Salome. Her friend shuffled away. Cassie took a step back and brought the broom up like a bat. Straining, she could hear the man banging into the counter then a bar stool. Bubbles was barking as though she'd like to bite him, and Cassie found herself praying the dog would find the courage to take a hunk out of his leg. Then the man swore and the dog yelped.

She had to take the offensive. It was only a matter of time before he found them. Though she was shaking, Cassie swung open the pantry door and leaped into the room with a yell. She brought the broom down on the man's head, and then whacked him in the stomach as he reeled back. He swore again and yanked the broom from her hands.

"Salome, run!" She yanked her friend from the closet and propelled her down the hall and out the broken door. Broken glass bit into her bare feet.

The man let loose with a string of profanity and started after them.

"The shed," Cassie whispered hoarsely. Salome ran toward it, and Cassie looked around for a weapon. Spying a broken branch, she snatched it up. Her bare feet slid on the wet grass, and she almost fell.

"Get in here!" Salome whispered.

"No, I want to see who it is." Cassie crouched behind the water fountain at the corner of the deck. She could hear the man's boots crunching over the broken glass as he stumbled to the door, then through it. The moon slid behind the clouds, and the backyard plunged into deeper shadows.

Just as he reached the deck steps, the moon came out again, and Cassie realized he was indeed holding a gun. Her stick would be no match for his weapon. The rough bark cut into the soft flesh of her hands, only used to holding Petri dishes and fine tuning microscopes. Her feet throbbed.

A tickle built in her nose, and she struggled to contain it. Her eyes watered with the effort, but a tiny sneeze escaped. The man whirled toward her and fired.

As Bree sped toward Cassie's house, she realized she'd come to care more for Cassie than she realized. The young woman had crept into her heart when she wasn't looking, in spite of the strain of today's dinner. Bree prayed for God to protect Cassie and Salome. Bargaining with God wasn't a good idea, but she asked him to give her a chance to get to know Cassie better.

Having called Mason and dropped Davy off at the safety of Anu's, Bree turned onto Cassie's street. A sheriff's car, lights and sirens going, zipped past her. She applied more force to the accelerator and sped after them. She pulled up behind Mason and jumped out, taking time to let Charley out as well. Mason and his deputy had their guns out.

"Sheriff's office, open up!" Deputy Montgomery shouted. He pounded on the door. No one came, but Bubbles was barking ferociously. "I'll go around back." His belly jiggling, he jogged around the side of the house.

"I'm scared for them, Mason," Bree whispered.

"Maybe she and Salome are hiding from the intruder." Mason tried the door, but it refused to budge.

Shouts echoed from the back. Bree and Mason turned and raced to the backyard. Salome, dressed in pajamas and slippers, was sobbing against Montgomery's chest.

"Where's Cassie?" In the face of Salome's hysteria, Bree was almost afraid to hear the answer.

"I don't know. She ran into the woods." Salome was sobbing so hard it was difficult to understand her. She turned and pointed. "There. Someone ran after her."

"Male?"

She nodded. It was too dark to see well, and a hat covered his face, but I heard his voice."

"Where's Cassie's bedroom?" Bree started for the house. "Charley will find her."

Salome made an obvious effort to collect herself. "I'll show you." She gingerly stepped past the broken glass from the patio door. Bubbles greeted them at the door and followed as Salome led Bree down the hall. "This is her room. Mine is on the other side of the house."

Mason followed them. "When did you become aware there was an intruder?"

"When I heard the glass shatter. I was in the kitchen fixing a cup of tea and heard them smash the patio door. Then Cassie screamed for me to hide. We hid in the closet. I thought I'd faint. Cassie hit him with a broom. He fell, and she yelled for me to run. I ran outside right behind her. She told me to hide in the shed, then she grabbed a big branch and waited for him to come out again. I begged her to hide with me but she wouldn't."

"Why not?" Mason asked

"She said she wanted to see who it was. So I got in the shed and peeked out through the window. She crouched on the ground by the water fountain. When the guy came out, he was holding his gun like he was ready to shoot. I think Cassie sneezed or something because he saw her and fired the gun at her. It hit the fountain and chipped it. She jumped and ran into the woods. He followed her."

Dread iced Bree's limbs. "Did you hear any other shots?"

Salome nodded. "Two."

Bree knelt and put her arm around Charley's neck. She pointed at a pair of socks lying on the floor. The dog bent his head and delicately sniffed the socks. Bubbles did the same. "Search, Charley!" she told him.

His tail came up, and he began to roam the room. His ears perked. He whined then raced down the hall and out the smashed patio door. Bree ran after him, nearly falling as her shoes slipped on the broken glass.

The dogs raced toward the woods. Bree plunged into the blackness of the thick trees. They would have difficulty tracking with the trees packed so tightly together. She flicked on her halogen flashlight, and the beams pushed back the edges of the darkness. She and the dogs had to slow their pace.

Mason panted by her side. He still had his gun out. "Cassie! It's Sheriff Kaleva. It's safe to come out now."

They heard thrashing off to their right. It grew more distant.

"Maybe a deer," Mason said.

"Or the intruder running away." Bree watched Charley. He still had the scent. His tail wagged as he wound his way through the trees. At least Cassie was still alive. Charley was giving off good vibes.

The flashlight beam bounced off rocks and downed trees as they trudged through the cool night. "Cassie!" Bree shouted periodically.

Her flashlight beam touched a rough outcropping of rock, and she saw something move. "Cassie?" She focused the light, and her sister's face jumped into focus. Bree inhaled and ran forward.

Cassie was on the ground. Blood trickled down the side of her face from a cut in her hair. "I fell," she muttered. "But he didn't find me."

Bree knelt beside her. "We'd better call for an ambulance."

"No, no, I'm fine," Cassie insisted. "Help me up." She grabbed Bree's arm and struggled to her feet. "It's just a scratch. I was thrashing blindly through here and ran into the stupid rock." She shook her head as if to clear it. "Did you catch him?"

"No, he got away," Mason said.

"Is Salome okay?"

"She's fine. Scared, but she'll be fine," Bree assured her. "Let's get you back to the house. You can't stay there tonight. I have plenty of room in my house."

"I can stay in a hotel." Cassie held Bree's arm and they turned toward the house.

"Absolutely not! You're my sister, and you're staying with me."

Cassie looked at her strangely. "That's a switch. You've acted like you don't want me around."

"I know, and I'm sorry. I've been a jerk."

"I wouldn't say that." There was a smile in Cassie's voice, and Bree knew it was going to be all right.

Anu had already put Davy to bed at her house. Bree showed Cassie and Salome to the lighthouse guest rooms, then went down to make popcorn and put in a pizza.

"This is like a slumber party," Cassie said, grabbing another handful of popcorn. "Got any good movies to watch?"

"*Princess Bride.*"

"Oh, that is the *best* movie!" Salome said. "I've been trying to get her to watch it, but she says it sounds too stupid."

"It *is* stupid, but that's what's great about it." Bree got out the DVD and put it in the player.

"No, don't make me watch it," Cassie begged.

"Inconceivable!" Salome and Bree said at the same time.

Bree laughed. "Naomi will be mad she missed this."

"I'll trade places with her," Cassie muttered. Her face sobered. "I'm only teasing. It was so great of you to have us. The company would have paid our hotel. You didn't have to be inconvenienced."

"I'm loving it." Bree hit pause on the remote. "We need to get to know each other. I wouldn't mind if you stayed for weeks."

Cassie studied her face. "I think you're telling the truth."

"I've never had a family to be close to. I'm sorry I've been such a jerk." Bree hadn't realized until now how much that had bothered her. Davy, Anu, Hilary, and Mason were her family, but she'd longed for the closeness she saw between Hilary and Rob when he was alive, that feeling of having shared parents. Though she and Cassie only shared a father, the blood ties could be strengthened if Bree had enough courage to do it.

"We can watch the movie tomorrow," Bree said. "Tell me how our father is doing. He seemed great today."

"Are you sure you want to hear this?"

"I'm sure."

Cassie took a sip of her Pepsi. "I feel so guilty for not taking care of him, but he has times where he forgets how to bathe or how to get dressed. He's still having some great days, like today."

"You had to keep him safe. He had wandered several times. I've had to search and find people like him often enough over the years. "

"I know I had to do it, but it's still hard. I've been all he has for so long, and I've always wanted to please him."

"Which is why you've pushed yourself," Salome put in. She stood. "I think I'll go to bed and leave you two to your confidences. I don't want to intrude."

"'Night," Cassie called.

"Does my mother know where he is?" Bree asked.

Cassie nodded. "He gets packages from her every now and then. The last letter said she might come see him. He wrote and told her not to come. I think he doesn't want anyone to see him like this." She bit her lip. "At least no one but you."

Bree started shaking her head. "What about the cancer?" The anger she'd felt over him leaving her in her mother's care was disappearing, she realized. Maybe she was coming to understand her life wasn't perfect. She'd made plenty of mistakes herself.

"He's got maybe three months." Cassie's face contorted with pain. "I don't know what I'll do without him. I think that's why I wanted to find you so badly. You'll be all the family I have left." She touched Bree on the arm as if she were afraid.

Bree felt the sting of tears at the backs of her eyes. "We can try," she said. "Just remember, God will go through those deep places with us."

Cassie pulled her hand away. "If he cared about me, he wouldn't take my father."

"I used to say that about Davy and Rob too. But when I reached the bottom of my well, I found God there."

"Let's not talk about it," Cassie said. "But I think I can work on learning to love you, Bree."

"And I you." Bree took her hand and squeezed it. "But only if you'll watch *Princess Bride* with me."

22

*T*he woman blew her hair away from her eyes in frustration. "I don't like this."

"We have no choice. We can't find the papers. The old man is our only link to our future." The man grabbed her arm roughly. "Let's get this done." He marched her toward the nursing home.

Nearly midnight. The residents' rooms were dark, but they knew which one was the old man's. Luckily it was near the front door.

They walked confidently inside. The woman in the office had her head bent over a book, and the TV played softly in the background. Perfect. They went to room 101 and stepped inside.

She shook the snoring old man. He awoke with a start and stared up at them in the moonlight streaming through his window.

"Cassie?" he muttered.

"That's right. We have to go, Dad. Right now. Come along."

Bree stared at herself in the mirror. She didn't feel like going out tonight, not when her sister would be here later, and they were enjoying the time together. But she didn't know how to get out of it with Nick. He'd been insistent about a date with just the two of them.

She brushed a bit of taupe shadow over her lids and added a touch of mascara. That would have to do. Elaborate makeup and fancy dresses weren't part of who she was. Shaking her head, she put her toiletries away and went down to wait for Nick.

Davy lay on the floor with his head on a pillow. His face was intent on the book in his hand. He looked up after a moment and saw her. "You look pretty, Mommy. How come I can't go with you? Nick won't mind."

"Lauri would be disappointed if she didn't get to spend the evening with you. You two are going to the party at Yancy's, remember?" Yancy had invited half the town to a cookout. Bree had thought she and Nick would go, but he'd nixed the idea.

Davy considered that, then scowled. "She could come with us. She could be my date."

Bree hid a smile. "You can come next time."

The lot at Syl's was full when Nick parked his Mercury Mountaineer. Bree hadn't felt like driving farther than Mass City, and Syl's had great food, though the ambience was backwoods hunter meets home cooking. Still, it was better than driving clear to Houghton.

"How's the investigation going?" Nick asked, opening her door.

"Nowhere fast. Mason ran ballistics on the gun I found, and it was the murder weapon. But the serial number had been filed off, and it was wiped clean of prints. So it's another dead end."

Nick nodded and led her inside. Once seated in a back corner facing the mural of mountains, Bree sipped her water and wondered what to talk about. She'd never felt so ill at ease with Nick—or so distant. He didn't seem to notice though, for he kept up a steady stream of banter about the goings on at the fire station. She made the appropriate noises at all the right times, but her thoughts were at a cabin in the woods. Kade never left her thoughts for long these days.

They ate their dinner, but the conversation never seemed to touch more than the surface.

"Want to go for a ride in the moonlight?" Nick suggested.

The moon over Lake Superior was a sight Bree never tired of. "Sure." Her smile felt plastered on. What was wrong with her? She wasn't being fair to Nick, feeling so disconnected. She told herself to snap out of it, but that seemed impossible.

Nick's warm hand clasped hers as they walked back to his SUV. Kade would have noticed her distraction, and it made Bree wonder how Nick saw her. Couldn't he tell she had something on her mind?

Nick drove out past her lighthouse to the turnoff that went to a tip of land jutting into the lake. He opened her door and, when she got out, tucked her hand into his jacket pocket to keep it warm from the cool breeze blowing off the lake. He led her to a bench with a vista of the water that nearly took her breath away.

He put his arm around her, and she leaned her head against his chest. Why didn't she feel safe and protected with him? He tried and did all the right things.

"Are you going to tell me what's bugging you? You've been as far away as Minnesota tonight. I was ready to get a boat and cross the lake to reach you."

"I'm right here." She didn't know how to answer something she didn't know herself.

He was silent for a time, and she looked up at his profile in the moonlight. His strong jaw and full lips reminded her of that statue of David by Michelangelo. Any woman would be thrilled to be keeping company with him, but all she felt was emptiness. He deserved more than that.

"What? You're staring."

"I guess I do know what's wrong," she said slowly.

He turned to gaze into her eyes. "Is it me?"

"No, it's me." She swallowed the fear that dried her mouth. "I don't think I'm ever going to feel about you like you deserve."

"What's that mean? You aren't attracted to me? I can make you love me if you give me the time." He cupped her face in his palms. "Just give me a chance," he whispered.

Shouldn't his touch make her pulse race? All she felt was pity. "I love Kade," she said simply. It was the truth she hadn't wanted to admit to herself. She loved the big-hearted ranger more than just as a friend.

Nick drew back and scowled. "He's not the man for you. You'll be stuck in this backwater forever. Once I make fire chief here, we can move on to a bigger, better place. It won't take long, not when there's no real competition."

"I guess that's what confused me for a while. Your dreams sound exciting, but I realized they're your dreams, not mine. I want to stay here, to raise Davy near his family. I want to have more children who can grow up safe and happy along the shores of this lake."

His arm fell away from her shoulders. "I guess that's it then. I couldn't stay here forever. Not even for you."

"And I couldn't leave for you." A part of her wondered what she'd do if Kade asked her to move. She thought she might be able to do it if he asked. That told her a lot about how she really felt about Nick. And about Kade.

"I'll take you home," Nick said.

"That might be best."

They drove in silence back down the road to her lighthouse. He parked in front and leaned across her to open her door. "What about Davy?"

"Try to let him down easy. Stop and see him occasionally."

"I do care about him, you know."

"I know. He loves you too."

His jaw twitched, and she hated that she'd hurt him. She got out and watched until his taillights disappeared around the curve. She thought she'd feel heavy-hearted, but the only emotion that came to her was something that felt like she'd been released from prison.

Donovan pulled Naomi close and kissed her. "Um, you smell good, like sunshine."

"It's my shampoo." She snuggled close to him, trying not to think of the stress of the past week. They'd just had dinner. Emily was doing her homework while Timmy played with his trains on the living-room floor. They had these few precious moments to themselves, and Naomi intended to milk them for all they were worth.

"We need a date, all to ourselves," Donovan whispered. "How about we see if Lauri can babysit tomorrow after church and we'll go to Houghton for the day, go shopping, out to eat, whatever you like."

"Sounds like a plan." The doorbell rang, and she groaned. "It never fails," she groused. "You want to get that while I stick the dishes in the dishwasher?"

"Sure." He kissed her on the nose and jogged to the front door.

"Mr. O'Reilly?" A woman's voice reached Naomi's ears, but it didn't sound familiar. Curious, Naomi stepped to the doorway. The smile froze. She'd seen this woman with her graying hair and chilly gray eyes before. Ellen Wright, the child welfare advocate.

The woman nodded to Naomi. "Mrs. O'Reilly. I'm Ellen Wright, child welfare. I'd like to discuss the custody situation with you. May I come in?"

Donovan seemed as shocked and scatterbrained as Naomi felt. "Ah, of course." He swung the door open wider and stepped aside to allow the woman to enter. "The kids are in the living room, so it might be best if we talk in the kitchen." He looked helplessly at Naomi. "Could you get Ms. Wright some coffee?"

"Nothing for me, thanks," Ms. Wright said. She followed Donovan to the table and pulled a notebook out of her briefcase. She took the glasses hanging from a chain around her neck and adjusted them on her nose. "Let's see, the mother has lodged a complaint that her son is being neglected and as a result his diabetes is out of control."

She smiled at Naomi, and the warmth in her gaze made Naomi breathe a little easier.

"Would you term that an accurate assessment?" Ms. Wright asked.

"I would not!" Naomi leaned forward across the table. "I love those children as if they were my own. I set a timer for Timmy's shot, and I plan menus two weeks in advance to follow his diet precisely." She reached for her meal planner on the counter and slid it across the table to Ms. Wright. "No one could do more than I have to make sure Timmy's blood sugar has been stable for months. I have no idea why it's suddenly gone out of control."

Ms. Wright flipped through the planner and nodded. "And you, Mr. O'Reilly, what is your part of the story? How often are you home to make sure things are rolling smoothly?"

"I run a business, as I'm sure you know," he said flatly. "I leave the house at six thirty every morning and I'm home around six at night. Naomi is doing a fine job with the kids. Marika's accusation is rooted in her attempt to gain custody after abandoning our kids. In the two years she was gone, she never so much as called the kids or sent them a card or birthday present. We weren't sure if she was dead or alive."

Ms. Wright frowned. "I don't have that in my notes. Is that accurate?"

"It most certainly is," he said.

Naomi had rarely seen Donovan so incensed. His face was red, and anger pinched his mouth. She touched his arm. The woman seemed to be on their side.

"I'd like to look at the children's rooms, if I may." Ms. Wright stood and pulled her glasses from her nose.

"Of course. Follow me." Naomi took her down the hall and showed her the rooms. Luckily they were spotless other than a few toys on the beds.

"Very nice." Ms. Wright's voice was warm with approval. She kept writing things down in her notebook. "I'd like to talk to the children now."

"Is that really necessary?" Donovan crossed his arms over his chest. "They've been upset enough by all this. There's no need to involve them in Marika's little game."

"I sympathize, Mr. O'Reilly," Ms. Wright said. "It's necessary that I ask the children a few questions. Alone. If we don't do everything by the book, someone not so sympathetic to your circumstances may be assigned to this case."

"I think I'll consult my lawyer before I agree to that." Donovan stared back at her.

Ms. Wright sighed and pinched the bridge of her nose with her fingers. "Very well." She dropped her notebook into her briefcase and snapped it shut. "But you're not helping yourself, Mr. O'Reilly."

"What kinds of things would you ask them?" Naomi put in.

Ms. Wright shrugged. "What kinds of things they eat, what time they go to bed, that type of thing. I won't ask them which parent they wish to live with. My job is to ascertain how well they're being cared for."

"It's okay, Donovan. Let her talk to the kids," Naomi said. "Let's just get it over with and put it behind us."

"I want to be in the room," Donovan said.

"Fine. I can agree to that as long as you don't coach the children on what to say."

"This way." Donovan stalked down the hall to the living room.

Emily looked up when the adults appeared. "I've got my homework almost done, Dad. You want to look it over?"

"In a minute, sweetheart. This lady would like to talk to you and Timmy."

Her eyes got round. "What about? Am I in trouble?"

"No, of course not. She—"

"I'll explain," Ms. Wright said, stepping forward. "Hello, Emily. I'm Ms. Wright. I'd just like to see how things are going with you and your brother." She seated herself on the sofa and leaned forward with a warm smile on her face.

Naomi tried to quench the burning in her stomach by sheer willpower. Things would be okay. She just had to leave this in the Lord's hands.

"Now, I'd just like to know what you had for dinner tonight."

"Pizza!" Timmy put in.

"We did not," Emily said. "That's what you wanted, but Naomi wouldn't let you have it." She fixed Naomi with a haughty stare. "Our mother lets us have pizza, but Naomi won't." The resentment in her voice let everyone know pizza would have been her choice too. "She made us eat grilled chicken and baked potatoes. Ugh! And peas. I hate peas," she said.

"I like peas," Timmy said. "I had a bunch of them."

"And sugar-free Jell-O with pears," Emily added. "Artificial sweeteners are bad for you."

"And broccoli salad," Timmy reminded her.

"Sounds like a good dinner," Ms. Wright said.

"She never lets us eat good stuff," Emily said.

"It was good," Timmy said. "Not as good as pizza, but Naomi is a good cook."

"Mommy is better," Emily said. "And she lets us go with her to play Bingo. Naomi says gambling is bad, but it's just a game, not gambling. Mommy says we don't have to be a hypocrite like her."

Naomi wanted to cry. How did she reach the little girl and assure her it was okay to love her and her mother both—that she didn't have to choose sides?

"What time do you go to bed?" Ms. Wright wanted to know.

"Eight thirty, like we're babies!"

"Yeah, babies," Timmy echoed.

A twitch of amusement lifted Ms. Wright's lips. She shared a commiserating glance with Naomi. "I think I've heard enough," she said, standing and turning toward the door. "You've both been very helpful."

23

*S*he had fifteen minutes to meet the team for the Wisconsin FEMA training. Would Kade want to come with them? She'd like some backup when she met with the guy at Jackson Pharmaceutical whom Cassie had on the payroll. She wouldn't know unless she asked. She wished she'd thought of it sooner. Bree dialed her cell phone.

"Hi, it's me. Are you busy this weekend?"

"No, but you are. Aren't you going to Wisconsin with your students for the FEMA certification?"

"Yep. Would you be up to sharing a room with Ryan? I want to go talk to Jackson Pharmaceuticals while I'm there, and I could use some backup. Want to come with us?"

"Now?"

Was that happiness in his voice? "Yes, right away. Can you get here in half an hour? We can wait for you."

"As long as you don't care if my clothes match." There was laughter in his voice, then he paused. "Thanks for asking me. Want me to drive?"

"We'll take my Jeep so there's room for Naomi and Davy. I'll meet you at the center."

Driving to the center, she couldn't deny the way she felt inside. All warm and soft like a toasted marshmallow. They'd have the weekend together, though it would be mostly business. She wanted to get to know this new Kade better.

She stopped outside the O'Reillys' house and honked. Naomi and Charley came running out. Naomi slung her suitcase in the carrier on top. She and Charley got in. "You're late," Naomi said.

"I know." Bree put in an Elvis CD and turned up the first song, "It's Now or Never." She began to sing along with him.

"What's up?" Naomi's forehead wrinkled with suspicion. "You look like Charley when he's found something particularly noxious to roll in."

Bree laughed. "I invited Kade to come along this weekend."

"What?" Naomi screamed, and Charley began to bark. She lowered her voice a notch. "You sly thing. You didn't say a word."

"I just now did it." Bree couldn't stop smiling. "You're right. I love him."

Naomi whooped and the dog started barking again.

"What's wrong?" Davy asked plaintively from the backseat.

"Nothing. Aunty Naomi is just being goofy," Bree said.

"And you're finally wising up," Naomi said with a smug grin.

Bree parked behind Ryan's SUV. "Not a word," she cautioned.

Naomi gave her an offended look. "As if I would. I don't see his truck."

"I gave him half an hour. He'll be here."

The team was assembled by the front door. They were talking with excitement and enthusiasm. Bree let Charley out to run until Kade got there. "You all ready for this?"

"You bet!" Eva was dressed in a sleek red pantsuit that showed off her stunning figure. Ryan had already noticed, in spite of them being on the outs.

Karen, Lauri, and Eva were riding with Ryan. Bree had room for Naomi, Davy, and Kade. His truck pulled behind her Jeep by the time everyone was loaded up. Kade embraced her, pulling her against his chest. Her nose buried in his chest, she inhaled his masculine scent overlaid with the aroma of soap. He wore a hint of aftershave today too, something spicy.

He bent his head and kissed her, his lips sparking a response she tried to hide. She pulled away. "Thanks for coming with me. But we won't get very far if you keep that up."

He grinned. "That's the plan. Keys?"

"In the Jeep." They linked arms and strolled to her Jeep. Naomi was waiting with Davy in the vehicle. Charley followed at her heels. With the sunshine glimmering on the full summer foliage, Bree inhaled a breath of pure enjoyment.

"So why are we going to see a pharmaceutical company?" Kade asked, starting the Jeep and pulling onto the road. Naomi was entertaining Davy in the backseat.

"Denise told me Jackson Pharmaceuticals had offered Phil a job. And a half-million-dollar bonus if he'd come work for them and bring the formula with him. He refused."

"So you're wondering if they killed him? What would be the point?"

"To gain time for them to catch up in their own research. What if they're also behind the attempts on Cassie's life? It makes sense."

"Maybe. But I can't see a big company pulling something like that. It could bring them down. There are lots of research projects going on. They could just focus on another one. Besides, they couldn't legally use any work that had been done by MJ."

"They could if no one knew it was the same research. If the researchers were dead."

"What research could be that important?"

"Denise and Cassie have both said this project is special. That it has applications for Alzheimer's. The company that brings it out will make billions of dollars."

"That certainly ups the stakes," Kade admitted. "And it sounds dangerous. I don't want to see you put yourself in the line of fire."

"But this is my sister we're talking about. I have to help her."

"I know. I just don't want to see you hurt. Whoever is behind this is dangerous."

"I have you to protect me. Besides, I'm just going to talk to a guy Cassie says might know what's going on." She gave him a cheeky smile and leaned over to fiddle with the CD player. Soon Elvis's mellow voice filled the Jeep with the lyrics of "Love Me Tender."

Kade reached out his hand, and Bree took it. The warm touch of his fingers laced with hers made her feel melancholy for some reason. The intense emotion made her want to cry. She felt ready now, ready to accept Kade's love. She wasn't sure how to let him know. The anticipation grew in her until she realized she was holding her breath. She should say something, but she didn't know how. All these months of holding him off had turned into a habit, one she didn't know how to break.

She licked her dry lips. "Um, Kade?"

His thumb traced patterns on her palm, and she felt her temperature rise. "Hmm?"

"I . . . I just wanted to say . . ." She trailed off, feeling stupid and tongue-tied.

"What?" His voice sounded more alert. He took his eyes off the road a moment and glanced at her, then focused on the highway again.

She was not going to say it. Not until he did again. "Nothing." She pulled her hand away and folded it into her lap.

A smile teased the corners of his mouth. "Chicken?"

Her face flamed with heat. "Of course not. Just drive."

"I have to go potty, Mommy," Davy called.

Kade pulled into a gas station. "Perfect timing."

"I'll take Davy in." Naomi unbuckled Davy's car seat and got out. She took him inside the mini mart.

"What were you going to say?" Kade took her hand.

"Later."

"Now." He pulled her hand to his lips and kissed her palm. "You ready to talk about us?"

She couldn't look away from the intense blue of his eyes. They seemed to glow from within. She nodded. "Maybe."

"Maybe?" He sighed. "Bree, quit it, okay? Just stop. Don't play around with me anymore. I love you. That's the bottom line. We've got a future together if you'll admit it."

"Okay," she said in a small voice.

"Okay, what?"

"I'm admitting it. We've got a future together. I broke it off with Nick. There, are you happy? You're the only man in my life."

His face lit with a joy she'd never seen. It awed her to think she was the reason for it. He took her in his arms and buried his face in her neck.

"Ah, baby, that wasn't so hard, was it?" He pulled back and cupped her face in his hands. "You love me. Say it."

"I love you," she said.

"Say it like you mean it," he commanded playfully.

She searched his gaze, seeing only unconditional love and acceptance there. "I love you, Kade Matthews. I love the way you tilt your head to one side when you're talking, and I love your strength of character and your sense of humor. I love everything about you, including your stubbornness and determination to do what's right."

He closed his eyes and sighed. "That's what I've been waiting to hear. You're going to marry me, okay?"

She nodded. "Okay."

"When?"

"I'm too happy to think straight. Let's see what Anu says. I'll need her help to plan the wedding." Ridiculously, Bree felt her eyes burn and blur as tears found their way to the surface.

"Why are you crying? You're supposed to be happy." His alarmed gaze searched her face, but a slow smile started at his eyes. He bent his head to kiss her.

The sweet touch of his lips on hers blotted out every problem and worry she'd had over the weekend. She clung to him and felt her world rock to the tune of "Wear My Ring around Your Neck."

Kade pulled away first. "We'd better get going if we want to make it before dinner." He sounded as rattled as she felt.

Bree knew her grin had to make her look manic. She tried to temper it, but it stayed right there, stretching her lips from ear to ear. "I'm not sure I can keep this from anyone," she said. "Maybe this wasn't the right time for this conversation."

Kade's smoldering look made her giggle. "Ooh, tough guy, you don't scare me." She touched his cheek.

He grinned then and reached out to take her hand. "Maybe we'll look for a ring this afternoon," he said smugly.

A ring. Somehow the word made panic rise in her belly. A ring was so . . . so . . . permanent. And real. She forced herself to breathe in and out, in and out. She loved Kade. This was right and good. He'd love her and Davy, and any other children who came along, with his whole heart.

She smiled. "Okay."

Davy and Naomi came back out, and they headed for Wisconsin. It was after six by the time they found the hotel.

"Davy and I have a date with a pizza," Naomi announced when they got out. "You and Kade go out on the town."

"You sure?" Bree asked.

"Yep. Go." Naomi leaned over and whispered in her ear. "Don't come back without a ring."

They checked into the hotel, then Bree kissed Davy good night and went down to the lobby to meet Kade.

"Where to now?" he asked.

"Maybe we'll check out the jewelry stores," she said.

He grabbed her hand and hustled her to the Jeep. "We're going before you change your mind!"

By the time Bree stepped back into the hotel, she had a rock on her hand the size of the famous Ontonagon Copper Boulder. At least that's what she told Kade when he kissed her good night at the door.

Bree hardly slept a wink. By the time she'd told Naomi everything, it was nearly two. Then she kept waking up and looking at her ring in the moonlight. Engaged. She was engaged to marry Kade. It seemed almost surreal.

Now to tell Davy.

She ordered room service for breakfast. No way was she facing Kade looking like a hag. Davy sat on the chair swinging his legs as he ate his oatmeal.

She sat in the chair beside him. "I have something to tell you, Davy."

He looked up at her. "Am I in trouble?"

"No, sweetheart, not at all. This is good news." She bit her lip. There was no breaking this easy. "You're going to have a new daddy."

His eyes brightened. "Yay! I love Nick."

"It's not Nick, honey. It's Kade."

His face fell. "No! You're lying, Mommy."

She pulled him onto her lap. "Kade loves you very much, Davy. We'll do lots of things together. You and he are going to build a tree house in the backyard."

But nothing she said stopped the tears. Naomi finally took him and told her to go get her shower. "Don't cater to him," she said under her breath. "He'll adjust, Bree."

"I'm not so sure," Bree muttered as she went to the rest room.

But he was calmly coloring by the time she got back to the bedroom "What did you do?" she whispered to Naomi.

"Talked about how jealous Timmy would be of that tree house. And said he'd probably get to help Kade with the baby animals."

Bree watched her son and knew it would be all right. He would feel their love and grow secure in it. "Thanks." She grabbed her backpack. "Ready to go train?"

Today would be hard, watching the other dogs and knowing Samson should be there. Bree wasn't sure how she'd get through it, but she gritted her teeth and went toward the door. Her students needed her.

The weekend flew by. Her students and their dogs spent hours climbing over concrete debris and bombed buildings. They were all still dragging when they got up Monday morning. Bree asked for a late departure for their room so Naomi could take Davy swimming in the pool while she and Kade checked out Jackson Pharmaceutical.

They rode in companionable silence to downtown Milwaukee. "There. There's the building," she said.

"Looks impressive," Kade said, pulling the Jeep into a parking place. "You ready?"

"As ready as I'll ever be." She unfastened her seat belt and got out.

At the door, Bree told the security guard, "We're here to see Mr. Leif Lindell."

The guard looked over his chart. "I don't see your name."

"Just tell him Bree Nicholls and Kade Matthews are here to see him about the Rock Harbor project."

The guard shrugged and went to the phone. While he was talking, Bree looked around. Affluence betrayed itself in the gleaming furnishings of the reception room and in the expensive art on the walls.

The guard returned. "Mr. Lindell has just a few minutes." He showed them the elevator. "Top floor," he said.

They rode the elevator to the sixth floor. The elevator stopped smoothly, and they stepped out into a busy lab. The receptionist's smile beamed a bright wattage. "Leif is over by the centrifuges." She pointed out a balding man who reminded Bree of Danny DeVito.

Leif was drying his hands. Bree's stomach clenched with anticipation. "Mr. Lindell?" Bree said, extending her hand. "Thank you for seeing us without an appointment."

He nodded to them curtly. "Follow me," he said. He led them to a stark conference room and shut the door behind him.

"You shouldn't have come here," he whispered. "You should have called and I would have met you outside the building. If my boss hears about this, I'm in big trouble."

"I'm sorry. Cassie gave me your name, and we were in the area," Bree began.

Leif sighed and sank onto a chair. "It can't be helped now. What do you want?"

"People are turning up dead in Rock Harbor. Scientists at the lab. Is it possible someone here is paying to get rid of the scientists?"

He blanched. Shaking his head, he held out his hand as though to ward off her accusations. "Absolutely not. No new drug is worth murder. We have plenty of other things in the pipeline. I'm not denying we'd like to have it, but no one here would stoop that low."

"Why were you feeding information to Cassie?" Kade wanted to know.

Leif looked away and shrugged. "Money, of course. Her boss pays me enough to compensate for my pitiful salary here. Murder, you say? Who was killed?"

"Phil Taylor was shot, Ian Baird was killed by an explosion, and Cassie has had two attempts on her life."

"Oh dear, I had no idea. You must believe me when I say Jackson Pharmaceuticals had nothing to do with any of it. In fact, I think they've given up all hopes of getting the drug."

"Then why did they offer Phil money to turn over information?" Bree pressed.

"I heard that offer was withdrawn. I couldn't find out why."

He stood. "Now I'd better get back to work before I get fired."

Withdrawn. Bree frowned as she went toward the elevator. Could it be they had someone else willing to betray MJ Pharmaceuticals?"

24

Cassie waved to the nurse behind the desk at the end of the hall before entering her father's room. The bed was empty. He was probably playing euchre in the rec hall. She laid her purse on the bed and followed the noise of a blaring TV.

Poking her head in, she didn't see her father's familiar balding head. She didn't know any of the residents in the room. A TV played an afternoon soap opera, three women sat knitting and talking in one corner, and four men were playing euchre.

She ducked back out and went to the nurse she'd seen earlier. The woman's blond head was bent over a crossword-puzzle book. She looked up when Cassie cleared her throat.

"I'm Cassie Hecko, and I'm looking for my father, Bernard."

A panicky expression crossed the woman's face. "We have him signed out to your supervision," she said. "Last night. See here." She pulled the logbook around so Cassie could read it.

The sheet was signed Cassie Hecko. "That's not my signature," she said. She stared at the script. It wasn't her father's scrawl either. Bree, maybe?

"Did you see the woman who signed him out?"

"No, see the time." She pointed a finger tipped in red at the checkout column.

"Nearly midnight. Isn't that unusual?"

"When I saw it, I assumed there was a family emergency of some kind."

"Let me call my sister and see if she has any idea what's going on."

The phone rang just as Bree was headed out the door on another search for Samson. Her hope always rose when the phone rang. "Kitchigami Search and Rescue."

Mason's deep voice came over the line. "Bree, I thought you'd want to know right away. We got the man who tried to attack Cassie last week."

Adrenaline tingled along her nerves. "Who was it?"

"Some guy protesting the genetic altering of plants going on at the lab. He doesn't seem to have any ties with NAWG as far as I can tell."

"You think he killed Phil and changed Cassie's prescription?"

"All we know for sure is he broke into Cassie's house."

Bree thanked him and hung up the phone. Still so many un-answered questions.

"I thought I'd find you here." Naomi came through the door with Emily and Timmy in tow. Davy ran to meet them, and the children went out to play with Charley.

"Yeah."

Naomi shot her a questioning look. "You sound tired."

"Just discouraged. It's been nearly three weeks. I'm afraid Samson is long gone." She pressed her fingers to her eyes.

Naomi's smile faded. "We can't give up hope, Bree."

"I'm trying not to. But we have so little to go on."

Naomi squeezed her arm and dropped into a chair. "I'm bushed. The house is spotless, and I decided we'd get out before I succumbed to the urge to go buy paint and redo the kitchen cabinets. Besides, a cer-tain bride-to-be needs to be giving me wedding gift ideas."

Bree smiled. She still couldn't believe it. "You're quite the Martha Stewart. I never knew you had it in you."

"You should see me with a toilet brush in my hand. The sight would terrify you." Naomi stretched her legs out in front of her and pulled her long braid over one shoulder. "You need a break. I thought we'd go shopping for school clothes. And Davy's birthday is next week. I bet you haven't even bought anything yet."

"No, but it would be hard to buy something for him with him along," Bree pointed out.

"I could always buy it and he'd never notice."

"It's hard to think about shopping when Samson has been kidnapped."

"I wish someone would kidnap Marika." Naomi sighed.

"Any more word from the welfare office or the lawyer about when you go to court?"

Naomi shook her head. "I wish we could just get it over with."

"There's no way Marika can win," Bree said. She wished Donovan's ex-wife would go away for other reasons. Cassie would probably be safer with the environmental group out of town.

"I keep thinking that, but I can't quite bring myself to believe it. She's gotten this far and disrupted our family until we can hardly have a pleasant meal without Emily saying something hurtful."

"She's just a kid and doesn't get it."

"I know. I love her to pieces, but she doesn't see it. She's swallowed everything her mother has told her about how bad I am."

"She'll figure it out sooner or later. Just give her some time."

"I know, I know." Naomi twisted her braid in her fingers.

"How's Timmy been doing?"

"Still not so good. His blood sugar has been all over the charts. I can't figure it out. I've been following his diet to the T. I've had to take him to the hospital twice in the past week. Donovan is beside himself. He's half afraid to go to work."

"Do you think Marika is giving him stuff he shouldn't have?"

"Oh, I've no doubt she is! But his sugar still shouldn't be so hard to control. He only sees her every other weekend and maybe once a week for a few hours. But his blood sugar goes up and down like Superior's tides."

"Makes no sense. Unless . . ." Bree frowned, remembering Cassie's close call.

"When did you get his insulin filled last? And from what pharmacy?"

"We get it through the mail from somewhere in Ohio, a place Donovan's insurance pays better. We got a new shipment a month ago."

"Right about when Timmy started having problems. But it's not the pharmacy here in town."

"Why are you asking?"

"I was thinking about how someone broke into the computer and altered Cassie's prescription."

"He's taking the right stuff here," Naomi said. "He takes fast-acting and the slower kind both. But what if Marika isn't doing it right when he's at her house?"

"Would she deliberately do that?"

"I would hope not. She used to give him shots before she left. She knows the protocol."

"Would a mother do something like that to her own child? What if he died from it?" Bree tried to keep the censure from her voice. They were just guessing.

"No normal mother would put her child in harm's way. But Marika isn't normal."

"You want to keep the kids and let me go talk to Marika? She might talk to me where she wouldn't talk to you. I've been wanting to ask her some questions about the lab explosion anyway."

Naomi hesitated then nodded. "I'd like to be there, but I know I'd just muck it up. She and I rub each other the wrong way."

"I'll be back as soon as I'm done. We'll go shopping then." Bree promised.

She drove through town looking for Marika's blue Honda. She found it parked outside The Coffee Place. She pulled in beside the Honda and stepped inside.

The aroma of coffee made her mouth water. She saw Marika at the corner table with Yancy. That woman had more men hanging around than anyone she'd seen. Maybe he'd leave if Bree hung around long enough.

Bree knew she shouldn't have anything but decaf, but her craving overcame her good sense, and she ordered an iced double mocha.

She sat at a table and watched Marika. Strikingly beautiful, her lustrous hair was tied loosely at the nape of her neck with a ribbon. The simple but dramatic hairstyle suited her patrician features.

Yancy finally took the last swig of his coffee and stood. "Call me if you need any more information," he said. He nodded to Bree as he left.

Now was Bree's chance. She walked to Marika's table. "Hello. You're Marika, Donovan's ex-wife, right?"

"That's what I hear." Marika smiled up at her. "Who are you?"

Bree tried not to wince. "I'm Bree Nicholls. I'd like to talk to you a minute."

"Oh yes. I recognized you. I've heard wonderful things about you."

The woman's smile seemed sincere. Bree sat down. "I'm investigating Phil Taylor's death and the incidents at the mine. Did you know Phil at all?"

"I came to town after he died."

An answer that adroitly answered without actually answering, Bree noticed. "The firm that employs you—NAWG—how did they learn what Phil's lab was researching?"

"A tip, same as we hear everything." Her smile widened. "Don't believe everything you hear about our organization. Things are changing with us."

"Who tipped you off?" Bree wanted to rattle her somehow but wasn't sure how to go about it.

Marika shrugged her slim shoulders. "That's privileged information."

"It wouldn't have been Phil Taylor, would it?"

"Why would he try to sabotage his own project? I've never talked to the man."

"What about the bombing at the lab? Your organization has been known to use violence in the past."

"We've put violence behind us. The evidence will show we had nothing to do with it."

"But you have to admit it looks suspicious." Marika just smiled and shrugged. Bree thought she'd try a shot in the dark. "I hear you're a computer whiz."

"So?" Marika said. She looked away.

Bingo. "How'd you learn so much about computers? Someone said you even know how to hack into the government computers. Is that how you learned about the research here? You're a hacker?"

"There are two kinds of computer work, Bree: hackers and crackers. A hacker is someone who does no damage. They just like to go look around, a cyber–Peeping Tom if you will. Crackers, on the other hand, do more than just look. They do damage or steal information. So yeah, I'm a hacker. And proud of it. But there's nothing to be ashamed of in what I do. I'm the IT person for NAWG, and I scan the Net learning what I can about the atrocities capitalists are perpetrating on the world. I know a lot of people look down on our mission, but someday they'll thank us when they still have clean water to drink and fresh air to breathe."

"Why did NAWG target the lab? They're not affecting our water or air."

"The jury is still out on that. Something is killing the fish in the area. Something more is going on there than what it appears. Or ask your sister."

"Kade thinks someone deliberately dumped toxic chemicals in the river to make it look like the lab was to blame."

"A gut-informed guess."

"He found the five-gallon buckets used to do it."

"So he says. For all I know your fiancé is just protecting your sister." She sighed. "Look, I don't want to fight with you. I want to be part of the community here, make amends for my past mistakes."

Marika's face was soft and pleading. Bree almost bought it. She switched topics, hoping the other woman's confiding manner would trip her up. "Naomi has been really worried about Timmy lately. Do you have any idea what might be going on with his blood sugar?"

Marika's smile faded. "I told child welfare what I think. Your friend is not taking good care of him."

"I know Naomi loves the children. She would never do anything to hurt either of them."

"I'm not saying she's deliberately neglecting them. But she's busy with the search and rescue. And they're not her children. She wouldn't give them the same care and devotion their own mother would."

"What about Donovan?"

"He's gone too much. Just like he was when I was married to him."

"He's home by six, same as most men."

"That won't last. The store is his mistress."

"Are you here to get him back?" Bree asked.

Marika barked a laugh. "I wouldn't take him back if he begged me! He's so staid and unimaginative." Marika drained her coffee cup and got up. "I have an appointment. It's been nice talking to you, Bree." She grabbed her purse, left a tip on the table, and walked away without a backward glance.

Bree took her iced mocha and followed slowly. Was it possible to put a cyberdetective on Marika to track her online activity? She didn't want to jump to conclusions, but Marika had something to do with all of this. She was sure of it.

She jumped in her Jeep and drove back to Naomi's. The kids were playing in the sandbox in the backyard. Charley came to greet her when he heard the Jeep. He rubbed against her leg, and she petted him, then walked to the house.

Naomi met her at the door. "Well?"

"She's a computer hacker. She seems to genuinely care about the kids though, Naomi. I'm not sure she's callous enough to hurt her own son."

Naomi stepped aside to let Bree in. "You've swallowed her 'I've changed' routine too."

"Not necessarily. I'm not sure she's hurting Timmy, but I think she might have something to do with what's been happening at the mine." Bree followed her into the kitchen.

"What other explanation is there? I'm doing everything right here. Someone who would endanger her own child like that isn't fit to have them, not without supervision. Oh, I feel so bad for Emily! She loves her mother so much." Naomi's eyes filled with tears.

Trust Naomi to be thinking of someone else. Bree squeezed her friend's hand. "I'm going to start trailing her to keep an eye on where she goes and whom she sees. We'll figure this out. I need to call Mason and clue him in."

Bree took the portable phone Naomi handed her and dialed the sheriff's office. After talking a while, she hung up and turned to Naomi. "Guess what? Hilary's ready to talk about adoption."

"Great," Naomi said absently. "Maybe things will all work out." She glanced toward the sandbox. "If only Emily would listen."

"Let's try talking to her." Bree stepped to the door and called her. Emily got up and brushed the sand from her jeans, then ran to her. Bree put her hand on the little girl's head. "Hey, sweetie, I hear you're having a sleepover this weekend."

Emily nodded, her face bright. "I know." A glimmer of a smile touched the little girl's face.

"How many friends are coming?"

"Five. Daddy said I could have five."

"Do you like them all the same?"

Emily frowned. "Hannah and Olivia are my two bestest friends."

"Which one is the best?"

"They both are."

"What if you had to pick one?"

"I won't pick one. They're both coming to my party! *She* can't make me tell one to stay home."

"I'm not doing that," Naomi soothed. "But it's like me and your mommy. We can both love you just like Hannah and Olivia love you. You don't have to pick just one."

Emily said nothing, but Naomi could see the thoughts whirling in her head. "Mommy won't like me if I'm friends with you."

"I won't tell her," Naomi said. "And no matter what you say or do, I'm going to love you, Emily. Nothing will ever change that."

Were those tears in Emily's eyes? Bree couldn't tell as the little girl turned her head.

25

$\mathcal{B}$ree wanted to hear Kade's voice. She twisted the ring around on her finger. She pulled her cell phone out to see how his day was going. Dead. No wonder she hadn't gotten a call all day.

She parked in front of her lighthouse and carried her sleeping son inside. She put him on the couch. It was too late to let him sleep long, but she could clean the kitchen while he dozed. The message light was blinking on the answering machine. She punched the button and heard her sister's voice.

"Bree, do you have Dad? He's missing. Call me."

Bree grabbed the phone and dialed Cassie's number. "It's me. What's going on? I don't have him. I've been with Naomi all day."

"Someone signed him out last night at midnight. They signed my name. I called Mason when I couldn't get you. He's here now, talking to the nurses. No one has any idea where he is. What are we going to do?"

"I'll be right there." She clicked off the phone and carried Davy back to the Jeep. He awoke when she put him in his car seat. Rubbing his eyes, he started to cry.

"It's okay, sweetie. You want to go back to Naomi's and play with Timmy?"

"I want Samson," he wailed.

Jonelle peeked outside the cabin. Zane was prodding Samson with a stick again, and the dog was grabbing it and growling. She sighed. She felt sorry for the poor thing.

"Breakfast is ready," she called through the screen door. She went back to the stove and slid Zane's eggs onto a plate. Over easy, with the edges of the whites crisp, just like he liked. Toast practically burned and slathered with real butter and thimbleberry jam from their own patch. Bacon practically raw, to her mind.

Zane came in wearing a pleased smile. "That new dog will give Bruck a run for his money. He was worth all the trouble we went through to snatch him. I think I'll keep calling him Samson. It suits him."

"I hate to see you turn him mean. He's a sweet dog."

"Have you been petting him again?"

Too late Jonelle realized she'd given herself away. "I couldn't help it. I think he misses his family."

"From now on, I'll feed him. You probably gave him too much food anyway, didn't you?" Zane threw himself into the chair and grabbed his fork. "I don't know how many times I've told you this, Jonelle. You never listen. But he's meaning up now. I just shot him full of steroids again."

She sat in the chair opposite him. "Do you ever think about getting out of here, Zane? Just you and me taking off somewhere else? I don't want you caught and put in prison for what you're doing. Now that we got a baby coming, we need to think about the future. There's no future in this dogfighting, Zane. You don't want your son growing up without his daddy around."

For a few precious moments, she thought she'd gotten through to him. His face softened, and he reached out and touched her face. "You're gonna be a good mama, Jonelle." Then he pulled his hand back and frowned. "Maybe I can cut back after this big score. We got the big boys coming in from Chicago for this fight. I'd be stupid to turn my back on all that money."

She stared at him wearily. "And after that there'll be another big score and another. The law will hear about you sooner or later, Zane. Can't you see that?"

"I just see you're turning into a nag like your mother." He shoved back from the table. "The law don't care about dogfighting! It's on the books, yeah, but they don't go looking for us. You worry too much, Jonelle. I'll be at the dog pens putting Bruck through his paces."

He stormed out of the kitchen, and Jonelle sighed, then scraped his half-eaten eggs onto a paper plate. He could use them for the dogs. Her gaze wandered through the window to the backyard. Samson had his head hung over the fence. He was drooling, and the dazed look in his eyes about broke her heart. Zane would be in the barn with Bruck. He'd never hear her over the treadmill he had the dog on.

She picked up the paper plate and stole out the screen door. Glancing around to make sure Zane was nowhere around, she stepped quickly to the pen housing Samson.

"Hey, Samson," she whispered. "You hungry, boy?" She put the food under his nose, and he gobbled it up like he was starving. He probably was.

Jonelle didn't think he could ever turn this sweetie mean. She could see him defending his loved ones, but those soft, intelligent eyes didn't have a mean streak in them, not even clouded with steroids and cocaine. She caressed his head, and he turned and licked her hand. She wished she had the courage to turn him loose. Zane would know she had to have done it, and she'd never hear the end of it. He hadn't hit her, but she was never sure if he might, and she didn't dare risk it now with the baby coming.

She gave him a final pat and took the plate. She'd throw it away before Zane saw it. Samson whined as she walked away. It was all she could do to keep going.

Jonelle had just crammed the paper plate into the bottom of the trash when a car pulled up outside. The sheriff's car. Her heart jumped to her throat. She flew out the back door and ran to the barn.

"The sheriff's here!"

Zane blanched. "Stall him while I hide the dogs!"

She ran back to the house and through the back. A uniformed man was knocking on the door. She spared a glance through the window and saw Zane leading Samson to the barn. Smoothing her shirt, she forced a pleasant smile to her face and went to the front door.

She took a deep breath and opened the door. "Oh, hello. Can I help you?"

The man outside nodded. "Ma'am. I'm looking for a lost or stolen dog. Answers to Samson. He has tags." He held out a picture. "This is the dog. His owner is very eager to get him back."

Her fingers icy, Jonelle took the picture and forced herself to study it. The little boy had his arms around Samson's neck. Poor kid. Careful to keep her voice regretful, she shook her head. "Sorry, Sheriff, I've never seen the dog. Looks like a nice one though. And the kid seems fond of him."

"It's Deputy, ma'am. Deputy Montgomery. Samson is a favorite around town. He's a search-and-rescue dog and very valuable. You mind if I take a look around back?"

"No, of course not." She started to step outside.

"Don't trouble yourself. I'll just take a gander in the back and be on my way. Thank you kindly for your help." He tipped his hat and went around the corner of the house.

Jonelle shut the door and ran for the kitchen. Peering out the window, she saw that Zane had removed the dog cages as well. The backyard looked bare and safe. As safe as they'd be for now. But what if one of the dogs barked while he was out there? Or maybe Zane had muzzled them. He might have had time while she kept the deputy talking.

She had to find some way to get Zane to quit this crazy business. Once this big fight was over, maybe he'd listen to reason. She just hated that it meant Samson was going to get hurt. Or worse.

Cassie paced the worn carpet in the nursing home hallway. She felt stunned and dazed. Who could have taken her father—and why? He was an old man without any real value to anyone except her and Bree.

The front door flew open, and Bree rushed in. Cassie turned and practically fell into her arms. She wanted to share her pain with someone, and she knew Bree would be just as concerned.

"What's going on, Mason?" Bree demanded after giving Cassie a fierce hug.

"No one saw a thing. The nurse was taking a potty break, evidently, or she fell asleep, though she's not admitting to that. No one noticed him gone until this morning, and they found the sign-out sheet filled out."

"Why would anyone take Daddy?" Cassie wailed.

Mason turned a penetrating gaze on her. "They might be planning to demand a ransom."

"Ransom! We don't have any money."

"Could it have anything to do with what's happening at the lab?" Bree asked.

"I wish I knew. I'll put out an APB on Bernard, but I'd advise you to go home and wait for a call. I'll put a tap on your line," he told Cassie before exiting to his car.

"This makes no sense," Cassie moaned when Mason was gone.

Bree put her arm around her.

Cassie's cell phone rang. She grabbed for it. "Dad?" she said breathlessly.

"Cassie?" His querulous voice made her dizzy with relief.

"That's all." The electronically altered voice was familiar. "If you want to see your dad again, you'll do exactly what I say."

"Who are you? What do you want?"

"Your dad has something that belongs to me. A file. I want you to find it."

"What file?"

"It's marked 'Top Secret,' he says."

"I've seen it."

"Good. Then it should be no problem to find it. When you've located it, put it in a plastic bag and dive down to where you've been harvesting algae. Put a weight on it and a marker, then leave. I'll retrieve it. If it's the right file, I'll let your dad go. Don't tell the sheriff or your dad's dead."

"Don't hurt him," Cassie whispered. "That file is old and out-dated. It can't possibly be of interest to you."

"You have twenty-four hours." The phone clicked off.

Still shaking, Cassie dropped the phone back into the cradle. "We have to find the file and leave it at the bottom of the lake where I go diving" she told Bree. "I think I know where it is."

"We have to let Mason handle this," Bree said.

"No! The kidnapper said he'd kill Dad."

Bree took her by the shoulders. "God is in control of this, Cassie. We have to trust him here."

"You and God. How can you be so sure he's even there?"

"I can sense him in my soul. He's my constant companion, no matter what I go through. He'd be there for you too, if you'd just let him."

She must be having a weak moment, because what Bree said actually sounded appealing. "It can't be that easy."

"It is. All you have to do is drop that pride and admit you are a sinner and can't save yourself. He'll be there to answer."

She didn't have time for this. "We'll talk about it another time. We have to find Dad."

"I'm going to tell Mason about the call."

Bree tried her cell phone. "I forgot it was dead." She went to the nurses' station to use their phone.

Cassie pressed her fingers to her eyes. She had to do something. Mason would spoil it all, and her dad would pay the price. Bree's back was to the door. Snatching up her purse, Cassie slipped out.

Cassie eased her tanks onto her shoulders and adjusted her mouth-piece. It would take a while for Bree to figure out where she'd gone. She'd told Bree she was to drop the folder on a dive, but she hadn't said where. She hated to disappoint Bree. She and her sister were finally bonding, and even Bree's constant talk of God was beginning to make Cassie think.

She saw a glint on a nearby hill and forced herself not to look. But knowing the kidnapper was watching her made her hurry even more.

Cassie cleared her mask, then jumped into the water. The underground world enveloped her. She felt as if she were on another planet, one where light and color were different. She hovered in the water and watched a school of fish swim by before gathering her strength and moving downward.

She was going against all the rules of diving. The buddy system was one of the most important rules taught in scuba lessons, though going alone didn't frighten her now. She never felt threatened or in danger in the water. It was like coming home. She glanced up to orient herself against the shadow of the boat and checked her compass. She never took chances, but she had to hurry.

There were so many places to go in Lake Superior, so many wondrous sights to see. She could live here her whole life and never see them all. Caves, underground mountains, shipwrecks, the list went on and on. She found the spot the caller had mentioned, dropped the sealed bag onto the lake floor, and released the marker.

Then she saw it. Bree had said something about several shipwrecks off this point, but Cassie had never seen one until now. Covered with silt and barnacles, there was no mistaking the steamer stacks soaring above the lake floor. A massive outbreak of bubbles escaped in her excitement. Cassie swam to the boat and circled it. On a shelf of rock only thirty feet from the surface, it was remarkably well preserved.

She swam closer and rubbed at a barnacle-covered window but couldn't clear it enough to peer inside the hull. Tugging at the door into the hull, she was surprised when it pulled free. She should leave and come back later, but a part of her wanted to see if the kidnapper would come down after the file. Flipping on her flashlight, she shone it inside and saw all kinds of interesting shapes that beckoned her in. She glanced at her watch and saw she only had an hour of air left. That should be enough.

She didn't trust the kidnapper to release her dad. It might be up to her to track him and find her father. She watched her bubbles and debated. No, she was going in. It was perfectly safe.

26

*C*assie paused and shone her light around the room. Looked like a hold for cargo. Wooden boxes drifted past her line of sight, and several kegs played bumper cars in the corner.

A thump outside startled her. She heard another sound like something sliding across the hull. If this were the ocean, she'd be worried about a shark or barracuda, but there was nothing that predatory in Lake Superior. Another fifteen minutes and she'd go. She still had forty-five minutes of air time left.

Then the door shut behind her, and she heard the dragging sound again. She swam to the door and shoved at it. It didn't budge. She gave a gasp, and bubbles burst from her regulator. Her knife was still in her hand. She used the handle to thump on the door.

Pressing her ear against the door, she listened. There was no sound on the other side. Panic clawed at the edges of her consciousness, but she pushed it away. She'd get out of this. Glancing at her watch, she saw she had forty minutes of life left. Forty minutes to figure out how to get out of here.

Bree glanced at her watch. Nearly three o'clock. Charley nosed her hand as if he sensed her agitation. Cassie had been gone an hour. Bree had done the only thing she could think of and had called Salome to have her meet at the lighthouse. At least they'd be close to the water and ready to go after Cassie.

"Think, Salome. Where is a diving spot she would have recognized when the kidnapper mentioned it? We have to find her."

Salome was tugging on her wet suit. "She knows better than to go out alone." Salome glanced at her watch and frowned. "Do you have binoculars?"

"Upstairs in the light-tower room." She followed Salome up the steps. "I was on the phone with Mason for several minutes, and her car was nowhere in sight when I went out."

"She should have called me. All kinds of things can happen underwater."

They reached the light tower, and Salome grabbed the binoculars. Scanning the horizon, she bit her lip in concentration. "Nothing," she said. "Let's go out in the boat."

Bree called to Charley while Salome grabbed her diving gear. Driving down the access road to Lake Superior, Bree prayed silently.

Her boat wasn't fancy, but it got them around in its seventy-horsepower motor. Bree fired up the engine, and they putted out into the lake. The water was calm today with only mild swells of white-capped waves.

"Which way?" Bree shouted.

"I'd guess south." Salome said.

Bree pushed the engine as fast as she dared and stayed close to the sheer walls to her left. The boat bounced as it hit the swells, and she fought with the wheel. Cold spray hit her in the face. She didn't often drive this fast. Superior could be capricious, and it was best to treat her with respect.

"There's her boat!" Salome pointed it out. The powerboat rocked in its mooring with the swells. "She's got to be just about out of air. If she had two tanks on, she'd only have two hours, and she's been gone an hour an a half. Even allowing for boat time, there can't be much left."

Bree cut the engine and tossed the anchor overboard. "Now what? You shouldn't go down there alone."

"I have a spare set of equipment in my bag if you're game."

"I went down once in Hawaii with an instructor. Remind me what to do." She listened closely as Salome explained how to breathe and how to manipulate the weights.

"I've only got one wet suit though," Salome said, beginning to pull it on. "You'll only be able to stay under a few minutes before hypothermia sets in."

"If I get too cold, I'll come up." Bree put on the tank and swim fins.

Salome shook her head. "No, if you start getting confused, come up right away. Confusion is the first symptom. In fact, keep an eye on your watch and come up in ten minutes."

"Got it." She turned to Charley. "Stay, boy." Knowing the dog, he'd jump right in and come along for the swim. He whined but lay on the bottom of the boat.

"Ready?"

Bree nodded and adjusted her regulator. She sat on the edge of the boat and tipped backward into the water like she'd been taught. The shock of freezing water made her gasp and then expel an explosion of bubbles. The cold settled deep into her bones like an ache. Trying to ignore it, she turned and followed Salome into the deep.

She was going to die.

There was no way out. The portholes were too small to get out of even if she was able to break them or pry them open. She'd broken her knife trying. The door refused to budge no matter how Cassie struggled with it.

No one knew she was down here. She'd told Bree she was going diving, but Bree would just assume time got away from her sister. If Salome got home in time, she might raise an alarm, but it would come too late for her. They'd find her dead body floating among the kegs and boxes.

Tears blurred her vision. She didn't want to die. There was so much left to do with her life. Who would take care of her father? And with her gone, the research would fall apart. Even more than that, she knew she wasn't ready to face God.

Was God really in this deep place with her? Bree said he was everywhere, that his ear was tuned to listen even to a sinner's prayer, but Cassie didn't know how to pray. And she couldn't speak, not here with the cold seeping through her wet suit and the fish swimming around her as though they knew a meal was only a few minutes away.

Her eyes never strayed from the air gauge. If she stayed very quiet, she might last another five minutes. Then it was all over. Best not to think about that though—it would just make her respiration go up. She grabbed a box and pulled it to the floor, then sat on it.

She was cold, so cold. And alone.

But was she alone? She reached out with her spirit.

God, are you there? Could you help me? I'm so cold. I'm sorry, God. Sorry for not believing in you. Is it too late? Can you hear me down here? Can you forgive me?

She tried to remember the prayer she'd seen in the back of Bree's Bible one night when she couldn't sleep. A sinner's prayer, the title said.

Lord, I know I'm a sinner. Forgive me if you can.

Her eyes flooded with tears again. She'd be seeing whether it worked in a few minutes. Some people didn't believe in deathbed conversions, but now, with death staring her in the face, Cassie knew she didn't want to live without God for all eternity. It had nothing to do with hell, really. It was all about knowing she wanted to be clean.

She wished she had a chance to live life as a Christian. She sat on the box with her head bowed forward and gradually became aware of another presence with her. It wasn't the fish. It was something warm and approving that spread from her heart outward, warming her hands, her toes.

Is that you, God?

She was afraid to hope. But if this was death, she would welcome it. Gladness radiated through her, a joy that warmed her even more. Her only regret was for Bree and her dad. Without her pushing, she doubted Bree would ever go see their father.

It was getting harder to suck the air from her tank. How would death come? Would she claw at the tank, maybe even rip it off? Or would her vision just grow darker until she blanked out? She tried to take shallow breaths, conserve the air. Speckles danced in her vision like tiny, brightly colored fish.

She dragged desperately at her mouthpiece. This was it. God was waiting for her.

Salome tugged at Bree's arm and pointed to the bubbles coming from below. There weren't many, but she could see them. They both began to swim down to where they seemed to be coming from the ground. Only as they drew nearer did Bree realize it was a sunken ship, half buried in the silt.

Three minutes now. Another seven and she'd have to go up. The cold numbed her, making it hard to think, to move. They paused above the deck of the ship, and Bree pointed to the door. It was blocked by two heavy rocks. She moved forward and Salome followed. Between the two of them, they managed to shove the rocks away from the door.

Bree couldn't see the bubbles anymore. Were they too late? Dragging hard on her regulator, she wrenched at the door. It finally opened, but it was too dark to see clearly inside. Salome flipped on her flashlight and shone it inside. The beam illuminated Cassie's face, eyes closed behind her mask. She floated freely inside, moving with the eddies created when the door opened.

Bree darted in, moving her flippers as fast as she could. She pulled the regulator from Cassie's mouth. Bree grabbed the octopus regulator on her tank and pressed the purge button, then thrust it into Cassie's mouth. She shook her sister.

Breathe! Breathe!

Cassie's eyes opened groggily. She inhaled, and her bleary gaze found Bree's. Her eyes closed again.

Where was the door? Bree found it hard to think, to move. Movement wavered in her vision. Salome grabbed her arm and pointed. They swam out of the sunken vessel. Bree stopped swimming and tried to clear her head. Which way was up? The cold had settled into her bones. She couldn't concentrate.

With Salome on one side of Cassie and Bree on the other, Salome pointed and Bree followed her directions, swimming slowly to the surface.

Bree's head broke the wave. Her limbs felt like cold lumps of clay, but she forced herself to swim toward the boat. Cassie. She had to get Cassie to safety.

"You can do it," Salome panted. "Keep your legs moving."

"Sleepy," Bree mumbled. She just wanted to close her eyes for a few minutes.

"Move, Bree. Kick!"

Salome was shouting in her ear, and Bree just wanted her to be quiet and let her rest. She could swim in a minute. But with Salome screaming at her, she kicked out weakly. And again. Finally she was at the boat's side.

Salome looped Cassie's arm through the ladder. "Hold her!" She scrambled up the ladder and grabbed Cassie's arms. "Help me, Bree."

Bree forced herself to focus. She had to help her sister. As if from a distance, she gathered every ounce of strength and shoved Cassie. With a final tug, Salome got Cassie aboard the boat. She turned and held out her hand to Bree.

Bree couldn't hold on to the ladder anymore. Her muscles wouldn't respond to her commands. She tried to kick, but it was as if she were paralyzed. Drifting away from the boat, she swallowed a mouthful of water. Her head submerged. She'd just sleep awhile. Dimly, she heard Salome shouting at her. Why did she shout so much? It was getting tiresome.

Just when she was beginning to feel warm, she heard a splash. She felt something on her face. Charley. He licked her again, then his teeth clamped on the shoulder strap of her swimsuit and he struck out confidently toward the boat. She tried to put her arms around him. Good dog, good boy. She'd use him as a pillow.

Her head touched the boat, then Salome grabbed her by the hair. Bree winced and fought weakly.

"Grab the ladder," Salome panted.

Bree reached out and grabbed the ladder.

"Now put your foot on the step and push up. You've got to help me."

The pain in her hair helped sharpen her senses. She couldn't feel her foot, but when she tried to stand, she found herself going up, so she must have found the step somehow. Seconds later she was lying on the bottom of the boat with the warm sun beating down on her face. Cassie lay gasping beside her, her face white.

"Samson," Bree muttered. But it wasn't Samson, was it? Her dog was missing.

"I've got him." Salome hauled the wet dog into the boat.

He shook himself, then whined. He licked her face. Bree wrapped her arms around Charley and pulled him on top of her. "You saved my life, boy." He whined again and nuzzled her face.

"I'll get blankets." Salome stumbled past her to the storage compartments under the wheel. She pulled out a blanket. "There's only one. Both of you curl up together. We've got to get you warm."

Bree still couldn't feel her body, but she managed to scoot over beside her sister. Cassie turned her head and looked at Bree.

"I thought I was dead," she whispered.

"I thought you were too," Bree admitted.

"I met God down there," Cassie murmured. "You're right. He goes into the deep with us. He saved me."

Was she hallucinating? Bree smoothed her sister's hair back from her face as Cassie's lips turned in a beatific smile. "What are you saying, sweetie?"

"God was there. I felt him. And he answered my prayer. He saved me."

"I'm sure he sent us," Bree agreed.

"No, you don't understand. He saved me. I wasn't afraid to die anymore. You were right, Bree. About everything. He was what I was searching for all along."

"He'd been searching for you," Bree corrected. "You were finally ready to be found."

Bree stood out under the stars and watched the lake. Inside, Anu hovered over Cassie with hot tea and cookies. There was still no sign of their father, though the folder had been retrieved. She needed to think about things, figure this out. Their father—no, *her* father—was depending on her. So was Samson.

She felt like wailing herself—just sitting down in this patch of moonlight and howling like a three-year-old. Samson had always been her comforter. She wanted to bury her face in his fur and smell his doggy scent. To hear the sound of his bark and run her fingers through his curly hair. She'd never complain about the dog hair on the furniture again.

If she could just get him back.

And her father wanted to leave his legacy with her, to share what was left of his life. How could she find him, and without Samson's help?

She heard a sound and turned to see Kade coming across the yard. He pulled her against his chest, and she burrowed close.

"You need to get some rest," he said.

"I'll rest when my dad is home," Bree said. "The rest of the team should be here, and we'll search for him."

"Wait until morning. I'm sure he's inside and safe."

"We don't know that."

The back door opened, and Mason stepped under the porch light. "You out here, Bree?"

"I'm here. Anything on Samson?"

"Nope. I just heard from Montgomery. His sector is clear. He's been to every house he can find. Nothing. I'm sure you'll understand—I had to pull him off Samson's trail to help with Bernard's case. No new leads there either, though."

Bree nodded, squeezed her eyes shut, and pinched the bridge of her nose. "What's next?"

"It's hard to say," Mason said staunchly. "It's been several weeks, Bree. Samson may not even be in this area anymore."

"What if they've killed him?" Bree could hardly bear to voice her anguish and fear.

"Stop it, Bree!" Kade took her by the arms and shook her. "Have some faith. God will help us here."

"God doesn't always stop bad things from happening," she whispered. "I don't think I can go through this again. Looking, always looking. First Samson, and now my dad." She finally gave in to the tears, rubbing her eyes like Davy did when he cried.

Kade hugged her close. "It's okay," he whispered. "I think we'll find them both, Bree. Don't give up now."

Bree pulled away. "I'll never give up—never!" she cried.

"I know," Kade soothed. "Let's keep looking."

Bree sat on a chair and rubbed her throbbing head. She had to think this through. Emotion wouldn't find her dad or Samson. It was going to take some sleuthing. "I still think Dad's disappearance—and maybe even Samson's—is connected to the lab somehow."

Kade sat beside her. "How could it be?"

"I don't know. It's just all these strange things started happening when the lab came to town. I know it makes no sense, but let's detail what we know." Any action was better than sitting around waiting for results. Bree grabbed a pen and pad from her backpack. "Okay, someone killed Phil Taylor. Samson was taken. He was definitely a target, since it took more than one attempt to snag him. Cassie's prescription was tampered with, and someone broke into her house. The intruder came back a second time when Cassie was home, and this time shot at her and chased her into the woods. Now my dad is missing, and some file containing the scribbles of a half-delusional man is the only ransom the kidnapper has demanded."

"Is it possible Samson was stolen to get you off of Phil's case?" Mason put in. "Maybe that was a distraction."

"Maybe," Bree conceded. "I'd like to believe whoever has him isn't mistreating him. But if that's the case, then who took those other dogs? And why?"

Silence. It seemed impossible to try to connect Samson and the violence against the scientists together. "Let's get back to searching," she sighed, putting her pen and paper away. "This is getting us nowhere."

"No more tonight, Bree. The deputies are exhausted and so are you. We'll hit it first thing in the morning. Nothing makes sense when you're tired."

"Have some tea," Anu said, holding out a cup.

"Is everyone else asleep?" Bree asked. "You shouldn't have waited up." She'd stayed out under the stars with Kade for several hours. He'd prayed with her, and she felt enough peace to rest for a few hours.

"I couldn't sleep. All day I have prayed for you, your father, and for our Samson. I've struggled to find peace in this, *kulta*. I have been filled with a sense of urgency. You must find Samson. Soon. My heart feels he is in grave danger."

Bree's eyes filled with tears. "I'm trying, Anu. Keep praying. What about my father?"

"I don't feel the same sense of urgency. Your father will be fine, I believe this. But Samson is calling to my heart. I feel you must find him tomorrow. I know it's likely emotion filling me with panic, but I cannot help this fear that wells in my heart."

"Davy's birthday is tomorrow."

"I know. But the party is in the morning. Then you must find Samson."

27

*B*rightly colored streamers waved in the breeze from trees and the porch posts. Today her son turned five years old. It was a miracle he was even alive, and the whole town wanted to celebrate this day with her. What had begun to be a quiet celebration had quickly turned into something of a festival. Molly from the Suomi Café had brought her famous cinnamon rolls, Steve Asters was hanging a piñata filled with goodies for the children, and Naomi's mom, Martha, had been cooking all week and had brought in all kinds of goodies. The tables out back were groaning under the weight of all the food their friends and neighbors had brought in.

Mason had assured Bree he had every resource under his power out looking for her father and there was nothing she could do, but after Anu's sense of urgency, she felt especially eager to get out and look for Samson. He could find her father.

Samson was conspicuous in his absence. There was a forced gaiety to the laughter, and Bree realized she was straining her ears to hear her dog's bark. She saw Davy's long face and knew he felt the loss. They both wanted their dog. She told herself she wouldn't think of it for a few hours. Just for the party, she'd throw herself into forgetting. Davy deserved a fun day today.

Bree stood by the food table and made sure everything was going smoothly. She caught snippets of conversation around her: Steve Asters was flirting with Cassie, Molly was telling Karen Siller about a new recipe she'd tried, Eino Kantola regaled Anu with a too-much-information description of her bunions. Everything seemed so normal. But Samson's absence left a huge hole in her heart.

Kade put his arms around her and rested his chin on her head. "You're putting a good face on it, but I can see it's a struggle. I've been praying for you today."

Bree rested her cheek against his chest. "What would I do without you?"

"You never have to find out."

He kissed her, a lingering touch that bolstered her courage. "I forgot the cookies. I'd better go get them."

"Did they escape a fiery death this time?"

She punched him in the stomach, and he grunted, then grinned to show her he was teasing. "I'll have you know these cookies are *perfect*. Lightly browned, exact ingredients. They will melt in your mouth."

"I don't doubt it a bit," he said solemnly.

"You'll see, oh ye of little faith." She was quite proud of the way the cookies had turned out. After all this time of trying to be a better cook, she was finally getting the hang of it.

Inside the house, she heard voices in the living room. She went down the hall and peeked in. Hilary and Lauri were talking. "Hey, you two," Bree said.

Hilary's eyes were bright. "Bree, did you realize Lauri's coloring is almost exactly like mine?"

Bree looked at the two of them sitting next to each other and nodded. "I hadn't considered it before, but you're right."

"I'm not making any promises yet, but I'm willing to talk about it," Hilary said. "We'd have to work out all the details."

"And Hilary has even invited me to live with her and Mason if we decide to go ahead with this," Lauri said.

"Would you want to do that?"

Lauri shrugged. "Kade might decide to sell his cabin and move here when you guys get married. I wouldn't want to be in the way."

Bree's face flamed with heat. She was engaged to be married. It still felt unreal. "You know you'd be welcome no matter where we are. You're part of our family."

"I know, but I don't want to be a fifth wheel. We'll see." Lauri turned back to talk more with Hilary.

They barely noticed Bree tiptoe out as they resumed their conversation. Bree went to the kitchen and grabbed the Tupperware container of cookies. She put it on the food table outside, and Cassie motioned for her to join the group of researchers under the giant oak tree. Bree smiled and held up one finger as she checked first to make sure Davy was having a good time. He was playing horseshoes with Kade and some of the other children. His long face had brightened a bit.

Bree waved at Kade—Davy was too intent to notice—then went to join Cassie and her friends.

"Have a seat." Yancy stood and pushed the yard chair toward her.

"Thanks." Bree settled into it, glad to rest her aching feet. She'd been running around all morning.

"Any news about the murder?" Nora asked. Her no-nonsense voice was more intense than usual.

"Nothing that I've heard. I did talk to Denise about two weeks ago. Did you know Jackson Pharmaceuticals offered Phil half a million dollars to join them and bring the new drug protocol to them?"

"Half a million!" Yancy burst out. "They'd never—" he broke off.

"You think that's too much? The process is worth billions," Chito said.

"They must have been desperate for that formula."

"Enough to murder for it?" Salome asked.

"I don't know. I can't tell you just why, but I think they didn't have anything to do with Phil's murder." Bree watched Yancy excuse himself and jog to a little girl.

"You're still thinking it's NAWG?" Nora suggested.

"Maybe." Bree was suddenly tired of it all. It was a gnarled mass of thread she couldn't seem to untangle. She nodded toward the children. "Who's the little girl? I've never seen her before."

"Yancy's daughter," Cassie said. "He doesn't get to see her much. Her mom married our boss now, Marcus Simik, and Yancy has to toe the line pretty tightly to get to see her. He's been pretty bitter about it all."

"His wife had an affair with your boss?"

Cassie nodded. "It caused a huge ruckus in the company. For a while I thought Yancy was going to kill them both. But he's settled down now and has accepted the situation. He didn't have any choice."

"Probably not." Bree's thoughts began to race, and she felt the blood drain from her face.

"You look funny, Bree. Are you okay?"

"I'm fine." Bree left the group and went to find Mason.

"I need to talk to you," she whispered.

He put his punch down. "What's wrong?"

"In private." Her heart hammered as she led the way inside. Hilary and Lauri were outside now. They wouldn't be overheard. She was right, she knew it. But how could she prove it?

She leaned against the kitchen counter. "I think I know who the murderer is."

"Who? Marika?"

She shook her head. "Yancy Coppler."

Mason grinned. "Our resident Santa Claus? Is this a joke?"

"Do I look like I'm joking?" Her thoughts racing, Bree flexed her jaw.

He stared at her. "Tell me what you're thinking."

"He has a personal grudge against the company. You remember you said you checked out all the researchers' criminal records and all you found was one charge against Yancy for breaking a restraining order and threatening his wife and her boyfriend with a gun. The charges were dropped."

"So? That's a far cry from murdering Phil Taylor."

"What if that boyfriend owned the company he's working for now? And what if he now is married to Yancy's ex-wife and makes it hard for him to see his daughter?"

Mason scratched his chin. "Okay, I see the picture developing. But you have no proof."

"Not yet. But it's him, Mason, I know it. Phil was offered half a million. Yancy started to say something. He said, 'They'd never.' What if he was going to say they'd never offer that much? And the reason he knew what they'd pay is because he had taken the offer."

"Maybe." Mason still sounded unconvinced.

"Cassie said she had to make good on this drug; otherwise they'd all be out of a job because the company was on shaky financial ground. Maybe Yancy saw sabotage as a way to get back at his wife and her new husband."

"Seems pretty extreme."

"He is a scuba trainer. He could have trapped Cassie in the ship and retrieved the file."

"There are plenty more who know scuba in this town. What other motive could Yancy have to kill? Jealousy doesn't sound like enough."

"The money itself? Money can be a powerful motivator. Maybe he's in financial trouble."

"He makes good money as a researcher."

"That doesn't mean he doesn't spend everything he makes."

"I can check that out," Mason said.

"I want to follow him tonight," Bree said.

Mason looked distressed. "I can't come with you, Bree. Hilary is having a dinner party. Wait until tomorrow."

"How about if I take Kade with me?"

"I'd rather go."

Bree leaned forward. "I know this is it, Mason. And what if it's tied in with Samson's disappearance somehow?"

"We went in circles over this last night, Bree. What possible connection could Yancy have with your dog?"

"I don't know. But I have to find out. I'm going crazy just searching the woods and getting nowhere. At least I'll feel I'm *doing* something!"

"All right. But take your cell phone and call me if there's the least hint of anything going down. I think you're wasting your time though."

"I know I'm right," Bree said. "And I'm going to prove it tonight." And she prayed that proof led to her dog.

Jonelle watched the darkening sky and chewed on her lip. She hated to see nightfall come. She knew what this night meant for that dog out there in the pen. All day long she'd tried to screw up her courage enough to let him go but couldn't do it. Zane said their future was riding on this night. She couldn't wreck it for him, much as she liked the dog.

Trucks began to pull into the yard around six. They came from as far away as New York and Maine. Big dualies trundled in, their massive tires sinking into the mud. Some bore deer antlers on their grills and carried high-powered rifles in a rack behind the seat. Some cars were sleek and shiny testimonies to their owners' wealth. Many unloaded cages of snarling, barking dogs.

The stench and noise made Jonelle nauseated.

Zane's face was exultant as he watched them come. "I told you this would be big," he hissed to Jonelle. "We got plenty of food?"

"I think so."

"Don't just think so; make sure. If you need to make a run to town, do it now." He jogged off to greet the visitors.

Jonelle turned and went into the kitchen, letting the back door slam for emphasis. A slave, that's what she was. Just a slave. Do this, Jonelle, do that, Jonelle. When did she get to do the things *she* wanted to do? She was sick and tired of living this way. All she did was clean and cook. What kind of life was that?

She glanced around at the laden table. Ham sandwiches, mounds of potato salad, cookies galore. If this didn't suit them, they could go to town. She wasn't going to put herself out any more. She was done.

Stepping to the back porch again, she watched the people begin to file into the barn. Maybe Zane should have built a pen outside for this. She wasn't sure the barn would hold everyone.

Her gaze was caught by a stern-faced man with two boys in tow. It never ceased to appall her that men brought their kids to watch this gruesome ordeal. Didn't they care they were scaring their children, desensitizing them to cruelty? She wouldn't let her child grow up like this. If Zane didn't give it up after tonight, she would leave him.

Her heart constricted at the thought. Whatever Zane was, she loved him. Leaving him would be like cutting out part of her heart, but she'd do it if she had to. He wouldn't let her go though. She was sure he would see the reason in it. He might be gruff, but he loved her.

The crowd's excitement was palpable. Eyes glittered with avarice and bloodlust. She shuddered and tried not to touch anyone as she found her way to the pen. Bruck was already pacing the enclosure. He could smell the other dogs, sense the coming battles. His legs stiff, he growled as he pranced.

Jonelle's gaze wandered the barn until she found the cage she was looking for. Samson. He raged around the cage, his eyes glazed with drugs. She wondered if he'd even know his owner if the search lady showed up. Zane had gone too far with the cocaine and steroids this time. She swallowed hard. If only she'd done something sooner. She could do nothing for him now. Nothing. He blurred in her vision as tears stung her eyes.

He and Bruck wouldn't be the first dogs to fight. The lesser dogs would fight first until the crowd was howling for the highlight of the evening. And even before Bruck got to Samson, Zane intended some sport with the two smaller dogs he'd taken first. He'd want Bruck at a fever pitch before he turned him on Samson. Her hands shook as she grabbed a bucket and carried it to the cages. The dogs all needed to be well hydrated so they performed their best.

Bruck and Samson would be saved for the final show in about two or three hours, depending on how long it took to get through the rest of the animals. Most of them looked ready to fight. Their teeth were bared as they paced their cages. Several snapped at her as she slid water dishes in to them.

Jonelle's hands already bore the scars of other bites over the years. These dogs weren't safe. None had touched her heart quite the way Samson did though. Her gaze went to him again. He was still watching her. Even drugged, he drew her. Samson wouldn't run from a fight. It might be better if he did. He wouldn't have a chance against Bruck.

"Let's get started," Zane shouted over the melee. "First up, we have Mickey from New York and Dixie from North Carolina." The crowd roared with approval. "If you haven't placed your bets yet, now's the time. I'll be at the table if you want to lay some money down. And if you haven't bet on the big fight yet, let me draw your attention to Samson. You all know Bruck and his reputation. Samson is a new dog, but what a fighter! He's heavy with muscle and has even defeated one of our North Woods wolves, so you know he's a lean, mean fighting machine. I might lay some money on him against my dog myself." His bragging about Samson had brought a murmur of excitement, and dozens of people crowded Samson's cage to get a better look at Bruck's challenger.

Jonelle knew he was gauging Samson wrong. Samson hated Zane, but he wasn't a killer. Bile choked Jonelle's throat. She told herself it was the heat and smell, not the thought of what lay ahead for Samson. But she couldn't quite convince herself.

28

$\mathcal{B}$ree glanced at her watch. Eight o'clock. Lauri was with Davy and Timmy, who was spending the night for Davy's birthday. The boys would be happy and content until she got back. But she had to do this tonight. She had to prove her certainty that Yancy was the guilty party before he harmed anyone else.

Kade drove his truck. He'd thought it might be less familiar to Yancy than Bree's Jeep. They were parked in a pull-off down the street from Yancy's house. The fading afternoon shadows hid them from view. A stiff breeze blew sand across the road.

"He's leaving!" Bree leaned forward.

"I see him." Kade started the truck. He waited until Yancy's car turned left at the corner, then pulled out of their hiding place and followed.

"He's probably just going to the store," Bree said. Sure enough, Yancy turned in at the convenience store. He came back out in five minutes with a fistful of lottery tickets in his hand. Lottery tickets. Bree gasped.

"What?"

"I just remembered something Naomi told me. The first day she saw Marika, she was buying a bunch of lottery tickets. And Emily mentioned her mother took them to the bingo tables. What if gambling is the connection between Marika and Yancy?"

"Maybe. It's worth telling Mason about. He's probably already run a check on her, but give him a call." Yancy's car turned left and Kade followed, driving smoothly, well back from the car in front.

Bree dialed her cell phone and told Mason her suspicions. He confirmed he'd run a check on her, but only on her criminal record. He promised to have Deputy Montgomery run a check on her financial status.

Yancy turned left and took Jack Pine Lane out of town. "There's nothing out here but wilderness and cabins," Bree said.

"He has to be coming out here for a reason."

"A dogfight?" Bree suggested, her heart surging at the thought of her dog.

"I hope not."

"Me too. But I can't get rid of this hunch that he's linked to everything, including Samson's disappearance." Her cell phone trilled, and she grabbed it. "Bree Nicholls."

It was Mason. "Bree, my deputy called with the report back on Yancy. He's in hock up to his eyebrows. And get this: He charged twenty thousand dollars on his credit card at Vegas. I'd say he has a gambling problem."

"Bingo," she said softly. "Dogfighting."

"Maybe." He sighed heavily. "I wish I was with you. Call me if you get in trouble. Just don't presume too much. And just watch. My deputies will come if you see anything."

"He's got my dog, Mason. I know he does. And I'm going to get him back." She clicked off the phone and told Kade what Mason had said.

"Sounds like this could be it."

"You sound doubtful. I'm sure of it, Kade." Bree tried to quell her irritation. Why couldn't everyone see it? It was clear as the sunny sky above Lake Superior.

"Don't bite my head off. I'm trying to keep your feet on the ground."

"I know exactly where my feet are planted," she snapped.

He kept his gaze on the road.

A long, uncomfortable pause heightened her senses. After several minutes she sighed. "I'm sorry."

Kade reached out and squeezed Bree's hand.

They drove on, staying a safe distance behind Yancy's car. Yancy seemed oblivious to the fact that he was being followed. Soon the road changed to gravel in front of them, and Kade dropped even farther behind. "We don't want to tip him off," he said.

After about thirty minutes, the plume of dust from Yancy's tires turned right. A long lane led into a thickly forested area. The woods swallowed up the car and the dust in its wake.

"This is it," Kade said. "There's a cabin back there. One of those survivalist sorts with no electricity or phone, though he has a generator for outside lights. He likes to be left alone. I wandered onto his property one day, and he ordered me off."

"Did you leave?"

"Sure. It's his property, not park property."

"Maybe we should park somewhere and walk back," Bree suggested.

Kade nodded. "I know a turnoff to the creek. We'll leave the truck there." He guided the vehicle into a lane barely wide enough for the truck and killed the engine.

Bree nodded and hopped out. She wouldn't put it past some of the people who would go to a dogfight to vandalize his truck. She hoped Kade wouldn't pay with his property for helping her tonight. Her heart was pounding like the surf in a Superior nor'easter. Was Samson down that lane? It was all she could do to fall in beside Kade and trudge through the brush with him when she wanted to run on ahead.

Her breath sounded loud in her ears as she gripped Kade's hand and scurried through the thick brush. A sound began to drift through the trees, a roar of some kind. Bree couldn't tell what it was. Then as she got closer, she realized it was a crowd. A raucous one.

She felt icy, nauseated when she realized what it had to be. "A dogfight," she whispered to Kade.

"Yep." He started jogging.

Bree clutched his hand and ran to keep up. Samson was in there.

Jonelle wanted to clap her hands over her ears. The roar of the crowd nearly deafened her. She glanced from face to face, searching for some scrap of decency in these people. All she saw were eager eyes and mouths shouting for blood. No pity there.

The winning dogs from the previous fights were being tended. Most of them suffered from bites and even broken bones. But what did the crowd care? They'd gotten their pound of flesh in the bodies of the vanquished dogs.

It was time for the big fight. Already in the pen, Bruck kept lunging at the cage containing Samson. Zane was grinning like an idiot, and Jonelle wanted to slap the smile off his face. He was looking forward to seeing Bruck kill Samson. But first he'd throw the little dogs in to Bruck as bait. Her husband would do anything to make sure Bruck lived up to his killing-machine reputation.

She couldn't bear to watch. Not one more minute. Drawing air past her tight throat, she turned and pushed her way through the crowd. Bursting through the doors, she drew a deep breath of sweet, clear air, free of the taint of blood, sweat, and feces. She leaned against the barn until she could get enough strength to get to the house. It was sick. Why had she never before realized just how sick? How could she stay married to a man who took pleasure in so much violence? Even if he gave it up, she'd always remember it.

There had to be some cruel streak in people like that, some piece of their soul missing. And Zane was a ringleader. So what did that make her?

She straightened up and heard a sound. Rustling in the bushes to her left. She squinted and tried to see through the twilight made even darker by the thick trees. Through the gloom stepped two figures. Probably more thrill seekers. But why were they moving so stealthily?

The motion-sensor lights detected their movement, and the sudden glare of light made them flinch. In that moment Jonelle recognized the woman and felt a stab of wild joy.

"Quick," she panted. "You have to save your dog! In there!" She pointed toward the barn.

⁂

When Bree saw the woman step out of the shadows, her heart sank. But one look in her face, and she knew she had an ally. She raced toward the door the woman had pointed to.

Kade stopped her. "Wait! We have to call for backup."

"There's no time," the woman insisted. "He's about to go in the ring with the deadliest killer in the country."

Bree tore herself loose from Kade's grasp. The roar of the crowd covered his shout of "Wait!" She opened the door and plunged into the barn, all her senses assaulted at once. The screams, the sharp odor of fear and blood, and the sight of nearly sixty people converged around a pen. Thrusting her elbows into stomachs to get to the front row, she fought her way through the crowd.

"Stop!" she cried, but her voice was drowned out in the din of howls. Panting, she dove through the last row of men. Wildly she looked around and saw Samson snarling at a man poking a stick in his cage. A dog in another pen beside him was raging and snapping at the bars as he paced the cage. A rough-looking man was beginning to lift the cage door where two small poodles cowered.

"No-o-o!" Bree shrieked. She launched herself into the air and landed on the man's back. She began to pummel him with her fists. "That's my dog! You get away from him!"

The man whirled round and round, trying to dislodge her. "Get her off me," he roared.

He slammed her against a barn pole, and the breath left her lungs.

She struggled to hold on, but her fingers lost their grip on his shirt, and she fell into a pile of hay. She came up fighting, her fists clenched. She darted past him to the cage. "Samson, I'm here," she crooned. She thrust her fingers through the cage. Would he know her? How had he gotten in this state?

He growled and lunged toward her. She almost pulled her hand back but forced herself not to flinch. Still crooning to him, she wiggled her fingers.

His teeth stopped mere millimeters from her hand. The snarls died, and he whined then licked her fingers. Tears came to her eyes when she saw how thin he was. The man must have starved him for the past several weeks.

The man grasped her around the waist from behind and hefted her away from Samson. "This is my dog. You're going to be sorry you barged in here."

Bree wrenched away, falling to the ground again. Her knees and the palms of her hands stung with the impact. She jumped up again. The crowd was roaring its approval of the way the man was handling her. She felt a stab of fear. Where was Kade? She needed some help here.

Samson was snarling now, biting at the cage. Bree knew he would fight to the death to defend her. She backed up to the cage then climbed on top of it. "This man stole my dog," she proclaimed at the top of her lungs.

The roars of approval faltered then burst out in full bore again. "Fight, fight, fight," the crowd chanted.

They pressed closer to where she stood on the cage. "Kade!" she shrieked.

Kade burst through a line of men. His face was red with exertion. "Get back! The sheriff is on his way here now."

Women shrieked and men cursed. They began to fight to get to the door. In moments the barn was nearly empty. Kade moved to the cage by Bree. "Let's get him out of there."

"I don't think so." Yancy stepped from the shadows with a gun in his hand.

His face twisted with hatred, Yancy looked nothing like the easy-going scientist Bree knew. The loathing in his eyes took her aback.

"You're despicable," she whispered. I know you're in hock for gambling. But why Samson? You know how much he means to me and Davy. And you have my father too, don't you?"

He shrugged. "I needed the money. He's an amazing dog." Regret touched his face. "I think he could have beat Bruck, and I had a lot of money riding on it. But now you've ruined it."

"Where's my father?"

"I let him go. He should be back at the nursing home by now."

"What was so important about that file?"

"He had the missing piece of the puzzle."

"The cure for Alzheimer's?"

"Nothing so mundane. It's a memory booster. It turns idiots into geniuses. The military will pay a fortune for it. They won't care where it came from."

Bree absorbed the revelation. Everyone would want it, not just the military.

Yancy moved toward the money table and pulled out a satchel from underneath. He began stuffing bills into it while keeping the gun trained on Bree and Kade.

"That's my money!" Zane moved toward the table but stopped when Yancy pointed the gun at him.

"Stand back with the rest of them."

Yancy gestured with the gun. "I'll take the dog with me. He'll fight just as well later as he would now."

"No!" Bree started to move and Yancy casually pointed the gun at her head. "Don't try it. It wouldn't take much for me to shoot you, Bree."

"You don't want to do that," Kade said, holding up his hands. "Right now you're just facing a count of dogfighting and maybe racketeering. You don't want to add murder to the charges."

Yancy smiled, a slight twitch of his lips. "Your girlfriend already has it figured out, isn't that right, Bree? She knows everything."

"It started with revenge, didn't it? Making your wife and her new husband pay." Bree edged closer to the front of the cage's top. If she could keep him off center, maybe she could tackle him, make him lose the gun.

"I see what you're doing. Don't move another inch, or I'll blow a hole in your boyfriend." He angled the gun to Kade's head.

Bree froze. Her gaze met Kade's and he gave a slight nod. Her muscles coiled to jump when he gave the signal.

"I'm not moving," she said, putting her hands in her pocket. "There's surely more than revenge. Did Jackson Pharmaceutical pay you too?"

A figure stepped up beside her. The woman from outside who'd told her to hurry. "Yes, he was paid. Read this."

"Jonelle, what are you doing?" Zane hissed.

Bree felt the crackle of paper in her hand and glanced at it. It was an offer of half a million dollars to Phil. And Yancy.

Jonelle looked at her husband. "Doing what we should have done a long time ago. Telling the truth. You were wrong, Zane, and I was wrong for letting you do this. But I'm not shutting up any longer."

Bree turned back to Yancy. "It wasn't really the money that tempted you, was it?" she said, drawing his attention back to herself. "You wanted revenge on Marcus Simik. He stole your wife and would soon take credit for your new drug. If you could hurt him where it really mattered, take away his business and his prestige, you'd be getting back at him *and* your ex-wife."

"She's keeping my daughter from me!" Yancy cried. "Did you know today was the first I'd seen her in three months? A kid should be allowed to see her dad. I had him right where I wanted him. His love of dog-fighting outweighed even his hatred for me—so I was able to use him to get your dog. When he lost the bet on Samson, he would have been poor."

"Cassie's boss was in on this too?" Kade didn't hide the surprise in his voice.

Bree nodded slowly. "And so was Phil." She held out the paper. "I have proof now. But why kill him?"

"It was an accident. He was running scared, worried about going to jail and leaving his kids. I told him we'd be fine, but he didn't believe me. He pulled a gun on me. It went off in the struggle."

"What about Marika—did she crack the pharmacy computer for you?" It was a stab in the dark, but so far her intuition hadn't led her astray.

He smiled. "How'd you figure that one out?"

"Kade saw you with her one day. And I saw you meeting at The Coffee Place. I knew you hate computers. Phil used to take care of that side of things, and someone had to do it for you. Did you offer her money?"

"Some. But mostly I gave her information for how to get her kids back. I explained how she could make Timmy sick without any lasting damage."

Bree's gut churned. "What if he'd died?"

"He didn't though, did he?" He glanced at his watch. "Zane, drag the cage to my car."

Zane grinned. "You got it." He moved toward the cage.

It was now or never. Bree yelled and jumped on Zane from her perch. Yancy jerked toward her, but Kade had the gun yanked out of his hand before he could blink. He knocked Yancy to the ground then ran to help Bree with Zane.

Bree sank her teeth into Zane's hand. He yowled and jerked his hand away. "Get away from my dog," she panted. She draped her body over the cage.

Zane glanced away. His eyes widened when he saw the gun in Kade's possession. He held up his hands. "Okay, okay. Take your dog."

"Good decision," Kade said between gritted teeth.

Behind her Samson was still growling and snarling to get out and get to the man who had been tormenting him. Bree grabbed the cage and twisted it around so the side was to the opening into the pen and the door to the cage was facing her. Her fingers were so stiff it was hard to pry the cage open. "It's okay, boy," she crooned. The dog began to settle down. He whined and pressed against the cage door.

She was still fumbling with the cage latch when she heard a guttural roar behind her. Brandishing a pitchfork, Zane prodded her with it.

"Drop the gun or the girlfriend will leak water," Zane warned.

"Zane, no!" Jonelle started toward her husband.

He backhanded her, and she fell onto a pile of hay. A trickle of blood oozed from her mouth. "I'm leaving you, Zane," she muttered. "I always told myself the day you hit me I'd be gone."

"He's going away for a long time," Bree said. She itched to get to Jonelle and comfort her.

Zane jabbed at Bree with the pitchfork, and she moved back.

Kade's eyes narrowed. "I'll shoot you where you stand if you move again."

"I'll fall and she'll be a tasty treat for Bruck," Zane said with a casual grin.

With her back to the cage and her hands behind her, Bree continued to work on the clasp. When Zane's attention was on Kade, she took a quick step aside and swung open the door. Samson flung himself out of the cage and launched himself at Zane.

Zane shouted and scrambled back, but seventy pounds of snarling dog landed on his chest. He threw his arm across his neck, and Samson's teeth latched on to his jacket. "Get him off me!"

Bree rushed forward and grabbed Samson's collar. "Samson, release," Bree said. At first he continued to snarl, but she gave him another tug and he whined and released his hold. He licked her hand, then sat back on his haunches.

In the distance she could hear a siren wailing. Stragglers outside the barn heard it as well. They ran for their cars and trucks, leaving their dogs behind.

Bree looked to Yancy. "Was it worth it, Yancy? You tossed your life away for revenge, for money. Tell me, was it worth it?"

He scowled. "I'd have been fine if you would have kept your nose out of it."

"You're the one who brought me in. You took my dog and threatened my sister. I feel sorry for you. You had so much—a great career, a daughter who loves you, a good name. You treated it like trash."

"Shut up," he growled. "I don't need any sermonizing from you."

Bree knew she had to forgive him, but the words stuck in her throat. She'd told God she would not go through life bitter about anything from now on. But this man didn't deserve her forgiveness.

But then neither did she deserve God's. She swallowed hard. "I just want to say I forgive you, Yancy."

He rolled his eyes and looked away without answering.

29

$\mathcal{S}$amson had his head stuck out the window, a doggy smile on his face. His ears whipped back in the wind. Bree sat next to Kade in the truck with her right arm around Samson's neck. His coat was rough, and he smelled bad. It was horrible how quickly mistreatment had shown on his body. He was too thin, but she'd soon fix that.

She felt like crying and laughing at the same time. Now that it was over, she could admit to herself she'd thought that they'd never find him—that he had gone to some terrible fate. And that fear had almost come true. She shuddered to think how close she'd come to losing him.

Her cell phone had rung on their way home, and Cassie reported their father had come wandering back to the house. Life couldn't be much better.

Kade slipped his arm around her shoulders. "Happy?"

"I can't even begin to say how happy," she said, leaning her head back against his arm. "I wish we didn't have to go to the jail to make a statement. I'd just like to go home and watch Davy with Samson. At least we get to reunite them first. It will take a while for Mason to book Yancy. He'll have to arrest Marcus Simik too. I think Cassie said he lives in Milwaukee." She glanced at her watch. "We're supposed to meet at the station in an hour."

Kade turned the truck down Negaunee Street. Samson whined and his tail wagged furiously, swishing Bree in the face. She laughed. "He knows where we are."

Kade parked the truck out front, and Bree leaned over and opened the door before Samson jumped out the window. "Davy," she called. Samson barked and ran toward the lighthouse.

The screen door opened. "Sam!" Davy called. He jumped off the front step and ran to meet his dog. Timmy followed, an excited grin on his small face.

Bree watched, her heart so full it overflowed into tears. She thought Davy had given up on finding his dog too. Her son threw himself against Samson, and the dog pushed him to the ground, then stood over him licking his face. Davy giggled and squirmed. Samson finally lay down with his head on Davy's tummy.

Davy turned his head to look at her. "You found him, Mommy! You found him."

Bree knelt beside him and Samson. "God helped me. God and Kade."

"We should thank God for helping you," Davy said solemnly. He shut his eyes, his face turned to the stars. "Thank you, God. Thank you for bringing my dog home."

"Amen," Bree echoed, making no effort to control her tears. She smoothed the hair back from Davy's face.

"Amen." Davy's eyes popped back open, and he smiled. "Thanks, Kade."

"You're welcome, big guy." Kade squatted beside them.

"What is the commotion?" Anu stood in the doorway of the house. Lauri was behind her. "Oh!" A smile spread across her face when she saw them clustered around the dog. She clapped her hands. "Samson!"

Samson jumped up and ran to her. Bree thought he was going to wag his tail right off his body. Anu exclaimed over him, running her hands over his rough coat. "You need some food," she said. "Davy?"

Davy rolled over on the grass and stood. "Okay, Grammy. Come on, boy. Let's feed you." Samson and his boy went inside.

They sat on the porch swing with Anu. Bree explained how they'd found Samson and Yancy's role in the summer's events.

"Does Naomi know about Marika yet?"

Bree shook her head then glanced at her watch. "We have to go. Kade and I heard Yancy's confession, so Mason wants us to give a statement."

Anu hugged her when they stood to go. "I'm proud of you, *kulta*. You have grown much in this past year. I see you strong and confident again. I see the glow on your face when you look at Kade. The future stretches before you so brightly. Put this all behind you now and get on with your life."

"We're going to do just that," Kade said, slipping his arm around Bree's waist

The promise in his gaze made Bree's mouth go dry. She smiled. "We'd better go."

Kade kept his hand at her back as he escorted her to the truck. "You nervous?"

"Not really. I just want Marika's troublemaking days to be over."

"She did more than cause trouble. I imagine she'll be charged with attempted murder and child abuse. Cassie could have died. Timmy too."

"Yes, I know. At least Naomi and Donovan won't have to worry about her anymore. But I feel bad for her kids. What's it going to do to Timmy to someday know his own mother altered his medicine to make him sick for her own purposes? And Emily . . ."

"Maybe they'll never have to find out."

"This is a small town. And it will come out in the trial. They'll hear about it at school."

"Yeah, you're right." He shook his head. "Poor kid." He parked outside the jail.

Inside, they found Mason filling out paperwork at his desk. "I'm about ready; hang on a minute." He scribbled a few more seconds then put the pen down and got up.

"You were right about Marika. She was up to her ears in debt too. She was home packing. Somehow she got wind of what was happening."

"I just want to know why," Bree said. "What would make her a willing party to murder?"

"I just interrogated her. She says she met Yancy in Las Vegas a couple of years ago. He knew she was a computer whiz and told her about the money they could make if they got rid of the rest of the researchers. And she really did want her kids back. She joined NAWG and used the organization as a cover to come back here."

"She dumped stuff in the river to kill the fish, didn't she?" Kade asked.

Mason nodded. "She admitted everything when I told her Yancy was singing. She wanted to make sure I knew he was the ringleader."

He took their statement, and on the way out of the interrogation room, they passed Marika. She stopped in the middle of the hall.

"This is all your fault," she spat. "You were determined to frame me and get me out of the way of your best friend. My lawyer will have me out in no time."

In spite of Marika's bravado, Bree thought she detected a trace of fear in the other woman's eyes. "I had nothing to do with it," Bree said. "I just wanted to find my dad and get my dog back. You brought this all on yourself. I want to know why you would want to hurt Timmy. He's your own son."

"He wasn't hurt," Marika said. "You're all blowing it out of proportion."

"Did you hate Donovan and Naomi so much it didn't matter who got hurt as long as you got your way?"

"You make me sound like some kind of monster," Marika said.

"Aren't you?" Bree asked.

"It wasn't like that!" Marika shouted after her.

Kade's warm hand enveloped hers, and Bree walked on without responding. The courts would figure out all the whys and hows. Her family was safe now. And Naomi's. She glanced up at Kade. "Can we go by and tell Naomi what's happened? I don't want her to hear it from the evening news."

They had to awaken Naomi and Donovan to tell them what had happened. Naomi began to cry when she realized Samson was safe.

Then her tears turned to anger, and it was all Donovan could do to keep her from going to the jail to confront Marika when she heard Timmy's own mother had altered his medicine.

It was nearly midnight when Kade walked Bree to her door. "Can I come in a minute? I know it's late, but there are some things I think need said."

"Sure." Samson met her at the door when they stepped inside.

"Looks like Lauri gave you a bath," she told him, running her fingers through his clean coat. His nails clicked against the hardwood as he followed her and Kade to the living room. "Want a Pepsi or a cup of coffee?" she asked Kade.

"I'd take a soda," he said. He sat on the sofa and patted his lap. Samson jumped beside him and sprawled on his lap.

Bree grinned and went to get the sodas. Kade's head was back against the couch when she came back. His eyes were closed, and he was breathing deeply. She studied his face. This was the first opportunity she'd ever had to look at him when he was unaware and vulnerable. The strong jaw was relaxed with a dark stubble on his cheeks.

"Hey, sleepyhead," she said softly, setting the sodas on the coffee table.

Samson whined and scrambled off Kade's lap to throw himself on hers. Kade flinched, then rubbed his eyes.

"I was almost a goner," he said.

"Almost?" she teased. "I'd say it was a done deal. Sorry I had to wake you. Your soda's on the table."

"Thanks." He reached forward and grabbed it, swallowing half of it in one gulp. "Guess I need the caffeine to stay awake."

"You want to stay here tonight? You can sleep on the couch. Lauri's here too, so we're safely chaperoned."

"No, I'll be fine in a minute." He put his Pepsi back on the coffee table and studied her face.

"What? Do I have a smudge on my nose?" Bree laughed and rubbed the dog's ears.

"It's midnight, we've had a grueling day, and you look good enough to eat," he said softly. "Good thing I'm not hungry or you'd be in trouble."

She chuckled. "I feel like yesterday's leftovers though."

"I shouldn't have asked to come in," he said. "I wasn't thinking. I just knew I had to say this before I lost my nerve."

"Say what?" Her heart began to thump against her ribs at the look on his face. She wanted to look away but couldn't tear her gaze from the soft expression in his eyes.

He took her hand, his callused fingers rubbing along her palm. "I don't want to keep dropping you at your door. I hate only seeing you a few times a week. I want to marry you right away, Bree, not next year. I want to wake up to your green eyes every morning. I want us to give Davy a brother or sister, to build a life together. Now."

"I already said I'd marry you." She lifted her hand to let her ring catch the light.

"I know, but it's one thing to say you'll do it and another to say yes to saying our vows now. How long would it take to get a wedding ready?"

For the first time the thought of a secure future with Kade didn't scare her and tempt her at the same time. Panic didn't well in her stomach at the thought of marriage. Not to this man.

"You're not saying anything," he said. He put her palm against his cheek. "I'll take care of you, baby. I can't always promise I won't be grumpy or that I'm perfect. But I can love you like no one else. Can't you say something? I can't tell what you're thinking."

"I'm thinking you're the most wonderful man I've ever met," she said softly.

"Is there a 'but' in there?"

"Not this time," she said. "I think my answer has to be yes in three weeks."

Samson barked.

Kade took her in his arms. "I think his answer is yes too."

Epilogue

"Quit fussing with your hair. It's perfect," Naomi commanded.

"I can't help it," Bree wailed. "I'm so nervous."

"What's to be nervous about? You're marrying the man you love." Cassie flicked a piece of lint from Bree's creamy lace dress. "That tea length is great with your legs. You look beautiful. Kade is going to wig out when he sees you."

"I hope so." Bree stared in the mirror. Her hair had grown out a bit and was curling up on the ends. A dusting of freckles from the summer's sun sprinkled her nose, but in spite of that, she decided she'd do.

"I have something for you, *kulta*," Anu said. She pulled out a long box. "You wore these when you married my son. I would be honored if you'd wear them again today as a reminder that you are still the daughter of my heart." She opened the box to reveal a lovely pearl and emerald necklace.

Bree's vision blurred. "Drat, you've gone and made me cry," she muttered. She grabbed the tissue Naomi handed her and dabbed at her eyes. "I was thinking about the pearls yesterday and wished I could wear them again." She lifted the strand and fastened it around her neck.

"The perfect touch," Naomi whispered in awe. "You look just like Princess Buttercup."

"The hair's wrong," Bree reminded her.

"Okay, you look like a red-haired Princess Buttercup."

Bree smiled. "Do you think Kade looks like Westley?"

"He's better looking," Cassie put in.

Naomi looked at her in surprise and Cassie shrugged. "Bree got me down and forced me to watch it. It was better than I expected."

Someone pounded on the door. "It's time," Martha called.

"Be right there, Mom," Naomi said. She adjusted Bree's short veil. "Take a deep breath."

"I'm okay. Let's go." Bree followed Naomi and Cassie to the door.

Davy and Samson were waiting at the entrance to the sanctuary. Bree watched while Martha got her son into position, then he and Samson walked down the aisle together. A ripple of laughter rustled through the church at the sight of the ring pillow strapped to Samson's back. Bree knew she had to get it together or she'd ruin her makeup with crying. The day was turning out to be too perfect.

Bernard Hecko stepped forward. His bright, clear gaze told her it was a good day for him. "I'm here to escort my oldest daughter down the aisle," he said.

"You're nearly as handsome as my groom," she said, her throat tight.

"Only almost?" He patted her hand. "But that's the way it should be. Shall we go?" He pulled her in line behind Naomi and Cassie.

Naomi and Cassie grabbed their bouquets from Martha. Naomi winked at Bree then turned and faced the church and began the march to the altar. Bree admired her grace and poise in the periwinkle dress. Looking beautiful in something other than army fatigues, Cassie followed.

Then it was Bree's turn. She clutched her bouquet, and she and her father stepped out to the melody of "The Wedding March." Samson barked when he saw her.

"I feel like doing the same, boy," Kade said, standing with Donovan and Steve. He placed his hand on Samson's head.

The congregation laughed, but Bree couldn't tear her gaze from the love and awe she saw on Kade's face. She barely noticed the walk to the altar. All she saw was her family waiting for her at the end of the aisle.

Her father passed her hand to Kade and he gripped it with warm fingers. Samson growled and pushed between them. His muscular body pushed Bree away from Kade.

"I think he's trying to rescue her from a fate worse than death," Donovan said loudly.

The congregation roared with laughter. "It's okay, Samson," Bree whispered. She gripped Kade's fingers. They turned and faced Pastor Alan. Bree knew she answered in all the right places, but the ceremony passed in a blur where she was conscious only of Kade beside her, promising to love, honor, and cherish her in his deep voice.

"The ring," Pastor Alan said.

As Bree fumbled for the ring, it rolled off the pillow on Samson's back. "Oh no!" She fell to her knees and ran her fingers over the carpet. Kade knelt to help her. Soon the whole wedding party was on its knees.

"I've heard of asking friends to pray for the new marriage, but this is going a bit too far," the pastor joked.

The ring was nowhere to be found. After the stress of the day, Bree felt near tears. Then she spied the pillow on Samson's back. Untying the pillow, she brought it around to Samson's nose. "Find it, Samson, find the ring."

He woofed and began to nose around the carpet. He began to bark at the communion table.

"It's under the table," Donovan said. The men moved it, and the ring sparkled up at them.

Bree scooped it up and turned to Kade. "You're not getting off that easy." She slipped the ring on his finger.

Kade lifted her veil. As his lips touched hers, Bree knew God was in the deep wells of their love as well. And she was finally home.

Acknowledgments

$\mathscr{H}$eartfelt thanks to the following friends and colleagues:

To my fabulous agent, Karen Solem of Spencerhill Associates. When the doubts come, all I have to do is call and hear your voice and I'm ready to get back to work. Your amazing grasp of the business keeps me on track. Thanks for being a friend who always tells me the truth.

To my extraordinary, wonderful editor at WestBow Press, Ami McConnell. Her knowledge of the publishing industry is light-years ahead of everyone else, and she's just plain fun to be with. She can sniff out a fresh story like Samson can find a missing person. And to brilliant freelance editor Erin Healy, who can resolve problems in a plot that would otherwise run amok. I learn something new from you both with every project. You make the editing process almost as fun as eating DeBrand mocha truffles.

To those who gave technical assistance: Dr. Mel Hodde (half of the writing team of Hannah Alexander) helped me figure out what drugs to change to cause problems for my characters. Pharmacist Liz Swindler gave me much-needed information about how prescriptions are filled and what drugs look similar.

To those who read my manuscript in the early stages and pointed out the glaring holes: my husband, David Coble, who reads every word and makes me feel like the world's best writer. Love you, sweetheart! Friends Kristin Billerbeck, Denise Hunter, and Diann Hunt are always there to offer advice and an iced latte when the going gets tough. I'm so blessed to have such great friends!

To my prayer partners: Kristin Billerbeck, Lori Copeland, Carol Cox, Diann Hunt, Denise Hunter, Crystal Miller, and Deborah Raney. What a wonderful thing to know we can depend on one another to drop everything and pray for our needs.

To my family and church family: New Life Baptist Church.

Please visit my Web site at www.colleencoble.com and e-mail me at colleen@colleencoble.com. I love hearing from my readers!

THE ROCK HARBOR SERIES

Without a Trace

BOOK ONE IN THE ROCK HARBOR SERIES

*B*ree Nichols, along with her search-and-rescue dog, Samson, won't rest until she recovers the lost bodies of her husband and son, who were killed in a plane crash.

Meanwhile, the quiet town of Rock Harbor is disturbed by a violent crime. Bree soon discovers a personal stake in the solving of the murder, and in the course of her investigation, discovers links to her husband's plane crash. Could solving the crime bring her peace with her own loss? Or, more incredibly, reunite her family?

ISBN: 0-8499-4429-5

Beyond a Doubt

BOOK TWO IN THE ROCK HARBOR SERIES

*B*ree Nichols is finally beginning to settle back into the routine of life in the quiet town of Rock Harbor after the death of her husband and reunion with her son, once thought to be dead. While rebuilding her relationship with her son, Davy, Bree embarks on a remodeling project alongside the area forest ranger, Kade, where they discover a skeleton. This launches them into a decades-old missing person's investigation. With Bree's hopes for quiet routine shattered by frightening personal attacks, she must work feverishly to find out who is after her, and why.

Beyond a Doubt is a novel that skillfully combines the elements of mystery and romance with the day-to-day happenings of life in a small town and the challenges and rewards of family relationships.

ISBN: 0-8499-4430-9